Michel Zohar Ben-Dor

No part of the material in this book may be replicated, copied, photographed, recorded, translated, stored in a database, transmitted or intercepted in any way or through any electronic, optical, mechanical or other means. It is strictly prohibited to make any kind of commercial use of the material included in this book without explicit, written permission from the author.

The Women of the Berlin Salon is a work of fiction based on actual events and characters, and real people. It was written following extensive research based on the sources cited at the end of the book, as well as additional sources. This book should not be viewed as a faithful re-creation of these actual events and/or people, but solely as a literary work of art. The book mingles fact and fiction, per the creator's artistic license.

Producer & International Distributor
eBookPro Publishing
www.ebook-pro.com

The Women of the Berlin Salon
Michel Zohar Ben Dor

Copyright © 2022 Michel Zohar Ben Dor

All rights reserved; No parts of this book may be reproduced or transmitted in any form or by any means, electronic or mechanical, including photocopying, recording, taping, or by any information retrieval system, without the permission, in writing, of the author.

Translation: Yael Schonfeld Abel

Contact: michel@mila-tova.co.il
ISBN 9798414865643

To my beloved Shimon, Dor and Dana

THE WOMEN *of the* BERLIN SALON

MICHEL ZOHAR BEN-DOR

PART ONE

"What is man without his history?
A product of nature—not personality."

— Hannah Arendt

Prologue

Three houses stood on Jägerstrasse Street in Berlin. From the narrow sidewalk next to them, it was possible to peek inside through the open windows, sneak a look beyond the curtains blowing in the wind, perhaps even take in the aroma of food cooking in the pots simmering on the stove.

The story of the purchase of these houses and the nature of their residents surely did not interest anyone striding past them on that sidewalk. Such a passerby was probably contemplating the day he had experienced and the portion of it still remaining, or meetings that required his attention, or an acquaintance he was about to meet in a café or a public house. He would certainly have a hard time imagining how many letters the residents of these houses had needed to send out. How many connections they had needed to make use of and the considerable bribes they had to pay the clerks in order to purchase the houses at a time when they were prohibited from doing so.

This street was different from those streets where, from the moment one set foot upon them, it was clear that Jews resided there, as in eighteenth-century Germany, everyone knew that Jews dwelled in streets surrounded by walls. This was the case in Bon, in Koblenz, in Meine, and in the most famous city of all, Frankfurt. Distant and sequestered, they lived in unbearably crowded settlements, until even the rays of sunshine could not infiltrate the wall. The stench of standing water rose from the streets, and the residents suffered from illnesses as well as fires that consumed entire houses and their residents with them, leaving behind soot and stifling air and great sadness, for many days after they were extinguished.

Jägerstrasse Street did not resemble those streets in any way and also did not hint at the identity of the residents of its houses, other than the fact that they held good jobs and did not lack for money. This was evident in their outfits—in the fur coats and the polished leather shoes—in the carriages that drove them to and fro, and in the well-tended façades. Perhaps in the freshly painted wooden beams and in the fresh, uncracked plaster, in the gleaming windows and the polished stairs that led visitors ceremoniously into the house from the outside world. Sunny days or sidewalks heaped with freezing snow did not reveal what was going on inside, and definitely did not disclose that the residents of those houses were Jews, while all their neighbors were true Germans.

Germans were not invited to visit these houses, and if they were, they needed to decline. After all, a Jew, however high in status, was inferior by definition, with few rights and the social standing of an outcast. If you were German, you had no interest in being seen in his company or, heaven forbid, upon his doorstep. You would not want to be the subject of gossip among your neighbors, in any society of which you were a member or at your place of employment. You would not want them to say, perish the thought, that you were a Jew-lover.

The Jews, the residents of those houses, were also not invited to afternoon tea at their neighbors' houses, even if they were well-mannered and greeted them when they met and paused for a minute or two of small talk. It was mutual, and so long as everyone understood their place, life carried on peacefully.

And then there were the exceptions.

Such as Markus Levin, for example.

1 | 1771

The bohemians of Berlin visited Markus Levin quite frequently. Just a short time ago, the sidewalk had filled with a young, colorful group on its way to his home. They arrived immediately once rehearsals at the theater had ended and, despite the cold weather, crossed the significant distance on foot. They told Mr. Levin, who had been awaiting their arrival, that they had decided to walk as it was the best way to stretch their legs, but the true reason was precisely what had brought them to his home. In the house, filled with the heat of the blazing fireplace, the group members peeled off their coats, hats and warm garments and remained in their colorful clothes: the women in breezy, bright-hued silk dresses and thin stockings peeking through a slit in the dress, and the men in light linen shirts and trousers that were blue, green or burgundy-colored. After they had sorted out the financial matters that had brought them there and signed promissory notes, and after they had thawed out from the freezing walk, Mr. Levin diverted from his usual custom and invited them to have some wine. He also sipped some himself, settling in to hear them delve into their true love: theater and poetry.

He was about the same age as the group members, closer in age to some than to others. However, he had needed to provide for himself from a young age, after learning the secrets of commerce from his father and grandfather. The members of the group were free spirits, with a carefree, irreverent attitude toward life. They did not heed society's edicts and perhaps even despised them. For its part, society returned the favor and therefore, they had no choice but to rely on Levin, the canny merchant who was also a moneylender under particular circumstances.

After a few sips, he would manage to don a narrow and rather stingy smile upon his face. By nature, Markus Levin might have been even more German than they were, prudent and reserved, with a deep sense of rage suppressed within him, calculated and sparing in displays of affection. He was especially withholding with his wife Chaya, whose belly had been gradually swelling in recent months with the promise of a first offspring who would continue his legacy. He should have rejoiced along with her and been grateful to her for carrying his firstborn in her womb, as this was the entire essence of life. It was even stated: *"Therefore shall a man leave his father and his mother, and shall cleave unto his wife, and they shall be one flesh."*[1]

But the two of them, Markus and Chaya, resembled two parallel sidewalks on either side of the street. When he was out and about tending to his affairs, she breathed more easily for a few hours; however, when he returned, she stilled her footsteps, pacing between the walls of the house in utter silence so as not to disturb his rest or evoke his fury, which readily erupted. She knew that although the young Levin was considered a good match, he would bring her no joy, despite his good looks and his wealth. After their marriage, for quite a while, she tried to appease her husband, who was tall and robust, and had set her up in a respectable home in a good neighborhood, outside the dense Jewish community based in the old city, with its nosy residents.

Her attempts to draw closer to him failed one after the other, until, after a while, she stopped trying and gave up. She actually preferred *Alt-Berlin*, old Berlin, and wanted to continue living in the old quarter, crowded though it might be, nosy though it might be. She preferred to live among women like her, drawing energy from them and raising her children alongside them. They would certainly have cooked together in a communal kitchen, and during her husband's business trips, she would not have been left alone in

---

1   Genesis 2:24

the big, cold house. "There's no need to waste good wood on one person," he had told her immediately at the beginning of their shared life when he returned from his business to a nice, warm house, after being gone for three weeks. And yet she knew she was fortunate and complained only to herself. After a while, she managed to make friends with two Jewish women, her neighbors, Fromet Mendelssohn and Esther de Lemos.

Fromet was married to Moses Mendelssohn, the spiritual leader of the new stream of the Jewish *Haskala* (Enlightenment) movement, which encouraged progress and did not view it as a threat to Judaism. He was well-known throughout Berlin to both Germans and Jews, and so was his wife, Fromet. Fromet told Chaya Levin all there was to know about the course of pregnancy with tales from her own pregnancies and those of her friend and neighbor Esther de Lemos, promising they would help her get through it all safely.

The moment arrived. It had been many hours since the tortuous contractions began, and Fromet Mendelssohn and Esther de Lemos had come to the birthing woman to hold her hand, just as they had promised. Chaya Levin struggled with the refusal of the infant in her belly to emerge into the world, and for more than twenty-four hours, was tormented by contractions that began with a comfortable slowness and intensified more and more as the hours went by.

What had begun with joy over the arrival, at long last, of the long-anticipated day, and with excitement from all three women, who had forged a covenant of friendship as if they had always known each other, turned, over time, into great apprehension. With every hour, Chaya's energy was depleted, while the contractions—those had a life of their own. They struck her at full force, as if hinting at what was about to take place. Chaya reached a point of utter exhaustion, until she was nearly swooning. Despite all her friends' goodwill, she would have to do the pushing on her own, which now seemed impossible. She had already begun to feel anger toward the infant that seemed to be tormenting her, one that was bringing no joy to her bad-tempered husband, while causing her unbearable pain. In the short reprieve provided by the contractions, a thought crossed her mind: what if the infant got stuck inside her? It would sentence her to death, while she had only begun her adult life and had yet to accomplish anything. And perhaps this was for the best; what would she have to accomplish? A life of endless housework and a scowling husband? A life without love? Perhaps her imminent death was a blessing. If this was what life was like, who needed it?

If it were not for Dr. de Lemos, Esther's husband, the whole affair might have ended badly. However, the doctor came to her quickly. After a short stay in Chaya Levin's room, a thin cry sounded. Throughout this time, Esther held Chaya's hand, wiped her brow with a damp cloth, preserved her modesty and adjusted her dressing gown, until, at last, she handed her the baby girl. While Chaya, who was utterly exhausted, rejected the baby, wishing only to escape from it all.

This was also the case on the second and third day. On the following day, the bohemian theater group was replaced by a different group, from *Alt-Berlin*, consisting of men with beards and powdered wigs and women fussing in the kitchen and delivery boys knocking on the door to bring provisions and, of course, their next-door neighbors, the Mendelssohns, who brought along their oldest daughter Brendel, and the de Lemoses, with their firstborn, Yente.

At the center of the Levins' drawing room, a weak cry emanated from a box placed on the carpet, with a scrawny body rolled up in a wool blanket inside it. For a moment, it seemed to move, while in the next moment, it froze. Yente and Brendel stood over the box, marveling. They had never witnessed such a sight. Brendel had two brothers and a sister and from the moment they were born, they had been plump, their cheeks red, their legs chubby, and they ate constantly. While this baby was rolled up like a ball, her coloring pale, and did not behave like other infants. She did not cry or screech or demand; she just lay there, abiding.

Brendel whispered to Yente that she had heard from her mother that they were waiting.

Yente did not understand. "Waiting for what?" she whispered as well, as she, too, sensed the heavy atmosphere in the Levin family home.

"Waiting," Brendel whispered again.

Prayers and charms were recited. A small Torah book was placed in the wooden box and the rabbis entered and exited the home. Chaya, who just several days ago was still celebrating the arrival of her firstborn, was crying. Markus Levin was silent, gazing at her. There was no compassion in his gaze; even two seven-year-old girls could sense it.

They tiny baby had still not been given a name. Everyone thought a name was pointless; after all, at any minute, her soul would return to her Maker. Dr. de Lemos, Yente's father, believed so as well. And the doctor was never hasty to declare that any of his patients were doomed. On the contrary, he would always focus on the bright side.

Yente approached him, tugged at his coat and asked, "Papa, what are they waiting for?"

And her father, the doctor who was always equipped with some salve to be applied, pills to hand over, or an injection of some sort if it proved necessary, or even just a word of encouragement, stood helplessly, stroking his daughter's pretty head, a porcelain head with a ponytail as black as coal, its top secured with a red ribbon, extending down nearly to her bottom.

Fromet, Brendel's mother, stroked the new mother. Brendel knew those caresses. They were reserved for situations where compassion was needed. Like that time Brendel had been stricken with severe whooping cough "that almost cost her her life," as Dr. de Lemos often recounted. Or like that time her brother Joseph broke his right arm and his left leg in the sort of fall that was not convincingly explained. However, those caresses—there was something else about them. A kind of sadness. And Brendel's mother was not a sad woman. She was smiley and polite and outgoing and always had patience for all of Brendel and her two mischievous brothers' tomfoolery, unlike other mothers, who were constantly busy with laundry, and cooking, and tidying up the house, and shopping for provisions and all kinds of tasks both inside the home and outside it. Sometimes, she would even tell jokes and tickle the children.

Fromet allowed Brendel to approach the little box. The baby was so tiny, with a round little head, her fingers as thin as strands of yarn. Her eyes were closed and looked as if someone had replaced them with a drawing of two lines, her mouth pursed. Brendel reached out with a tentative hand, wary that this might be forbidden and therefore looking around to seek permission. No one stopped her and she began to stroke the baby's thin skin, rubbing her with her finger with all the gentleness she could summon, so as not to harm the tiny one or hurt her, heaven forbid. With an instinct of sorts, the baby grabbed on to Brendel's finger, and the girl let out an embarrassed giggle. Fromet's eyes grew bright, as if a little miracle, or an act of grace, had just taken place.

"God did not place us on His earth like foam upon the waves," Moses Mendelssohn, Brendel's father, broke the silence. "The baby needs a name." And even before anyone present in the Levins' home could respond, Moses proceeded earnestly. "Death deprived me of a daughter who lived innocently upon this earth for a mere eleven months. But, thank heavens, her life was cheerful and full of hope. Her short life was not in vain."

Brendel was caught by surprise. Her father's current openness first revealed to her that she had had another sister. A murmur passed among those sitting and standing, entering or on their way out, both due to such a personal, intimate revelation and due to the demand that the baby be named right there and then.

Moses Mendelssohn approached Markus Levin and grasped him with both hands. Mendelssohn was short-statured, his back curved due to the scoliosis that had afflicted him in his youth, while his friend Markus Levin was tall and erect. And yet he directed his gaze down at the floor at that moment. Markus owed Moses many debts, in addition to Moses's status as a good neighbor and a friend, and to the wives' support for one another. Mendelssohn, who had connections throughout Berlin, had frequently helped Markus in forging connections for his business. The last favor was the most significant one, making Markus Levin's greatest wish come true—leaving *Alt-Berlin* and moving to a good neighborhood, becoming one among many, a German like any other German.

Moses Mendelssohn grasped Markus Levin with both hands and waited. A moment of silence filled the room. It was obvious that Mendelssohn was prodding Levin. Mr. Levin withdrew his hands, clearly uncomfortable with the situation that this baby had imposed upon him. However, he knew he could not evade the demand and had also promised himself some time ago that if he had a daughter, he would name her after his mother. He had not consulted his wife.

"Rahel," he whispered, and it seemed as if a weight had been lifted off his chest. As if, after all, he had only been waiting to be asked, to be commanded, for someone to take matters into his own hands and put an end to the spectacle that had been taking place in their home for several days now.

"And Rachel was beautiful and well favored,"[2] Moses Mendelssohn boomed out. "And now let us recite *Shehecheyanu*."[3] And like the murmur of a swarm of bees arriving from afar and growing louder, the voices of the attendees began to come together and swell: "Blessed are You, Lord our God, Ruler of the universe, Who has given us life, sustained us, and allowed us to reach this day."

And all that time, little Rahel Levin held on to Brendel's finger.

---

2 Genesis 29: 17

3 The *Shehecheyanu* ("Who has given us life") blessing is a common Jewish prayer said to celebrate special occasions.

2 | 1774

A carriage carrying a woman, a man and two sleepy children rolled slowly down the streets. At this time in the evening, the members of the Levin family should have already been at a roadside inn, resting from the travails of their journey, but Rahel had begun to vomit before they left. Markus Levin, who was so caught up in his own affairs, only noticed the matter when they were due to leave. Why couldn't she be like her little brother, quiet and obedient, who did not require so much attention? Why couldn't she be healthy this time? During all the other times she had been ill, he had not been affected, while now, she was delaying him.

Chaya had already asked him that morning to postpone the journey, or to allow them to stay behind. She had even summoned Dr. de Lemos, hoping he would sway her husband in this matter. She did not understand why he needed the three of them with him. Why should she brave the bumpy roads in a carriage, along with a sickly three-year-old girl and a two-year-old toddler, for days on end, all the way to Wroclaw? Up until now, he had seemed to be comfortable on his own. From the day they had gotten married, he had not taken her anywhere, and suddenly, he announced they were going to see relatives. He had not asked Chaya whether she wished to join him, or explained the purpose of the trip. He simply laid down the law.

Summer had already passed and winter had not quite arrived, but sent ahead a chill announcing it would soon land in full force. Little Markus, born about a year after his elder sister, was sleeping safely beside his mother, while Rahel, who had not stopped throwing up since the moment she boarded the carriage, had not closed her eyes the entire way. Even now, as darkness threatened to obscure their path, she sat with her eyes open, listening. Listening to the crickets, which had begun their nightly tunes, and to the sound of the wheel flattening the moist gravel. Listened to her little brother's even breathing and to the howls of the jackals, drifting in from afar. All the night sounds that sent shivers through her mother's body sounded to her like a melodic refrain, making her alert and sharp.

She sat tall and tensed while her mother, Chaya, sat bent and curled on the hard seat, her back already shooting out small pains. The longest journey she had ever taken in her life was from *Alt-Berlin* to her current home on Jägerstrasse. The two sites were separated only by a few kilometers, and yet they resembled two different countries, and the way from one street to the other seemed alien and never-ending. Chaya was not an adventurous woman and any dream she might ever have had, and whose contents she certainly did not remember now, had crumbled a long time ago in view of her current life. She had not had time to recuperate from Rahel's birth and from constantly taking care of her before Markus had planted another seed in her, just a short time before leaving on a business trip, one of many. If she had been living in *Alt-Berlin*, her friends could have taught her tricks to avoid the arrival of another child at an inconvenient time, of another offspring that would surely purloin a bit more of her. However, the seed gradually grew and swelled and emerged into the world quietly and peacefully with the help of her dear neighbors, Esther and Fromet. At least this time, he had made his way out into the world without much effort. A plump baby, with flushed cheeks, wailing and crying and demanding attention in a loud, strong voice, just as a man should. This baby did not even wait for his father to return from one of his frequent journeys to make his appearance. Markus Levin returned home to find his son waiting for him there.

One look at the baby was enough for his father to know that this was the offspring he had been waiting for. Waiting so eagerly that he insisted that the circumcision ceremony be held in the synagogue of his youth, the same synagogue in which his bar mitzvah had been held, the same synagogue in which his wedding had been held, and for that reason, they had to travel to *Alt-Berlin*. Chaya had had no idea that her husband could be so happy. And as he recited the blessing, "Blessed are You, Lord our God, King of the universe, who has sanctified us with His commandments and commanded us to enter him into the Covenant of Abraham our father," she saw that his eyes were sparkling and knew that this child had entered his heart. And when the *mohel*[4] declared, "His name in Israel shall be called," she was not at all surprised that he had given his son his own name—Markus.

Now, on the way to Wroclaw, Mr. Levin was sitting in the carriage with his eyes closed. Occasionally, he opened one eye to glance at his sleeping son. Occasionally, he exchanged a word with the coachman. Even during the circumcision, she had realized she must protect the boy above all else and treat him gently. Perhaps she hoped that by doing so, she would also succeed in finding a way into her husband's locked heart. If Rahel had not been so demanding in her illness, perhaps Chaya could have devoted a little more attention to little Markus. However, each time Rahel emerged from one illness, another arrived a few days later, and with every illness, Chaya was afraid her daughter would die. Chaya noticed how much anger Rahel evoked in her father and when she looked at his face, she saw him wondering whether that was the reason she was born. Nevertheless, she liked the little wretch; after all, she was her daughter. Perhaps, deep in her heart, she wanted Markus to be the firstborn. He deserved this status more than the sickly daughter she had brought into the world, who might yet cause her parents an inestimable amount of sorrow.

When they entered Wroclaw around noontime, after a journey of several days, Chaya's back was bothering her greatly and her body bore the bites of the bedbugs at the inns where they had stopped to spend the night. The only advantage she could see to the journey was that perhaps from now on, she could be forgiving regarding her husband's absences, as now she

---

4   The *mohel* is a religious official who performs the Jewish ritual of *milah*, or circumcision, on the eighth day in the life of a Jewish boy.

understood the difficulty they entailed. If only he had told her, she would have been more welcoming as she greeted him. But he had never talked or told her, merely scowling as he returned home from the road, his hands empty of gifts, unlike Dr. de Lemos and Moses Mendelssohn, who always returned home with their arms overflowing with bounty.

However, from the moment they entered Wroclaw, which was vibrant and bustling, something changed in Markus Levin. As if he had shaken off a burden or load, or a kind of heavy blanket that enveloped him. There were so many kinds of carriages driving on the roads, with tall, lavish buildings by the sides of the street, and people walking on the sidewalks, men in suits and women in elegant dresses. The city was reminiscent of Berlin but there was something livelier about it, sparkling, a sense of things incessantly happening. Where was everyone hurrying to? What did they find so urgent?

Little Markus sat beside his father, who patiently explained to him that Wroclaw was a crossroads, between two seas, the Adriatic and the Baltic, and between Eastern Europe and Western Europe. Rahel sat and listened. They had never spent so much time together, just the four of them. He never explained anything patiently. It was true that he was speaking to Markus now, but Rahel felt that what he was saying was addressed to her as well, and although her father was something of a stranger to her, she asked him to explain a bit more about the crossroads, since she hadn't really understood. Her mother Chaya did not shush her this time. Markus explained and his gaze did not contain the familiar spark of anger directed at Rahel.

"As Wroclaw is approached from all directions, it constitutes an important axis of commerce, which is the reason for the heavy traffic there."

Rahel questioned him about himself. Was this where he went on his travels? Was this where he worked? What exactly did he do? What did he buy? What did he sell? What people did he meet? Rahel asked more and more questions. Perhaps, deep inside, she knew this was an opportunity that would apparently not recur, and therefore, she gathered her courage. Chaya, her mother, taut in her seat, also wanted to know these exact same things. Markus answered everything patiently and during those moments, his wife Chaya saw him in a new and somewhat different light, which felt to her like something she could not explain to herself, something that was not bad.

Later, Rahel would not remember exactly which relatives they visited, whether they were close or distant family members, or precisely who they were. Who were the ones with the ear locks and the black hats and who were the ones who resembled the people walking on the street where she lived. Who were the women toiling at housework in the homes they visited, and who were the ones who made her marvel at their handsome figures within dresses that fit them admirably, at their meticulous hairstyles and the knowledge they exhibited in the conversations she heard. In any case, the visit definitely left an impression on her and found its way into her heart, and she would carry her memories of it for many days to come, perhaps even forever.

On the first evening, after they had taken a tour to get to know the city, which was significantly larger and more impressive than Berlin, they stayed with a nice family. Before they arrived, Markus had mentioned that their host was a second cousin, or something of that sort. It did not really matter to Rahel. They reminded her of the Mendelssohns, pleasant and agreeable, constantly looking after their needs. Her mother, Chaya, was suspicious about this; she was unused to having anyone fuss over her. Perhaps she also feared she would do something wrong and evoke her husband Markus's rage, and who knew how this rage would erupt in the presence of those distant relatives. Therefore, she sat quietly the whole time, maintaining her silence, as if attempting to be invisible.

Rahel felt different. There was not a single cough, weakness, nauseous spell, or any other sort of ache. All her ailments appeared to have evaporated and she allowed herself to mingle freely and easily with people who were, in some manner or other, a part of her family. She expressed interest, asked questions and even leafed through the books, which smelled heavily of print. Occasionally, she even walked over to stand beside her father. On one of those times, she also dared to try to hold onto his large hand. She inserted her tiny fingers between his own, their tips yellow with nicotine, and for a moment, she could feel the warmth of his hand. But only for one brief moment, because immediately afterward, her father withdrew his hand from hers, ushered her out of the room and closed the door after her. A closed door was not an unfamiliar concept, neither to her nor to her mother Chaya, as the business conversations conducted by her father always took place behind closed doors. However, in this case, it was accompanied by a sense of insult, because the relatives' four sons were allowed to remain in the room, as was Markus, her little brother, who at the time was only interested in sleeping, while she, who was highly alert and equally curious, was not allowed to stay.

During the visit to Wroclaw, Rahel spent her time solely in the company of women. The men gathered in one room, drinking and smoking and talking about their business, while the women in the other room chatted about raising children and household matters, teaching each other a new stitch or an interesting recipe. This was the case in the homes of all their relatives, other than the one house that seemed to her like the residence of a king.

On their last day in Wroclaw, in the late afternoon hours, the Levins embarked on another visit to one of the houses in the city, which turned Markus Levin into a different man than Berlin Markus. One day, Rahel would discover that this was the reason why Markus Levin had been forced to subject his family to the rough trip from Berlin to Wroclaw: not out of a desire to spend many days in the company of his wife and children, but due to a demand posed to him by that aristocrat, von Bismarck, who was considering the option of conducting business with Mr. Levin. As far as Markus was concerned, he would have preferred to travel alone, as he always did, but what were a few days with his family compared to the possibility of accruing a significant fortune by doing business with a well-established German aristocratic family, and, more importantly, forging connections that could certainly be of use to a Jew like him in a country striving to limit his progress.

Von Bismarck believed that a business owner's family was a reflection of his soul, and therefore, the first test he set for anyone who wanted to engage in commerce with him was to meet the merchant's family. Many found this theory ridiculous, and it was also a topic for jokes cracked behind his back. Von Bismarck was familiar with these jokes and they had no effect upon him whatsoever. He relied on two things that supported his belief—the first was the great amount of money he had made with the help of trustworthy partners who had never cheated him, and the second was a wife he loved with all his heart and greatly beloved offspring. Unlike his aristocrat friends, he did not need mistresses and did not frequent brothels. All his needs were fulfilled by the woman living by his side, who also occasionally advised him on his business.

Markus Levin also considered him an odd duck. He himself did not subscribe to this theory, but he had already overcome more challenging obstacles when conducting business, and would overcome this one as well.

The day before, the cousin's wife, a gentle, reserved woman who was precisely kind enough, had provided Chaya Levin with a dress that was different from all her everyday dresses. The dress was a light blue color that shone a bit, and Rahel could not hold back, stroking it with her tiny hand in order to feel the shimmer, which was pleasant to the touch. Her mother Chaya also caressed the pleasant fabric again and again, but her caress seemed to be intended to ease the confusion she was feeling as a result of the flurry of her recent experiences.

When they disembarked from the carriage after driving for several minutes along a boulevard lined with tall trees and meticulously trimmed shrubs, they sighted a handsome building.

"Those are Greek columns," her father explained, some tension evident in his voice.

When they entered, they were greeted by a lavish staircase of a type Rahel could never have conjured in her imagination. They walked upon a red carpet decorated with a pattern of pink, light yellow and sky-blue flowers, which was laid out from the front door to the broad living room at which they arrived. With every step, Rahel experienced a kind of pleasant springiness in her feet, until she almost felt like laughing. The walls of the drawing room were adorned with giant paintings—portraits of strangers who all had the same expression: a stern gaze that scared her a little. There were many wooden items of furniture in the room, as well as curtains and covers made of a pleasant, light green fabric, a glass cabinet full of silver and china figurines, and mirrors in gilded frames. Apparently, her father was not as impressed as she was; perhaps he had visited this house before and was already used to the grandeur erupting from every corner, perhaps he did not attribute any importance to such things, or perhaps she could simply not read his expression.

Rahel and her mother were treated like princesses. Waiters donning fitted black suits offered them a seat and asked how they were and proffered beverages and assorted delicacies, precisely like the ones they had seen the day before in the window of one of the bakeries on the street. Rahel behaved politely. She sat on a sofa that was large for her small figure, closed her eyes and imagined herself living in a house exactly like this one, wearing a fancy dress like the pleasing dress her mother had on, eating special dishes and feeling well.

"Did you remember to say the blessing?" Rahel's father asked just as she had put the cake in her mouth. He looked at her before she bit into the first piece of cake and continued looking at her as she shoved the second piece into her mouth. And now the third was on its way, too. She simply put a piece of cake in her mouth and then another, and they melted inside instantly, with no blessing at all. Rahel nodded and Markus knew she was lying. As far as he was concerned, she had doubled her offense by both failing to recite the blessing and lying about it. This, in itself, charged him with anger that began to bubble inside him. Markus Levin never skipped a single prayer, short or long. Not with regard to himself, or to his wife, or to his daughter. Although, he knew they did not understand a word of the prayers they were required to recite. He believed prayers had to be said precisely at the right time; that was their purpose and they should not be treated lightly.

Perhaps Rahel picked up on the imminent anger, or perhaps she did not. In any case, she began to mumble something that sounded like *Birkat HaMazon*, the blessing said after the meal, mumbling and eating, mumbling and eating more and more sweets, until nausea spread all throughout her body, and a stormy wave purged her little body of all she had stuffed inside it.

Throughout the visit, Chaya Levin had felt as if she were in a dream. Her husband introduced her to their hosts in a pleasant, respectful way and also introduced Rahel and little Markus as if they were exemplary children. For once, he had allowed her and Rahel to taste a little of the refreshments served to them so as not to insult his hosts, despite the fear of violating Jewish dietary restrictions by eating non-kosher food. In this lavish house, she was allowed to peek into a life she had not known was possible; actually, she did know, but had never been able to imagine it, and even if she had tried, what actually took place there was beyond anything she could have conjured in an imagination diminished by the circumstances of her life. She was very tense but tried to be, for a moment, the woman Mr. Levin asked her to be, producing, almost through sheer willpower, expressions she was unused to wearing. She almost felt as if she had succeeded and thought that maybe, from now on, things would change between them. Even if they changed only a little, that would be beneficial to her, because then she would know that there was hope, that there was something to look forward to, and she experienced a flutter of excitement. However, the flutter instantly transformed into a mayhem of sorts, which came upon her from inside.

She felt worst about the dress. Immediately when she put it on, she was afraid that something bad might happen to it, and therefore asked not to wear it at all. However, she succumbed to the pressure of the cousin's wife, who had been sent on behalf of Markus Levin. When they entered that large, elegant house, she understood that, indeed, she could not have shown up here in one of her simple dresses. She could not sit that way on the antique sofas and mingle with the esteemed guests and listen to the heavenly piano playing and taste the delicacies served to them on small platters. She could not stand beside her husband, who had taken particular care with his outfit that night, although he was always a dedicated follower of fashion, who returned from every trip with a new bespoke suit or shirt. There was no doubt that he had been more concerned about his appearance than her own, and now his appearance had been tarnished.

Markus Levin was furious, oh so furious. But with so much on the line, he could not direct his rage, which resembled lava bubbling up to the surface, at his wife or at his daughter Rahel. The room was full of people whom he had made many efforts to impress throughout the evening, and who were now frowning and drifting away from the smell gradually spreading through the air and from the whitish chunks scattered on the rug, and on the sofa and in other places that would be revealed when the room was cleaned.

And never mind the vomit of a little three-year-old girl. Never mind the accompanying shame, which would probably have been scrubbed away once the servants cleaned up, and in a moment, all would have been behind them. Even worse was the palm surprisingly raised by Chaya Levin, landing on Rahel's small, pale cheek, while she was still recovering from the act of vomiting.

The entire image of a happy family shattered at once. The impression Markus Levin had toiled to create in the previous days was now equivalent to those chunks of cake that had yet to be digested and had ended up on the floral carpet. Von Bismarck, who had invited Markus to come to Wroclaw with his family, and insisted on getting to know the family before establishing business ties, did shake his hand and smile warmly when they parted, but Markus was certain that the episode had already sabotaged their shared business venture before it even began, and his rage at his wife now encompassed the future loss still awaiting him.

At night, Chaya Levin tried to suppress the sobbing emerging from her. She cried and cried for quite a while and could not manage to stop. Her husband Markus was indeed justified when he assaulted her with a barrage of fury; this time, all his rage was warranted. Every word he said was right—she was stupid and ungrateful; there was no other way to describe her. Small and useless when he took her, she would remain that way her entire life. The sorrow and tears held on to her tightly, and she could not manage to lull herself to sleep.

Rahel was woken up by the murmur of her sniffles. After a deep sleep, she had almost forgotten what had occurred, or perhaps she had not. Perhaps the sobbing erupting from her mother pained her so much that she chose to suppress the event, chose to remember her mother in the dress that made her look like a high-class woman, among all the other elegant, beautiful women, amidst the cabinets displaying lovely china, while in the background, the piano played and wineglasses chimed. Perhaps it was not her mother she was picturing, but rather herself.

Rahel would always bear the pain of the sound slap she had received; however, it was not just due to that silly incident, but because of the heartache still to come, because of the attempt to clamber up and establish herself alongside the von Bismarcks and their ilk. To try and attain what people like her would never attain. She was only a three-year-old girl, but the seeds had already been sown, in that large, lavish aristocratic estate, surrounded by an enormous garden.

3 | 1778

Rahel wasn't a big talker—she usually preferred to listen—and although a long time had passed since that visit to Wroclaw, she was still talking about it. Talking about the experiences, the memories, the sights, the scents, the words—she talked about all of these endlessly, as well as about what she had learned there and her plans for the future. So long as Brendel listened, she kept telling and talking. What she did not talk about was what had happened at home since the day they returned. Those were the things she wanted to diminish, to ignore. As far as she was concerned, there was no need to talk about it; there was nothing exciting there, only tension, anger and distress, all of which she tried to keep at bay.

Since the day Brendel Mendelssohn had taken hold of Rahel's tiny hand, she had felt a need to take part in the life of the little soul who had bravely faced the death stalking her. Yente de Lemos, Brendel's friend, was busy with theater plays, with reading and mainly with the engagement that had come to pass shortly after her twelfth birthday, exactly two years ago.

Dr. Herz, a man of thirty or so, was one of Yente's father's—Dr. de Lemos—best students, as well as his close friend. Yente, who knew him, had not thought that this man, whose age was nearly twice her own, would be her husband.

"The doctor is requesting your hand in marriage." This was what her father had told her about two years ago, with no formalities or preliminaries, and Yente felt heat flooding her doll-like face as she gradually flushed.

"I barely know him," Yente said, her eyes downcast.

"He will be a good husband to you, I promise," her father told her. "He comes from a good, modest family and he has good manners and is financially well off."

Yente did not reply. If her father had decided that Dr. Herz was the right groom for her, she could not disobey him but must resign herself to her fate and hope that he was indeed correct, as he had been during all the times he had made promises to her and kept his word. And ever since, Yente had been preparing for her new life every day, while Brendel had been like a little mother to Rahel.

Yente chatted on about her dowry, which was coming together, about the dresses being sewn and then required to be undone due to her growth spurt, while Brendel told her about the development of her protégé, Rahel. Yente could not understand her mature friend's attraction to a snot-nosed, sickly baby who was seven years younger than her. Brendel, too, could not always explain the source of their connection to herself, but to Yente, she said, "Her mother, it's difficult for her sometimes. And Rahel is sickly. I'm only helping. My father is very proud of me and says that treating others well is just as important as fulfilling religious obligations, and might even be more important."

A slight sense of envy flitted through Yente's heart. While she was immersed in her own affairs, Brendel was tending to others, which meant that Brendel was a better person than she was. Although, if Brendel had been asked, she would have immediately and honestly confessed her envy of Yente. How could she not be envious of her? Yente was as beautiful as a porcelain doll while Brendel greatly resembled her hunchbacked father. And not only had Yente been blessed with extraordinary beauty and a carefree approach to life, but she had also been fortunate enough to find a good match, and was even overjoyed about it. She wondered what would happen to their friendship after Yente's wedding. The whole idea of being matched off did not appeal to Brendel, regardless of Yente's constant declarations of how happy she was. Brendel was certain that her own experience would more closely resemble Goethe's Young Werther, who was in love with Lotte. Reading the story of his love for her for the first time nearly took her breath away, and ever since, she had fervently wished she, too, would end up with a suitor who would love her to death, and that she, unlike Lotte, would be utterly won over by him.

In the meantime, the three of them met occasionally, and Rahel and Brendel were required to hear about the engagement again and again until sometimes, Brendel felt the urge to cover her ears. It was only the fact that she was a role model to Rahel that kept her from doing so.

Yente told them about the fabrics sent from Paris for the bedroom she would share with Dr. Herz. About fresh white linen with lace embroidered and entwined all around it. Matching pillows with their initials embroidered upon them: her initials on one pillow and the doctor's on the other, along with another pair of matching larger pillows. A light blue bedcover was also being sewn for the same set of linens. Yente provided a detailed description of the stitches, which were a darker shade of blue. She described where they began and where they ended and Brendel felt as if the description of the perfect bedroom intended for Yente and her future husband was about to put her to sleep. She tried to steer the conversation in a different direction, but Yente did not bother to listen and continued to provide details about fabrics and dresses and lampshades and curtains, as if she had not heard Brendel at all. Brendel appeared interested, but privately, she mused that she had never dedicated even a moment's thought to her bedcovers or the sheets or the tablecloths. When she snuck a look at little Rahel, she almost burst out in laughter when her young friend rolled her eyes at a dizzying speed.

Rahel was only seven years old, but sometimes it seemed to Brendel that her conversations with her were deeper and more stimulating than her conversations with Yente, who, since her engagement, did not seem to be using her brain anymore.

In the two years that had passed since the engagement, Yente had begun to limit her reading to books recommended by her fiancé. All the books she had Brendel had read before were now of no interest to her. She explained that Dr. Herz wanted to ensure her development so that she could fit in well within his social circles and take part in the conversations he would conduct in their home. And when Brendel finally succeeded in steering the conversation in her own direction, she mentioned that her father often consulted her mother in matters that did not pertain to the household, and that he greatly valued her opinion.

"My mother told me that after they fell in love, she and my father, he had to go back to Berlin while she stayed in Hamburg waiting for a permit to reside in Berlin and a license to get married there. And while she was waiting, my father hired a private French tutor for her and recommended books she should be reading. And so, when she arrived in Berlin about a year later, she was ready to be the wife of a philosopher."

"Your mother just plays the hostess in your drawing room," Yente said dismissively. "Ultimately, her role comes down to serving raisins, almonds and beverages to your father's guests, and no more. It won't be like that for us."

Brendel, who did not like her friend's criticism of her parents, felt the need to defend them.

"My parents are special people. My father married my mother out of love. It wasn't arranged." *Unlike you*, she wanted to say, but did not dare. "He traveled to visit a friend named Aaron in Hamburg, and that was where he met my mother. For an entire year, they corresponded, and every letter Father wrote to her began with the words 'My most beloved Fromet.'" Brendel looked at Yente. "One day, I'm going to love like that too."

Yente listened. Her father, Dr. de Lemos, had never told her how he had met her mother, whether he had fallen in love with her or how the match had been arranged. He was openly affectionate toward her, but Yente had never heard him utter words of love addressed to her mother.

Rahel, too, listened to Brendel and thought precisely the same thing. She did not understand the nature of her parents' connection, but knew she would only evoke their anger if she tried to ask them.

"Every birthday we celebrate at home, my father blesses Aaron Gumpertz twice, then raises a glass in his honor."

"Why twice?" Yente asked.

"Once because Aaron introduced him to his good friend Lessing and twice because he introduced him to my mother."

"We don't celebrate birthdays," Rahel said suddenly. She had been listening to the conversation the entire time while also reading a book.

Brendel and Yente exchanged a big-girl look. A baby who had come back from the dead deserved to have her birthday celebrated. Both of them were thinking the same thing, but they did not say a word to each other. They merely looked at Rahel, who was memorizing words from a book.

"You know," Brendel whispered to Yente, so that Rahel, who was somewhat distant from the two of them and busy with the booklet she was holding, would not hear, "she's right. The Levins don't celebrate birthdays."

"That can't be," Yente said. "They already have two children. Maybe they did celebrate and didn't invite you? There's no home where birthdays aren't celebrated!"

Brendel insisted, "They don't celebrate. Rahel is already seven years old, and they've never celebrated hers."

"We'll celebrate it," Yente declared and Brendel knew in her heart that despite Yente's good intentions, in a moment she would surely forget about her promise due to all the never-ending wedding preparations.

Rahel liked to be in the Mendelssohn family home. The toys, the dolls, the patience they exhibited toward her, the calm prevailing there and the mutual respect—all this attracted her. It seemed that she spent time in her own home only when she was sick. Lately, Brendel had begun to teach Rahel to read. Chaya Levin did not encourage this, and little Rahel did not understand why, but had gotten used to her mother complaining about her every action, regardless of what it was. She was already constantly complaining about the fact that Rahel did not leave her time for anything, that she was always sick, that she did not help her around the house, that she was "underfoot." This was the case regarding reading, as well. Rahel proved to be a quick learner and picked up the letters immediately; it seemed to come naturally to her.

Surprisingly, when it came to reading, her father did not object. "It wouldn't hurt her to know how to read and write," he once said when her mother tried to redirect his mounting fiery rage from her to the girl. "It wouldn't hurt if you yourself knew how to read and write," he told her. "You could have been more useful."

Rahel tried to stay out of the fights between her father and mother, which seemed to have gotten more intense and frequent ever since they returned from Wroclaw. When the fighting broke out, she would escape to her room and barricade herself in with her books. In the past, she would look at the pictures and make up stories, guessing at what the letters, which were foreign to her, were saying. But since Brendel had started teaching her, it seemed to have become easier. A whole world was gradually opening up before her, a world that led her even farther away from her bickering parents.

***

One day, the girls were spending time together at the Mendelssohn home. Rahel coughed and Brendel adjusted her coat, wrapping it tighter around her so that not even an iota of autumn wind would invade her frail body, wreaking havoc there. The house was otherwise unoccupied, and Yente produced a booklet with an elegant cover from her coat. Since Dr. de Lemos had announced his daughter's engagement and the event had been celebrated, she had been receiving gifts from all over Berlin and even beyond the city. One of the numerous gifts she had received thus far caught her eye when the courier had brought the delivery the day before. No more candlesticks or another casserole pot, no more bedcovers or a lavish porcelain set, no more of the variety of possessions that would serve her in her new home with her new doctor. No more of all that, but rather, a book.

And since there was nothing that pleased Yente more than a book, she had already sat down in her room and started to read. And when she reached Chapter 10 and began to read it, she grew furious, quickly closed the book and tossed it to the other end of the room. Now that she was sitting with Brendel and Rahel, she took the book out of her coat and read from it out loud: *A Woman's Guide to Marriage*. In a low voice, fearing that someone would enter, she read the opening of the story: "A story. *A queen had a daughter, whom she gave to the young king. She wrote a will declaring that she must be married. She sent the daughter off to her wedding and addressed her daughter. 'My beloved daughter, I am sending you away. I am handing you over to a stranger, although I don't know what manner of person he might be.'*" Even at this point, the three of them were already frowning, but Yente went on to read all ten rules teaching a woman how to conduct herself with her husband. All the rules explained what to do so as not to evoke the husband's anger, and were ultimately summed up by the seventh rule, which was not the last: "'*The seventh thing, my beloved daughter, is not to rebel. Do everything he commands you to do, whatever he says.*'"

From the moment Yente had read the contents of the story, she could not shake it off, while having no desire to follow its edicts. In her heart, she cursed the person who had made sure the book would end up in her possession, and for the first time, it occurred to her that she might be too young for all this. Brendel was silent and Rahel continued to occasionally let out an adult cough, as if she were at least ten years older than they were. And what could Brendel say, other than silently thanking her father, who was in no hurry to find her a match? Brendel had heard him talking about it with her mother. "It's too soon. She's still a child, and what's the big hurry?"

"These are different times," Brendel finally said, wanting to encourage the dejected Yente. "I'm sure you'll be happy with Dr. Herz, you'll see. And besides, those are just words written on paper and that's all." Privately, she thanked her father for his opinions, which were different than others' opinions, perhaps more progressive.

"I'll never get married," Rahel said, much to Yente and Brendel's surprise.

"Never?" Brendel teased. "And how do you know? What do you even understand, little girl?"

"Never!" the little one decreed, stamping her match-like legs. Yente and Brendel laughed and Rahel joined them.

Brendel then recalled Chaya-Hendelle, a childhood friend of theirs. She was older than them and her family was less wealthy, but she was still a friend. Brendel had heard that Hendelle's husband beat her. "Once she even tried to run away. She fled to her mother and father's house, although she was nearly sixteen years old. She said he beat her and even showed them the marks on her body." Rahel and Yente listened as if it were a thriller novel. "The rumor spread, and emissaries began to show up at the parents' home. They came and tried to talk her into going back home, to convince her. They talked about the importance of domestic peace and asked her to forgive; after all, he was not young like she was and spent most of his day studying the Torah while also required to provide for the both of them. Then they said that he was a scholar and she was an uneducated girl and finally they blamed her for the fact that he was beating her. She was the reason, that was what they decided."

"'Beat' means to hit?" Rahel asked.

"It's hitting," Brendel replied earnestly, stroking little Rahel's head. "And in spite of it all, she went back to his house. She didn't have a choice."

The three of them were briefly silent before Brendel added, "And then one day he came home and found her hanging."

"Hanging?" Rahel looked at Brendel in disbelief or incomprehension, yet her gaze was sad, as if she could feel that Chaya-Hendelle's pain.

"But such things won't happen to Yente," Brendel concluded, feeling as if she might have made a mistake by telling them. "Right, Yente?"

Yente, still shaking from the story, nodded slowly.

"It won't happen to any of us. We'll take care of each other," Brendel added determinedly. And now Rahel, too, nodded.

4 | 1778

The book Yente had received as a gift left her unsettled. There was an internal bubbling inside her, like a bothersome stomachache climbing nearly up to her throat, and heartbeats that were also discernible outside her chest, and thoughts that began and constantly returned to the same point, leading nowhere. Yente had never troubled herself with too many thoughts; she was always moving forward. But now she found herself thinking and thinking, as if she were an old woman with all of the world's troubles upon her shoulders, and no one to share these thoughts with. Lately, she seemed to have lost something. Her inability to put her finger on it awakened an anger in her that erupted uncontrollably. Yente noticed that this anger of hers also contained a bit of power. She saw that after each such outburst, her parents became more gentle, more considerate, less rigid toward her, seeking to fulfill her requests so long as she did not lose her temper. Perhaps they feared that she had lost her mind or that some demon had gotten into her, and she, in turn, took advantage of it. Some part of her regretted the worry they experienced after each of her tantrums, while another savored the accompanying sense of power.

This went on for a considerable period of outbursts and tantrums, during which she canceled her plans and rarely saw Rahel and Brendel, merely isolating herself. She even stopped reading the books recommended by her fiancé Dr. Herz, as if she was in a contrarian mood that encompassed the entire world. She paced back and forth in her room in a thin gown, watching herself, wanting to know who this girl or woman or figure looking back at her through the mirror was, trying to think what would become of her in the day after her marriage. Would he continue to be nice? Would he respect her? Would he allow her to do the things she loved? Could she keep on singing and accompanying herself on the piano, or would he forbid it? Would he be like her father, who loved her more than anything else in the world and was willing to do anything for her?

One day, she traveled with her father to visit an ailing member of the community. He asked her to accompany him and as always, she agreed immediately. She loved those trips, which always ended up in some café where they sat and drank and ate something sweet, just the two of them. Then she felt like one of the esteemed ladies of Berlin. She sat beside him clad in an elegant dress, attracting attention due to her beauty. People who knew her father stopped to say hello or to ask a question, some commenting on how lovely she was, and all that filled her with bliss.

On that day, Dr. Herz, her fiancé, joined them on the visit as well. When he was not looking in her direction, Yente allowed herself to glance at his face, hoping she would not be caught. His face was clean-shaven, his head encased in a smart bowler hat, from which strands of hair, tied back in a ribbon, trailed down. He did not don one of those powdered wigs that certain men placed on their heads, which was already one point in his favor, Yente thought then. As she looked at him, his gaze was drawn to her and their eyes met. She did not look down and neither did he, until her face grew flushed and she was flooded by heat. In her room, in her thin gown, the same sense of heat spread through her when she thought of Dr. Herz and immediately afterward, the same anger swirled through her belly. Fortunately, her father had to leave urgently for Hamburg, and succumbed to her pleas to let her join him. She could thus briefly escape from herself and from the reality that would soon become her life.

In Hamburg, she did indeed find a certain calm. Yente could not lock herself away in her room and was obliged to accompany her parents on every visit they made to their relatives and acquaintances. She also did not allow herself to have outbursts in the presence of strangers, and therefore she held herself back. And in general, she privately had to admit that she liked the change. She liked spending time with her relatives and liked to visit the lavish homes of Hamburg. After her marriage, she would live in a house with her doctor and be the mistress of the house, and although the dowry was piling up, it was obvious that she would still have to decide which items of furniture would go in her home and how she would design it. Therefore, she began to pay more attention to the houses they visited. She noticed that in quite a few of the houses, portraits of the family members hung on the walls. Sometimes it was a portrait of the father and sometimes of the grandfather. There were also paintings of the entire family, occasionally including a dog or two as well. She also noticed that such paintings appeared mostly on the walls of wealthy families that were not Jewish. And as she was still on her way home, she came to a decision. She, too, wanted a portrait to adorn her drawing room. Now she had to find someone to paint her, and she wanted to do it on her own, without her father's help. Soon she would be a married woman, and if she was old enough to get married, she was old enough to find an artist for the portrait that would hang in her home.

Yente knew the best person to consult on this matter was Princess Anna Amalia, the sister of Frederick the Great, who was the king of Prussia at the time. Anna Amalia was particularly interested in the Jewish holidays and had asked Dr. de Lemos to invite her to the family's home during the holidays. The de Lemos family had a hard time understanding what charmed her about the house, bourgeois and wealthy though it might be, when her own home was glittering with wealth, brimming with grandeur and grace, and overflowing with every manner of bounty. However, Anna was intrigued by the change that took place in a Jewish home when a holiday arrived. And they had plenty of holidays.

"So many holidays, and each holiday seems to be unique," she said every time she arrived at Yente's family home. She loved the blessings recited in a language she did not understand, and accompanied by sipping wine at the table or distributing the bread. She liked the customs that were a part of each holiday—eating matzah on Passover, lighting the menorah candles on Hanukkah, eating a fish head on Rosh Hashanah, the Jewish New Year, or the custom of purchasing new clothes, which had nothing to do with religion, as she was told. Most of all, however, she loved to observe Yente. She was like a doll in her dollhouse, with her delicate face, her immaculate clothing, and her coal-black hair, constantly braided in a different style. The princess found a special pleasure simply in watching her and did not care if this looked odd. Dr. de Lemos and his wife Esther always put her up graciously. After all, she was the king's sister. It never hurt to nurture such connections; who knew when they would need them.

And now Yente made an appointment to meet Anna Amalia, who had become her friend. She knew the princess would have the perfect recommendation.

Anna Amalia knew immediately who would be the best person for the task. The painter was actually a woman, named Anna Therbusch. Yente felt in her gut that this was the right thing to do, perhaps knowing that her father would object if she had to spend hours with a strange man. Mostly, though, she felt that it would be right to allow a woman to paint her. One thing was clear to her—she was about to get married, and this was her time to make decisions for herself. In addition, beauty was fleeting and should be immortalized when it was at its peak

Anna Amalia took her to her brother's home and showed her Anna Therbusch's paintings.

"If she's good enough for the king, she'll certainly be good enough for me," Yente told her.

Anna Amalia offered to pay for the painting. "A wedding present," she told Yente. This freed Yente from the need to manipulate her father in order to get money, and the entire process became more personal to her. Now she would not have to be accountable to anyone until the project was completed.

***

While Yente paved her way to her married life, her friends were ensconced in their homes, each of them experiencing a different sort of familial crisis. Rahel, who had always hoped she and her brother Markus would forever remain two and that she would never have to share her parents with more children, was waiting anxiously for another birth. Rahel possessed no great love for Markus, but knew how much her father valued her little brother, and when she wanted to obtain something from him, would offer Markus various temptations and apply various manipulations until she got what she wanted. Now their mother was about to give birth to another offspring, and Rahel was certain the balance would be disrupted.

Brendel's home was suffused with mourning after the departure of Zisse, a smiley baby girl who spent a mere three months on earth before being abruptly plucked.

Yente was sufficiently self-aware to avoid bothering them. She was dealing with luxury while they were dealing with the labor of life.

The three girls were scheduled to meet again only at the *bris*, the circumcision ceremony for Ludwig, Rahel's new brother. Brendel and Yente's family had been invited to the humble ceremony held in the Levin home, but Brendel and her family had not attended.

Rahel spent the *bris* in Yente's company, hoping that some of Yente's joy and great excitement in preparation for her new life would rub off on her as well. Dr. de Lemos provided a short explanation for the name given to the baby. "'*Hlud*' means fame and glory, while '*wig*' means battle or war," he explained to the few guests staying at the house. Rahel was glad that her new ally would have something of the warrior about him and would be able to protect her when necessary, although she preferred him to be interested in the things she liked.

After the *bris*, Yente and Rahel went outside and Yente told Rahel about Anna Therbusch.

"I want Anna," Yente told Rahel proudly. She was proud of sticking to her guns. "Anna has painted Frederick the Great and Catherine the Second, the greatest Russian queen of them all," she explained to Rahel. Rahel found the idea exciting and secretly yearned to be like Yente.

***

Yente's portrait was of great interest to Rahel, while Brendel had no interest in it at all. The last thing she wanted was for someone to paint her. "It would be a waste of paint," she said when the three girls discussed the painting, thus excusing herself from the enthusiasm and from the entire affair, which she saw as unnecessary. Rahel was allowed to visit on painting days, watching from the sidelines while Yente posed for the painter, erect and determined, for hours and hours.

Anna Amalia suggested that Yente pose in the de Lemos family home. As the artist did not stay in any one place for long, she would usually paint in her patrons' homes, and before Yente could say a thing, Anna Amalia volunteered to come speak to her father. Both of them knew that Dr. de Lemos would be unable to refuse her, and this proved to be the case.

The artist arrived with her apprentice, a young, smiling man whose entire role was to carry the paints, the paintbrushes and the rags, clean them and restore them to their places at the end of the day, serve Anna food and drink, and take care of her every need. He was a man of a kind Rahel and Yente had never seen before, neither at home nor in their immediate surroundings. His gestures were delicate, almost feminine, and his clothes odd. He did not wear a suit and a bowler like most men, but rather simple clothing that reminded Rahel somewhat of the theater actors who occasionally arrived to see her father. He was courteous and obedient and seemed as if his only desire was to please Anna. However, after a while, this began to seem natural to them. On the first day, Anna gave him precise instructions regarding the location, after choosing the most appropriate room, with the desired amount of light. She examined the direction from which the light flowed and calculated the times when it would change, picking the spot accordingly.

Her apprentice brought her the easel and opened a suitcase full of paints and brushes. After emptying it out, he turned it over and installed additional accessories on it, turning it into a kind of three-legged table on which the equipment was placed.

Anna produced thick fabrics and multi-hued powders from the suitcase. "Each powder," she told them, "was brewed from a different source. The pink and the crimson were brewed from berries and trees, the Prussian blue was discovered by accident when someone was boiling bones and blood, and the white lead had a strong smell that required opening a window. There were other powders that, when mixed with a certain liquid, became paste."

Rahel tried to show up whenever she could. She was the only one allowed to enter the room, so long as she was not a bother. She always came, other than the times her mother forced her to stay home and complete some task, and other than one week when she was afflicted, once again, with a severe cough, fever and a rash all over her body. Between shaking and coughing, she regretted who she was: a small, weak, indistinct creature that, even when sick, was left alone with its illness. She envisioned Yente sitting on the sofa with the light-colored, regal dress designed and sewn especially for her, with a neckline trimmed with lace in the front and sleeves edged with ribbons, savoring the attention bestowed upon her. Rahel wanted such attention, consisting of praise and compliments, rather than the kind she received from her angry mother and father.

Yente herself was not always pleased with all the fuss surrounding her. Recently, she had asked her father whether she could stop attending school due to all the harassment on the street, which had initially been bearable, but lately kept swelling. The staring was one thing, she could deal with that, but lately, she had started to experience comments and physical proximity from men, and these comments were coarse and unpleasant. But the tipping point was a hand extended to her body, which did not stop even when Yente asked the man to step away and even when she informed him that she was connected to important, influential people, even mentioning Frederick the Great. If a man who recognized her distress had not happened to pass by at the moment, she did not know how it would all have ended. The next day, private tutors started to arrive at her home, and the school chapter of her life came to an end. Now, with the whole matter of the portrait, she had to skip some lessons, and hoped her future husband would not be too angry about it, as he valued her education.

Yente did complain somewhat about the difficulty of being a model, about the many hours of sitting mutely, about her aching muscles, about the required discipline, but she persisted religiously. Of course, she complained about the odors she had to put up with and the immense effort she was putting in, but she and Rahel agreed that the most fascinating part of the entire process was the conversations with Anna.

Anna was in her sixties but very vigorous. She took care to arrive for work wearing her finest dresses, without a work gown. "My father taught me how to paint, along with my sister Rosina," she told them, after Rahel could not hold back any longer and asked her how she had learned a profession that was usually confined to men only.

"My father, may he rest in peace, was born in Poland. He was born in the exact same city in which the king of Poland was born." She was as proud of this fact as if she were still his little girl, and as if his birth in the king's home town made him regal as well. "In 1692, he was a part of the entourage of the court architect, and came with them to Prussia," she recounted, directing Yente with the paintbrush in her hand. She asked her to tilt her head slightly to the left and not to move, all wordlessly, like an orchestra conductor.

"He was a painter and he taught us to paint. My sister, Anna Rosina, and I, Anna Dorothea, were considered *wunderkinder*. Wonder children. We were full-blown painters at such a young age. A true wonder."

"Then she got married," Rahel told Brendel, "and from that moment on, she stopped painting."

"Why did she stop?" Brendel asked, although she could guess the answer.

"Since she had to help her husband. He ran an inn with a restaurant."

"And she didn't paint that entire time?" Brendel asked.

"She didn't paint for many years," Rahel said, shaking her head oddly to emphasize that statement. She then paused for some time, as if thinking something over, before she continued. "And after a few years of living with him, she left him and her children, all in order to paint again. Later she painted in Stuttgart, for Duke Carl Eugen. She worked vigorously and completed twelve portraits in a very short time. They were so impressed with her work for the duke that they invited her to be the guest of honor at the Stuttgart Academy of Fine Arts." After another brief silence, she added, "I want to travel to Stuttgart when I grow up."

Brendel shrugged.

"She also spent time in Paris. And she achieved true acclaim there. But no money, and so she returned to Prussia." She paused again, then added, "I'll go to Paris, too."

The days went by and Rahel and Yente's curiosity only increased. They asked to peek at the painting. "Just for a moment, and we won't tell anyone, we promise."

However, Anna firmly refused. "An agreement is an agreement."

After a few weeks, Anna Dorothea Therbusch announced that in a day or two, the portrait would be ready and that during that time, she would make some corrections and then the painting must dry, and she would bid them farewell.

That night, Yente did something she had never dared to do before, and apparently would never do again. She rose silently while everyone was asleep, tiptoed down to the drawing room holding a lit candle, and peeked.

5 | 1779

Three years after the engagement, the moment arrived. Yente was married in the drawing room of the de Lemoses' large, spacious home. Brendel and Rahel were already utterly prepared for the wedding, and yet both of them were seized with excitement at the moment when Yente stood below the *chuppah*,[5] with a *tallit*[6] for its ceiling and thin sticks as its posts.

"God willing, your turn will come as well," Fromet told fifteen-year-old Brendel as they huddled around the *chuppah*, while Brendel responded with a smile that did not disclose what was going through her mind. On the one hand, she understood that marriage was an important, inevitable step, but on the other hand, she knew it all depended upon her father and prayed he would make the right choice for her when the day came.

Rahel did feel some excitement, but it was only on Yente's behalf. She knew how important that moment was for her friend; she had been waiting for it for three years before it finally arrived. And now, under the *chuppah*, the groom and his elderly parents stood on one side, while on the other side were Dr. de Lemos and his wife, Esther. And above them all, Yente was radiant in her puffy lace dress, with its high collar, the delicate ribbons adorning its sleeves, and the gems embroidered upon the chest, seeming to

---

5   A *chuppah* is a canopy under which a Jewish couple stands during their wedding ceremony.

6   A *tallit* is a fringed garment, traditionally worn as a prayer shawl by religious Jews.

drip down to its hem. Yente looked like a fairy-tale princess.

Rahel recalled the story Brendel had told them about Chaya-Hendelle and hoped that Yente's story would have a happy ending. She wanted Yente's husband to be good to her, and to ensure this, was even willing to say a prayer, if she knew the appropriate prayer and if she could understand anything from all the prayers in a language she did not speak. When she grew up a bit, she wanted to learn the Hebrew language. She would ask Yente to teach her, as well as ask Brendel to teach her French, so that she would be ready to travel to Paris, which seemed so distant from her. If she had a husband, she would certainly have to ask his permission every time she wanted to travel, and how could she know whether he would agree? And how could she know whether he would be nice like Yente's doctor? Or like Moses Mendelssohn, Brendel's father, who was constantly affectionate? Or like Dr. de Lemos, who made his daughter Yente's wishes come true? Perhaps her father would want to match her up with someone like him, who would constantly be angry at her and treat her the same way he treated her mother? For all of these reasons, she would not consent to any match her father offered her. Deep in her heart, she was glad she was still young and far from all that, and that she still had time before she became a woman. If she prayed for anything, this would be it; she would pray that no husband would be found for her.

After the *chuppah*, and the ceremony, and the blessings, and the traditional breaking of the glass[7] and Dr. Herz's tentative kiss on Yente's porcelain cheek, Yente slipped away to her room. Her cheeks were flushed and her body cold due to the sweat that had flooded her when she was under the *chuppah*. She wanted to take a few minutes to herself in order to recover and get used to the new status she had taken on as of that moment. On the bed was a beautiful headscarf, decorated with pearls, sent from Paris especially for the bride. Starting tomorrow, as a married woman, she would be obliged to wear the scarf on her head, hiding all her coal-black hair under it, as her

---

7   At the end of a Jewish wedding ceremony, the groom breaks a glass by crushing it with his right foot. The primary reason for this custom is the belief that joy must always be tempered.

mother had taught her. This had been her guidance—all women did so.

Yente sat down on the bed, which responded with a creak. She had never noticed that creak before, and now it sounded discordant, almost betraying her, and any moment now the guests would enter her room to find out that she was there, sitting rather than participating in the ultimate celebration. Yente was not sad; on the contrary, Dr. Herz was a nice, pleasant person, and there was something non-threatening about him. It was true that some of her friends were already talking about him behind her back, saying he was ugly and short, but she chose to see his internal qualities, which she found to be radiant and beautiful.

Now she only wanted one moment to herself. One moment of quiet, without being congratulated, or kissed, or hugged, or any feminine advice being whispered in her ear. Just one moment. Across from her was the portrait painted by Anna Therbusch, which had been taken down from the wall in order to be sent to her new home—their home.

It had been almost a year since she betrayed her painter friend's trust and peeked at the painting, which had yet to dry then. She had been stunned and a cry of alarm nearly escaped from her lips, but she stopped herself, fearing that one of the household members would awaken and she would have to deal with what she saw on the canvas on her own.

Under the brush of an artist who had been greatly praised for her paintings of kings, princes and aristocrats in Germany and outside it, the Jewish Dr. de Lemos's daughter, a beauty already engaged to a man who was just as respectable as she was, had been transformed into Hebe, the Greek goddess of youth. Her hair was loose, adorned with flowers, her shoulders bare. It seemed as if, just moments ago, her white dress had slipped off and glided down her left shoulder, and soon what should remain discreetly concealed would be exposed. The Jewish goddess's right hand was holding a glass full of nectar and ambrosia. At any moment, she would distribute it to the gods, who would be blessed with eternal life, and she along with them. Yente would acquire eternal life upon the taut canvas, sitting there with her pinkish skin that was permitted to all.

She was not Jewish in the painting, and there was not the slightest spark of guilt in the expression of that goddess of youth looking innocently at all who gazed upon her. All of the Jewish history seared inside her disappeared without a trace, absent from those lines of paint and brushstrokes. A woman-girl exposing herself, as innocent as youth itself is innocent, no more and no less.

Anna Therbusch was pleased, and Dr. de Lemos had no say in the matter, as she had received her fee from Anna Amalia, and even if he chose to convince the princess not to pay due to the shame the painting would soon bring upon them, Anna would consider it fair, as this was not how they had expected her to paint their oldest daughter, and in any case, she never painted according to expectation. She was not one of those painters who copied what their eye perceived; she included an interpretation as well.

Yente would have preferred to forget the chaos that broke out after the whole matter was revealed, as well as her father's expression when he first viewed the painting. She had never seen her father so angry, an anger that made his face flush and caused him to bury his face in his hands as if he were a child who did not want to see something that had frightened him. If he were not a level-headed man, he would certainly have picked up some object and thrown it at the painting until it was destroyed and had vanished from the world. But her father was endowed with great restraint, acquired over time thanks to his work, and after gazing at the painting for a long time, he retired to his study and barricaded himself inside. Yente knew she would have to tiptoe around him, and that it was possible that her father would be unable to look her in the eye for a while. She was already sorry for the initiative she had taken, although she truly loved the woman reflecting at her from the painting as well as the daring she had exhibited, and mostly the fact that she could not be blamed for all this, as Therbusch had done whatever she wished.

Dr. de Lemos's non-Jewish friends had been the ones to appeal to his heart and mostly to his mind. Of course, first they had to come and see the painting that had become the talk of the town. The portrait that had remained upon the easel long after the painter's task was done, long after the paint and oil had dried, and long after the anger and the shame. After all this, people began to come to the house especially to see the goddess Hebe, the Jewish daughter of Dr. de Lemos.

Art. That was precisely the thing. No more and no less, it was what adorned the homes of kings and earls and all of the top nobility. "And what is this world without art?" one of the women visiting the house, whose opinion he valued greatly, told the doctor. "Your daughter is very beautiful, and that is indisputable, and everyone is envious of her beauty and talking about it. This beauty of hers is as rare as a precious gem and now it is laid out on the canvas and does not indicate anything about her nature, but only about the nature of the artist." And perhaps that was the strongest argument, the one to convince her father and reconcile him with his daughter.

"Where shall we hang the painting?" Yente asked her husband. The guests had already left and Yente felt as if the entire evening had passed her by, as if she had not been present but rather more of an observer from the sidelines, and all the anticipation and the preparations and the excitement preceding it had come down to three or four hours, and after dawdling for a while longer in her parents' house and agreeing that the wedding party had been a success and kisses and "good night," Yente and her doctor climbed into the carriage that led them to their new home, but not before Yente had taken the painting with her.

When Dr. Herz viewed the painting for the first time, he was embarrassed. It happened in the presence of his bride's father and the entire situation seemed strange to him. The only thing he was thinking about at the time was not the nature of the art, the quality of the painting or the circumstances under which it was created. The only thing he saw in it was that bare shoulder, taunting him and invading his mind with thoughts he tried to shake off, and which aroused his body in a manner that mortified him.

Now the two of them were sitting on their bed and the young doctor, her husband, the man who had been her father's apprentice, reached out for her tentatively. He was permitted to do so now, she was his and he was hers and the two of them were bound by the covenant of marriage through the blessings and the ring and the ceremony concluded and sealed with the breaking of the glass. And yet his reach was tentative. By force of habit and due to his respect for her father and for her, and because of her sharp tongue and her directness, and mostly the beauty of his wife sitting beside him and looking at him tauntingly from the painting propped against the wall. Yente brought her mouth closer to his and she too reached out her hand, straight for his dark, tangled hair. They kissed, a kiss of which he had dreamed for many days along with its taste and softness, a sweet, fierce kiss. Yente's delicate skin was flushed, and his face became flushed as well. He felt his heart beating and his blood flowed swiftly, now concentrating in his trousers.

"We'll hang the painting wherever you decide."

Yente smiled. The doctor peeled off her dress until her shoulders were left exposed to his eyes only, just as she was in the painting. He felt the shiver than ran through Yente, the shiver of one who desires something but is simultaneously also terrified of it. She was so young and delicate. He continued to caress her, quietly explaining to her what was about to happen and kissing her all over her body. Slowly, she felt she was returning to herself and the shivering stopped. Only then did the doctor's body take action, with great gentleness. That night Yente understood she would always be safe by his side and surrendered herself to him. The covenant was signed with their bodies.

∗∗∗

When she was invited to a ball several weeks after her wedding, she was very excited, as she knew this would be the first event she would attend alongside her husband, Dr. Herz. And in all the excitement, she forgot that as a married Jewish woman, many rules would apply to her. Now she stood in front of the mirror in her new room and put on her clothes, sewn in accordance with her status as a married woman. She did not recognize the woman reflecting back at her. The elegant headscarf, adorned with pearls and tiny flowers, and a new dress with long sleeves and a modest neckline, all these brought her to bitter tears and a refusal to leave for the ball. Dr. Herz, her new husband, inexperienced and helpless, summoned her mother, who must know the way to her heart.

"These are our customs, Yente," her mother tried to console her. "At first, the appearance is strange, but only because it's new, and later, you grow accustomed to it." As she consoled her, she adjusted the headscarf so that the hair rebelling against it and poking out would return to its proper place.

"I won't grow accustomed to it," Yente whimpered. "I never will."

And yet, she showed up to the ball covered up like a modest Jewish woman. And throughout the evening, an intense emotion, already familiar from a different time, bubbled up inside her, and seeds of loathing were planted within her. Self-loathing due to that appearance, and loathing toward the religion that forced her to walk down the streets of fashionable Berlin with her religion displayed upon her head. She also felt loathing toward her mother, who urged her with sweet words to leave for that ball, and loathing toward Jewish society as a whole, which pressured her to suppress her beauty, the same beauty granted to her by the God of all of them. Later, she also tried on a wig made especially for her, another idea originating with her mother, who tried in any way she could to keep her within the bounds of Jewish society.

Yente stood across from the portrait painted by Anna Therbusch as if attempting to draw a bit of courage from it. In addition to the mark Anna had left behind in the form of the painting, there were also the conversations that Yente retained in her heart, not sharing them with anyone. Back then, when the two of them were on their own while Rahel was sick, they had conversations about freedom and independence and choices and the price paid for all of these things; a price Anna paid and was willing to pay even in three more incarnations. Anna Therbusch went back to her life and left Yente behind, trapped behind laws and rules. And Yente, who wished to make her own choices, knew those choices would not be accepted without a fuss, just like the painting that created an uproar in her father's home, and yet she chose to persevere.

Despite all her mother and her aunts' attempts to convince her, Yente decided she would no longer wear anything on her head and that she would dress as she saw fit. If she wanted, she would cover up her body completely, and if she did not, she would not.

And just as her doctor agreed to hang the painting in their drawing room, over the fireplace, so, too, did he agree to her requests not to abide by the laws of Judaism with regard to her attire and the headscarf. And every time he agreed to her whims and requests and suggestions, she loved him more and more.

6 | 1780

"People, people, when will you stop all this?" Moses Mendelssohn muttered with simmering rage.

"What did we do to them, Papa? Why do they always chase us and curse?" ten-year-old Joseph asked, and Brendel, who was six years older, hugged him and looked at her father as red drops trickled down his forehead.

Sunday was the Mendelssohn family's favorite day. After Friday, when there were plenty of preparations to be made, and Saturday, the Sabbath, devoted to prayer and rest, came Sunday, the day of rest for their Berlin neighbors who were not Jews like them. And on that day, the Berliners went out for walks throughout the city, as did the Mendelssohns—Fromet, Moses and both the young and older children.

They walked on Unter den Linden Boulevard, a long, broad avenue lined with old linden trees. The trees were so tall that their roots were probably branched underground along the entire boulevard. And during that early morning hour, as the Mendelssohn family walked down the boulevard that ended with the hunting grounds that were popular with the nobles—the Tiergarten—they experienced an incident that the passersby chose to ignore.

A group of noisy boys, around Brendel's age, were lurking there, seemingly waiting for the Mendelssohns to approach. Then they began to call out, their shouting rhythmic and taunting, "Jews, Jews." In between the calls, they threw stones they had prepared in advance in their pockets, small, large and medium, with a kind of malice that surprised Brendel, a malice she had not suspected that her peers possessed. The stones hit her parents and little Joseph. Apparently, Brendel was the only one who was not hurt by the barrage assaulting them. Moses pulled his young son by the hand, hastening his steps, and Fromet followed his lead. The boys, pleased with their success, ran after them, alternately shouting and laughing.

The panic on her father's face, his helplessness in front of his family and the sight of the blood trickling down his forehead to his face, all of it angered Brendel. And where could she direct her anger? At her father, who did not hold his own when confronted with the young boys and chose to flee? At Berlin, which never protected its Jewish citizens? Perhaps at those "good" Christians who filled the churches every Sunday, praying to Jesus, but did not have an iota of compassion in their hearts for them, and chose not to interfere in what was not their business? The rage within her threatened to erupt and Brendel did not know how to contain it.

A few hours later, Fromet convinced Brendel to go meet her friends. Although her mood was glum, Brendel complied. She sat with Rahel and Yente for a cup of afternoon tea in Yente's yard and swore to herself that she would not tell them of the incident that had so shamed her father. But after a short time, she felt that if she left it all inside her for much longer, it would burn her up and she would burst into flames. Ever since that morning, her heart had been beating wildly and would not stop. She had never seen her father so angry, and although his words only emerged in a gritted mumble of rage, she could sense his insult and internalized it as well. To hell with the Chosen People and to hell with those *goyim*,[8] with their hatred, which, like burning embers, occasionally ignited into wildfires.

She swore them to secrecy. She also told them about the letter her father had written to his good friend, the monk Peter Adolph Weinkopf. She had never peeked at his letters before, but this time, perhaps because he was in a state of emotional upheaval, he had left it open on the table and Brendel could not stop herself from taking a look. Her eye was particularly snagged

---

8   Non-Jews

by four lines that she could not believe her father had written. Words full of outrage and anger of the kind she had never known him to exhibit. She read the words again and again until they were engraved in her mind:

"The country in which I live is supposedly called 'a tolerant country,' but in fact I live there under intense pressure and the intolerance oppresses me from every direction. What should I do? Perhaps lock up my children with me all day at the silk factory where I work, like you willingly confine yourself to the monastery? Would that be the way to spare them such brutal experiences? This situation certainly does not inspire an intellectual's literary and philosophical muse."

Tears that she had thus far forcibly suppressed burst from Brendel's eyes. Her father had always believed in respect and tolerance. He never maligned others and always insisted that they, too, refrain from doing so in his presence or at all. He was an important man who was respected by many—both Jews and gentiles, Berliners and non-Berliners, common people and dignitaries.

"Brendel, those were just children, they don't have a brain in their head," Yente tried to console her, although she knew this was not quite accurate.

"Whether they're children or not, the fault is ours, and ours alone." And from the moment Brendel came out with the tale, it was as if some dam had broken within her, and the words flooded out.

"We Jews do our very best to separate ourselves. Look at the ones who still haven't been exposed to progress. They walk around the streets of the city in Jewish attire and with Jewish side locks, confining themselves to their own company and ostracizing anyone who doesn't walk their own path. They condemn anyone who holds independent views and hopes to live his life based on education, enlightenment, joy and love for his fellow men. On the other hand, look at the ones calling themselves 'devotees of reason.' They consider themselves enlightened, but instead of adopting values of love and tolerance, they exile and ostracize those who behave differently and reject the 'Berlin mentality,' as if they were better than us."

Yente was silent. Brendel was right. Now that she was married and out and about in society alongside her husband, she was better acquainted with the intrigues and infighting within the self-isolating Jewish community. She and her husband were among the rather small number of Jews who wished to live their lives like all other citizens of the world, which made them the target of plenty of gossip whispered behind their backs, and even resulted in their being shunned. Because her husband was a doctor, his services essential, they were spared much of this, but it still happened. Anyway, some envied them and only talked about them behind their backs, while others hated them and avoided all contact with them. And in any case, such sentiments came from the mouths of people who were part of their own society.

"Judaism is despicable," Brendel added.

Yente nodded and warned her not to voice such opinions too loudly.

"A Jew should be a person first, and only then a Jew," Rahel added. She knew precisely why she had come out with such a statement. She did not need to venture out into Jewish society; she had learned this lesson in her own home. Her observant Jewish father, who was equally strict about both minor and major religious edicts, who contributed to the synagogue and was guaranteed a place of honor there—that same esteemed man forgot all about the edicts governing a man's relationship with his wife and children the moment his anger flared. And his anger flared from the moment he entered the house until the moment he left it. And how did all this Judaism of his help them if he treated them the same way Gentiles treated Jews?

"Brendel is right," Rahel said, not taking care to lower her voice. "Judaism is despicable and hypocritical."

7 | 1782

Once again, Dr. de Lemos was summoned to the Levin home. Rahel had been coughing all night and her father had no choice but to retire to his study and close the door so as not to hear the barking cough issuing from her. Only a short time ago, she had recovered from a severe cold. Her mother, pregnant with her fourth child, was forced to stay up nearly all night long because of her.

The doctor examined her and heard sounds he did not like coming from her chest. Her tiny bones seemed to be on the verge of flying apart due to the cough, and would be impossible to knit back together again. He handed her mother a tincture to mix and give to Rahel and instructed her to lower her fever with a cold dip.

If there was one thing Rahel hated most of all, it was the cold dips, in summer or in winter. Her mother would take off her clothes and walk her to a bath full of cold water. She immersed herself as warm, salty tears trickled down from her eyes, disappearing into the freezing water. She wanted to grow, to be stronger, and to turn into a young lady like Yente or Brendel. The two of them were only rarely ill, and when they were, the members of their families supported them until they recuperated completely. A short time ago, Yente had told her that her throat felt like it was burning, as if she had swallowed a little ball of fire. And until that ball of fire disappeared, her mother came to her home and brought clear chicken broth and delicacies reserved only for such occasions. The Mendelssohns treated any illness with much gravity due to the many losses they had suffered, and Rahel knew that anyone who was ailing received the greatest attention from the moment the disease first made an appearance and until it faded away.

Meanwhile, in her household, other than that cold dip, Rahel's mother was busy with her own affairs, her father was busy earning a living, and Rahel was laid up in bed burning with fever or coughing or suffering this or that pain on her own. She could not even read, which, in and of itself, caused her much anguish. Her body hurt when she even raised her head from the pillow. When she recovered, she would read twice as much, she swore to herself.

She yearned to return to the library. That alone motivated her to get well as quickly as possible. Yente had once told her that the lending library was a relatively new thing. It first opened to the public when she herself was a child. She revealed with a smile that she had read plenty of "bad romances and comedies," in the words of her parents' friends, educated Jews who were greatly surprised that her father, a devout Jew, allowed her to read such books. As she lay confined to her bed, Rahel imagined herself walking to the lending library. After she took the stairs right down to the street and walked about forty-five steps, and after turning right to the boulevard leading to the library, she would stop. She had an ongoing ritual of sorts—a moment before she walked in through the heavy wooden door, she stopped to look at the structure with the wood-framed windows and the coarse iron handles. She looked left and right in order to see who was about to enter the library and who was just passing by on the street, and then she extended her right leg forward and strode into the library, not before listening to the usual creak emitted by the heavy door.

The first time she had arrived on her own and roamed among the wooden shelves, the many books on the shelves made her head spin and a true sense of timelessness enveloped her. She had loved the smell, imprinted upon her nose the moment she entered, right from the start: a heavy scent of wood mixed with a light smell of dust, and each additional inhalation revealed new layers of the scent of print and of book covers, leather covers and cloth covers, thick paper covers and special binding threads holding the pages together. All these mingled with the odor of cigarette smoke invading the space she had created for herself and ruining the magic. And just as she tried to understand where the smell was coming from, she heard a man's voice behind her.

"Young lady," the voice said, "you cannot walk around here on your own. Please come back with your mother or with your father." And Rahel felt all the magic fade away as her dream drew farther away, almost vanishing.

Her father and mother had no time to waste on her and her desires. As far as her father was concerned, it was quite enough that he had paid for her education, as if she were a son, which he had only done to achieve equal status with his friends, like Moses Mendelssohn and like Dr. de Lemos and like other Jews of their class. Soon, she would grow up and he would find her an appropriate match and then the burden of providing for her would fall upon her husband. And as far as her mother was concerned, it was bad enough that she had not managed to convince her to learn how to do housework, or the craft of sewing, or embroidery, or other skills that would serve her well after her marriage when she would have to manage the housekeeping. Her mother had lost her to books, and certainly had no desire to accompany her to the place that had caused her to shirk all her responsibilities as a young woman.

The smoker with the low voice stood and pointed his plump finger and his overgrown nails at the door.

Rahel told Yente she had been thrown out of the library, and the two immediately boarded a carriage that was always waiting at the entrance to the Herzes' home and returned there. When they entered the library, they were greeted by the smoker and tall, lovely Yente extended her hand to him. She introduced herself as the wife of Dr. Herz, whose name was already well-known in Berlin, and now a big, rare smile dawned on the squat man's face and ever since, he had allowed Rahel to show up and read as much as she wanted. She, too, read the same romances and comedies that Yente had read. Luckily for her, she had learned to read in German and did not require translations, which, in many cases, negatively affected the story. Most Jews, and certainly Jewish women, did not read German, only translations into Yiddish, and yet she, little though she might be, had risen above most of them.

Now she lay in her bed, burning up, when suddenly she heard a knock on the door. At first she thought she was hallucinating due to her high fever, but the door opened and Yente came in. Ever since her marriage, she had been asking everyone to call her by her full name, Henriette, but Rahel and Brendel found it hard to get used to the change.

"Yente, you shouldn't be here, I'm sick."

"Anna Therbusch passed away." Yente was distraught, as if she had just been told that one of her family members had died. They had not spent much time with Anna Therbusch, but the time in which they were with her had left an impression on both of them. The woman who arrived day after day with her apprentice had managed to crack something in Yente, whose path in life had been paved by her father and was known in advance. Meanwhile, Rahel, who lay covered up to her nose in winter blankets, also felt Yente's sadness. If she had known the extent to which Anna Therbusch had actually gotten under her skin, she would have been much sadder.

Yente did not stay long and stormed out of Rahel's room, just as she had stormed in. Apparently, she only wanted to relay the news and proceed with her mission of further disseminating it.

Rahel let out a cough that almost took her breath away and found herself alone in her room again, sleeping and waking between one cough and the next, with no sense of time. And now the door was opening swiftly and somewhat alarmingly and Brendel appeared, her face as bleak as Yente's face had been. Rahel tried to say she already knew about the painter's death, but Brendel was just then bursting into tears and could not be stopped. If Rahel were not sick, she would have approached Brendel and hugged her.

"Does your father know you're here?" Rahel asked. If Moses Mendelssohn knew his daughter was in a room where an invalid was laid out, he would be furious.

Brendel produced a handkerchief from her small handbag and blew her nose. She wiped her tears and only then said, "He's the reason why I'm here." Once again, tears burst from her eyes and she needed a few more moments to calm down.

And then Brendel began to talk. "He's not particularly handsome, but I'm not pretty, either. Father says he's kind and moral and generous." Rahel could still not grasp what she was talking about.

"And it's my fault, no less than the damn tradition's. Father came and introduced me to this Simon Veit of his, whom he appreciates so much because of the fact that he's already managed to stockpile a lot of money for himself. He came and introduced me and I sat there like a little girl and stayed quiet and nodded agreeably and didn't object."

Now Rahel understood.

"I should have run off and slammed the door after me or maybe cried and stamped my feet. I should have smiled that polite smile of mine and retired to the other room and then tried to explain why it's not an appropriate match. I should have objected." Brendel burst into tears again.

Rahel tried to cheer her up. "Tell your father that you don't agree. Nothing has happened yet. Say that you changed your mind."

Brendel said that she would rather die than disappoint her father. If she said she had changed her mind, she would bring shame upon him. How could she reconsider after she had already agreed? After the deal had been sealed and she—the merchandise—would soon be transported into the hands of the man who would become her husband? And how could she live with a man for whom she felt no love whatsoever? She was not like Yente; she was not an innocent fool who would follow a husband she did not know. And what about her dreams? About a lover who would sweep her off her feet, and together they would sail into the sunset? Brendel sat down on Rahel's bed, as close as she could get. Rahel asked her to keep her distance.

"Maybe I'll catch your disease and die. That way, I won't have to marry any man I don't love."

"Maybe, like Yente, you'll find out he's good for you," Rahel said.

But Brendel refused to cheer up. Unlike Yente, who was flexible in her opinions according to what suited her purposes, Brendel was tremendously stubborn. Rahel's words of encouragement could not break through her decision to devote herself to melancholy.

She did not stay with Rahel for long, and silence prevailed in the house once more, but in a way that was unusual. Rahel continued to shiver under the winter blankets, appreciating the quiet; this way, she was left alone and would not have to encounter the cold bath. And as her body trembled and her breath wheezed, her head on fire and her hands as cold as ice, she suddenly heard the cries of a newborn baby.

8 | 1783

"And he shall rule over thee."

(Genesis 3:16)

"It is even so! As nature puts on her autumn tints, it becomes autumn with me and around me. My leaves are sere and yellow, and the neighboring trees are divested of their foliage."[9]

The words of young Werther, in love and on the verge of insanity, echoed within Brendel. She copied them onto the page, inserting corrections as she saw fit.

"Yes, this is where things stand. As nature tips into spring, and as the Israelites were already making their way from Egypt to liberation, winter is refusing to leave me and it is obvious that from now on, my life will be one long, ongoing winter. The man I will marry is pleasant, but uninspired. Although my father claims he is a kind-hearted young man, moral and generous, highly esteemed traits. And my father, oh, my father, is as happy as he could be, as if he were the one who was about to marry Simon Veit," Brendel wrote as she tried to imagine how the rest of her life would unfold. "He is not handsome, but is not particularly ugly, either, and if that were his only shortcoming, I could resign myself to living beside him, as I am not pretty at all, either."

---

9   Goethe, *The Sorrows of Young Werther*. Translated by R.D. Boylan. https://www.gutenberg.org/files/2527/2527-h/2527-h.htm

She tried to fight off the oppressive feeling that had landed upon her shoulders and her back and her heart and had already settled in and turned her body into its home. Continuing to vent at the paper, she wrote down what she could not share with anyone.

"She does not feel, she does not know, that she is preparing a poison which will destroy us both; and I drink deeply of the draught which is to prove my destruction."[10]

"Like young Werther, sipping down the draught of poison until it is gone, so, too, did I enter the same trap with my eyes open. Soon I shall become a married woman. I will be an uninspired bourgeois woman, just like the man with whom I will share my bed. Soon I will start bringing children into this wretched world and become my mother, hosting and smiling, cooking and smiling, caretaking and smiling, with nothing else in her life other than all the work and taking care of my father and his guests."

All her words were collected on paper, etched in black ink, and could have no effect whatsoever on the decision that had already been made and the arrangements that had taken place and the dowry items purchased in advance and piling up in one of the corners of the house.

The day of the wedding drew nearer and Brendel withdrew increasingly into herself. She refused to go out and meet Rahel and Yente, while they wanted to come and take part in all the preparations and lift her spirits and attempt to change her outlook, but were refused. She consented to come out to the drawing room for fittings of the dress that was being sewn slowly and patiently and had to be undone and sewn again and again due to her many comments and dissatisfaction. One time it was the fabric she objected to and once it was the embroidery she did not like, one time it was too puffy and another time its collar was too tight. And so she would make her comments and her mother, with great patience, listened and despite her discomfort, asked the seamstress to make alterations. She could also not

---

10 Ibid.

escape the family's shared meals and made a supreme effort to be nice to her father, who had sealed her fate, and to her mother, who was in seventh heaven. How could parents be so blind to their daughter? Fromet explained Brendel's withdrawal to herself as overexcitement, and Moses Mendelssohn was so busy inviting the guests and making wedding arrangements at the large, opulent synagogue located at the corner of Rosenstrasse and Spandau streets that he had no idea what went on in the house during the day.

Only Yente and Rahel understood what was going on inside her and could not do a thing. Yente brought Brendel some books she knew she would like, so that escaping to a world that was not her own would make her forget the sorrow to which she had so avidly devoted herself, at least for a few hours.

"Maybe Brendel's thoughts will air out a little," she told Rahel as they walked to Brendel's house together.

Rahel was silent. What did she understand about such matters, anyway?

But the books only reinforced the despair in Brendel's body. In every book she read, she found something that made her sadder, something she already knew would be missing in her own life, whether it was a story about the heroine's success, or a moving description of a sunset, or some rich meal that one of the characters in the story was eating with great appetite, of the kind Brendel had lost some time ago. The world became gray and dreary. For her, everything had ended before it even began.

***

All of Berlin's high society attended the wedding. Brendel looked pretty in her sumptuous white dress. Moses Mendelssohn was busy excitedly shaking hands with the important guests, and Fromet did not leave her daughter's side even for a moment. Occasionally, she fixed Brendel's makeup or whispered something in her ear about this or that guest. It might have appeared as if Fromet was keeping an eye on her daughter for fear she would try to run for her life. However, Brendel had no intention of fleeing. She was there, a martyr utterly dedicated to her role.

Simon Veit, soon to be her husband, stood on the sidelines, embarrassed by all the fuss taking place around him, one to which he was not accustomed. He would have preferred a small, intimate wedding, but just like Brendel, he, too, did not dare oppose the request of the man who was soon to be his father-in-law, and followed his wishes, just as she had done. He had felt so honored when Mendelssohn offered him his eldest daughter that anything he requested from him, from here to eternity, would be willingly, happily and whole-heartedly provided.

The day on which the offer was made started out as an ordinary day and ended with much excitement and anticipation. Simon Veit was only twenty-four years old and had to wait several more years to get married, but the agreement was sealed with a warm handshake and he had no doubt that it would be carried out, even if it was being kept secret for the time being. It was a good match for both of them. Mendelssohn had ensured a quiet, secure life for his daughter when he matched her up with a groom who belonged to one of the few families that had been granted a "writ of protection"—his family was among the Viennese Jews exiled to Prussia and granted the right of permanent residency there. In addition, he was also a wealthy banker. Veit, in turn, was granted the privilege of becoming like a son to Moses Mendelssohn, which was, in itself, a dream come true. It was true that his father was a respectable man, a major manufacturer of cotton and the founder of a bank; but Mendelssohn was an intellectual, an innovator renowned throughout Berlin and beyond it, too, the epitome of all that Veit would like to attain for himself and could never achieve. He had liked Brendel right from the start, although there had been no contact between them. Even as a young girl, she was clever and witty and the fact that she physically resembled her father did not bother him in the slightest; on the contrary, he actually saw it as charming and was certain this fact was also reflected in her personality, secretly hoping that it would come to reflect upon him as well.

When his elderly parents heard about the match, they tried to implore him to get married as soon as possible. "Who knows when our Maker will summon us back," they told him. However, he asked them to have patience and swore them to secrecy until Mendelssohn allowed him to share the news, and now they were standing under the *chuppah* with him, overjoyed.

Brendel wanted to be moved and really did wish to be carefree and get swept up in the great celebration. However, not only did she not feel a thing throughout the celebration, but during the ceremony, she found herself far away from there. She did not hear the rabbi's voice, the prayers of the attendees, the hymns or the blessings. She was immersed in the pages of Goethe's book, imagining the trail of blood seeping from the young, besotted Werther's head, imagining the puddle forming under his head after he shot himself and fell from the chair to the ground, a puddle that gradually spread around his body. She saw him laid out on his back, wearing a blue jacket, a yellow vest and boots on his feet, and nearly burst out of the *chuppah* to hold his hand as he breathed his last. Her hollow gaze met the eyes of Simon Veit just before he broke the glass, and before she could return to reality, her husband was already grabbing hold of her and pulled her body against his for an excited kiss. Immediately afterward, she was swarmed by her parents and his and the rest of the attendees who hugged and congratulated her with smiles that appeared fake to her.

After the ceremony and the masses crowding around her to congratulate her with the traditional "*mazel tov*," everyone turned to the food. Brendel felt nauseous and revolted as she watched the mouths chewing and talking and laughing, the occasional drink being poured down their gullets. Now she would be forced to observe daily this husband for whom she did not feel a thing. Every day, she would have to watch him chew and swallow and listen to him talk and, in general, do as he instructed her. And, beyond that—she would have to put up with his passion. The very thought of it made her shudder. She was flooded with a cold sweat, her heart beating rapidly. She was on the verge of fainting.

Yente recognized Brendel's distress, grabbed her hand and took her out of the cramped room and into the fresh air. Outside, Brendel allowed herself to discharge some of the tension that had been gathering within her, and after stopping the tears that had begun to trickle onto her makeup, she gathered her courage and asked Yente about her first night. Yente blushed; she was not used to talking about intimate affairs between herself and her husband. But she immediately came to her senses, took Brendel's hands in her own, and asked her to promise to give her Veit a chance.

"You dismissed him before you could even know him," she said. "Be patient, at least initially. You might find out that ultimately, he is the right man for you, like your father thought."

The wedding ended. Fromet said it went by too fast. "All those preparations and it's all over in a minute." To Brendel, it seemed to have lasted an eternity. She thought about what Yente had told her and summoned up all the good thoughts she could. However, the first night left her with a feeling of great emptiness and shame. She had to take off her dress in his presence, the corset she wore under it and her slip. This in itself was enough to leave her with the feeling that someone was invading her. Strange fingers helped her undo the laces, slowly peeling off the layers that protected her, and in another moment, her intimate parts, now permitted to him, were already exposed to his gaze. And when she wanted to slip under the covers and conceal herself, he whispered out a request that she stand a moment longer so he could look at her and she, much as she longed to refuse, could not. And what if he was like her and did not know what to do? And what if she resisted? All these thoughts raged in her mind and diverted her from the intention to give him a chance. He looked like someone who was sure of himself and knew the way, and this in itself angered her slightly more, but she did not say a thing, held back and gave herself over to suffering. And under the force of this surrender, every caress and every kiss he bestowed upon her and every word of love he dared to whisper only increased her discomfort and her disappointment with herself. She tried to be fully present, but her body opposed her and struggled against her, just as she opposed and struggled against her heart.

Any enthusiasm, joy or sensual arousal remained confined to words printed on pages and bound in hard or soft covers and placed motionless on shelves. There was nothing in that night of what she had read or heard about, and she lay there awake long after Veit had fallen asleep. Another eternity went by before morning dawned.

***

"Such great suffering must I bear!" Werther said, his voice her own and her heart his own heart.

Just a short time after her wedding day, Brendel complained to Yente again and again, and Yente stopped trying to convince her to give him a chance and began to implore her to leave him. But Brendel could not do that to her father. After all, if she could, she would have refused the match from the start. And besides, she was pregnant. Something was wriggling and growing inside her and soon everyone would be able to see it, and she had not yet managed to take in the fact that she was married to this strange man and soon she would become a mother. She still had to learn how to cope with the many emotions that flooded her from the moment she opened her eyes and until the moment she closed them. One moment, she yearned for her husband to disappear from the world and leave her to her own devices and, while she was at it, silently cursed her father for the match he had made for her, and the next, she regretted the thoughts going through her mind.

Suffering. It was what she felt and nothing could change that. And as if to add to her suffering, the Creator had chosen to impregnate her and strand her in her current situation forever. Now she would be even more shackled to this fertile man, who would probably impregnate her again and again. If she had at least enjoyed having sex with him, like she read in her stories, or if at the very least she liked him, things would be more bearable. However, the memory of the first evening refused to fade away. Again and again, she remembered his white, scrawny body and the member pushing into her forcefully. How he had taken off her clothes and left her exposed to his gaze, which seemed alien to her at that moment, and to his breath, which had a sour smell, and to the rubbing motions that hurt her. Pleasure? All her books had deceived her. None of what they said was true regarding her, and she wondered whether any woman could enjoy being penetrated in that manner.

She realized her life was an enforced game inside which she would have to live, a game in which she was no longer the only player. Now she was responsible for another life that was gradually forming inside her, whether she wanted it or not, whether she was ready for it or not, whether it was formed out of love or out of necessity. Her father's God was sitting and laughing at her. Yente, for example, had been married for quite a while and yet her womb had yet to bear any fruit. She was living happily and doing whatever she fancied, while Brendel had just gotten married and in a moment, would become a mother and spend her entire life chasing babies who would annoy and harass her, and her mind would remain troubled from the day of the birth until the end of her days, just like her parents.

However, every time such thoughts arrived, Brendel tried to banish them. She had some unresolved issues with God, but she did believe in the devil's handiwork. After all, she had seen what he wrought upon her siblings who were no longer with her and was afraid she might bring on the effects of the evil eye upon herself. If, heaven forbid, the baby felt that it was not wanted, who knew what sort of trouble might descend upon it and upon them. It was still the flesh of her flesh, and if this creature felt a desire to arrive so early, perhaps she should rejoice in it. And if a baby did have to arrive, it would be better for it to be a boy, she thought. That was her preference. A daughter's entire destiny was to be a receptacle for growing offspring, while a son would have so many options that she wished she'd had. She definitely preferred for it to be a boy, and even prayed for it.

Veit witnessed Brendel's suffering and his heart shrank inside him. This was not how he had imagined his marriage. In the first few weeks, he attributed her suffering to her young age and to the age gap between them. Ever since she told him she was with child, he was certain she was dejected due to her pregnancy. But as time went by, he understood that she was simply not happy with him. He did not give up and was convinced there was something he could do for her, something that would prove his love for her, something that would make her trust him, trust that he would be hers alone.

One evening, when they were both sitting silently at the dining room table, he suggested they establish a small cultural association in the drawing room. Brendel could not believe her ears.

"It will be a society dedicated to intellectual lectures," he said, and she felt something awakening within her.

"Once a week, let's say every Tuesday evening or any other day you choose. What do you say? Would that make you happy?"

Brendel nodded excitedly, secretly unable to understand why he had proposed it. For him, everything ultimately came down to profit and loss and she could not think of any material profit he might gain from such a lecture society. On the contrary, such a commitment entailed only expenses. Perhaps there was something to him after all. She almost liked him.

"Once a week, on Tuesday evening," she repeated his words, and for the first time in quite a while, a fleeting smile dawned upon her face.

9 | 1785

"You are cordially invited to a ball celebrating Rahel Levin's fourteenth birthday!!!"

In the month of May, Rahel decided to take action. She felt mature enough to celebrate a birthday. She had planned it many months in advance and now the time had come. She knew she was diverting radically from her father's instructions and was willing to accept the consequences.

She folded the missives and wrapped each one in a pretty ribbon she had taken from her mother's sewing kit. Rahel addressed the invitations to Yente and Brendel, to neighbors, to other acquaintances and to her father's actor friends. Every day, she approached several of the invitees and personally handed them the invitation, imploring them all to attend the celebration. She asked them to keep it a secret.

A week before the celebration, Rahel had conducted all the necessary preparations. She discussed with the housemaids how the drawing room would be arranged and what provisions should be purchased. She decided which cakes and pastries to make and where the gifts she received would be placed, and throughout these preparations, she was as excited as if she were being reborn. In her new life, there were no prohibitions or dictates, and it was possible to be rowdy and sing and rejoice. In her new life, her mother and father had prepared the entire celebration for her, and for this purpose, a dress had been sewn and a pair of doll shoes in a matching shade had been purchased along with a shiny ribbon for her braid. In her new life, she was no longer sick and no longer acutely needed the sun to warm her and heal her with its rays.

She had attended a birthday celebration only once. She had been invited to the Mendelssohns, and as her father could not refuse the esteemed Moses, she had gone. It was a birthday party for Brendel's younger sister, also called Yente. Rahel had only been eight years old, but the celebration was firmly engraved in her memory, as if the entire event had been captured by some paintbrush, and the painting had been seared into her mind. Musicians in bow ties played and the notes filled her heart. Decorations has been sewn, adorning the drawing room with colors uncharacteristic of everyday life, and the table was overflowing with delicacies—thin spongy dough rolled up and filled with light cream and sour halved cherries, balls of dough fried in butter, filled with plum jam and powdered with sugar, crispy poppy-seed dumplings, sugared fruit, baked apples, meringues and whipped cream and orange pudding in small crystal bowls. Everything was so vibrant, and above it all presided the gifts. They were piled up in the room and soon became a high, colorful mound. For many months later, every time Rahel wished to escape to a better place, she would close her eyes and observe that happy image retained in her mind. She remembered the sounds and could almost feel a sweetness edging to the tip of her tongue, the same sweetness that, in their home, was mostly reserved solely for her father's guests.

The fierce desire for a celebration had been planted inside her in the previous year, when she met Brendel at the lending library where she spent so many hours. They had not seen each other since her wedding and were glad for the surprising encounter. They sat and chatted and when Rahel congratulated her on her pregnancy, which was now readily apparent, Brendel recalled the day when she had first met Rahel and a grin surfaced upon her face.

She told Rahel how she had been born and survived against all odds, about the box and Rahel's firm grasp on Brendel. She added that she truly believed that Rahel was a particularly strong creature and did not explain why she thought so. But she did go on to say, "You were born on May 19, in the year 1771." And that exact date, which had never been known to Rahel, was revealed to her and opened something within her that she could not understand at the time.

Until that moment, Rahel had never dedicated any thought to the day she was born or to birthdays. She had never heard her parents talking about it, one way or another, and had never asked. Even if she had asked, she would not have received an answer. At best, they replied, "That's the way it is." Otherwise, they simply ignored her.

But a short time later, a bubbling of sorts appeared within Rahel. Initially, she did not notice it, but over time, it grew stronger. Rahel did not know what she should do and did not dare reveal it to anyone. From the bubbling emerged emotions that she experienced for the first time, such as the desire to have something that others had and the reluctance to accept things as they were. The sweet memory of Yente Mendelssohn's birthday was no longer as pleasant as it once was. It was now tinged with something bitter and the image seared in her memory became an image of missing out, of something kept from her, maliciously taken.

And why should she not be entitled to it? Was she inferior to Yente Mendelssohn? Any less smart than she was? And her father, did he have less money than Moses Mendelssohn did? Fewer acquaintances? A lesser status? And why couldn't he do it for her? All those questions surfaced and returned and pecked at her mind and brought her again and again to the same understanding—that the source of all her problems was Markus Levin, her father. It was the first time that Rahel grasped that her father did not love her and would never love her. It did not matter what she did; she would never win his love or affection. And how could he love her? After all, she was a daughter. And a Jewish daughter's entire purpose was to attain maturity and produce offspring. In her case, it was also to be healthy and not cough all the time. Beyond that, not a thing was expected from her, and soon, he would sell her—convey her to the highest bidder, and thus be rid of her. Therefore, she decided not to try any longer. And perhaps this understanding came as a relief to her, a liberty she claimed for herself, to do as she wished, come what may. And therefore, although her father had forbidden commemorating birthdays in the Levin household, she decided to celebrate.

She then had to wait many more months for that date, the next birthday, to arrive. Rahel prepared a chart with all the days in May until that longed-for day—the nineteenth. Within each square she wrote the date and her allotted task for the day in cribbed handwriting.

Every evening, before she went to sleep, she produced the chart from a thick volume on the shelf, crossed off the passing day with a large X, recited the task awaiting her on the following day, and prayed that she would only be healthy and would not get sick on the day of her celebration. For that purpose, she was willing to call upon all the prayers, even if she did not truly understand their contents.

She went to Yente to deliver her invitation. Yente invited her to choose a fancy dress for the celebration, saying she would help her arrange her hair on the day of the party. Suddenly, her expression darkened, and she asked Rahel if her actions would not hurt her father.

"My father's dignity is the only thing he cares about and that dignity will be on my side that day. He won't dare cancel it." Rahel was certain that even if he found out, he would exhibit restraint in order to continue portraying them as a perfect family, and as for the rage that would follow, she was already prepared for it. It seemed like a fair price to her. Yente had never seen Mr. Levin raise his voice or treat any members of his household harshly, but she believed Brendel's accounts. She recognized the terror in Rahel's body language and in her eyes, and in the things she said occasionally. She was afraid that Rahel would be hurt, that her father would be truly violent toward her. Most of all, she was afraid that all this would cause Rahel to be seriously ill.

"The dignity of Markus Levin—your father—might be the very reason why he would retaliate against you with a very harsh blow. The ruins of dignity might bring about great force, intense hatred and a lack of judgment," Yente further clarified.

However, none of her statements deterred Rahel from the goal she had set for herself, especially now, when the coach had begun to roll down the slope and could no longer be stopped. If Mr. Markus Levin had paused for a moment to observe his daughter, as a father should, with a bit of attention, perhaps he might have liked her. After all, her character was a reflection of his and her nature resembled his own. He would have found her to be determined, brave, and goal-oriented, as well as clever, possessing an intellect that only a few others possessed. He would have found she had inherited those traits from him; he had made good use of them when he took his first steps in the field of commerce, when he was around her age, and, in fact, continued to use them to this day.

Throughout all the preparations and the excitement, Rahel's mother was busy with her own affairs and immersed in her fifth pregnancy. Four-year-old Rose scurried hither and thither in the house, seven-year-old Moritz was in and out, and Markus, who was old enough, was wrapped up in affairs about which she knew nothing. During the last two weeks, their mother spent the majority of her days laid out in her bed on the top floor, under doctor's orders, and household matters took place under their own steam, with the help of the laundress, the cook and Herr Berthold, who was in charge of minor and major repairs, the upkeep of the yard, and various errands. *It's a sign from above*, Rahel thought to herself, praising a God of whose existence she was usually unaware. She felt He had sentenced her mother to bedrest, thus allowing her to make all the preparations she wanted without being asked about them. As if He wanted her to celebrate her birthday at least once in her life. She was greatly optimistic.

And indeed, about a week before the party, she received another sign. Her father departed abruptly on one of his business trips and Rahel heaved a sigh of relief. As she was swept up in her preparations, she had not fully considered whether her father would be home or on a business trip. Her father's trip was one more sign indicating that all would be well. The guests would arrive and rejoice along with her and her father would not know a thing. And even if he did, he could not thwart her birthday party while it was going on.

***

On May 19, Rahel woke up with a tingle in her throat and immediately ran to rinse it out with salt water, as she always did when she felt that way, praying it would go away. But as the hours went by, the tingle gradually turned into a pain that only grew worse. Nevertheless, she put on the dress she had borrowed from Yente. The dress was slightly too long, which turned out to be an advantage, as it covered the shoes that did not match its peach hue. She arranged her hair as best she could although Yente had promised to do so; however, Yente was delayed and Rahel no longer had the patience to wait. The much-anticipated hour had almost arrived and she felt a stabbing in her throat as if she had swallowed needles. She did not know how she would be able to greet the guests and be merry and taste all the delicacies prepared for her, and yet she rinsed out her throat again and again and tried to ignore the pain.

Rahel's fourteenth birthday was her first life lesson. A lesson about the power of a man of great wealth whose fortune relied on knowledge and rumors spreading through the grapevine and machinations and manipulating people and debts owed to him and those people's attempts to earn his favor.

The only ones to arrive on that wretched day were Yente and Brendel. Despite the letter delivered to them that morning, announcing the cancellation of the party and signed by Markus Levin, they chose to come, bearing the presents they had purchased for her along with various pastries and sweets they had picked out at the last moment. They knew something was about to take place and came in order to be with Rahel and protect her and perhaps even to cheer her up, although, deep inside, they knew this would prove impossible.

Markus Levin, who had returned unexpectedly from his journey, was in the drawing room when the two arrived. They did not say hello to him and took the stairs up to Rahel's bedroom immediately. She was sitting in her room in her nightgown, her brow furrowed and her eyes sad but dry of tears. The festive dress was ceremoniously folded on the chair, ready to be returned to Yente with utter resignation. Immediately when the two girls entered, they saw a large red blotch adorning Rahel's left cheek, one that would probably fade away within a few days, but that would linger upon her soul forever.

"There could not be a more tortuous experience than this in youth," she said. "No one could be sicker or closer to madness."

Suddenly, the sound of a baby's cry rang out within the house, but even this cheerful exclamation of life could not console Rahel.

10 | 1786

All night, Brendel's father lay in his bed, and the house was illuminated as if it were mid-day. Everyone was awake. When dawn broke and the first rays of a cold, wintery morning emerged, everyone expected him to rise, walk over to his *tallit*, wrap his skinny body in it, use his white fingers to extract the *tefillin*[11] from their velvet case and place them on his hands and on his head. Everyone awaited the murmur of his prayers. But Brendel's father did not rise to his morning prayers, or to his *tallit* or the *tefillin* stored in its velvet case. He lay in his bed, his soul having already departed his body.

On the morning of that day, saturated with a chilly sun, the coffin was borne all through the city. At ten o'clock, its journey began in a polished carriage whose wheels moved through the streets, from the center of Berlin to the old cemetery on Grosse Hamburger Strasse. A large crowd followed the mahogany coffin, accompanied by a stillness of mourning. They paid their last respects to the renowned philosopher from Berlin, an esteemed scholar and a symbol of hope for the future. For her, for Brendel, the man was not a scholar, a philosopher or a symbol, but a father. A beloved father. And as angry as she might have been at him in recent years for the match he had made on her behalf and for failing to notice her unhappy marriage, she respected and loved him, particularly now.

---

11 The *tefillin*, or phylacteries, are a set of small black leather boxes containing scrolls of parchment inscribed with verses from the Torah. *Tefillin* are worn by observant adult male Jews during weekday morning prayers.

"I implored him not to hurry so much," Fromet recounted again and again to anyone who was willing to listen. Brendel sat beside her on the drawing room sofa, her dress torn in accordance with the Jewish custom of mourning and her eyes red and exhausted. Her usual pain, the one accompanying her every day from the moment she rose and until the time she went to sleep, now seemed to her like a light prick, the kind one receives when being careless while darning a sock or sewing a button on a shirt. While now, her body was filled with a different pain, of a kind she had never known existed.

"I implored him not to hurry so much, to take care of his delicate health, and at the very least to put on a warm coat to protect him from the chill in the streets of Berlin in late December," her mother continued, her tears flowing constantly. "He didn't listen to me."

Brendel added, "He left once the Sabbath was over, hurrying off urgently and eagerly to hand over the manuscript to Herr Christian Friedrich Voss, the publisher. As if he knew there was no time and he had to hurry." And her mother nodded, confirming the story.

Simon Veit stood at the corner of the room, ready to faithfully tend to all the needs of his mourning wife, her mother and all the residents of the house. He had to be strong and could not fall apart, but he, too, felt the same blade notching his heart vertically and horizontally.

Dr. Herz, Yente's husband, gave his testimony as well. "I heard a noise from the sofa and I ran back to his room. He was lying there and I saw his head tilted back and foam on his lips; there was no pulse or signs of life. We tried to revive him in several ways but to no avail. He lay there, with his familiar, friendly smile on his lips, as if an angel had taken him from this earth with a kiss."

Yente had heard the same story repeated for several days now, and each time, her heart went out to her tormented husband as if she were hearing it for the first time.

"The light in the room had gone out," he continued, "because the lamp was out of oil. In the first moment of terror, I immediately grabbed his head and stayed frozen in that pose, for God knows how long. All I wanted was to drop down next to him and die along with him."

"If he had only listened to me and taken a coat," the widowed Fromet said. "If he had only listened."

Brendel joined Yente and Rahel, who were sitting on the purple velvet sofa, each immersed in their own ruminations. Rahel was imagining her own father lying in that mahogany casket and tried to think what the people who were always coming and going from their house would have said about him. Deep in the secret chambers of her heart, she yearned for his death, so that she could be rid of her troubles. If she had thought previously that her father did not love her, after that birthday that never occurred, she was certain that he loathed her. The slap he had delivered to her face, which sealed that story, made things clear for her once and for all. And what she had not told Yente and Brendel at the time was what she had tossed in his face. "You're sorry I was born, and so you don't let me celebrate," she had yelled at him, while he remained silent, neither confirming nor denying.

Yente was contemplating practicalities. Now that her husband was in mourning, she would have to temporarily pause the ongoing literary meetings held in their home. Perhaps she would suggest that they travel to the spa in Pyrmont to recuperate somewhat. And there was also the matter of purchasing new furniture for their drawing room, which they had discussed quite a few times. And in the midst of all these thoughts, she felt embarrassed, for while everyone around her was deep in mourning, she was considering such trivialities. The great Moses Mendelssohn had died so abruptly, and here she was reducing life to the smallest bits of currency.

As for Brendel, a new idea was surfacing within her. She still did not understand its significance and preferred not to share it for now.

"I had a major fight with Veit on the eve of my father's death," Brendel whispered to Yente, glancing at her husband, who was standing to the side. "While my father was fading away, I was dealing with trivial matters. I was angry that he was late for dinner and even when he sat down to eat, he was constantly silent. I was angry when he tried to draw closer to me and appease me and I stayed angry before we went to bed, too. All evening, I confronted him with the dreariness of that day, and when I tried to talk about some poem, I grew furious when he could not contribute a thing to the conversation. After all, I had known in advance that this would be the case, and seemed to have acted on purpose in order to ignite the fight. I was so wrapped up in my anger and did not know what was going on in my parents' house." Brendel palmed her face with the hands that were left to her as a memento of her father, and Yente did not say a word, but merely stroked her head. She, too, shared that pain, as they were almost sisters. In addition, her husband, Dr. Herz, could not save Mendelssohn and was now full of guilt, as if he had been the one to kill him with his own two hands.

The visitors arriving to console the family were constantly in and out of the house and there was no day and no night. Many tales were told about Moses Mendelssohn and much praise was heaped upon him. Thus, the image of the deceased loomed larger and larger, appropriated from his daughter Brendel and his widow Fromet and his young children, who received the many visitors and the letters and telegrams, as well as the large amount of food that gathered in the house kitchen and was discreetly sent off to the poorhouse for fear that it was not "strictly kosher."

"There was no one with such stellar qualities among his generation of learned Jewish men," the Jewish scholars stated. Christian friends sent telegrams. "An eminent scholar," they wrote about him, "who fought with his pen for truth and served as a role model with his excellent words." And among all the things said and disseminated everywhere, they used his own words to describe his legacy: *"Strive for truth, love beauty, aspire for goodness and do the best."* They also wrote, *"Without love, the world is chaos,"* and *"Love truth and peace."* Even the Austrian ambassador in Berlin took the time to update his minister of foreign affairs in Vienna by telegram of the scholar's death.

During the days of mourning, the house was bustling. A medley of languages, words and prayers mingled together, and other statements began to surface regarding his premature death, things that had thus far remained unsaid and accusations that had remained unspoken. There was even a name ascribed to the battle upon whose altar Moses Mendelssohn had sacrificed his life. "The battle of pantheism," his friends termed it, pointing an accusatory finger at Jacobi[12] of Dusseldorf, the sworn enemy of the late Mendelssohn, whom he had only encountered on the written page.

Fromet stated that ever since his good friend Gutthold Ephraim Lessing[13] had passed away, something had broken in her late husband. As she spoke, she turned to look at the bust of Lessing, which stood on the drawing room cabinet, and was now covered up, as was the portrait of Isaac Newton, whom Mendelssohn had admired, and paintings of the Greek philosophers.

"Moses informed everyone that after finishing his book *Jerusalem*,[14] he intended to devote himself to writing an essay that would describe the character of his close friend Lessing." Fromet then paused, and after a silence that lasted several moments, added, "But Hamann[15] from Königsberg and his friend Jacobi—damn them both—spread a rumor that Lessing had confessed to them that he was a Spinozist."[16]

The attendees grew silent. It was one thing for Mendelssohn's friends to accuse Jacobi of spreading lies about Lessing, blatant falsities about his heresy. But when such accusations came from Fromet—the woman who had shared Mendelssohn's bed, the mother of his children and his confidante—it was quite a different matter.

---

12   Friedrich Heinrich Jacobi (1743–1819) was an influential German philosopher, literary figure, and socialite.

13   Gutthold Ephraim Lessing (1729–1781) was a prominent playwright in the Age of Enlightenment.

14   In *Jerusalem*, Mendelssohn called for religious tolerance and for an acknowledgement of the rights of the Jews.

15   Johann Georg Hamann (1730–1788) was a German Lutheran philosopher from Königsberg known as "the Wizard of the North" who was one of the leading figures of post-Kantian philosophy.

16   Dutch philosopher Baruch Spinoza (1632–1677) was considered a forefather of secularism, skepticism and modernity.

"For two whole years, Moses tried to clear Lessing's name. Two whole years!"

Brendel placed a hand on Fromet's shoulder. Her mother was being quite vocal and saying things she might regret airing in her sorrow. She was sitting in the company of strangers and exposing the secrets of her husband's heart, even as his body lay freshly buried in the ground.

However, Brendel's mother was oblivious to her daughter's signals. "And if Lessing is a disciple of the teachings of Spinoza, it also implicates him, my Moses, of being a heretic. How could you believe such a thing? For entire nights at a time, he didn't sleep because of such lies, and that is how his health began to abandon him."

Moses Mendelssohn was a philosopher who tried to understand the world and grant it meaning. He was constantly striving to repair and improve and pave the way for his children and their peers. Brendel felt paltry in comparison to her father. One thing and one thing only was constantly pecking at her mind—the happiness she did not feel. She believed it was related to her marriage, but there was something in her character of which she was not aware, something that had troubled her father much earlier. He had often told his wife Fromet that Brendel had arrived in this world dissatisfied and would apparently leave it the same way. And despite his comprehensive understanding of the world, he did not understand this trait in his eldest daughter.

However, despite her preoccupation with 'trivialities' such as happiness, Brendel was constantly striving to understand her thoughts and emotions and was growing better at it every day. From an essay to a manuscript, from learning this or that language, from attending the theater to attending concerts, all in an attempt to understand herself and the meaning of her unhappiness, which remained unwavering.

"*Never grow tired of uprooting the flaws you discover in yourself,*" she wrote to her sister. "*The only path to happiness is to constantly improve yourself.*"

***

Tomorrow, the family would rise from its seven days of mourning and the house would empty out. Brendel would return to her home and to her daily routine, which remained dreary even after the gesture her Veit had proffered by establishing a literary salon in their home. Her mother would remain alone with the smells of her husband, which would gradually fade away until it seemed as if he had never been there at all.

11 | 1789

Brendel was familiar with "Monday Club" from the time she was a child. One of her earliest memories of her father was when he returned home after attending the weekly meeting with his friends. He was proud that a Jew like him could sit down to intellectual gatherings with members of the Academy of Sciences, with musicians, with artists and with philosophers who were not Jewish. He called it "a new era" and was proud of the change that the new age had brought with it. After every such meeting, he would come home, seat Fromet beside him and tell her, in great detail, what had taken place there, expressing his sorrow that she had missed it. Brendel did not understand why her mother could not be there with him. But as she grew up, she did understand. She was somewhat angry at her father about the hypocrisy he displayed with regard to her mother, for coming and brandishing these meetings in her face when she herself could not attend them, talking to her as if they were equals while this was not true; she was angry at how all his enlightenment came to an end outside the house, where he behaved like everyone else.

In her own generation, however, things were gradually changing, and in recent years, Berlin was being taken over by a new fashion and "literary salons" were popping up and flourishing, and were open to all. An interest in Romanticism, fraternity, literature and art was sufficient to serve as an entry pass to join them. And if there was one thing that thrilled her and which she anticipated, it was the meetings held by such clubs. In recent years, Yente too had joined in, opening her home to such gatherings. Even when they first got married, her husband Markus Herz had already been hosting his students in the living room of his home. They were a group of tedious men of science who arrived to hear his lectures and discuss them. Sometimes they also stayed for dinner. Yente, Brendel and Rahel also joined the lectures sometimes, as auditors only, denied the right to respond and voice their opinions.

But the change actually came by chance. One evening, Markus told Yente that he had met a handsome couple. He encountered them in his clinic, immediately grew to like them and invited them home. Yente was truly happy; she loved the company of people. It offered her the opportunity to dress up and garner more compliments than usual.

The attractive, pleasant couple arrived. The wife, Leonora, was dressed with the sort of restraint characterizing respectable women. Yente did not think she was pretty but did not find her ugly, either. In contrast, her husband, who was slightly shorter than her, was wearing a wool suit with a blue-gray hue and was certainly handsome. From the moment the two entered their home, it was obvious to her that they were not Jewish; but this did not change a thing, since what was the importance of such a trivial fact while conversing about poetry and literature and plays produced in the theater? If she felt any discomfort in the course of the evening, it was caused by the fact that Leonora did not contribute a thing to the ensuing conversation. Nevertheless, she hurried to give Yente her address so that she could report to her about the new fashions arriving from Paris, as if they were already good friends.

The handsome couple was greatly satisfied by their encounter with the Herzes. The rumors of that successful, productive encounter began to spread and Dr. Herz's esteemed patients began to request to come over to his home. Thus, their residence became one of the "open houses" where a guest did not require an explicit invitation, but rather could arrive following a recommendation from a friend.

In one room, Markus lectured on nature, science and the medical world, while in the other room Yente hosted the most prominent artists and writers as well as those who wished to write or only wanted to listen and rub shoulders with Berlin's cultural elite. There was such pleasure and joy and cheer in these gatherings, which gradually flourished until there was sometimes not enough space to contain all the attendees. Brendel, too, would come, and although she always enjoyed spending time at Yente's, lately, that pleasure had been tainted with sourness. In her own home, traffic was sparse and the guests were few, while the Herzes did not have enough room for all comers. It was true that Brendel had not been blessed with Yente's beauty, but she surpassed her in knowledge and wit. However, this detail was no help when it came to salons. Could it be that people judge others only by their beauty?

Yente told Brendel about the important people who dined at their table during the first year of her marriage, intellectuals whom her husband had invited. "And although I was young and ignorant, they talked to me at length. Perhaps they thought I was smart because of my beauty." Could intellectuals possessing a sharp mind, achievements and acclaim be so biased when it came to physical beauty? If that was the case, her salon was doomed to failure in advance.

Rahel took care to attend Yente and Brendel's gatherings equally. She found pleasure and interest in both of them and did not compare them, as some people did. Yente's gatherings were full of drama; they were loud and colorful, mostly due to the characters who took part in them, but also because of the things they talked about. Brendel's gatherings were calm, inspiring her with deeper thoughts. She always left them enriched by one or two things, which pleased her. Rahel admired Brendel because, despite her daily misery in her marriage, or that her first pregnancy had not come to fruition and had almost brought about her collapse, and although she rarely left her home due to her many tasks—despite all of this, she did her best to live her life as fiercely as she could. Brendel clung to the guests who attended her salon and prepared for their arrival, assembling reading material and varied refreshments. She read books almost obsessively, wrote endlessly to her friends, and most importantly, attended Yente's salon and other salons taking place in Berlin, in order to listen and converse. She considered herself a capable woman of opinion and the thought that she would never be able to write anything beyond letters to her friends or lists for herself, that she would be unable to present what was inside her to a larger audience, brought her to despair. She did not wish to be merely an implement for producing children. She had more than that to give to the world. She was fighting for her life and mainly fighting the evil spirits inside her, trying her best to oppose them. When Simon Veit sang her the traditional song "Who Can Find a Woman of Valor"[17] on Friday, he had no idea the extent to which the words truly described her.

***

Brendel's salon was only packed full when Yente was sitting *shiva*[18] over her father. He did not die suddenly like Brendel's father had done, but rather withered away slowly, so that when his soul departed, everyone heaved a sigh of relief due to the suffering he had experienced. And in that month of mourning, Brendel's salon suddenly filled with the sounds of witty quibbling and arguments and poems read aloud and piano playing. People came and went and in one evening, the composition of the crowd could change several times. Brendel was pleased, there was no doubt about it, and yet still reserved a slice of sadness in her heart as she knew this state of affairs was temporary and soon Yente would rise from her *shiva* and then the month would be over and her salon would empty once more in favor of the one held by her good friend.

Yente wanted to tell her she was too serious and solemn, and in addition, there was also the matter of Veit, who could not understand a single thing about modern literature, and therefore did not take an active part in the

---

17 The lyrics of this song are taken from Proverbs 31, and detail the attributes of a good wife or an ideal woman.

18 The *shiva* period is the seven days of mourning prescribed by Judaism.

salon, which further cast a shadow upon things. Markus, too, was not a proponent of the latest style and despised all the Romantic literature that Yente and her friends worshipped. However, he was sociable and chatty and knew a thing or two about canonical literature and thus contributed his part. Ultimately, Yente did not say a thing to Brendel, not about her or about Veit, and particularly not about what people were saying behind her back, and there was plenty such talk. They talked about her appearance, about her drawing room, which was always dark, about the glum expression with which she greeted her guests and about her husband's money, which she did not spend. They talked and talked, spreading wicked gossip, and Yente, who was herself often the subject of such talk, knew the feeling. She only repeatedly suggested to Brendel, "If you're unhappy, leave him."

12 | 1790

"A man's life is a poem like this:
with a beginning and an end. Only completeness is missing."

— Goethe

Rahel's father died suddenly, with no warning at all, in an unusual manner. When the person bearing the news arrived with his bitter message, the house grew silent. Instead of brokenhearted cries like the Mendelssohns or hushed weeping tinged with relief like the de Lemosses, with the Levins, it was quiet. Perhaps it was the shock of being left on their own, of losing the man who had moved the members of the household around as if they were marionettes, and now, they would have to learn to move by themselves.

For Rahel, it was the quiet of suppressed joy.

After the pit was covered with dirt and the Mourner's *Kaddish*[19] prayer, with its *"Yitgadal VeYitkadash,"* was recited and the tears and the whispers, and after the name Markus Levin was written on a piece of wood and affixed at the head of the mound of moist soil, she walked home alone. Her mother and siblings—Markus, Ludwig, Rose and Moritz—quickly climbed

---

19 "The Mourner's *Kaddish*" is recited as part of the mourning rituals in Judaism in all prayer services, as well as at funerals. Its central theme is the magnification and sanctification of God's name.

into the carriage placed at their disposal, while she preferred to stride alone and ruminate. No one implored her to board the carriage or encouraged her to talk.

Her father had been wrapped up in a shroud and ceremoniously lowered into the pit. He was covered by a pile of dirt and would never rise again. Now she strode among the houses of the city and with every step she took on the long way home from the Jewish cemetery, something came loose inside her. She observed the structures she passed and wondered how life took place inside them. Were the people who were living inside happy? Were they like her, trapped within a religion that smothered them? Perhaps they, too, were stuck in a place where no one appreciated them? Perhaps they were actually happy in their lives, in the choices they could make, in the freedom they possessed by virtue of being Christian Germans.

Rahel did not know how long she walked, nor did she care. As far as she was concerned, the route could go on forever and ever. At such moments, she did not think about the visitors who would begin to show up at their home, or about mourning customs, or about her mother, who would certainly need support, or about her younger siblings, who would also require care. She thought only about herself and her life and the way she would conduct it from now on.

When she got home, she stood in front of the door, lingering. She knew that the moment she came in would be the first moment of the beginning of her life as she had often imagined it. She was excited. True happiness was pulsing within her, but she needed a few minutes in order to assume the appearance of sadness.

Mourning can be misleading. People come to the house, some of them familiar, others are not. Some of them are liked, while others remain dim and transparent. But there is one thing that all of them have in common: all of them speak kindly of the deceased. They mention his positive qualities and his good deeds, telling stories people have never heard before; perhaps they have actually arrived for some other dearly departed. But all of them are united in the sanctity of that person who is no longer among the living.

The Levin family's mourning contained something of all this as well. Rahel sat and listened and although she wanted to yell out, "Which Markus Levin are you talking about?" there was also something within her that wanted to hear more. More about how her father adopted an impoverished family from *Alt-Berlin* and provided them with a tithe[20] at the beginning of every month, about how the group of actors tricked him during one of the performances to which he was invited, and when he arrived, he found himself alone in the auditorium. His face flushed until they thought something was about to happen to him and then he burst out in laughter until they were afraid he was on the verge of choking. The men from the synagogue described what a scholar he was and how he always arrived in time for the prayer, even if there was a deal waiting for him around the corner. Her mother nodded constantly in agreement, as if she knew all this.

Whether the visitors were speaking the truth or whether they were exaggerating due to his irreversible state, they made Rahel see her father in a different light, as a man who could have been a real father to her, the kind who talked to her about things the way he talked to the friends and acquaintances to whom his door was open. A father who smiled and laughed. A father she had often dreamed of having and now the traits she had sought were indeed a part of him. They were, and yet they were not manifested in her relationship with him and at home in general, and this was something she could not understand. Instead of rejoicing over the new aspect of him she had discovered, she grew even angrier at him, filling with a burning animosity. She thought that once he died, she had locked the doors of her soul after him, but that week brought with it an anger over all that she had missed, and over what would be his absence from now on. The only good thing about her father, she thought, was the fact that he had afforded her some security in her fragile life as a Jewish woman in rowdy Germany. And now the thought surfaced within her that despite his behavior, she still needed him. Thanks

---

20 Tithes are a form of mandatory charity in Judaism, and are linked to a seven-year agricultural cycle. The tithe was distributed locally "within thy gates" (Deuteronomy 14:28) to support religious officials and assist the poor.

to her father, as bad as he was, she still retained what few rights she had. He constituted an insurance certificate for her and for the entire family, and what would become of her now? What would become of them?

Her brother Markus tried to take up the reins. He was familiar with the business and it was only natural for him to keep it going. If she hadn't known him so well, she would have thought that he, too, was happy over this death, based on the way he walked around the house and greeted the guests visiting them. But she sensed his confusion and panic and knew it was all a result of the scope of the responsibility that had descended upon him. He would now have to carry the entire burden of the family on his shoulders, and he was still so young. From now on, all the people with whom their father had conducted business would constantly be comparing Markus to him.

***

Four years had passed since Moses Mendelssohn's death and it seemed as if death refused to leave. First, there was the embryo that did not hang on and then her son, Moses-Judah, born two years ago, had died when he was only a month old. Brendel lived with the feeling that the good part of her life was over. Gone were the days when she was protected in her father's house, far from all the troubles of the world, which now invaded her home and set up residence there. If she had thought the worst thing of all was the lovelessness in which she lived, she would soon learn first-hand that additional calamities still awaited her. Simon Veit constantly consoled her, promising things would get better, thus only further inflaming her anger and intensifying the distance she felt from him.

All that was swirling within her: the accusations she leveled at herself and at her father and at Judaism, which had dictated her way of life, the lack of love she felt and the anger at all of these, all of it was expressed in one place, directed at one person—her husband, Simon Veit.

"What do you care?" she flung at him one evening as anger distorted her thoughts and she could no longer hold back. "There's only one thing on your mind—shoving yourself inside me and making more and more children who will end up dying."

His face went gray and his body shrunk back. She saw the insult upon him. Moisture filled his eyes. The knowledge that she held the power and that she had managed to infiltrate his optimism and his constant desire to be good to her only armed her with more daring.

"I'm the one who carried all those deaths. I'm the one who killed them all and it's all because of this wretched marriage that you insist on having." She went on and on in this manner, until he could no longer hear it and went to his study, barricading himself there. He did not provide the pleasure of a decent battle, either, just like the other things she sought in him but failed to find.

Later she regretted it, but her dignity was stronger than she was. She could not bring herself to apologize and also did not want him to take advantage of the apology to edge closer to her again. It suited her to keep her distance from him. And, indeed, it seemed as if something in him began to crack and he became even more quiet than usual. Meals were eaten silently, and they did not exchange a word, not during the meal or throughout the rest of the day. She knew she had crossed the line and secretly hoped that he would ask her to leave, ask not to see her again, realize that she was not good for him and banish her back to her mother. But this was not the case.

He stayed in the same house, and she stayed as well, and after a while, he began to once more demand his natural right. Demand that she satisfy his urges, that she lie with him, and it did not matter to him whether she wanted to or not. As far as he was concerned, she should lie there quietly and obey until another baby began to grow inside her. And so she lay there, naked and exposed, once on her back and once on her belly, and waited until he was done and prayed that his seed would be weak or defective. But as for him, from the moment he entered her, he forgot all her accusations, forgot all his anger and loved her. He would whisper to her that he was sorry, whisper that he loved her, and tried to appease her with every such act of love, wanting her to enjoy herself, but he was disappointed every time.

Afterward, he would fall asleep while she stayed awake for a long time. The nights were particularly hard on her. Images and sounds and smells of babies and births mingled together, repeating again and again, and one tenacious dream she first had after her father passed away began to recur almost every night.

She was lying in the cradle. She was about a month old and had just returned with her father and mother from the synagogue. It was the first Sabbath in which she was taken out of the house. At the synagogue, her father was the first on the list of those celebrating a happy occasion and therefore obligated to ascend to the Torah. He approached the Torah, kissed the scroll and blessed her with a good, healthy and happy life. All the children gathered around the cradle built especially for the *Hollekreisch*[21] ceremony and hoisted her up into the air.

"What shall we call the child?" the required question rang out.

And all the children yelled out together, "Dorothea, Dorothea, Dorothea."

One morning, she realized that this dream, which visited her again and again, was the key to something in her life. That name, the new name, was apparently her deep desire for change. She decided she would call herself Dorothea. Cast away the child Brendel, thus leaving behind what was and summoning a new fate for herself.

She was pregnant again. In a few weeks, she would give birth. She wholeheartedly wanted the embryo inside her. She wanted to prove she was not defective, that she could produce a being from inside her that would live and have meaning in the world. But how could it have meaning in the world if she was still utterly immersed in the past? Therefore, she wished to confuse the Angel of Death by changing her name. She did not know the meaning of the name or its origin, but was certain it would bring about the happiness she so yearned for.

***

---

21 The *Hollekreisch* is a ceremony held four weeks after the birth of a baby girl, in which the newborn is named.

Yente missed her father. She was her papa's girl and always had been. Now only her mother was left.

"My mother is supposed to be beautiful, and yet she no longer displays any remnants of beauty," she told Brendel.

Yente had had an older brother who had passed away before she was born. "And Mother's crying over him all those years created a strange problem with her eyelashes. They became ingrown, turning her face strange and sickly."

It did not matter how much her mother had done for her all her life; Yente still maligned her. It was only her father whom she worshipped. He was handsome, he was always meticulous and fashionable in his attire, his beard was trimmed precisely as it should be and his hair well-coiffed. The fact that he was greatly respected and managed the hospital in Berlin also won him plenty of credit with his daughter. She was resentful of her mother.

"My father was the one who gave me love and education, as well as my beauty, which was why I also offered him the first dance at my wedding," she told Brendel. She acted as if the stork had brought her into the world, as if her mother had nothing to do with it. Her mother sensed her hostile attitude.

"If you had children, perhaps you'd treat me differently," she said to Yente.

The arrow she had shot out hit Yente hard.

She had been married for eleven years now and the children refused to arrive. God sat and laughed to Himself up there and all her father and her husband's medicine could not do a thing. Yente had long resigned herself to this fact and might even have been glad that the only person she needed to take care of was herself. Markus Herz had also stopped talking about it and their life proceeded as if the whole matter did not exist. He had the patients he tended to and Yente as well. He was certainly aware that taking care of her was like taking care of a child. He pampered her with pretty clothes, jewelry and trips to spas and did all that she asked of him, and she had quite a few requests. In return, she made him godlike as well, just as she had done with her father. Ever since she lost her father, Markus was all she had left, and she clung to him more than ever now, fiercely protecting him and making sure he would always love her.

13 | 1790

It had now been a week since the day Markus Levin passed away. A week in which Rahel fulfilled her role in the play called Markus Levin's *shiva*. And once her obligations to her mother, her siblings and her late father were done, and the pretense to which she had subjected herself was at an end, she prepared to go out into the world. When they returned from the cemetery, she went up to her room, took off the mourning outfit that had encased her body all week long, filled the tub with hot water and sat inside until it was cold. The chill in the bathtub brought back things she wanted to forget. All the illnesses that frequently plagued her and the dreams that did not come to fruition. However, before she began to delve into her bitter fate, she remembered that her father was no longer around. This reminder filled her with excitement and shame. She was excited about the new future that would soon open up to her and ashamed of her joy. Her father, the man who had brought her into the world and provided her with the means to obtain the knowledge and education that were a part of her, had died, and she was happy about it. If any of her family members could read her mind, she would find herself cast out. But there was no need to read her mind—they only needed to look at her and observe her actions.

After a week of wearing rags, Rahel put on her favorite light blue dress, plaited her hair into a swept-up hairstyle that had always flattered her, gathered up her small reticule and prepared to leave the house.

"Where are you going?" Markus barked out.

"To Yente's."

Markus knew that Yente would be holding her usual gathering that night. He also knew the piano would be playing and that people would be singing and laughing, while Rahel was still in mourning. What would they say about her? What would they say about them? And how dare she think it was permitted to go to Yente's salon when the thirty days of mourning mandated by Jewish law were still in progress? When she was still in mourning? Markus's face grew flushed. He resembled his father in one thing only—the redness that covered his face when he was excited or angry. The red flush turned purple when he saw that Rahel had no intention of changing her plan. They had just returned from the cemetery, the house was still in disarray after the past week, and instead of spending time with her family, tidying up and cleaning and supporting their mother together, Rahel had dressed up and was about to leave the house.

Markus blocked the door.

"Move away from the door and let me out," she asked quietly. She saw no point in raising her voice or getting angry. Deep inside, she knew she was attempting an inconceivable deed, but she decided to proceed anyway, willing to bear the consequences. She knew people would gossip about her but did not care. What she cared about, more than anything, was starting her life the way she saw it. She wanted to firmly assert herself both in the house and outside it. Those who wanted to would accept her as she was and those who did not were unworthy of her anyway.

Markus did not move away from the door.

"Please let me out," she said again in a moderate, cold voice, but Markus did not move. From this day forward, he was the man of the house and everyone would have to respect his authority. He too knew that whatever happened now would determine the shape of things to come.

Rahel was unimpressed by his determination, but knew she could not win the day by force. Therefore, she turned back submissively and began to walk toward the staircase, back to her room.

A short time later, when Markus was busy, she swiftly snuck out.

Yente, who for some time now, had insisted on being called by her

German name, Henriette, was surprised to see Rahel. She stood in the entryway to her home with a big smile on her face, as if they had not met just that morning at the cemetery. She did not make any comments, knowing there was no point. Pulling Rahel inside, she hugged her tightly. She then seated her in the living room, still saying nothing. Rahel merely said, "Thank you, Henriette."

Rahel was careful this time. Several days ago, a slip of the tongue had caused her to call her friend 'Yente,' while she, as if gripped by madness, had assaulted Rahel angrily and threatened that if she did not call her Henriette, she would never talk to her again. "Anyone who doesn't respect me isn't worthy of me, including my good friends."

That statement had been like a mantra to her for several months now. When she decided on the change, she had not known how hard it would be for people to adjust to the new name, especially within the Jewish community where she lived. Brendel, now called Dorothea, had gone through a similar experience. In her case, the resistance came primarily from home, from her mother and siblings. They did not understand why she needed this change and none of her explanations satisfied them. Luckily, Henriette felt the exact same way and for the first time, she felt that she was just fine, that her feelings were normal and that she was not fighting against the current on her own. However, Henriette's new name made sense, while for Brendel, it had popped up out of nowhere. Either way, both of them agreed that people were simply dismissive of them, as if they were still little girls and not the respected women they were, and no one bothered calling them by their new names. Therefore, for some time now, they had replaced their pleasant tone with aggression. It seemed to be more effective.

The salon was thronged and bustling. Henriette sat and smiled. She liked this state of high spirits as it was proof that the cultural endeavor she had founded in her drawing room was indeed worthwhile. There were not many places in Berlin where the aristocracy could argue with the bourgeoisie. Where else could Jews voice their opinion? Where else did their Christian friends value their opinion? Where else could literature and poetry inflame people with utter seriousness, if not at her salon?

At such moments, the guests of her husband, Dr. Markus Herz—young doctors and other well-educated friends—would also frequently abandon their discussions, held in the adjacent room, and listen in on the arguments in the salon. For Henriette, this constituted a small victory over her husband, of her lust for culture over his for higher learning. From Markus's perspective, any writer who was not blessed with Lessing's clarity was not worthy of his time. Henriette and her friends agreed with him on that score, not primarily due to Lessing's dramatic output, but due to his status as an iconoclast; for this, they were willing to proffer their respect, as if he were a contemporary writer. Iconoclasm was the essence that imbued their lives with many hues.

At this point, it was impossible to know who had started the argument. Someone said to the person beside him, "There are many people, quite a few, who find satisfaction in books, and yet their reading is not true reading."

And that person replied, "Why, that's obvious, as each of us derives from a book what we have put into it, from our own internal musing."

And from the moment the duo's conversation was overheard, each of the attendees contributed his or her own ideas to the developing discussion.

Von Humboldt said, "It is a known fact that people differ from each other in their character, in their emotion and thought, and by way of their degree of education and knowledge of life and, of course, their experiences. They cannot be equal in the great spiritual joy they experience after reading a novel or an essay."

Friedrich Hermann supported his opinion: "A person whose mind is numb, his senses dull and his imagination exhausted cannot possibly gain the sort of satisfaction from a novella that would be experienced by someone whose thoughts are lively, whose senses are refined and who possesses an agile, vibrant imagination."

In contrast, Karoline Dittmann said, "Pleasure is pleasure, regardless of the education or the quality of the imagination a reader does or does not possess. A book or an essay is meant to be read by those who can read it, and the meaning of what is read is insignificant except to the person reading."

Rahel wandered into the argument after it had already begun, which did not lessen her pleasure in the slightest. She did not take part in the lively debate. She had opinions to contribute but she was very tired and preferred to listen and enjoy it quietly. At such moments, she knew that no future fight with her brother could decrease the immense bliss that had taken hold of her body.

"Some people turn to books to discover pleasures there," said Ulrich Guggentag, who had stood up as he wanted to be heard. "The same pleasures that they could find outside of books as well, for example in a game of cards or in drinking. And if that is the case, this is a sign that such people have no affinity for literature, and their reading is lifeless. Therefore, I would recommend to them that they do not bother reading." Once he was done speaking, he let out a healthy cough and sat down once more, exhausted.

"Even if reading merely brings pleasure, in the course of dull, dreary daily life, reading of that sort should not be dismissed," said a young lady whom Rahel did not recognize. "Reading for pleasure is a worthwhile pursuit. Just like other things we do for pleasure and still value." She looked at von Humboldt, who appeared to have been the one to bring her along that evening, then looked down at the floral carpet upon which she was standing.

"Naturally, such a thought would be voiced by a lady," said Albert Müller, a paunchy man and the oldest among the group. "Most women, as well as quite a few men, read uselessly. For them, reading is entertainment. It is not meant for refinement or wisdom or enlightenment. They read idle tales and therefore value reading by the amount of pleasure it provides."

The only time Henriette intervened in the discussion was to suggest that Müller clarify his statement regarding women's vapidity. And he, greatly appreciative of Henriette, had to qualify his statement, explaining that he had been speaking in generalities, his assertion aimed at the lower classes. However, since everyone knew Albert, they knew he was expressing his frustration with regard to women.

The same young lady, her face no longer flushed, added, following the support she had received from Henriette, "Even a paltry, lightweight book of idle tales might awaken and enliven a person, diverting him to a new path."

"Would the young lady be willing to explain the matter to us?" came a call from the end of the room, followed by a murmur of agreement passing among the attendees like a breeze.

"A false intention may become a true intention." She shifted a strand of light hair away from her forehead in a graceful gesture. "Let's say there is a Jew who had read only sacred texts his entire life, and believes that behind the small town where he has lived his entire life, the sky descends into the earth and the Mountains of Darkness begin. One day, he picks up a book, even if it is the most trivial, paltry and lightweight of books, and after reading, discovers that there are such places as Paris and London. And there are places where roses grow and where there is love of a kind he has never known. And therefore, his eyes have been opened."

"And after he has learned all that?" the same voice called out again, followed by that same breeze passing through the crowd. "What additional contribution has he received from the books?"

"If he persists and reads additional books," the young lady said, with absolute conviction, "gradually, he will learn to discern the internal and artistic flavor of the narrative."

Paunchy Albert, whose balding dome sported droplets of perspiration both in the cold and in the heat, tried to improve the impression he had created earlier, saying, "Women, you have a compassionate view. Therefore, you can find the good even in a reprehensible deed." But in this case too, he evoked his listeners' wrath.

"And what about those who read a book not as a way to spend time, but merely to boast?" Ernst asked. "There are people, some of whom I know personally, who pretend so they can brag to their acquaintances. Just as a person buys the latest fashionable suit, so, too, does he buy a famous book."

A peal of laughter echoed through the room, after which the laugher, who had kept his silence until now, asserted, "And that reader! It is precisely this reader upon whom the book avenges its violated virtue! Oh, the torments experienced by the person whose heart yearns for the dictates of fashion! Such great torment he feels as the story is locked before him like a flower shuttering before the cold, such great torment he feels as it hides away its scent, its inner glory." Another burst of laughter, thundering even louder, rang out. "Oh! Such torment. And the boredom he feels. Heaven help us."

The quarreling group let out a burst of uninhibited laughter, as if pausing before another round, and then another question was released into the room. "And how will the deceptive reader discover the contents of the story so he can talk about it among his educated friends?"

"Easily," Friedrich said coolly, as if he had just woken up from a slight nap. "After all, that is the exact purpose of a literary critique. And the deceptive reader, as my friend so succinctly defined him—and I might yet write something on this topic—uses it as a mere ruse. As, after all, his entire desire is to pretend he is not falling behind."

"Hypocrisy!" Ulrich cried out in his hoarse voice, standing up once more so that everyone could see him. "After all, what is the virtue of a book? The fact that it can be closed while being read as the reader retreats into contemplation. A wise reader will use this to his advantage and remain immersed in the book even when it is not in front of his eyes."

Rahel began to ruminate. She ceased to hear those around her and began to hear the inner voices that were shouting repeatedly within her. Those voices led her to a decision regarding the way she would proceed and navigate her life from now on, in order to make use of the education of which she was so proud. One decision followed another, her mind teeming with plans for the future. Only one thing might delay them. She must pray for good health.

PART TWO

"It is not possible to live pleasantly without living wisely, honorably, and justly."

— Epicurus

14 | 1791

Rahel and Henriette were sitting in the well-tended garden of Henriette's house and drinking afternoon tea. The air was precisely cool enough and the rose bushes were the perfect background for the evening that had started to fall. They drank without speaking until Henriette broke the silence and asked Rahel if she had noticed that she had not been ill for some time.

It was exactly that week that Rahel became ill, afflicted by a bothersome cough as well as a fever and severe headaches. As if the devil had been sitting and listening to them and picked up on their satisfaction and wished to sabotage that happiness. Or perhaps she grew sick due to what had taken place the day before.

Her oldest brother summoned the entire family—his mother Chaya, Ludwig, Rose and the younger siblings were invited to sit in the family's drawing room. Markus wanted to introduce them to the candidate—a respectable Jewish businessman he had chosen for Rahel and whom he wished to invite to join the family. He explained to everyone that together, Rahel and the businessman would establish a proper Jewish home and his sister's livelihood would thus be ensured from now on and into her dotage. The deal was nearly signed. Rahel only had to do one thing—consent.

"Under no circumstances," Rahel replied, seeing no cause to elaborate or explain. She had just broken free of her father's chokehold and had no desire to be reeled in once more into an institution that would oppress her. She knew with certainty that avoiding marriage would be harder than marriage itself and had prepared herself to face this battle.

She was willing to bear the consequences of her refusal and to live in the sort of social isolation she would surely face as time went by. But, in any case, her life to date was more a world of words and sentences, of pages and leather covers and dreams, than the kind of full, lively social sphere of which she had dreamed. She dreamt of balls and theaters and resort towns and summer houses, dreamt of carriages transporting her throughout Berlin and of young men who would admire her and be her lovers. And within all those dreams, she knew her Judaism would always constitute an obstacle and that the entrance to her dream society was barred to her. Now, as she had rejected the good match offered to her and her family, she would also be rejected by her own world. However, the world in which she lived—Jewish society—did not interest her anyway. A world of religious edicts, of 'thou shall' and 'thou shalt not.' A world in which women could only follow one path, and were forbidden to divert from it. A path that led to only one place, precisely the place where she did not want to go, although some time ago, she had given Henriette Mendelssohn, Dorothea's younger sister, precisely the opposite advice in the letter she sent her:

"In our given social situation, what could be better for a physically and mentally sound person than the consoling, gentle bond of marriage?" She added, wishing to clarify, *"You are surprised to see me defending something I so objected to last summer. In fact, I do not direct all these appealing arguments at myself—as I no longer can—I am already spoiled. It is precisely for that reason that I am warning you so emphatically. You should be wary—this is great trouble."*

But Henriette was not won over. *"Great trouble indeed,"* she replied, *"and an even greater trouble is to be shackled in ties of marriage to a man whom you do not love or like and being wretched with him for your entire life. I see Dorothea. She is miserable and all the knowledge and languages she has acquired and her fluency in the humanities and her daring and her opinionated nature, what is the point of all of them? Just to say, 'Yes, my husband' and to obey? And to be subject to his whims? And to give birth to tots who waste her days away? I do not seek such a fate for myself."*

Immediately after the intended groom departed, the shouting began in the Levins' drawing room.

Markus did not understand why Rahel had rejected the groom he had brought. He did not possess any visible flaws. He was not particularly tall or particularly short and was not poor— quite the contrary; it was true that he was not among the best educated, but he was also no fool. He was elegantly dressed and was polite and had not looked at Rahel inappropriately. He was gentle and polite and was even willing to commit to offering her a certain independence when it came to her reading.

Rahel knew that the minute the ring was on her finger, she would be at his mercy and any promise he made at the moment, even if sealed into a contract, would immediately be broken and no one would stand by her on that matter.

"It is my life, and as that is the case, I will decide by myself how I wish to live it!" She was really yelling. "You're doing all this in order to shirk off the concern of my livelihood. One less mouth to feed and one less body to dress and one less soul to worry about!" she shouted at him and he retorted in kind.

"You're ungrateful and always have been!" Markus bellowed. "You always put yourself ahead of others, regardless of what's going on around you!" He lost control, his voice rising and falling, occasionally turning discordant, as if he had a horn stuck in his throat. Rahel saw his lips moving, his face growing red, the tips of his ears turning purple, and the beads of sweat on his forehead. German words mingled with Yiddish and even English. There was no language he skipped.

"Who do you think you are?" he screeched. "After what happened here today, no one will want you!"

This statement made its way into her mind and a big grin spread across her face. "Excellent! That's exactly what I wanted. You finally understand."

She had never witnessed an outburst of that sort from him. Such outbursts were reserved for her father and had been his exclusive domain when he was alive. And now, just a short time after Markus had taken on the role of head of the family in their father's stead, he had already adopted his negative qualities. If she thought that with the death of her tyrannical father her problems had come to an end, and she would no longer have to deal with being scolded, humiliated and mocked, she had been wrong. Apparently, she had just been passed around, while those qualities in their household remained as they had always been. From now on, she would continue to be at the mercy of the brother who had control of the family funds.

Her mother, who had always been like a leaf swept helplessly in the wind and had never protected her from her father's eruptions, did not say anything now, either. Rahel had expected that now that she too was free of the burden of her despotic husband, she would open her mouth and speak up for her, as she, too, had married a stranger and had not experienced even one day of grace with him.

A doormat, a broken vessel, a shadow—these were some of the descriptors Rahel silently attributed to her mother, but did not dare utter out loud. Although she did not respect her mother, she had no desire to further hurt this woman, for whom pain had become an integral part of life. But the silence frustrated Rahel. After all, her mother was the one who had given birth to her; she had grown in her mother's belly and her mother had undergone much suffering to bring her into this ruined world, standing over her bed and praying over her when she had been suspended between heaven and earth. And despite all that, she did not see fit to stand by her side on one of the most important moments of her life. On the contrary, she chose to support her brother Markus by not saying a thing and even allowing him to raise his voice at her in her own home.

Markus could not believe that this was truly what Rahel wanted. What woman did not want to get married? To establish a home? To have children? It was inconceivable to him. After all, why even live if not for all these things?

"You're going to beg me to bring you a groom, I promise you, and when you do, I'll bring you the most pathetic man in all of Berlin."

His words made no impression on her, precisely as her father's words had not managed to hurt her after a while. She was immune to both of them. However, the more indifferent she looked, the more Markus was motivated to hurt her.

"Who do you think you are?" he repeated the same statement he had already hurled at her several times. "You're just an ugly little woman with no skills to keep house. You think all your reading and studying will help you in this life. But it won't help you at all. You'll see."

Rahel had long distanced herself from that place. From the drawing room, from that house, from that family. She saw his lips moving, but she was already far away from there. And so he shouted and shouted and once he saw she was no longer answering him, he stopped. At that exact moment, she turned and went up to her room in the attic.

***

From that day onward, Rahel regularly attended all the cultural gatherings in Berlin to which she had access, as if her father's death marked a new era that arrived not only within her, but throughout Berlin. A new tolerance of sorts gradually spread through the city, allowing Jews, and primarily Jewish women, to speak out outside of the community. Perhaps she could still not attend the opera or the theater on her own, requiring an escort for such outings, but she could go to the meetings of the literary salons by herself. Not only did such gatherings allow women to attend, but they were even run by women, under the patronage of a father or a husband. Such clubs were not only for women or only for Christians, not only for the nobility or for the commoners. These gatherings were open to anyone who wished to talk about culture, art and poetry, and mostly about Romanticism—both men and women. Some arrived in groups and others on their own; either way, all were welcome.

Rahel left her house every evening and returned late at night. She could not disappoint her brother and her family any more than she already had.

And her reputation was no longer stellar since the rumor spread among all the 'good souls' within the community. Therefore, she was free, and from day to day, she acquired many new friends. Her refusal might have denied her grooms and mothers-in-law, brothers-in-law and nephews and nieces, but did open up an entire world of possibilities before her. Some of the women running the salons were childhood friends of Rahel's, while others were long-time acquaintances. Was this not what she had sought for herself? Had her dream come true, and her torments come to an end? Had a new life begun for her?

***

Now that she was already familiar with many salons, Rahel knew that she preferred the gatherings taking place in Henriette's residence, where she also felt at home. Lately, she had sat and assessed Henriette with inquisitive eyes in order to understand what made these gatherings in her home so successful, and why so many people wanted to attend them. She envisioned her own home as bustling and hectic as this house was; if only she, too, could host people like this. But would it work? Did she possess what Henriette possessed? The secret of Henriette's success was in her classical beauty, her great intellectual aptitude, her passion for all that was new in literature, her social skills, as well as her respected, worthy husband. All these attracted respectable folks, who were ultimately won over by Henriette's carefree approach—the approach of a child who refused to grow up, one that Rahel would never attain.

How could she compete with all that? She had no beauty, no money, no respected husband. She did not possess even one of these.

She felt that she was deluding herself. This must be another dream that would live on forever in her mind, never coming true, like many dreams she had had. Why did she think her father's death would change her luck? Had she not stayed on in the same house? With the same family? Her fate had been sealed on the day she was born and any attempt to change it was doomed to fail. Suddenly, she felt that she had been arrogant when she determined to create a new reality for herself that was different than that of her mother and her grandmother and any other woman in her immediate circle. If only she were a simple, foolish woman, the kind that did not want much, and therefore was not disappointed. If only she wanted to get married and have children and make her brother and her mother and all their Jewish friends proud. But as much as she tried to imagine herself that way, she could not. The thought of belonging to a strange man filled her with disgust.

She was stuck with desires that did not fit in with the world where she lived and this was her true fate, a fate with which she had to deal.

15 | 1791

If there was one thing Rahel loved about her father, it was his friends—French noblemen and bohemian theater people, whose colorful nature attracted her. They were graceful and elegant, wearing the latest in Parisian fashion and exotic clothes originating in places she did not know, but not the kind that could be found in the windows of Berlin's shops. Their behavior differed from the meticulous attitude of her father, who was both a devout Jew and a German like any other. Perhaps, like her, he too was attracted to characters who were unaffected by any dictates. Or perhaps it was due to other things, related to money and loans and usury. In general, she noticed that since his death, she had stopped clinging to her hatred for him. Something about that fervent emotion she had nurtured all her life crumbled somewhat, allowing other memories to enter. Perhaps because he no longer posed a threat to her, she was calmer, less intimidated. In any case, the fragments of things that had taken place a long time ago, but were folded in somewhere between all the bleak occurrences, began to sneak in.

Some time ago, she had heard his voice as she was haggling at the spice booth in the market. "Whether it's a minor matter or a major one, negotiation is always the same," he once said when a fabric merchant visited their home. Now she made use of his wisdom. Ever since Markus had asked them to limit expenses, she found herself bargaining more and more. Her father would surely be pleased with her if he were currently alive. Perhaps he would even have granted her a little smile.

He had not always been volatile and short-tempered. Sometimes, when the spirit moved him, he allowed her to sit with his bohemian friends. There were also several occasions when he permitted her to read poetry to them. She never understood why, but also did not ask. She could even remember one time when she had joined the group, although he had not approved it, and he did not retaliate in any way. But although she spent time with them, although she tracked them, she could not adopt even a single feature of their easygoing nature, of their carefree attitude, of the irreverence with which they treated life. They were glamorous while she felt like an outsider. Not due to her mind, which was just as sharp as theirs, and not due to her tongue, as she was wittier than most of them, but because she felt like a *schlemiel*—someone unimportant. It was interesting, as these actors and artists were not elevated in their social status and usually did not have any money, either. After all, this was at the root of their connection to her father, who was a moneylender. And yet they were happy and proud, feeling that the whole world lay at their feet. While she was the exact opposite. Her feelings of inferiority and her status in society tormented her constantly, and these feelings grew more heightened when she was in their company. Why couldn't she be like them? It frustrated her. She had no doubt that the blame lay in her Judaism.

"It seemed as if, immediately when I was flung into this world, some celestial power, some non-terrestrial entity, used a dagger to stab the following sentiments into my heart: yes, take some sensitivity, see the world as very few people can see it, be elevated and high-minded, but I will add something else—be Jewish! And now my life is bleeding away slowly and will do so until the day I die."

Rahel would write these words in the years to come to her friend David Veit after he left to study medicine in Göttingen. But for now, something began to happen in her life, as well as in the lives of her friends.

Dorothea became submerged in her life while a toddler scrambled at her feet. Another infant had been born a short time ago but was no longer with them. After the death of her first baby she had an intuition that more trouble still lay ahead and now the proof had arrived. Apparently, death had turned her home into its residence. Simon Veit mourned this early death, but although sorrow over the baby tore at his heart and, for the first time, undermined the foundations on which his easygoing nature was built, he felt even greater sorrow for his wife. Two dead babies were like a mark of Cain. How could he ask her to believe all would be well if he himself no longer believed it? How could he ask her to try again? How could he look at her if the third baby, too, did not want their company?

This baby reminded Dorothea of the circumstances of Rahel's birth; however, unlike Rahel, he did not wish to cling to life, but rather was in a hurry to leave it. She tried to appease him, spending a large part of her day trying to breastfeed, but instead of growing stronger, he grew increasingly weaker, as if what came from insider her was poison, as if he knew he could not be happy with a mother like that, in a house such as this. She saw that he was weakening, she said it to Simon, but he initially hoped that it was the fear speaking from her throat. Deep in her heart, she knew she was right, that the worst still awaited her, but she wanted to believe it would be all right as the fears had already extinguished every spark of hope within her. They named him Abraham, but his given name did not result in a miracle. Just as her own name had not granted her the change she yearned for.

Perhaps that was what happened when she sought a bit of happiness for herself.

She was cursed. She was convinced of it. Any shred of luck she once had disappeared on the day her father presented her with Veit as a husband. On the day she agreed. She herself had brought all this misery into her life. She did it with her own two hands. This was also true regarding the deaths of her children—both the unborn ones and the ones who were born.

Happiness. Did she even know what it was? Had she ever experienced the feeling it brought with it? And how did she even get the idea that it existed? From books? From stories? Those were fabrications by people who wished to sell books, publishers wanting to get rich by making use of the fantasies of wretched people like her. Happiness. Perhaps it had simply skipped over her? She was in a state of despair, but this time as well, she trusted her heart. If there was one good thing about the death of her children, it was her growing confidence in herself, in her intuitions. And if her heart yearned for happiness, it must indeed exist. Perhaps she simply had to seek that happiness elsewhere.

But what was that happiness, which was so elusive? Was it supposed to come from within her? If that was the case, why could she not feel it? And if it did not come from within her, this meant it was somewhere in the possession of someone she had yet to meet. Many stories, essays and plays had been written about happiness and its pursuit and she could only imagine how it felt, feel herself nearly touching it; it was there, waiting for her to come and pluck it. She was determined to make her way toward it, had tried to summon it by changing her name, and although it did not come, she did not give up. She was still seeking it.

A short time ago, Dorothea had met a handsome young man at one of Henriette's gatherings. Perhaps more than he was handsome, he was witty, and furthermore, he had been kind and attentive to her in a way she had not experienced for some time. She was no longer pregnant and had already shed the excess weight that made her even uglier than she was. She could easily fit into her old dresses and every time she left for a meeting for one of her reading clubs, she took care to dress up even more than usual. Sprucing herself up made her feel slightly better, as if she were putting on a mask and instantly transforming into someone else, someone who left all her troubles at home the moment she closed the door behind her.

During these gatherings, particularly the ones held by Henriette, the atmosphere was free, joyful and light-hearted, the opposite of what happened in her home. Perhaps it was due to the nature of the participants, who were carefree, uninhibited young people, mostly thanks to the alcoholic drinks. D'Alton behaved like a boy, giggled with her and told her tall tales, some of which she knew were fabricated by his fertile mind, but this did not bother her. On the contrary, she gladly accepted anything that was far from her own world, and this was far from it indeed.

She found herself thinking of him constantly. When she was performing the household tasks and when she was playing with Jonah, her toddler son, and when she was reading books and as she closed her eyes before sleep took her. Was this the feeling of being in love? The heaviness weighing upon her dissipated somewhat and a feeling of lightness enveloped her. She was even more forgiving of her husband. *A silly, harmless infatuation*, she told herself. She deserved to be courted, she deserved some joy; after all, soon she would be pregnant once more and the worries of the world would settle upon her shoulders yet again. She wanted to share what she was feeling with Henriette, but discovered that Henriette had been unhappy lately. With surprising honesty, she told Dorothea that her relationship with Markus was not so perfect, even if it did appear to be that way.

"When I ask Markus to show some emotion for me, he dismisses it. 'Silly, childish conduct,' he says, as if I'm some little girl."

Dorothea did not understand why Henriette had suddenly chosen her as a confidante with whom she shared her intimate life with her husband. "You always look so happy together. I'm always so jealous of you for that," she confessed to Henriette.

"Yes, it's a happy relationship. Not necessarily a happy marriage. We live in one house, share a good, active life together, but we're missing the intimacy of a couple in love. There's love between us, but the deep passion between a man and a woman is not there, for how could there be passion between the two of us when I can't exhibit any emotion?"

She then talked about the matter of infertility. For some time now, they had stopped talking about it, but deep in her husband's heart, the topic was still simmering. He thought she did not know it, that she could not sense his disappointment, but she knew him well enough to see and feel it on him.

"The Creator of the world sits there, high and mighty, and toys with us. His game is a cruel one. He gave Markus talent and a profession but did not give him the opportunity to use it inside his home. After all, we aren't fulfilling the most important religious edict, 'be fruitful and multiply,' which nullifies our entire essence in the world as husband and wife."

It was the first time Henriette had ever said anything of this sort and the last time as well. However, she kept her true thoughts to herself. Such thoughts should stay private; for example, the fact that she was not very sorry about all this, as it left her free to do as she wished at any time without time-devouring little creatures eating away at her day. And besides, she had never been all that enthusiastic about those tiny ones. Now that her friends were drowning in them, she was quite certain about it. Her marriage was not perfect, and her only regret regarding this deficiency was the disappointment experienced by Markus, who stayed with her despite her infertility, but was not whole-hearted about it.

This honesty made Dorothea realize that life was complex for her friends as well, and perhaps no one around her was happy, and the appearances were misleading. This wretchedness was the result of expectations. Their Judaism expected them to be mothers and give birth to as many offspring as possible, to be modest, to only do what was right, but gave them nothing in return. Heartache and no more.

Dorothea, too, kept a thing or two to herself, although she had meant to share what she felt with Henriette. But after her friend's candor, she felt it might not be the right time for it. One evening, after she left Henriette's house following another high-spirited gathering, D'Alton volunteered once again to escort her home. However, once they had drifted away somewhat and reached a dark area, he stopped, brushed his hand down her hair and brought his mouth to hers. Dorothea did not shy away; on the contrary, she gave herself over completely to their first kiss. She felt as if someone had lit a match inside her, which fired up her whole body, a fire she had never felt with her Simon. She did not know much about love, but there was no doubt that if there was desire in the world, this kiss was its epitome. Had he asked her, she would have surrendered to him right there on the dim street corner; however, a gentleman would never request such as thing, and D'Alton was a gentleman.

In their next encounters too, the kisses, caresses and canoodling went on and after a short period in which Dorothea floated in a fantasy world, she fell to earth when she began to see D'Alton as he really was: a handsome, cheerful and impudent young man whose head was full of nothing. If he had interested her intellectually, she would have demanded more from him. However, after a while, she found that he bored her and even the kisses and fondling that had reawakened her and filled her with a passion she had never known were no longer enough. She liked him, for the way he gave her attention, for listening to her, for introducing her to passion and proving to her that love did exist in the world. It was as if he had helped open something up within her. That which had once been closed and concealed was revealed to her, and now she needed to learn how to use it. That was the role of young D'Alton, to wake her up from the deep sleep in which she had been immersed, and that was enough. Therefore, when their relationship came to an end, there was no heartache, as she was not expecting a thing. She was not willing to give up intellect and interest. She had given them up one time and for her, there would be no second time.

Dorothea then fell in love with another man, Wilhelm von Humboldt, whom she knew from back in the days when he had come to study the writings of Kant with her father, and together they discussed the nature of enlightenment. If she was looking for intellect, this man had plenty of it. He spoke Greek, Latin and French, was full of knowledge, and the fact that he had recently married Caroline did not stop her from yearning for him. Von Humboldt was indeed an intellectual, but also a braggart and an insatiable gossip. She knew all this, but the thrill of another infatuation blurred her perception of reality and her success with D'Alton imbued her with courage and hope that were uncalled for. If she was making a fool of herself, she did not see it and there was no one around to tell her so. If she had known what he thought of her, her infatuation would have turned to resentment.

"That inexplicable woman," he called her behind her back, further maligning her to anyone willing to listen. "She's unbelievably miserable, married to a facile, vapid husband who is lacking in refinement and in masculinity. With a husband like that, her feelings for me can only increase," he boasted. "She loves me in every sense of the word. I find her to be a living portrait of the cruel destruction of a lovely, wondrous bud. Every time I see her, admiration and pity alternately fill my heart."

Even the worst of gossips spared her, as they knew she had indeed been unhappy and did not want to add to her misery. They spoke only behind her back and took care that their talk would not reach her. However, her husband was a different story. They did not spare him, and some of them took the time to tell him how his wife was allowing herself to enjoy being courted by other men, kindly advising him to keep an eye on her.

While Dorothea moved from infatuation to infatuation, and Henriette delved into questions regarding the nature of her relationship with her husband, Rahel was actually experiencing an awakening of sorts, a change that began to creep into her home.

"Could I come visit you occasionally?" she was asked one evening by David Veit, whom she had recently met in the gatherings she attended, just before the group assembled at Henriette's dispersed. David Veit was a young man about Rahel's age. He wasn't the kind of man who would cause female heads to turn, but there was something about him, a kind of stillness that came from within and projected outward, and a calm she could never find within herself.

Rahel was surprised. Why would anyone ask to visit her at home? Apparently, David interpreted her startled expression differently, as he immediately added, "It would all be conducted respectably."

Rahel thought this respectability of theirs, of the Jewish society to which she belonged, was overrated. If someone was asking to visit her home and be her friend, she would certainly not refuse. Perhaps David Veit would not be the one who would transport her to a different place and status in life, but she did find interest in friendship with him. There was something worldly about him; he knew things and strived to expand his knowledge. Through his eyes, she could experience a world she might never know.

"You are invited to come visit at any time you see fit," Rahel said and David looked overjoyed, or perhaps that was only her interpretation of his expression. It did not seem reasonable to her that she could ever make anyone happy. After all, she was not pretty, her body scrawny and bony, and she did not have Henriette's cheerfulness, and in addition, she was a Jewish woman who refused to obey the important edict of establishing a household and being fruitful and multiplying, and her economic status was also not as established as it once was.

In any case, the true hurdle was the one formed by her mother and her brother Markus, who would certainly have something to say about hosting men in their home. Perhaps she would not even tell them for the time being.

16 | 1792

Lately, something had begun to change in Simon and Dorothea Veit's home. Dorothea was happy in a way he was not familiar with, but that joy mingled with sorrow due to the gossip that had reached him regarding the reasons for his wife's new *joie de vivre*. He had already been described as submissive and limp, and these same things would probably be said about him now, but Simon Veit had no intention of taking a stance regarding Dorothea; he would merely keep an eye on her and make sure that all of these infatuations of hers would not ripen into a full-blown affair.

He loved her. From the first day her father had proposed a match between them, he had already loved her. First of all, she was rooted deep within a rich world of knowledge, even if he himself did not come from that world, or perhaps precisely due to that fact. Then there was her character, which was not submissive, a tumultuous nature he had not encountered in many women, and opinions she was not shy about voicing. As time went by, he loved her more, even though he understood that she did not love him. Deep in his heart, he believed that one day she would recognize all that he had done for her and realize that he was good for her, but in the meantime, he continued loving her despite everything. If he could ease her suffering, even slightly, as far as he was concerned, it was a small miracle he could produce for her. And if the attention she was getting from others raised her spirits, he would not try to oppose that joy.

Dorothea did not know whether he knew about her infatuations and did not dedicate any attention to the matter. On the one hand, she concealed them, but on the other hand, perhaps she did want to get caught. If he caught her, he might banish her and thus her troubles would come to an end.

But Simon Veit was still cautious, for both their sakes. He listened to the swirling rumors and kept his eyes open for fear things would deteriorate to a state that would prove to be irreversible. Finally, he decided it would be advisable for the two of them to distance themselves somewhat from their daily routine and from potential lovers. Therefore, he planned a trip for them. After all, he was not truly a distant observer as he wished to see himself and a bit of jealousy did settle inside him.

Surprisingly, Dorothea consented to the journey immediately and did not need to be convinced. Perhaps it was the failure with von Humboldt and perhaps she, too, wanted some distance from all that was familiar. She was not stupid and, contrary to popular opinion, she had heard the gossip. She simply did not care, as she had already been through the worst, and what was a bit of gossip compared to all the death swirling around her? This was what she told herself, but deep inside, she did care. Mostly, she felt Simon's concern and the way he protected her. She needed it.

Simon said they would travel to Sterlitz, and she truly did not mind if it was Sterlitz or the moon, so long as it was a change of scenery. When she told Rahel about the trip, Rahel said she had heard good things about the place, about its green meadows, the Baroque structures and the nice people living there. "Not like the Berliners, walking around with their noses in the air and thinking there is no place other than where they are."

Before they departed, Dorothea promised Rahel she would write to her in detail about everything she experienced: what she saw, what she heard, all the flavors, and especially the people she would meet there.

Rahel made her swear that she would keep her promise. "It's the only way I can see the world." She did not have a father who would take her, or a husband or lover, either. There was no journey on the horizon for her. "But that doesn't mean I can't be there with you, if not in body, then in spirit. In the meantime, that will do for me."

The moment Dorothea boarded the coach, she regretted having agreed to the trip. Why had she been in such a rush to agree? Now she would have to spend time alone with her dreary husband, just the two of them, for many days, and already, she could feel her body tense as her old anger and dissatisfaction seized control of her.

As they left the city, Dorothea closed her eyes. If she slept, she would not have to talk to her husband. And even if she could not fall asleep, she would pretend. For a short while, it worked, until Simon began to whistle various tunes. The fact that his wife had agreed to embark on such a trip with him was a good sign as far as he was concerned, and this alone lifted his spirits. He could not remember the last time he had whistled with such pleasure. In the streets of Berlin, it was not the custom to whistle, and at home, ever since Jonah was born, he had to tiptoe around. Now, in the wide open spaces laid out before them, he felt that anything was possible, including the whistling he had been suppressing for so long.

Dorothea opened her eyes. She was about to ask him to stop, but then caught sight of the green meadow spread out at their feet, and a moment later, they were inside it. The smell of fresh vegetation and greenery reminded her of a different path at a different time, when she had traveled with her parents and siblings to visit relatives. The reality of her life had caused her to forget the happy moments she had had with her family. All that was left to her was a past gradually fading away over time and a gray present.

Little Jonah began to wiggle inside the bassinet in which he had been lying since they left. He opened his eyes wide and smiled at Dorothea. Dorothea smiled back, reached out and plucked him straight into her lap. If she loved something in this world, it was Jonah. He was her true source of light. It was a joy that contained great fear and immense anxiety and the constant fear of growing more attached to him. As the months went by and Jonah was still with them, she loved him with greater and greater intensity, and her fear increased accordingly. She wavered endlessly between the desire to hold her live son to her and never let go, and the wish to establish some distance. To prepare for the worst.

After several hours, Simon stopped by a stream that flowed leisurely by the side of the road. He produced a basket containing apples and oranges, bread, quince jam and a wedge of cheese, as well as a checkered napkin with two pastries, one with cinnamon and the other with sweet cheese. There was no logical connection between the various food items other than his wish to sate Dorothea's hunger and to please her. Dorothea flashed him a stingy smile, took a bite from the apple and one from the cheese pastry, and walked away from the spot where Simon was assembling the meal he had prepared upon a starched tablecloth. If he thought this illogical meal would make her happy, she would prove him wrong. No apple or pastry or fine wedge of cheese would allow him entry into her heart. If he had been exuberant like D'Alton or smart like von Humboldt, perhaps she could have made an effort for him, for them. But he did not possess any of either man's qualities.

The two of them then sat silently the whole way, while in the background, the grass murmured and gravel crackled under the wheels of the coach. At some point, they began to hear the sounds of the bustling city preparing for the arrival of evening. In a moment, the carriage would stop at the entrance to a large, spacious house, whose residents, childhood friends of Simon Veit's, would be their hosts.

"*I have to tell you about the French opera in Reinsberg,*" she wrote to Rahel a week later. Reinsberg was a short distance away from Sterlitz and was the site of King Frederick's palace, a roomy estate built on the bank of the river, surrounded by a sprawling green lawn. The southern side of the palace sported two round structures, each headed by a spiky turret.

"Look how nature and architecture blend seamlessly," Simon Veit said when they passed by the palace on their way to the opera. If this statement evoked anything in Dorothea, it was merely contempt and no more. Was he trying to be someone else? And what did he understand about architecture and beauty, anyway?

"*Oh! I have never wanted you close to me as much as I did this evening. Lots of satin, lots of furs, lots of rich belts and powdered curls, lots of dramatic* expressions, but no spark of poetry, or style, or true acting, and it was all overshadowed by the scandalous seating arrangement. The best seats were allocated to members of the upper class, and heaven forbid that they meet or even see their inferiors, us. Therefore, they have a separate entrance and a separate sitting room, in a way that disgusted me."

All that she saw and felt was summed up in a critical letter, as if she were a publicist writing a newspaper article. From the opera, she continued on to politics.

Rahel laughed. Dorothea could always be counted on to find the darkness in anything good that happened to her. After all, what did she have to do? Let go of her worries and enjoy spending time in this quiet location along with her little son and her husband, who was constantly trying to please her. And what did she do instead? Constantly saw only the injustice taking place in every corner.

"You must already know quite a bit about Reinsberg. People here live for the prince and through the prince. This is how they are steered, to aggrandize the prince, and all they do is pray that he live long! All that absurd power and happiness revolt me. His house, his garden, and all that can be seen from his window are full of majesty and splendor. If you continue even one house further, you will not find a single whole roof, a single clean street, a single child who is dressed from head to foot."

Dorothea had traveled to get some fresh air and had become a warrior of justice. What had all that to do with her, and when had she begun to develop a conscience regarding all the ills of the world? She had to travel all the way there in order to see that the royal family lived at the expense of the common citizens? And what about the rights that German citizens enjoyed compared to citizens like her? She was concerned about the Germans? She should worry about the members of her own religion first.

"The opera we saw cost more than it would cost to renovate a decrepit shack. I imagined the whole of France like this and now I understand the French and their revolution. Forgive me for getting fired up, dear Rahel. If only you could see Reinsberg."

Had Rahel traveled to visit Reinsberg, she would have chosen to see its better areas and would certainly have enjoyed the opera. Dorothea's criticism was surely exaggerated, just as she exaggerated other things in her life. Rahel felt nearly angry at her close friend's inability to enjoy herself, even a little. As if she intentionally sought out the bad and did not give herself a chance. And yet Rahel knew she herself quite resembled her. Like Dorothea, she, too, believed the world was cruel to her and that she stood no chance against it.

But lately, things had begun to change for her, which made her see things in a somewhat different, less critical light.

Rahel chose not to write to Dorothea about what was currently happening in her life, about going out to the theater and the gatherings of reading clubs, about afternoon walks in the streets of Berlin and about David Veit's visits. It was an irony of fate that one Veit was causing misery while another Veit was bringing happiness, and the two were not related, and neither of them knew the other. And what would she write to her? That she was happy? Dorothea would surely find something critical to say about it and Rahel was not interested at the moment in hearing a critique of her life. Even her mother, from whom she had expected a world war, welcomed David Veit civilly and respectfully and without a single complaint.

Two weeks earlier, on Wednesday, David Veit informed her that he would be coming for dinner and she briefly reported this to her mother. "A guest will be coming to dine with us today. I want you to get to know him. He's a nice, interesting fellow and I think you will like him."

The very thought that a prospective groom might be coming pleased her mother, and perhaps she also liked the idea that Rahel cared about her opinion. No one had ever asked her opinion and no one cared what she liked or did not like, and now Rahel had asked her to meet this man, and this in and of itself made her want to prepare delicacies. She cooked the beef roast she had not made for a while, a dish her husband Markus Levin had liked greatly and since his departure, she did not see the point in making the investment. Not when she considered the cost of a slab of fine beef and the good wine, or the long cooking time required. But as she thought the fellow was a future groom, she saw the point of making the investment. Perhaps she would also add bread balls and some potatoes to the meal, and for dessert, she would make a tort cake with a layer of apples and frosting, of the kind Rahel liked.

The meal was wonderful and flowed along peacefully, but this did not change the fact that Rahel and David Veit were merely friends and neither of them had the desire to alter their status. They had plenty of common ground; he was like a close female friend to her. She felt as if she had known him all her life and there was almost nothing they could not talk about honestly and openly. But this friendship, so inspiring, was cut short one evening when David Veit told her that he was leaving soon.

"In the coming fall, I'll start attending the university at Göttingen."

Rahel felt as if she had sustained a stinging slap to her face. She was not inferior to him by any measure; on the contrary, she actually exceeded him in knowledge, certainly when it came to literature, poetry and culture, but also in additional subjects such as mathematics. And yet she could never attend university. David knew how she would feel when he told her, and therefore put off the telling again and again until he could no longer do so. Rahel tried to hide her sense of insult and be happy for him, but she could not.

"If you're leaving, it would be better if you already left now," she said angrily as they were standing in the entrance to the house, retreating inside with a slam of the door. She did not want him to see the tears streaming down her face.

Everything was easier with Henriette and Dorothea. They were both in her position, more or less, in that they were Jewish women. Their starting point was similar and apparently their ending point would be as well. However, with David, things were different. Although he was Jewish, he was a man, and the world was open to him, with possibilities that greatly exceeded her own. In their conversations, he tried to argue this point and claimed he was hampered by his Judaism as well, but when Rahel suggested that he change places with her, he knew she was right.

Now he lingered for slightly longer behind the closed door. Based on their rather brief acquaintance, he knew that the door would not open again that evening, and yet he could still not leave. He wanted to console her and tell her that everything would work out eventually, but he knew that nothing would work out, that soon he would leave to study in a distant city and find the right opportunities to soar, while she would forever remain stuck in the same place.

17 | 1793

Dorothea knew passion existed in the world and within her and believed wholeheartedly that someone was waiting for her somewhere and that one day, her sex life would be the way she imagined it, thrilling and full of satisfaction and pleasure. But in the meantime, she had to sleep with her husband. This was one thing Simon Veit was unwilling to give up. And in contrast to Henriette, the sex between them, though unsatisfying and not based on love—at least on her part—proved fruitful. A few weeks after they returned from Sterlitz, she discovered she was pregnant, which deeply unsettled her once more. First came the familiar fears and anxieties, which intensified with each passing day. She could not fall asleep at night and even when she did, she woke up terrified from dreams of dead babies. Some of the babies had faces she knew and some were strangers, and both kinds returned to her night after night. And as she was not sleeping at night, she was off balance during the day, both due to the fatigue created by her fears and due to lack of sleep. She could not go out to visit her friends' salons in such a state and even if she had the energy, what would she do among all these cheerful young people? And who would even look at a pregnant woman? At a body swelling and expanding? At a face marked with dark circles under the eyes? At a soul that was frightened and panicked? And besides, now that her mind was utterly focused upon one thing only, she did not feel like hearing which book had recently been published or about a poem composed by one of the participants who called himself a poet but did not understand a thing about poetry. It was all utter folly. Her world was now narrow and limited, focused upon one single goal.

The months went by and the pregnancy was a normal one and the birth, too, ended well and Philipp, the new baby, grew to be plump and active. And Dorothea's exhaustion merely increased as now her hands were full of the work of tending to two children who were healthy for now. She also had to make sure that this would not change.

Philipp was an easy baby from the moment he emerged into the world. He arrived suddenly. The contractions began at nine in the morning and Dorothea was already preparing for the worst—for long hours of painful contractions and possible complications. But much to her surprise, at ten after ten, the baby had already made his appearance. Simon, who had also been anxious from the moment the contractions began, thanked the Lord that it had all ended so quickly and that Dorothea had not suffered much.

"This is compensation for all your suffering," he whispered to her as the little infant lay between his palms, swaddled in a clean, warm blanket.

Dorothea merely answered, "No more." And when she saw that Simon Veit did not grasp her intention, she added, "God has given us two live boys and that is enough for me."

Simon Veit understood and agreed, praying to God with great intention that He would protect these two children. So long as she was happy.

Happiness. For Dorothea, it was Philipp, the baby whose arrival heralded a new era in her life. When Henriette came to visit Dorothea after she had recovered from the birth and after the baby had already acquired chubby cheeks and a healthy pinkish color, she found a different Dorothea, more focused, and not on her usual preoccupations but on her children. This now seemed to be the only thing in the world for her. Henriette could not understand it. For her, children were a nuisance, no more, and yet she was happy for Dorothea. But due to the maternal bubble in which she was enclosed, she did not tell her what was going on in her own life. It was obvious to her that Dorothea could not be interested in such things. Not at the moment.

***

Two things were making Henriette happy lately. The first was a man named Friedrich Schleiermacher, whom she had met and befriended. The second was being courted by men who had come to see her vibrant salon with their own eyes and stayed after being bewitched by her charms. The passing years and time, which was abusive to all, seemed to have passed over Henriette, who would soon turn thirty and yet was only growing finer and becoming ever more popular.

She liked the attention. To Rahel, she said, "Yes, I enjoy the compliments bestowed upon me and the words of admiration sent to me in scented letters and the little surprises delivered to my home. Yes, all of them testify that I am still worth something to someone."

Both of them knew she never let any of them into her heart because her heart belonged to her husband Markus, even if all passion between them had been gone for some time now. In general, it seemed as if, as time went by, Henriette, too, lost her passion, or perhaps had never possessed it. In retrospect, when Henriette surveyed the years of her marriage, if she was completely honest with herself, other than the first year and perhaps the one that followed it, her lovemaking with her husband had been unsatisfying for both of them. Sex that was initially characterized by the enthusiasm of two young people had become disappointing, a chore, an intimacy intended to achieve a need they could not fulfill. Now, when Markus was about to turn fifty, he seemed weary of it. And yet Henriette remained the most important thing in his life.

Henriette's sexual passion was replaced by a passion for social gatherings, parties, recreation, reading and research. All these filled her life with much interest and meaning. Now Friedrich Schleiermacher had come along and appeared to be sparking new interest in her life.

The Herzes had first met Friedrich Schleiermacher about two years ago, when they were introduced to him by Count Alexander von Dohna, and by a striking coincidence, he and Markus met again at Charité Hospital, where Schleiermacher was carrying out his role as the emissary of God and Markus as the emissary of science. Despite the significant difference between the Christian priest and the Jewish doctor, the two found common ground and enjoyed each other's company.

The Herzes then invited Schleiermacher for dinner at their home, and he arrived with his sister Charlotte, a woman with a pleasant, easy nature, just like her brother. From that evening on, Henriette and Friedrich formed bonds of friendship.

"I enjoy the company of women more than the company of men. Men have managed to understand me only in rare cases, while among women, I find understanding, tenderness, grace and more diverse topics of conversation."

He had made this statement back on that first evening and thus won Henriette's heart. There was a gentleness to him that she had not encountered in any other man, including her husband. A gentleness she was familiar with among her female friends. And the more they met, the closer they grew. Schleiermacher learned Italian from her while she learned Greek from him. And although he was a Christian pastor, her Judaism did not come between them. What he liked about her most of all was her ability to understand him.

18 | 1795

Summer was nearly here. Berlin was about to be emptied of its residents, who preferred to depart for spas, resort towns and other exotic locales. As was the case every summer, Rahel began to harbor an oppressive feeling. Her friends and acquaintances would disappear and she would be left with nothing but her letters. Her only solace now was the studies she had embarked upon.

Her brother Markus, who had resigned himself to the fact that no groom was forthcoming, had agreed to grant Rahel a monthly allowance and she hired a private tutor to teach her English, French and mathematics, thus complementing her education, which had never been formal on those topics. But, as always, her studies were repeatedly interrupted by illnesses that seemed especially numerous that winter. On one occasion, her temperature climbed and on another she was stricken with a heavy cough, and once she felt that her lungs were about to burst, and another time it was intense stomachaches.

Her mother said all the illnesses were caused by the way she was constantly running around during the day and at night. "You don't rest for a moment. You're constantly rushing from here to there and when you're not running around, the house is full of people and rest is impossible."

Rahel dismissed this claim. After all, her mother enjoyed the visitors to their home just as much as she did. Following an entire life of loneliness and condescending treatment from her husband, the people who came to the Levins' home were greatly attentive to her, inquired after her wellbeing and exchanged opinions with her. Rahel was surprised to discover that her mother was an excellent conversationalist.

But as summer drew near and the sunshine illuminating Berlin peeled people of their layers until they became more cheerful, Rahel's mood turned overcast and gloomy. Any joy she possessed thanks to her vibrant salon evaporated, and she returned to her habitual heaviness of spirit and to a melancholy that threatened to take over her.

Her mother suggested that she travel as well. "Heizel Berndhard, Moses and Esther's daughter, is leaving soon and she has agreed to have you join her."

Rahel wanted to say that they had nothing in common, but instead, she acquiesced.

"The plan was for me to join Heizel Berndhard, although the two of us do not have a lot in common. But at the last moment, she changed her mind and the trip was canceled. Now I shall have to watch Berlin empty of all my friends, while I stay here, along with my illnesses, for another year," Rahel wrote to David, who had also decided to leave for a holiday in Paris directly from the university. When she put down her pen, she tossed herself into bed and all her self-pity descended upon her. She was stricken with a bleak mood and immediately began to curse her Judaism and her father and the fact that she was a woman. If she had been born in England, she could travel on her own, unescorted.

"In England," her friend Esther Gad told her, after returning from there, "women travel by themselves with no apprehension."

Not only had she been born in Berlin, but she had also been dealt the weakest hand that the world could offer.

However, apparently, luck had not completely abandoned Rahel, as a few days later, she received another invitation from a completely unexpected direction—the actress Friederike Unzelmann, whom she knew through her father. Rahel did not hesitate and immediately agreed, and her mother urged Markus to give her some money for the trip, uncharacteristically not at the expense of her monthly allowance.

On Monday morning, a coach stopped at the entrance to Rahel's home, picking her up.

Years later, when Rahel wrote her memoirs, Teplitz would be mentioned as a crossroads that changed her life irrevocably.

From the road, Rahel wrote to David Veit that she had finally found an escort, imploring him to meet her at one of the sites where she would be staying.

"I will be in Karlsbad for four weeks and another three weeks in Teplitz, and I am certain there will be additional stops as traveling by coach is not a trivial matter. I am certain you can feel my great excitement. Since the first, accursed trip to my relatives in Wroclaw, I have never left Berlin, certainly not alone and certainly not to a place like this."

***

They made their first stop in Dresden. As they stood at the entrance to the city, Rahel told Friederike that in Ancient Sorbian, the word '*dresden*' meant "the people of the forest next to the river." Friederike Unzelmann remembered Rahel's witty puns and the knowledge she had exhibited back in the days when she sat at her father Markus Levin's table. She also remembered the birthday party that never materialized and now tried to draw Rahel out on the matter, to hear the story first-hand. But as for Rahel, at such a pleasant time, on her way to new, exciting experiences, freed from the shackles of her family, she did not want to relive that grim, bitter evening.

"Perhaps some other time," she said, not wishing to hurt the feelings of the person who had allowed her to be here.

The carriage stopped in a sprawling square, with a large, impressive church towering at its edge.

"Frauenkirche," Friederike said. It was now her turn to exhibit knowledge. She only knew the church's name because she had already visited Dresden several times and was already familiar with its views.

Rahel added, "The church was originally built in the Romanesque style, outside the walls of the city, and once it became too small for all the residents of the city, it was decided to rebuild it in a central location."

Friederike, who was accustomed to traveling with friends and acquaintances in the course of her work as an actress and for recreational trips as well, had never traveled with anyone who possessed such broad knowledge. Her friends were interested in simple, trivial matters, mostly drinking and dancing. She had not expected a person who had spent the majority of life cooped up between four walls to know so much more than those who habitually roamed the world, and even if she had known such a person, she certainly did not expect it to be a woman.

"Initially, it was a Catholic church, and after the Reformation, in the sixteenth century, it became Protestant. Then it was utterly destroyed and rebuilt. Construction took seventeen years, and it's very apparent, as this is not a run-of-the-mill church. I've heard that during the Seven Years' War, a hundred cannon shells were shot at it and it remained standing, unharmed. Look at the upper dome; it's made of sandstone." Rahel was truly excited. "Promise me we'll go inside."

Friederike promised. And since she was familiar with the devoutness of the late Mr. Levin, she did not understand this Jewish woman's great interest in a site that was holy to Christians.

They stayed in Dresden for another day or two and then continued on their journey until arriving in Teplitz.

***

During breakfast on their first day in Teplitz, Rahel extended her hand. "Pleased to meet you, I'm Rahel Levin."

Across from her stood a tall woman with hair as golden as wheat that was about to be harvested. She was dressed with discreet elegance and extended her fair, delicate hand. "Countess Josephine von Fichte," she said and once breakfast was over, she invited Rahel to accompany her to the hot springs at the edge of town. Friederike was not feeling well and Rahel happily joined the countess.

Here she was, a Jewish woman, along with Catholic Josephine, sitting and chatting as if there was no difference between them. As if they were both equally beautiful, as if they both belonged to the same class, and both shared the same circle of acquaintances.

They sat in the sulfur water, clad in a special garment meant for dipping in the lake. The smell of sulfur rising from the water dimmed Rahel's senses until she could no longer bear it.

"Come on," Josephine said to her as if she could sense her distress, and several minutes later, the two of them were already lying on a low bed. Each of them was covered in a towel, under which was only their fair skin, anointed in aromatic oils, and already, busy hands began toiling over their bodies, up and down, up and down. Rahel felt as if she were in a dream. She had not known that such things existed. Yes, she had heard of the hot springs and of the treatments, but all these were dwarfed by the magic feeling engulfing her.

If she had traveled to such sites with her parents in her youth, perhaps she would have been spared many aches and ailments and her body might have healed, but her father had never tended toward such pleasures. His strictness and rigidity were directed primarily at himself. Apparently, this was one of the reasons why he had never followed his actor friends who implored him to travel with them on healing trips to the springs of Karlsbad in Bohemia, or to Bad Pyrmont in Lower Saxony, or to Teplitz, the site she was so enjoying now. If he had allowed himself to loosen up a bit, to enjoy himself more, to be easier on himself, perhaps his family would have reaped the benefits as well.

She would not be like him.

Dinner required formal attire, and afterward, she attended a ball. Although she was somewhat weak from all the excitement of the day, she would not be deterred. She put on a dress borrowed from Friederike and set out.

"Pleased to meet you, I'm Rahel Levin." She extended her hand and across from her stood a tall, handsome man, his head fair and golden. He grasped her extended hand, looked into her eyes and politely kissed the back of her hand, a respectful kiss.

"Gustav von Brinckmann," he said, and the scent of a sharp, pleasant masculine perfume enfolded her.

"Before you lose your head, allow me to warn you," Josephine laughed.

"I won't lose my head because of beauty, however blinding it might be." Rahel winked mischievously and Brinckmann felt they were destined to be friends.

During the entire ball, Rahel and von Brinckmann were inseparable and after the dinner and the dancing, they went out into the courtyard. The official excuse was "to take in the air" but both of them felt that they wanted to be alone, quietly. Rahel told him about herself and her family, feeling free to share her harsh feelings about her Judaism. Von Brinckmann did not flee. He found that he liked her directness. She was different from many women he met, delicate women who did not speak much and waited to be addressed, diminishing themselves and living within the bounds of the tiny square they allocated for themselves, women of his own class. After several hours, he already felt as if he had known her for a long time, and therefore allowed himself to open up to her and read a poem he had written and had not dared to show anyone.

"It's obvious that the poem was written with great haste," Rahel told him without sparing his feelings. "If you had dedicated more time to processing it, the result would have been more impressive." He agreed with her and privately resolved to stop writing poetry.

As the evening neared its end, while he was escorting Rahel to her room, he told her he was posted in Berlin. He was a Swedish diplomat, the son of a devout man who had sent him away to be educated at a monastery when he was eleven years old. He, too, had a complicated relationship with his father, which, in itself, opened up a large, substantial topic of conversation between them in the days to come. Before they parted, Rahel invited him over to the attic in Jägerstrasse to meet her friends and take part in the conversations that periodically took place in her drawing room.

"Perhaps you might even improve your writing."

He, in turn, promised to introduce her to his aristocratic friends.

"Von Brinckmann is serving as the Swedish ambassador in Berlin," Rahel wrote to Henriette several days later. *"He is easily influenced, and yet unusually courteous and, most importantly, he is handsome and well-groomed to an admirable degree. He allowed me to read the letters he wrote to von Gentz and Schleiermacher. They are full of descriptions of his acquaintances, gossip and his flirtations with women; very salacious. Borgsdorf, his good friend, is incessantly chatty. He possesses the nobility of one who has never been rejected."* She then reported that he was also graced with integrity, and that she felt that he had an influence on the world around him, and certainly on her.

In the course of that summer, which lasted longer than usual and turned out better than expected, the two of them became her best friends. Two good friends who were total opposites, and yet each of them found his way into Rahel's heart, while she found her way into theirs. *"They are merely friends,"* she would note when writing David Veit of her experiences in Teplitz. *"Merely friends."*

19 | 1795

After the summer was over and the brief encounters in the resort town turned into memories, Rahel worried that they would fade away in time, and therefore put them all in writing in her letters to David, to Henriette and to Dorothea, as if she wished to hold on to them for a little longer, to sustain the living, breathing feeling.

She told them about the hot springs *"where one dips one's body and soul,"* about the balls on warm summer evenings, where high-class women *"exhibited their exquisite taste in clothes that seemed to have emerged from the most prestigious fashion houses."* She described the cream pies and the strudels and an intensely sweet drink she had never tasted before. *"It was warm, precisely at the right temperature, and it tasted divine! After tasting it, you could die knowing you had achieved the peak of pleasure."* She told them about the opera there, which, unlike the Berlin Opera, was *"another type of pure pleasure,"* and about a particular show that had actors" *with whom we spent an entire evening of excessive drinking and wild laughter, and, in retrospect, I cannot point out what in particular had struck us as so funny."*

It was only to Dorothea that she dared write about her less-pleasant sensations, as well. *"I felt shabby in my tatty dresses, in my graceless manner and in my clumsy figure. If it weren't for dear Brinckmann and Borgsdorf, who introduced me to everyone and sung my praises, I would certainly have withered up and fallen like a leaf in autumn."*

Her letter to David Veit, whom she had not ultimately managed to meet that summer, also disclosed some of her frustrations, albeit from a different direction.

"My stay in that place wavered between wonder and excitement, also mingled with a bit of happiness, I presume, and a descent to such depths whose meaning only you could understand. It could all have been different for me if only the thing with which I was born, the stain keeping me on the sidelines, would trickle off me and evaporate. There is no absolute happiness and never will be, but only brief intervals comprising particles of pleasure. A painful happiness that could have been mine and was taken from me on the day I emerged into the world."

Although she bared her heart to her old friend David, who was Jewish just like her, she did not dare do so with her new friends, and certainly not to an absolute degree. She now had to move between two worlds, between her official life, in which her educated and aristocratic friends, bookish men of letters, took part, and her unofficial life, the details of which she concealed from them. There, she was on her own, she and her misery. She sometimes shared this misery with her brother Ludwig, who was younger than her by seven years and yet very close to her, perhaps more so than the rest of her family members.

"I don't know," she told him honestly one evening, after he returned from a work trip. "It's as if, years ago, something shattered inside me and I derived cruel pleasure from the knowledge that from now on, nothing could break anymore. Although now, that shattered thing has turned into a place that I myself cannot reach. If there really is such a place within a person, then any possibility of happiness is blocked. I can no longer remember what it was. And if I can't succeed at the little things, I must immediately provide so many rational reasons for all my failures, so that no one else will believe me, and I myself will become timid. It's very frightening to consider yourself a creature that turns everything into grief. And as far as I know, that is my only accomplishment."

Ludwig's personality was completely different than Rahel's. He saw everything in a positive light and tended to be optimistic, perhaps because he was younger, and his father's poison had not seeped in. That was what Rahel always said when he berated her for her innate melancholy. This time, as well, when she said what she said, he could not understand her. After all, for the first time in her life, she had experienced something so powerful, as she herself had told him; apparently, the greater the experience, the deeper, too, was the plunge that followed it, as if she derived pleasure from it, as if she sought out that melancholy, to wallow inside it and dive into it.

* * *

That melancholy, there was something appealing about it, like a dark magic sucking in young, talented people. One evening, when the outside world was immersed in the white light of a full moon and night seemed to have turned into day, young Friedrich Schlegel sat with Rahel, keeping her company, or perhaps she was keeping him company. She had first met him one evening at Henriette's and was impressed by what he had read out loud—an original, unique essay by a daring young man. Since then, she had met him several more times, and on each occasion, he had read aloud a poem, a short story or an essay, which had impressed her as much as the first time. And now he had shown up in her attic and remained sitting after everyone else had left, and it seemed as if he had no intention of leaving. Although he was younger than Rahel by two years, he looked at least five years older than he was.

When it was only the two of them in her drawing room, he drew her hand to him, held it in his thick fingers, looked into her black pupils and said, "I must admit that I am not sociable. People find interest in me while simultaneously keeping their distance from me. I must also admit that I feel a constant incongruity within myself. Everywhere I go, joy immediately takes its leave." He said these words without lowering his eyes even once, nearly boring holes in her pupils with his staring. Was it the full moon that extracted such a confession from him? Perhaps it was the alcohol speaking from his throat? Or perhaps the fact that he felt a need to unburden his heart, and she knew how to listen?

If he was seeking her pity, he did not earn it even in the slightest. However, she could understand exactly what he was talking about. Perhaps not about the joy, but about his sense of discomfort. Perhaps not with regard to being unsociable, but regarding the feeling of incongruity. Either way, she understood him and yet did not see fit to console him.

Before she could say anything, he continued. "There is something depressing and oppressive in my presence. I am always viewed from afar as if I were something both rare and dangerous. I evoke a sort of fierce antipathy among some people, while others see me as self-possessed."

She, too, now felt an antipathy of sorts toward him. Out of all the people who could have come here, she was now stuck specifically with this despairing man, as if her own despair attracted others who were similarly afflicted, confused folk and other depressed souls.

"Take Hamlet, for example. We are two of a kind," he went on. "He knows he strides over the abyss and that he must overcome it. He wishes to find—on his own—his place under the sun, to create such a place for himself. He cannot live without being free, without being mighty."

Now Rahel knew that they, too, were two of a kind. Friedrich Schlegel was also seeking. He also knew he was destined for great things. He, too, was immersed in melancholy, which threatened to extinguish him if he did not achieve the purpose for which he was put on this earth.

"After all, heroic despair combines the highest mental traits. The logic of Hamlet's internal death surely lies in the scope of his intellect."

Schlegel spoke wisely. He was indeed young and confused, but Rahel predicted that this was merely a passing malaise and that soon, he would discover his calling and ascend to greatness. And as she came to this conclusion, sadness overcame her, as her certainty with regard to him equaled her skepticism with regard to herself. Ultimately, she still found the resolve to encourage him, serving up a bit of compassion.

"I'm glad you came and shared your personal concerns with me. They are worthy concerns," she said, staring at him until he was now the one to lower his gaze.

20 | 1796

Apparently, despite Rahel's fears, since that summer in Teplitz, her circle of friends had actually expanded and all thanks to Count von Brinckmann. He told all his friends about the special woman he had met, and they, full of curiosity, arrived at her home, attending the meetings of her salon. If she had thought, a year ago, that her dreams had come true, they now appeared to be coming true beyond her wildest expectations.

One evening, Rahel went to the theater with von Brinckmann. At the end of the intermission in the second act, a moment before they returned to their booth, von Brinckmann stopped to warmly and earnestly greet a person of his acquaintance. Dressed as usual in his best finery, polished and redolent in French perfume, Brinckmann stopped in front of the man, who was taller than him. The man was obviously a member of the elite aristocracy; Rahel could recognize his status in society from afar.

"Count Karl von Finckenstein," von Brinckmann introduced her to him. Rahel extended her hand and the count gently kissed it. "My cousin on my mother's side," he added proudly, clapping his back companionably.

Many years had passed since she was a young girl. Back then, when high-class people passed by on the street, sitting in their luxurious carriages, dressed in their finest apparel, she would stand frozen in her spot, staring at them, although she knew it was impolite. She would gaze at the beautiful women and the impressive men and be charmed by them. They seemed to be presenting her with a different world, as if through a window display, a world in which a fate different than hers existed. She was charmed not because of their money, or their status, not because of the fine jewelry and dresses, not even because of the expression of satisfaction she seemed to recognize in them, but due to the fact that they were free, or so she thought. Free to move around from place to place, to choose their fate, to be masters of their own life.

Ever since she met von Brinckmann, princes, counts, painters, composers, playwrights, poets, and many more intellectuals, and non-intellectuals as well, had all been over to sit in her home, side by side. They crammed into the small room in the attic of her house with joy and pleasure: Christian von Bernstroff, the Danish ambassador, and the Count of Casa Valencia, from the Spanish embassy. Prince Heinrich von Rausch—the Austrian ambassador to Prussia—and Italian Major Peter von Gualtieri, and, of course, her two good friends, the noble Borgsdorf and von Brinckmann. More respected nobles and less respected ones, nobles who had purchased their title over the years or those born to established, highly influential families. She knew aristocrats, counts and princes, and, more importantly—she knew their secrets.

Von Brinckmann told her about every affair he embarked upon, especially about his lovers, who were almost all married. "There is something thrilling and enchanting about a love affair with a married woman," he explained when she asked him about the meaning of his passion for them. "First, they possess a kind of gratitude. In addition, there is the thrill of the forbidden, the need to hide, the fear of being caught. It has often been the case that a jealous husband chased me, and on occasion, they have caught me, as well. I have also been laid up for more than a month with a broken rib." He recounted it all lightly, as if it were a normal thing to ruin a family or to sustain a beating.

Borgsdorf did not have secrets like von Brinckmann's, but more salacious stories about the aristocracy. The stories of one who had been born into its ranks and could view it with a critical perspective, condemning it without knowing that some people wished passionately to be a part of it.

The most personal thing he told Rahel was his secret desire to write. He wanted to draw closer to the intellectual world of writing, reading and research, and the fact that he could not do so saddened him. It was the only topic on which he was not verbose, merely mutely sorrowful, after having been strictly forbidden to follow this path by his father, whom he could not disobey for fear of being disinherited.

But the man who shook her hand now at the theater and kissed it gently and respectfully—there was something different about that man. The mysterious count, von Brinckmann's cousin, did not speak much during their brief introduction. Most of the talking was done by her chatty friend von Brinckmann. When they met again later, he was also sparing in his speech.

It was only a matter of time before von Brinckmann dragged his maternal cousin, Count von Finckenstein, to the attic on Jägerstrasse, and following his first visit, he took care to show up every Tuesday. He always arrived at the same time. He was not among the first to arrive, nor among the latecomers. He always sat in the same place, which, miraculously, seemed to be reserved solely for him. Entering the drawing room, he would take off his hat, place it on the shelf designated for this purpose, peel off his blue coat with the gold buttons and hang it on the rack. After his gaze spotted Rahel and she approached to greet him, he would take hold of her hand and kiss it gently. This went on for quite a while.

During his first visit to Rahel's home, he found Prince Louis Ferdinand already sitting at the piano and playing. The count had heard of various reading societies that had become fashionable in Berlin, but had never visited such a society, and the scene to which he was exposed surprised him. After the applause he received from the attendees who were all sitting in their places and from those who had joined in as he was playing, the prince abandoned his spot at the piano, wrapped his arm around Rahel's shoulder and planted a kiss on her forehead. He then declared he would commit the piece he had just improvised to writing immediately when he arrived home, as he was very pleased with it. This statement was greeted with another round of applause.

Friedrich Schlegel, who was visiting Berlin and arrived directly at the gathering, although he had not meant to do so, added, "The moment the piece is ready, I must, truly must, hear it in its entirety." And the prince promised to send him the score.

"Or perhaps I will come personally and play it for you," he said.

Count von Finckenstein did not say a word the entire evening. He sat there with an expression Rahel could not decipher, a kind of rigidity characterizing a high-ranking man. It would certainly require numerous attempts, and perhaps some trickery as well, in order to break through it. From that evening onward, Rahel tried to figure him out, and the more she tried, the more anguish she felt.

"You know you have a need to admire, to peer up at people. I know the feeling of being looked at from below. That's how the young fools look at me, the way you look at him. I know, Count von Finckenstein is that kind of man. I see you squirming next to him, trying to sound smart. I see the efforts you put into getting him to like you, trying to find a way into his soul, while he—just stays silent!" Henriette told her after a gathering in which, once again, nothing happened between them, one that ended with another fleeting glance, with another polite nod, with more disappointment.

"Do you think there is a reason why he stays silent? Do you think it is some sort of sign? I have never been unable to interpret silence the way I have with this man. Do you think it signifies something? Do I stand a chance?"

Henriette ignored the barrage of Rahel's questions. After all, she was not truly seeking an answer, and anything she would say in an attempt to explain the silence would, in any case, fall upon ears that were unwilling to hear. Therefore, she said something different. "Not just any nobleman. You are aiming as high as you could be. He is the son of one of the oldest aristocratic families in Prussia. As you always do, this time as well, you are aiming for the impossible, which somehow, with you, becomes possible."

"You have to dare, Henriette. This means you have to give yourself over to destiny, and I feel that von Finckenstein is my destiny. In any case, the rest of the time, things are too calculated, known in advance."

Rahel did indeed give herself over to destiny. The more silent the count was, the more she was attracted to him. The more attracted to him she was, the more his silences seemed significant and thrilling to her.

He attended these gatherings many times, and in all of them, he stayed silent. Listened and stayed silent. He sat erect in his chair, and seemed to be interested in what was being said, in the poems read and the music played on the grand piano brought to Rahel's home by her good friend, Prince Louis. During the last meeting, after he kissed her hand with the same gentleness as always, he stood close to her, waited for them to have a single moment alone, and then asked if he could make a request "which might sound a bit odd to you, perhaps even impudent."

His hand was warm, despite the freezing chill outside that evening, and he did not let go of her hand the whole time he was talking. Rahel nodded with a smile. "How could I refuse your eminence the count?" she said, feeling that she would like her hand to stay forever within his large, warm hand.

"If I may," he said, pausing briefly, "and if you would approve," he added, pausing once more, and before he could finish what he had intended to say, Prince Louis Ferdinand arrived, along with Rahel's good friend, the lovely Pauline Wiesel. The two of them were holding hands and giggling as if they were two children who had discovered something new, something forbidden.

Von Finckenstein waited for a moment until they were alone again before saying, "If it's possible, and so long as you do not think ill of me, and out of my great respect for you, I would like to stay behind this evening after everyone leaves."

Rahel was silent. She had not expected such a request from him. She was flattered that he sought her society, as if, in one moment, due to his statement, the entire Prussian nobility had acknowledged her existence. Acknowledged her, the non-pedigreed Jew that she was. A Jewish woman with no means or status. And perhaps, like Prince Louis, he thought she might amuse him for a while, and therefore wished to stay behind with her after everyone left.

Rahel was silent. She was not naïve. Men had courted her before quite a few times. And yet she wondered whether it was not arrogant of him to think that she would acquiesce only due to his elevated status. How easy did he think she was? She was not a prude, but was afraid that his desire was not real, that he merely wished to toy with her.

And before she could open her mouth to answer, the count tightened his grip on her and drew slightly closer, until she could feel his warm breath. If she had not been immersed in her own apprehensions, she could have seen that he was truly begging.

"Please, Rahel. I promise not to hold you up for long. I'll say what I have to say and be on my way."

Since the first time he had smiled politely when he met her at the theater, she had not seen him smile. Now he smiled again, a big smile exposing white teeth and revealing two crinkles extending from the corner of each eye, which she found irresistible.

"I'll be here," she said, feeling her head flushing, and before her face could expose her, she withdrew her hand and turned to her guests.

As he did at every meeting, this time as well, the prince played a new piece he had composed that week on the piano. This time, too, someone recited a poem. Beyond that, there was nothing new or exciting. No crucial conversations or some manifesto that had been published and required analysis. Or perhaps there was. She was unable to focus and felt the urge to send all her friends home. Perhaps she would say she was not feeling well. But then she grew angry at herself, about the way she had allowed someone to get to her and disrupt her routine. Beyond that, what could someone who had everything—divine beauty and a title that granted him entry to anywhere in this world—want from her?

Later, she would write to Henriette, *"Heavens, Yette, how ugly I felt when he was standing there so close to me as beautiful as a god."*

***

The attic drawing room emptied out. Everyone departed and only the two of them were left.

Rahel waited for him to open his mouth and tell her why he had stayed, perhaps even smile like he had before. But the count was silent, seeming as if he had lost his courage.

"The unexamined life is not worth living," Rahel began. She was confused and tense and felt a need to fill the quiet, dense space with words, and perhaps also to impress him with pearls of wisdom. The count looked at her with perplexity, as if uncomprehending.

"Socrates," she added, but no response was forthcoming from him.

It was now nearly midnight. Soon, the bells of the church located a few streets away from her home would ring. The count rose and approached the place where she was sitting. The closer he drew, the more the gap in height between them grew apparent. He was tall, rangy and towering, while she was short and slim. However, before she could continue thinking about the matter, her count kneeled before her and now his head was precisely as tall as she was.

She thought he would now undo the buttons of her dress and want to carry her to her bed or to make love to her here, in the center of the room, while the fireplace was lit and the room was still warm. She had already informed herself that she would not object, although her mother was on the bottom floor. After all, the man was handsome, and everything about him attracted her, starting with his shoes and ending with the way his hair was cut. She stroked his straight hair. Her closeness to this stranger, who had only come into her life a few weeks ago, surprised her. A man whom chance could not possibly have placed in her path if it were not for the little universe she had created in her home. A man who had been born and lived in a protected space and now wished to be close to her in a way that was still unclear to her.

"Dear Rahel," he began, the words seeming to refuse to leave his throat. He, too, was nervous. Rahel found it hard to believe that she, she was the one causing a man of his stature to lose his words. "Could you find room in your heart for me?"

He was the first man who had asked for her love. Openly requested that she love him. Him. Precisely so, that she love him. He promised to love her back and that was all that she needed to hear.

She nodded. Then she, too, got down on her knees and began to undo his shirt, button after button. He was surprised but did not object and stayed where he was, obedient. After the immaculate white shirt he was wearing was tossed to the wood floor, she took off his chemise—the only thing now separating her from his fair body. The entire time, she remained in her dress, expecting him to follow her lead and surprised when he did not take the initiative in that regard. She had never been with a man who had not taken hold of the reins and found that she actually liked it. Rahel stood, and now it was the count who was forced to look up at her. He was sitting in his long underwear, which was exquisitely sewn, an undergarment made of thin fabric, pleasant to the touch, emphasizing his manhood and causing her to impatiently undo her dress, which also fell to the wood floor.

Count Karl von Finckenstein was in no hurry. He did not have a wife waiting for him at home, or children. He was not immediately called upon to perform any service. He was master of his own time. And yet after a while, he rose and sought to get dressed and leave.

"It cannot be assumed that I will remain in your home," he said, "unless you invite me to stay." She pulled him back to her, covered him with the down blanket and brought her body to his. She liked the fact that he respected her and did not take anything for granted. She also liked that he did not try to impress her with a lot of talk. He was noble in every sense of the word, respectable and polite and courteous and decorous and well-groomed and considerate and gentle.

21 | 1796

The large house in which Rahel lived already displayed initial signs of neglect, and the tea and refreshments she served her guests were simple and sparse. She was also lacking in beauty, and yet one fact was indisputable—Rahel's room in the attic of 54 Jägerstrasse overflowed with visitors once a week. Anyone who considered himself cultured, fluent in the mysteries of poetry and prose, had heard of Miss Levin, visited her Tuesday salon and talked about it during the remaining days of the week.

For some time now, Henriette had closed her home to visitors during those Tuesday evenings and she, too, departed for an evening out at her friend Rahel's. She did it because she wanted to take part in those salon conversations, but mostly because on Tuesdays, the number of her own visitors had gradually declined. It seemed the cultural gatherings in her home were currently less interesting to the crowd, which now had a new, more thrilling place to visit. In actuality, these gatherings were currently less exciting to her as well. She now had a new interest in life, provided to her by Schleiermacher, who challenged her intellect in a way that could not find an expression in the company of the people she hosted in the living room of her home. With him, she felt that her opinion was valued and meaningful. Their shared discussions touched upon deep matters, rather than remaining suspended between piano tunes and idle chatter. They spent many hours together. She taught him Italian, they read Shakespeare together, he taught her some of what he knew about nature and, in the interim, they went on walks in the streets of Berlin, stopping to read a good German book or simply to talk. Those conversations produced many ideas that Schleiermacher would put in writing and send to Henriette, the ultimate arbiter, to be read and opined upon.

Markus had managed to hold back thus far, but when one of those compositions was about to be published, his anger increased. He felt betrayed, and not necessarily for the usual reasons. The manuscript was titled "On Religion: Speeches to its Cultured Despisers." Christianity filled every moment of Schleiermacher's life; he lived it, breathed it and mostly loved to talk about it. He was charmed by it and wished to charm those around him, especially Henriette, to whom he was close.

Markus knew each chapter was sent to Henriette for a meticulous reading. The book included actual attacks upon Judaism. And Henriette, rather than defending her Judaism, took it in stride when he wrote that Christianity was the pure, ultimate expression of true religion and that Judaism had died some time ago. *"Those who still don the uniform of Judaism are simply mourning alongside its mummified corpse, which does not rot, bemoaning its departure and its sad legacy, which persists as an unpleasant aftereffect of a mechanical movement, from which any spirit or life has long departed."*

How could Henriette object to such reasoning? In any case, she had never considered herself Jewish like those Jews living in the Jewish Quarter. As far as she was concerned, she was German first and foremost and only then Jewish. Therefore, if she felt an affinity for any religion, it was precisely the sensation Schleiermacher was describing: internal, personal and powerful to a degree that could not be conveyed in words. This was the true nature of religion and of divinity, and it was present within a person himself or herself and in the world as a whole. Schleiermacher claimed that "religion has no truck with the God of obedience and commandments," and Henriette felt that he had written precisely what had been in her heart for some time. He was attacking the rationalism of "the religion of intellect" that people like Kant and Mendelssohn wished to apply to religion.

In contrast, Markus Herz firmly objected to what he heard from both

Schleiermacher and Henriette. It was true that he himself did not observe the customs of Judaism and felt just as much of a Berliner as Henriette did, but unlike her, he disagreed with Schleiermacher's claims and felt hurt and betrayed, on behalf of himself, on behalf of Mendelssohn, who had been his good friend and patient as well as the father of Henriette's best friend, and also on behalf of her father, Dr. de Lemos, who, despite all his liberalism, would certainly be appalled if he heard that his beloved daughter supported such an essay.

Henriette disagreed with her husband. "My father taught me to think for myself and this is what I have always done, both then and now."

She had indeed been born to a religion that neutered many of its adherents, but she was not among them. Her eyes were open and so was her heart. And it was true that Markus had known her father, but not the way she had. She was the one who had roamed with him throughout Berlin, and even if he had tried to conceal from her his disdain for the Jews who lived in the crowded, smelly quarter, she had perceived it, along with his clear preference for treating German patients belonging to the bourgeoisie rather than poor Jewish patients.

Henriette's independent opinions now threatened to tear them apart. They had lived together for many years and throughout that time, there had never been a single subject on which they had not managed to come to an agreement. Until now.

These days, she had internalized the folly of her friend the pastor and could not be divested of it. Like him, she felt that Judaism was no more than oppressive, tasteless forms of expression, and shamelessly stated so. When Markus reacted with belligerence and anger, she added, "This does not diminish my respect and admiration for Moses Mendelssohn and for my father, may he rest in peace, who was a friend of Mendelssohn's and shared his opinions."

This statement on her part did not ease their heated argument. On the contrary, it merely flamed it more, as if she had poured on incendiary material that threatened to consume them both. Markus felt as if everything he had allowed, all his permissiveness, had come back to haunt him now.

"If I look at it today, with my eyes open, from what I understand, my father himself was endowed with Christianity's gentleness and love. And as for Mendelssohn, he himself was observant out of true, honest faith, but since he was not familiar with Christianity, he sought God through Judaism."

Markus could not believe his ears. It seemed as if she was channeling the pastor who spent so many hours with her. As if she were not the same woman he had married. He had understood when she refused to wear a head covering and understood when she refused to cover her body as a married Jewish woman was required to do. He understood that she too, like him, wanted to be a Berliner like their non-Jewish friends, and felt that all these concessions had brought him to this moment.

"You're spending too much time with him. We might have to limit these meetings."

Henriette was not impressed by his threat. "You've never imposed a thing on me, and you want to start now? Do you think you'll succeed?" And Markus raged and yelled and cursed as she had never seen him do before, even warning her not to test him. The fight lingered between them for many days. They stopped talking to each other and the atmosphere at home was tense. Henriette, who initially thought he would come to his senses and shift in her direction, as he always did, had made a major mistake. Judaism was a red line that Markus was unwilling to cross. "Talk leads to action," he said in the last argument between them. Rumors of Jews who had converted to Christianity were spreading through Berlin and Markus nurtured a great fear that Henriette was heading in that direction. Therefore, he firmly refused to listen to her talk of Christianity, of how beautiful and benevolent and kind to its believers it was. He had been born a Jew and would die a Jew, and so would Henriette, so long as she was married to him.

The silence between them led him to depart from their room and spend his nights in the guest room, as he had never done before. Henriette was not concerned. It had been a while since they had any guests over anyway and based on the circumstances, it would not happen anytime soon. But when Markus began to return home in the wee hours of the night, she panicked for the first time. His absence from the house could only indicate one thing, one that she could never accept—other women. The passion between them was dying and he had ventured out to find it elsewhere. The thought of Markus touching another woman made her anxious. Her heart rate increased, her body was covered with a cold sweat, and she was certain he was about to leave her. She was indeed independent in her opinions, but when she tried to imagine herself living without Markus, she realized she could not do so. She was utterly dependent upon him and, in fact, knew no life without him. But, more than that, she realized she did not want to live without him. Over the years, she had relied on the strong connection between them. She always knew that come what may, they would remain united. And now came the thing that was about to ruin them, something she had brought into her home and was unwilling to give up. If Markus left her, it would be the end of her.

Markus did not ask Henriette to limit her meetings with the pastor (he could not even call him by his name). He did not even try. If he had the will or the ability to impose anything on her, he would have done it a long time ago.

Henriette felt, with every fiber of her being—in accordance with Schleiermacher's description—that religion was "an orientation of the soul," endless, eternal power stemming from personal experience. She could not share all of these feelings with Markus, as she knew the earth that had begun to shake beneath them would swallow them both if she persisted. She knew things would gradually deteriorate to the point of utter destruction. Markus might do something they would both regret, something that would prove irreversible, and she did not want that. Therefore, she kept her silence on this matter, and the longer she stayed silent, the more Markus calmed down and returned to his former self. He thought the matter had passed. If he had known that the first seeds were sprouting within her, he might have taken extreme action in order to put a stop to it. But he did not know and never would.

***

Dorothea, too, took part in the Tuesday salon held in Rahel's attic. She rescheduled the gatherings at her own home to Wednesdays. How hopeful she had been back when her husband first brought up the idea of hosting scholars and intellectuals in their drawing room. For a while, she had wanted to believe that her life would actually be on course. However, that hope had dissipated a long time ago.

Lately, she, too, like Henriette, had been displeased with the way her salon was being conducted, with the guests visiting her home, and even more displeased by her husband's intellectual ignorance. She did not like it when he attempted to mingle with the attendees and mocked him when he discussed various subjects. As hard as he tried, he never managed to fit into the conversation. And how could he discuss Goethe and Schiller, whose play, *The Robbers*, had been recently produced and become a hit? After all, he could not understand how the character of Franz, the cold-blooded killer, could touch her heart and the hearts of her friends, and did not comprehend how his despicable qualities could be considered admirable.

Another thing was recently troubling Dorothea more intensely—the language in which he spoke. When they first got married, she had asked him to speak German and he had made an effort to comply with her request. However, during his workday and when he was conducting business, he was used to speaking Yiddish. He was surrounded by Jews and conversed with them in his mother tongue, in which he felt at ease. At home, he tried to speak only German and did so with his young children as well. And yet he never grew used to it. He found it particularly hard to translate the thoughts rushing through his mind and switch from the imagistic quality of Yiddish to the rigidity of German, which created additional misunderstandings between him and Dorothea. The more time Dorothea spent with her friends, with whom she shared a common language, the more revulsion she felt toward her husband Simon, who struck her as a limited little Jewboy.

She despised his appearance, the way he woke up in the morning, his manner of chewing and even the way he played with his children. She found his voice insufferable and no longer listened to what he said, and in general, tried to spend as little time as possible in his company. It seemed as if the more he tried to appease her, the more she loathed him, until she could no longer sleep with him. For many years, she allowed him to lay with her as part of her marital duties toward him, and now, after she had Jonah and Philipp and after she had made it clear to him that she was unwilling to become pregnant again, it seemed as if her duties had been fulfilled and she began to oppose him. At first, she found various excuses to refuse, saying she was sick, that it was the time of the month when she was forbidden to him by Jewish law, that she was suffering from an inflammation, that she had a migraine. Later, she simply started saying that she did not want to. Perhaps if she firmly resisted, he would finally understand that she did not love him and would cast her away from him. This would solve many of her problems. At last, she would be free. But her husband Simon did not choose to divorce her. He accepted her demands and hoped that this wave, too, would pass, as always, and that things would calm down.

***

While Henriette was in the process of life-changing revelations and Dorothea was yearning for an invigorating emotional experience, Rahel seemed to be experiencing good luck that had awarded her with both.

Many Berlin intellectuals had become her good friends, with no barriers or affectations of propriety coming between them. The guests felt liberated from the shackles of class; they talked to each other and exchanged experiences, regardless of the title, status or money that one might possess while the other did not. Their sense of ease was also expressed in singing or dancing together or even touching each other in a way they did not allow themselves to do outside the room, and the atmosphere was exuberant and carefree.

All of them came together around her and she held them close. Now that she was somewhat more sure of herself, she piqued their curiosity with a new topic of interest characterized by a unique style that she decided to reveal to them: Johann Wolfgang von Goethe. Just as she had been swept up in his writing ever since she was young, so, too, would her guests be swept up by him. Now that she had accrued popularity and confidence, she allowed herself to introduce him to her friends without being afraid they would mock her, misunderstand her or challenge her literary taste.

Goethe was no longer unknown, but was still not familiar to all, and it would be a crime, she thought, to continue to keep him to herself. The time had come to share her story, linked to his writing, and now she would have an audience.

And indeed, one Tuesday evening, as she was holding *Wilhelm Meister's Apprenticeship*, Goethe's most recent novel, published some time ago, she opened up to them.

"Frankfurt, on the Main River, is the birthplace of the one who became my soulmate. Both of us were born when the sun was in the sign of Virgo." This in itself was an omen to her that her fate was linked to his, even though they had never met and even if they never did. *"It is possible that thanks to the positive forecasts that the astrologists predicted with regard to my future, I survived,"* Goethe had recounted in a newspaper she had read some time ago and now she shared his statement with everyone. "Due to the midwife's inexperience, he emerged into the world stillborn, and after many attempts, was revived and opened his eyes. It is true that the circumstances of our births were not identical, but I too was born and remained suspended between heaven and earth." She did not add that her parents nearly let her die, rather than fighting for her as Goethe's parents did.

"I lived within his world. I loved, I suffered, I rebelled and I learned to know him. Each new volume by Goethe was a fête to me. He was a pleasant, sumptuous, beloved and respected guest who opened new doorways before me to a life that was unfamiliar and bright. Throughout my life, the poet has been accompanying me, with nary a disappointment, through love and anguish both."

Since first showing up in her life with *The Sorrows of Young Werther* and its hero's fatal love, she had been anticipating every word he spoke or wrote, every poem and every story and every play. She tracked the course of his life and once even briefly saw him in Karlsburg but did not dare approach him.

These days, she no longer had to dream and wish; it seemed as if she had the world in her palm. She now had three loves: Goethe, whom she worshipped, transmitting her admiration to her friends as well; the salon, which she nurtured and of which she was proud; and a third, thrilling love, the love between a man and a woman, in the form of von Finckenstein. He was not always present due to his professional commitments, but whenever he could, he rushed to be by her side. Rahel waited breathlessly for the days in which they could be together and every parting hurt her as if it were their last one. Whenever he arrived, he waited patiently until she concluded her interaction with her friends and acquaintances. He respected the fact that she was busy and never had a single complaint about her. He sat and waited until everyone left. Then he would extend his hand to her, take hold of her and bring her body to his, and like a recurring ritual, they would enter her room. Rahel would take off his clothes and then her own, until they were swallowed between the covers, surrendering to love.

Their nights were full of the passion of two yearning people. Von Finckenstein was good to her. If he was passive in his daily routine and in his relationship with her, from the moment he was left naked, he seemed to become a different person. He knew where to caress and touch and press down and let go, arousing places within her that she had never thought could arouse anything, and yet with his touch, like a marvel, sounds and heavy breathing burst out from inside her, forcing her to suppress them due to the thin walls. And when he touched her with his hands and with his mouth and with his hard member, she felt herself to be alive, that all she had ever wanted was about to come true with this man who, in her bed, performed all that she had read about in books, all she had imagined and even what she had not known to be possible. And although the nights of love with him were extraordinary and satisfying, something about him bothered her.

He did not talk to her, did not open his heart. At first, she thought he was a private person, and that once he felt at ease with her, he would open up to her and tell her things he might be embarrassed to reveal. She wanted to know everything about him. About his family, about the childhood he had been through, about life in a world she did not know and about the thoughts running through his mind.

But he was still silent, just like the first time. He did not share his impression of the books or poems he read, or of plays he watched. He did not indulge with her in the sort of intellectual conversations that could fill the heart and the mind and challenge the thought. He lay with her and yearned for her and thrilled her body, but no more than that. She did tell him about her life. She told him where she had come from and where she had gone, told him about her disappointment with Judaism and about the humiliations she had sustained because of the religion to which she was born. She told him about her various friends and about the writers she admired and, of course, she told him about her Goethe. She opened up her thoughts and emotions to him and did not keep a thing to herself. And still, he remained self-contained and mysterious.

22 | 1798

It had been two years since Friedrich Schlegel, Rahel's friend, had moved to Jena. "It's the center, where things are happening," he told Rahel on the evening when he came to say goodbye. He was early as usual, as he was every time he showed up at her salon and shared his dreams with her.

"If there is anyone in this world who believes that everything still awaits me, it's you," he said, openly and with gratitude. "Throughout all the evenings I sat in your drawing room, aimless other than the knowledge that something big would happen to me in the future, you listened and asked questions and encouraged me, while all the others mocked my dreams."

Rahel was sorry to see him go but was happy for him. In a way, she admired him for the way he was guided by his belief that a brilliant future awaited him. And now it had been two years since that evening and she was holding the first issue of *The Athenaeum*, the journal Friedrich Schlegel published with his brother Wilhelm. And all this joy was about to be overshadowed by the earthquake their reading group had experienced, now that the news had spread that Dorothea and young Schlegel were in love.

Dorothea was acquainted with Friedrich Schlegel, who came to Berlin occasionally and would visit Henriette and Rahel's salons. They were friends for a while and from the first moment, found topics in common to talk about. Although he was clearly interested in her and exhibited much enthusiasm, she did not feel the same. Perhaps she was still sluggish due to her dull daily routine, or preoccupied with dreams she had yet to realize;

perhaps she was not alert enough to grasp what was right under her nose. Therefore, Schlegel had no choice but to make the first move. He declared to her that she was the woman of his dreams.

"You're well-educated and mature, and you have a gift for poetry, wit and philosophy, and I'm sure you have a gift for love, as well," he told her one evening after the meeting at Henriette's had come to an end, and both of them were standing outside the door, a moment before they turned to walk down the street.

It took Dorothea a moment to process what he had said. As much as she yearned for new love, she took care not to stumble into a temporary blindness like last time, setting herself up as an object of mockery once more. She asked him to repeat what he had said so that she could focus upon his words and take them in and Schlegel repeated his statement verbatim. As if he had practiced it beforehand, as if he had prepared himself for their encounter. No one had ever expressed such sentiments to her, not in that way, not in the manner in which they emerged from Schlegel's mouth, with the excitement of one who held a single truth in his heart. Once he was done, he paused briefly, then extended both his palms toward her face, held it with a gentleness mingled with determination, and brought her face to his own. After his kiss, Dorothea no longer had any doubts. Passion existed and so did love, and this time she would not let it escape her.

Throughout the time Schlegel stayed in Berlin, Dorothea met him in secret. She did it in the evenings when literary gatherings were taking place in various homes all over Berlin. During the day, she made sure to tend to the household chores and to take care of her two children, to whom the majority of her attention was dedicated. She did so with a sense of freedom and pleasure only because she knew what awaited her in the evening, when she would meet her beloved.

In contrast, Schlegel declared his love for her to anyone who was willing to listen. He did not care what her familial status was, and when anyone dared to comment about the fact that she was married, he openly stated, "Marriage that is not based on love is not true marriage and must be annulled." He believed in this wholeheartedly. The Romantic faction to which he belonged was, to him, more than mere words written on paper in books and poems, as it was for some of his friends, but rather a way of life that he believed must be manifested. If love was called for, he would do so at full force, with heightened emotion, and if suffering was called for, he would do so as painfully as possible, giving himself over to agony.

"Life must be experienced at full intensity, at its full weight," he told Dorothea. "If you did not feel it, that means it passed you by. Life should pass through you, collide with you in all its might and leave its mark on you. That is the difference between being dead and being alive."

And Dorothea did feel it. The thought of meeting him in the evening made the blood in her body boil. As she was standing over the stove, as she was folding laundry, as she was teaching Jonah new words and singing lullabies to Philipp, throughout her most minute actions, she was thinking of one thing only—about her and Schlegel in his little bed, in the room he had rented in a filthy hotel in one of Berlin's alleyways. She passed the time recalling their last encounter and yearning for their next meeting, which would be in a few hours. And when she was snuggled naked into his body, she felt as if she was the most beautiful woman in all of Berlin, even more than Henriette. When he ran his thin lips over her body, gliding them between her small breasts oh so slowly and patiently, there was nothing in the world but the two of them, two naked bodies and the sounds and heavy breathing and moans emerging from inside them and filling the musty room.

This was what she had been waiting for all these years. She had known that it existed and had faith that it would indeed happen to her, just like the faith that Schlegel possessed. He was younger than her and handsome, had roamed the world and dared to demand from it what she never could. He had the ability to take all the intellect, knowledge and creativity within him, put them down in writing, publish them, and reap praise or criticism, all under his full name. He could make his dreams come true while for her, no dream could be manifested. And yet perhaps they were more similar than she thought, and now they were sharing one dream and that dream was shaking up the society with which they kept company in Berlin.

The shake-up was not caused merely by the fact that Dorothea was married to Simon Veit, who was respected within the Jewish community in Berlin and in general, not merely because of sixteen years together that were about to collapse and be destroyed, and not merely because of the fact that she had children. It was due mostly to the fact that she was older than Schlegel by seven years. Nearly a decade separated the two of them and this turned into the hottest, most exciting topic of conversation among those who defined themselves as their friends during those evenings at the literary salons. It was precisely those people who classified themselves as enlightened and as Romantics, those who allowed themselves to open up to each other and touch and flirt during the merry salon gatherings, who were particularly distraught over the age gap between Dorothea and Schlegel. If it had been the other way around, and Schlegel were the older one, not a single word would have been uttered. However, in this case, the gossip, the tongue-wagging and the disparaging comments leveled against both of them, but mainly at her, refused to subside and ease off. These comments were featured in small talk, social events and letters exchanged among friends. Words upon words piled up regarding their love story, which was appropriated from them and became public domain. Their intimacy was violated.

Skeptical questions were voiced regarding their ability to conduct a conversation, since Dorothea was a mother of two children while Schlegel was a single Lothario. "She could be his mother." Some spoke about Dorothea's physical appearance, unable to understand what Schlegel, a handsome youth by anyone's definition, found in her. Others pitied the cuckolded husband, the kind, submissive Simon Veit.

Rahel did not take part in the tempest as she had known their secret even during their first fumbling interactions. She had been there when their relationship ignited into a love affair, as well as during the moment when they realized it was not merely a fleeting liaison. Schlegel shared the developments with Rahel, telling her about the emotions that erupted from him when he met Dorothea and about the interest she added to his life, the intellectual stimulation she awakened within him. Dorothea told her the same things, but from her perspective, contributing additional descriptions that made Rahel blush and yearn for von Finckenstein, who was far from her.

After the couple's relationship was gradually established, turning into something that could not be unraveled, Dorothea retreated once more into herself, engulfed yet again by the melancholy that increasingly enveloped her, threatening to ruin her once and for all. She was stuck between Schlegel and Simon Veit, between her new, thrilling life and the life of dreary routine with an even drearier husband, and was having a hard time seeing a way out. Any decision she made, any path she chose, would doom her to great pain. If she chose to live with Schlegel, she would lose her children, who, by law, would remain with their father. In addition, her quality of life would suffer. If she chose to stay with Simon Veit, she might as well sentence herself to death. And the deeper she delved into it, the further she was drawn into melancholy. All the joy of infatuation and excitement she had experienced began to fade away, turning into a mass of confusion and anger, fear and helplessness. Dorothea seemed to be paralyzed and all she wanted to do was climb into bed, pull the covers over her head and sink into a deep sleep that would transport her to a place where she did not have to think or feel, a place where she would not have to make decisions.

Many days went by in this manner, and every time they met, Schlegel tried to convince her to leave her husband.

"You don't understand what it's like to leave two little children," she accused him when he once again expressed his desire to have her move in with him. "You'll never be able to understand."

She thought this would put him off, distancing him from her and thus making it easier for her to come to the decision she must reach, but he understood that it was only the sorrow speaking from her throat, nothing more. He never doubted her love for him. He never doubted her.

"We were meant to be together," he told her, and this statement made her laugh.

"You're living in romance novels, but this is real life, not a story fabricated by someone's febrile brain." And yet, much as she protested, deep inside, she felt that he was right.

One day, in the afternoon, Dorothea made her way up to Rahel's room. Rahel was immersed in writing letters and Dorothea's hasty entrance disrupted the absolute silence of the room, until Rahel let out a small screech that amused them both. There was something liberating about it. It had been a while since she had laughed. She lay down on Rahel's bed, her face turned to the ceiling.

"All the traits that Veit lacks are found in Schlegel," she said. "An uninhibited masculine spirit, passion, originality, the daring of youth and endless plans for the future. I cannot give up something I have dreamed of all my life. I will not give it up."

The only question remaining now was how to do it in the best way possible. She knew her heart would be shattered to smithereens because she would have to leave her children behind, but she also knew that if she continued to live without Schlegel, her entire being would be shattered and this was a price she was unwilling to pay. If she could not be with the man who completed her, who provided her with the intellectual world for which she yearned, who loved her as much as she loved him and made her feel life at its full intensity, then her life would be worthless and she would be better off not living it.

She did not love Simon Veit, but she did trust him. She saw how much he loved his children, the attention that he devoted to them, how he took care of them although he was not obliged to do as, since after all, that was a woman's role. She saw how they gazed at him with admiration, eagerly expecting him to come home after his long workday. She was certain that just as he had been patient and loving toward her all these years, he would also act that way with his children, who were the most important thing in his life. She knew he would continue to be a good father even if she was not around.

Rahel encouraged her. "What is this life without love?" she said.

"Marriage that is not based on love is not marriage, so that your divorce proceedings are merely a formality."

One thing saddened Rahel. Dorothea was clever, sharp and highly intelligent, resourceful and enterprising. Everyone acknowledged these traits in her and some therefore characterized her as possessing a "masculine nature." However, Dorothea was head-over-heels in love and was already willing to give up everything. Out of the two of them, Schlegel was the rising star and she was living in his shadow. Much as Rahel believed in Schlegel and nurtured him, and although he was her good, dear friend, she knew Dorothea surpassed him, and her willingness to relinquish herself hurt her. But she did not dare say anything, merely gave them her blessing and took care to silence all the gossips, men and women both.

"Anyone who has anything to say on the topic should look into his own heart and inquire and ask why it is so important for him to malign this relationship," she responded to anyone who badmouthed the couple, and everyone knew that in Rahel's salon, they could not discuss the subject, at least not to her face.

***

The sun had sputtered several moments ago and Rahel's guests were sitting, prepared for a proper argument, as usual. She was holding the first issue of *The Athenaeum*, and meanwhile, arrangements for Dorothea's divorce had begun, mediated by Henriette and her pastor friend Schleiermacher. Dorothea had entwined her life with Schlegel's and he cherished her for this, dedicating the essay "On Philosophy" to her in the journal's first issue.

Rahel read out Schlegel's words from the journal:

"If he thinks and creates and lives divinely, if he is full of God. If an aura of dedication and enthusiasm encompasses his whole being, if he does nothing out of obligation but only out of love, solely because he wants it, and if he wants it only because the Lord says so, meaning the Lord within us, then this is a man in whom religion dwells."

Schlegel defined the concept of religion in an issue he dedicated to his beloved. This was precisely the sort of religion Dorothea had adopted for herself, a religion that meant freedom, internal development and mostly remaining true to one's self. What, then, so angered their friends, who had revealed themselves to be primitive hypocrites? They were only angry at themselves, for despite the Romanticism they worshipped, many of them were still shackled by the bonds of status, wealth or family. But in the tiny world that Dorothea had created for herself and her beloved—and then publicly displayed—she could be herself, if only for a few hours. It was true that she had been the one among them to dare to burst out of bounds, but Schlegel, too, was utterly true to himself. He had fallen in love with a woman who was seven years older than him, married, a mother, and had not given her up despite all the obstacles. There was something groundbreaking about this couple.

***

Rahel's aristocratic lover, Count von Finckenstein, sat in the corner of the room and pretended to listen, but his face was frozen. After nearly two years together, Rahel had still not managed to decipher what was going on inside him. She already knew that he was slow and already realized he did not find interest in everything, but she maintained hope.

When he was not in Berlin, Rahel breathlessly anticipated his letters, but every time a letter arrived, she was somewhat disappointed. And after feeling disappointed, she came to her senses and explained to herself that the reason for the shallowness of his letters was the fact that he was not familiar with the writing, verse and epic poems that she and her friends knew. Deep in her heart, she thought he could have made an effort and used the services of a well-educated female ghostwriter; but, on the other hand, if he had indeed done so, she probably would have been very angry.

Henriette expressed her reservations regarding Rahel's relationship with the count, but Rahel found herself defending him to her friend. "Even if he does not write the sort of letters I would like to read, it is still his truth. A shortage of truth is the malaise of our race, which brings about all the plagues of the soul." Perhaps more than she tried to justify his conduct to Henriette, she wanted to justify it to herself. "It takes endless courage to be a person. It does not matter how and who a person is if he cannot be what he wants to be."

Henriette immediately recanted her statement, already adopting Rahel's stance. "You are right in every sense of the word. Utterly right! And I'm not concerned about you at all, and trust you to go where your heart leads you, as your heart is not at all disconnected from your mind."

One evening, Rahel shared her feelings with her friend Schlegel, telling him about von Finckenstein's slowness and asking his opinion. He replied that lack of understanding did not usually result from lack of intelligence but from lack of sensibility. His answer made her contemplative. Did he mean that the count was not sufficiently educated? That he had not read enough throughout his life? That he could not improve? Was he really afflicted with a lack of sensibility?

And now that sentence had appeared in an article Schlegel wrote in his journal. She was afraid that von Finckenstein would understand that the statement was aimed at him. He had already complained that she discussed him with her friends and she did not deny it. "My life has always been open to everyone. So are my letters and my affairs of the heart, and to an even greater extent, the affairs of the mind. I have nothing to hide, neither my life nor my thoughts."

He felt intellectual inferiority in Rahel's company, although he had never openly stated this. But Rahel noticed. She saw him shrink back in his chair, shift restlessly, exhibit boredom with words that seemed to fly over his head. Perhaps he also heard the mocking comments voiced about him. Her friends saw him as an empty vessel that could never be filled.

Rahel felt the need to make it up to him. She wanted him to feel good about himself and wished to endow him with the ability to ignore the gossip about him. But reality did not support her. She saw how von Finckenstein's fellow noblemen strived to evolve and change in accordance with the spirit of the times and many of them impressed her with the creativity they exhibited. Friedrich von Hardenberg, for example, had recently been calling himself "Novalis." He was indeed an aristocrat, but he was also, and perhaps primarily, a poet. Or her good friend, the nobleman Heinrich von Kleist, who had managed to serve in the army and be an officer, and had then become a playwright and a novelist. Now her count's sense of inferiority did not arise only in the presence of artists and scholars—her friends. His inferiority also reared its head in comparison to his own noble peers. And yet she remained focused on a single, supreme goal, a clear final destination—the aristocracy. She would still have to peel some layers off him and bestow him with others, but the effort was worth it. Therefore, all the comments circulating about him did not affect her, even if some of them were voiced by Schlegel, whose opinion she greatly valued. "To dare surrender to fate at any time when everything else is too calculated." Those were her words, and they were applied to her affair with the count.

"Class does not exist in this room. In my drawing room, everyone is equal," she repeated again and again, yet she knew this statement was only half-true. She knew with certainty that in her drawing room everyone was indeed equal, but the count equaled less.

She did not want to or could not understand that it would be hard for a man of his status to instantly become one among many. His entire life, he had epitomized the unobtainable, the enviable aristocracy, and now, not only was he not one among equals, but actually lower in status. In Rahel's salon, he was no longer an aristocrat, but he was also not well-educated or an intellectual, was not a connoisseur of poetry and did not know how to interpret a play. He simply sat there, staring into space, somewhat inferior.

She tried to appease him and make him feel good, choosing to distort the truth a bit rather than giving up. She was not afraid of battles and now needed to confront one that had several fronts. She had to fight herself first and foremost, moving carefully between the desire to instill culture within him and accepting him, since, much as she wanted him to be someone different, she was plagued by the fear that she might be applying too much pressure, that he might break. However, the greatest hurdle was his family and mainly his sisters, who refused to accept her.

He told her he had three pretty, elegant sisters, their hair fair like his, who were always dressed in accordance with the latest fashion and were always prepared for any event. His father had passed away after an illness and he was left as the only son, pampered and fussed over by his mother and sisters, as befitting the only surviving man in the household.

He told Rahel about the estate in which he lived and about the dynasty that had been inhabiting the large stone mansion from the day it was first built, describing the structures that had been added with every generation, the horses raised and the dogs that took part in hunting trips. and the maids and governesses that tended to his every need. These stories charmed Rahel as if they were part of a thick historical novel in which she yearned to become a character. Yet simultaneously, she also felt distant from the man who thrilled her body every time. His stories remained a paper-thin picture. There was nothing personal about them. Not the emotional experience of riding with his father, not a fall that resulted in a scar, not a sweetheart he took to the big meadow while no one was looking, not shenanigans he had gotten up to with a group of boys like him. Still, she shook off these thoughts, feeling grateful that he had finally opened up to her and told her about himself and his family. She was even happier when he informed her he had presented her to them as his fiancée.

The euphoria she experienced following this revelation lasted only a few minutes, until she realized he had concealed the fact that she was Jewish, the fact that she belonged to the bourgeois class and the fact that she was liberal in her opinions.

"But my sisters prodded and looked into you and discovered it all on their own." He did not lie or conceal and that trait in itself was the one she most appreciated about him.

"They accused me of lying to them and betraying their faith and said other things that, out of respect for you and out of respect for your Judaism, I won't repeat. But I did not break down and for that, you should be proud of me," he said. He asked her to finally be proud of him; he had openly said so.

Despite the difficulties, Rahel knew she would fight. She would not give up. She loved him and perhaps even more, loved the idea of being part of the upper class, belonging to the aristocracy at any price. Therefore, she consulted her friend Borgsdorf, who knew the von Finckensteins intimately, and he wrote her back:

"The moment you enter that house, you become part of that charming family. On the other hand, you lose all your freedom, you cease existing as an individual in your own right and you have no will of your own."

Nevertheless, she wanted to be his wife and to live with him at the estate. And during that time until they were married, she would bring him slightly closer to her world, turn him into an intellectual and imbue him with spirit. She knew she could do it and wanted to believe that he could as well. She would teach him to develop critical thinking, not to accept anything as-is, to examine and question and challenge things, perhaps including even his mother and his sisters.

"We must not give up. You'll see, they'll get used to the idea eventually."

He listened and nodded and was silent and accepted everything she said as if her words were carved in stone. And although she should have been happy that he agreed with her opinion, something was gnawing at her.

***

All that Dorothea had feared came true, in full force, but she was not expecting her mother's anger.

"You should love your husband and no one else," her mother told her during their harsh conversation immediately after she informed Simon Veit that she was leaving him. Her mother was unwilling to hear a single word about her beloved Schlegel and their true love and the place he held in her life. She saw it as "adding insult to injury."

"You've committed adultery and now you want to move in with a strange man without a proper wedding ceremony? You are a married woman and you want to live in sin?" Tears of pain filled her, washing over her face.

Dorothea loved her mother and was not indifferent to her bitter tears and to the pain she had caused her, but it was not enough to stop her now. Neither she nor her late father, her siblings or the malicious tongues wagging and spreading venom about her throughout Berlin. None of them would divert her from the path she had decided to take.

"It's my life and I have no other. You should congratulate me and be happy for me for finally finding my soulmate."

"You are casting off your mother and father and your roots for a man who is not even Jewish."

"If I am casting off anything, it's the bonds in which I was shackled. The slavery imposed on me by Father." She said what she had never dared say before and the sky did not fall and the walls did not tremble. But the moment the words were out of her mouth, they could no longer be unsaid and her mother immediately vowed that she would never forgive her.

She did not understand how her mother could not manage to feel what she felt. Why she was not even willing to try. Why she refused to accept that her daughter had found her happiness after many years of life without purpose. A life where her heart was not fulfilling its true function. How could her mother, who was supposed to have her best interest at heart, prioritize the interest of her husband, the interest of her children and the interest of Judaism, while her daughter's interest was not even part of her considerations?

That day, after the bitter conversation with her mother and the ensuing sense of suffocation, after she had left her childhood home and gotten some distance from it, her breath began to gradually return to her. That time in which the news became public knowledge was a difficult one, with a war on every front. Her city, too, betrayed her. Berlin, which was open to all the attitudes of the era, to all its changes, with its poets, writers and authors, the Berlin of plays, concerts and balls, the Berlin of aristocrats, scholars and the bourgeois, the Berlin that had been her father's—the great, famous

Mendelssohn—was now dead to her, just like him.

"Hypocrites," decreed Henriette, one of the few to side with Dorothea. She had been in the know since the affair between the two first began. Now Dorothea's divorce from Simon Veit was nearly complete, mediated by Henriette and Schleiermacher, who were both good friends of Dorothea's, but were also acceptable to and appreciated by Simon Veit. They tried to reconcile between the two and produce the best agreement for her. Dorothea was willing to give up everything: the house, the property, her social status, her familial ties, but not her children. She knew in advance that a woman who left her husband would be forced to leave her children behind. She had known it well the moment she came to a decision and yet found it hard to resign herself to the law, which she found to be despicable. If it proved to be inevitable, she could resign herself to it as well—her love for Schlegel was that great. But in the meantime, she was making every effort not to reach that point, and therefore she referred the hurt, humiliated Veit to those she thought would most excel at the task.

Kind, wretched Veit—all he had tried to do for her had failed and now he sat there with a broken, empty spirit, and did not even have the energy to rage and curse and hurl insults and threats of revenge at his wayward wife. Henriette and Schleiermacher sat across from him and praised his easy nature, diminishing Dorothea's worth, while overstating his own. They praised her qualities as a good mother without going overboard; Simon Veit even agreed with them. Despite the great pain he was experiencing, he still found the strength within himself to say kind words about the woman who had humiliated him throughout Berlin.

Dorothea was indeed a good mother. She invested in finding the best tutors for her children, taught them how to read and write different languages, and mostly to look and investigate and ask questions and not to take anything for granted. They learned to play instruments and about theater and fine arts, such as painting and sculpting, and despite her endless striving for independence, she found the time and the patience to sit with them every day, fully focused, and to ask and ascertain what they had learned in order to find out what they had yet to learn. Now she had to depart and leave then in the hands of Veit, who was a good father but was incapable of teaching them a quarter of what she did.

If Simon Veit had relied upon the statements of the people around him, he would never have agreed to do what he did and consent to what he consented to do. However, ever since he had married Dorothea, he tended to respect her wishes, tried to understand her and loved her whole-heartedly. Despite her restless nature, he always tried to make the best of everything and tended to ignore what others were saying and, ironically, almost like her, listened only to his own heart. He found sense and logic in Henriette and Schleiermacher's attempts to sway him, and believed it would indeed be for the good of the children, and therefore reached an agreement with them, but not about everything. There was one thing he was absolutely unwilling to concede.

23 | 1799

Since Henriette had married Dr. Herz, she looked up to him and avidly devoured everything he taught her. Thanks to him, she had made great progress in reading and learning languages and had acquired a desire and a curiosity to research anything that was interesting. He, in turn, encouraged and supported her, making sure she would develop and turn into the woman she became over the years. He placed food on her table and provided her with maids and ongoing upkeep for the house, supported her wish to host her young, noisy friends, whose minds and hearts were filled solely with the Romanticism that was incomprehensible to him, and not only did he allow her to have them over, but made sure to accommodate them in a manner fit for a king, glittering and ostentatious.

In the evenings when they hosted guests in the drawing room of their lovely home, the table was full of fresh pastries prepared by Henriette's beloved cook Mathilda, fruit bought at the market stall, and sweets that the doctor bought on his way home from the hospital at a shop he happened to come across one evening when he decided to divert from his regular route home. There were also spirits like cognac and wine, tea imported from England and sugared beverages. And the pastries were never ever the same two days in a row.

Everyone knew that in their home, in addition to the stimulating conversation, the poems read out self-importantly, the in-depth analysis and the music playing, the attendees could count on having their palate pleasured by those morsels, their bellies filled with a variety of delicacies, and their head spinning somewhat by the end of the evening.

Henriette had wanted to marry Markus Herz, unlike her friends who had married reluctantly—such as Dorothea, who had hated the candidate who had been forced upon her from the first moment, or Adele Ephraim, who drowned her disappointment over her marriage by immersing herself completely in the world of art. When the match had been proffered to Henriette, she was still a young girl, and all she could think about was the bonnets she could purchase and the barber who would come up with a hairstyle for her. She believed that when she broke free of her father's grasp, she would be able to lead a freer life than the one she had as an unmarried woman. And indeed, she had been lucky to end up with a husband like Markus Herz, who opened his world to her, making an effort to include her and sharing his friends, his money, all the knowledge he possessed and mainly his love.

"The child," he called her privately and when they were with their friends and when he talked about her in her absence. Initially, she objected and was offended, as if the word was an insult, as if he was belittling her as children were belittled. But although she did not like the moniker, as time went by and as she grew more renowned within high society, she realized it was his way of expressing affection toward her, a nickname he had found especially for her, which contained all of his love for her. It was a love he had a hard time expressing in words or gestures, but a love she knew without a doubt was there for her.

But all that was about to change on Monday evening when they sat down to dinner. Markus informed her unequivocally that from now on, he forbade her to see Dorothea.

Henriette felt as if the blood were draining from her body. He had never forbidden her a thing. Even when whispers and rumors spread regarding her relationship with young men, he trusted her whole-heartedly and did not forbid her from seeing them or corresponding with them. Even when everyone pointed out Schleiermacher as her lover, he allowed her to meet him, stroll throughout Berlin with him, and share with him the matters that the two of them shared. He never told her how to dress, did not ask when she was coming or going, did not examine what funds she was spending and on what. This was his only instruction. As if he had asked her to lop off some part of her body and now she must do so, with no objections.

"To shun!" was what he asked of her. "To shun Dorothea," in those very words.

Would he have asked her to shun her sister or her mother?

Henriette looked at him in disbelief. She did not say a thing and could not eat a bite. As if she did not know the man with whom she shared her heart and her life. As if he were a stranger. At that moment, all she could see was the male ugliness that everyone had talked about from the first minute. In a single moment, he had turned into one of those husbands she had heard about. And immediately, she was envisioning the image of Markus Levin, Rahel's father, who bullied his family, and already she began to imagine how her life would look from now on, when edicts such as these would descend upon her with no rhyme or reason. After several minutes in which thousands of thoughts rushed through her head, she came to her senses.

"And why should I shun my best friend?" she finally asked.

"She's a bad influence, and is giving her family and Jewish women in the community a bad name, and I don't want any of it to stick to you."

"So you're actually protecting me from her?"

"You and me and this thing we've greatly toiled to create here." At least he bothered to explain, rather than leaving her without an answer.

All night, she lay awake. She had known Dorothea long before he came into her life and now she was forbidden to see her, the woman who had been a true soul sister to her. All her attempts to explain were to no avail, as were her sobbing and the tears dripping from her eyes and all her tossing and turning; all of them merely prevented sleep, and did no more. The seeds of contention sown last year over her friendship with Schleiermacher had sprouted and grown and had now been reaped by Markus. As if what happened between them at the time had cracked something between the two of them, and that crack might now gradually widen until it became a true fracture.

In the morning, after Markus left for work, Henriette hurried over to see Dorothea and told her what had happened, with no shame or concealment.

"He asked me to shun you. Yes, he used that word, like a part of the herd of excluders and denigrators. Not I! I'm disobeying him, but from now on, we will have to keep our relationship a secret."

Dorothea took it in stride. She was currently engaged in saying goodbye to her old life and in the wars she was fighting in order to fit into her new life.

Rahel, too, was not overly excited by Henriette's news, both because it was clear to her that she, too, would not sever her relationship with Dorothea, as her brother had instructed her to do, and because she was busy with her own challenging love affair.

***

Dorothea now lived in a small house in the suburbs of Berlin, along with her young son, who was allowed to move in with her after she had agreed to the condition imposed by the betrayed Simon Veit: not to marry her beloved so long as her son was living with her. Perhaps this was his way of driving a wedge between the two lovers, making their life somewhat more difficult, even if he knew he had lost this battle a long time ago, a battle he had no chance of winning ever since the first day of his marriage.

For Dorothea, it was a decisive victory. And as for marriage, what was it but a hollow ceremony? The important thing for her was love, emotion and the inner connection between her and Friedrich Schlegel. Everything else was trivial to her, so long as she was able to raise at least one of her sons. Now she spent her days expecting her beloved Schlegel to arrive from the matters occupying him outside of Berlin. She was busy writing letters to her few remaining friends, in which she praised and celebrated Friedrich Schlegel. These letters exuded a spirit of optimism, youthful joy and exuberance that she had never known before.

"There is no man like him in whose hands one can deposit one's soul and redemption with utter confidence," she wrote to Rahel, peppering the correspondence with phrases such as *"that divine Friedrich"* or *"a rich abundance of spirit, soul and life."* As much as she had yearned for love and anticipated it, she had not thought she possessed the capacity for such love. All her letters, conversations and thoughts contained one thing only—her Friedrich. There was no room for anything but him,

"My greatest wish in life," she wrote to Henriette, *"is to serve my beloved."*

***

Lucinda, written by Friedrich Schlegel, reawakened the typical Berlinesque self-righteousness of those who called themselves intellectuals. Before writing the novel that was now the talk of the cultural world, he said to his brother Wilhelm, "I have a desire to write something raging, something resembling Burke[22] or Ezekiel. I would like to write a new bible." And now, indeed, it seemed as if in *Lucinda*, he had constructed new moral principles and changed the perspective on love previously prevalent in literature, including an erotic element in the novel by way of graphic descriptions that repeated again and again, making readers blush. At the end of the novel, the hero found the one woman with whom he could attain true love, pure and distinct.

The critical response came promptly and was harsh and rigid.

"Anything can be done, so long as we know how to do it," one of the newspapers wrote, and that was one of the gentler reviews that the novel and its author garnered. Novalis wrote, to anyone he could, *"This is still not a mature composition. The dust of the schoolhouse rises from it. Perhaps it*

---

22   Edmund Burke (1729–1797) was an Irish statesman, economist, and philosopher. He was a proponent of the belief that religion is the foundation of civil society and emphasized Christianity as a vehicle of social progress.

appeared too early." Tieck[23] deemed the novel "stale" while Schiller[24] wrote to Goethe, *"This piece better characterizes the man than anything he has written thus far. Thanks to it, he now appears even more ridiculous. As he saw he could make no progress in poetry, he composed in his imagination a certain ideal figure, skilled in matters of love, and as he thinks he holds endless torrid love within himself, he believed that anything was permitted to him."*

The critiques of intellectuals were one thing, but when his fellow writers began to aim their sharp tongues at him, mocking and teasing and mostly despising his writing, he was no longer able to stand it all. Letters traveled back and forth, containing statements of criticism, and criticism of that criticism, and the mail coaches were filled with overflowing mail bags and the newspapers heaped paragraph upon paragraph, while the intellectual salons spoke of one thing only—*Lucinda*, published in Berlin by Heinrich Frölich, who had dared to print such an inferior piece of smut.

"A manifesto written in the form of a novel and failing miserably," Schlegel read out loud to Dorothea from the newspaper he was holding.

"Utter hogwash," she pooh-poohed the entire matter, dismissing the words of criticism. "After all, Goethe himself said that if the classical is healthy, the Romantic is sickly, and what is *Lucinda* if not a Romantic creation, down to its very letters?"

"You've read it, after all. And you know I value your opinion more than anything. Did you not see these things? You yourself gave me your blessing to proceed." Schlegel kneeled before Dorothea in tears and she stroked his head, trying to soothe his emotional turmoil. She had indeed inserted the occasional improvement in the novel and made a comment here and there, but she had not thought, even for a moment, that the novel was bad. Had she failed to see what was before her? Had she been biased? Was she blind

---

23 Johann Ludwig Tieck (1773–1853) was a German poet, fiction writer, translator, and critic, as well as one of the founding fathers of the Romantic movement in the late 18th and early 19th centuries.

24 Johann Christoph Friedrich (von) Schiller (1759–1805) was a prominent German playwright, poet, and philosopher.

when it came to her beloved? The more she looked into her actions, the more convinced she grew that her comments had been valid and true. No review would manage to change her opinion, and certainly not when it came from the Berliners, who had revealed themselves to be hypocrites and persisted in their hypocrisy now, as well.

"One fact cannot be disputed. Remember that there is not a single person in Berlin, and perhaps even outside it—I mean the ones who read—who has not read this novel. Is that not the main point?"

Schlegel ignored her words and continued to read aloud from the paper, overcome by tears: "*Schlegel does aspire to elevate life to the highest level of poetry, but he does not possess the required tools or display any indications of the effects of any of the powers that might have given vivid expression to the emotions of the soul, or spiritual expression of sensual pleasures. This composition does not possess any style or any moral qualities.*" The heartache Dorothea felt for him was unbearable to her.

Several nights later, when Schlegel was once again finding it hard to fall asleep, he came to the decision that their lives in Berlin had been thoroughly exhausted and that they belonged in Jena. The next morning, he asked Dorothea to pack their possessions so that they could move to a place where people were more open-minded.

24 | 1800

At this point, everyone had something to say about the relationship between Rahel and Count von Finckenstein. Von Humboldt said that although he was highly sensitive, there was nothing complex or multifaceted about him. Mr. Genelli, who considered himself a good friend of von Finckenstein's, said honestly that he believed "the entire affair is an unfortunate mistake! My friend von Finckenstein is unsuited for the whole matter, and besides, he is too submissive." And Countess Josephine von Fichte, Rahel's good friend from that summer in Teplitz, also honed in on their relationship. "There is no true happiness there, only misfortune."

Some of these statements were made to Rahel's face and others were not; in any case, none of the speakers tried to hide their opinion. And like any other gossip, eventually, she heard it all. She was not upset or angry, neither at the statements nor at those making them. All of this gossip was meaningless compared to one crucial fact—she felt loving and loved.

"*He is original*," she wrote to David, with whom she had been exchanging fewer letters lately. This was how she convinced herself.

"It's true, his knowledge is limited and his perception is slow," she also told von Brinckmann, the friend who had introduced her to von Finckenstein. "And these are the things that make him original and real and different. And he has the ability and the desire to learn and change and make his way into my world, as he has indeed been doing."

Von Brinckmann replied, in an uncharacteristic manner, that perhaps he was already tired of hearing about the problems between them. "My dear, you took your little infatuation and turned it into a career without understanding the world from which your count, who truly does want to love you, comes. Well, allow me to tell you about us—the people to whom all eyes turn, the nobility. We who have everything. In a patriarchal aristocratic family, the familial structure is always the same. The person, the individual, exists for one reason only and is essential for one purpose only—representing our class. I am only essential in order to serve as a representative of our house—the noble house to which I belong. I am a representative of eternity and of the class's unalterable interests. Therefore, as a persona, I am all; I contain the whole world within me. But as an individual, I am nothing! There has only ever been one thing that was ever asked of me—to be a member of the family. And when I complied and did as I was asked, I received esteem and respect and, of course, money."

Rahel had never imagined that this was the case. In the living room of her home, von Brinckmann was a man in his own right. And so were other aristocrats—her friends—who impressed with their writing and musical talents. They possessed knowledge and opinions that were their own. In collaboration with intellectuals from the middle class, they wrote manuscripts and articles and contributed to the German cultural world. She had never heard anything of this kind from von Brinckmann. All his talk and stories always focused on the pleasures of life and his romantic conquests. He always had something to tell her about a good play or a concert that bored him to death. He never discussed anything more serious than the weather. Spending time in his company was always carefree and easy and Rahel had always been certain that von Brinckmann lived life as it should be lived, at full intensity, at full emotion, with full freedom. With no obstacles or fears or boundaries. With no limitations.

"Reading or intellectual conversation about literature is a total waste of time as far as my family is concerned. It does not contribute to the goals of the aristocracy and therefore it is unnecessary. Some of my friends gave up their intellectual studies under pressure from their families. Some of them were even offered money in order to give up such studies. And for some, insisting on getting their education cut off their supply of financial oxygen. Economic insecurity among my noblemen friends has made the decision to strive for an intellectual career a hard and painful one. We have everything other than ourselves," von Brinckmann concluded, and Rahel thought that she did have herself, and nothing and no one in the world would deprive her of herself.

And yet she found herself focusing obsessively on their relationship, expecting him again and again to change something in himself, to draw closer to her, for them to set the date. Instead, their days together grew further and further apart, she in her Berlin and he in the rest of the world.

"How do you see our relationship?" she finally asked von Brinckmann. His previous honesty had encouraged her to ask as she knew that at this moment, his answer would also be real and honest, and she was also ready to accept it.

"Berlin is a city of individuals. You have stripped him of what he is and forced him to become an individual. Now you complain that there's not a lot to him. Well—there was a lot to him. Everything you wanted for yourself. But that was not enough for you."

Although von Brinckmann was honest and direct, he did not manage to unsettle her or cause her to rethink the path she had chosen. Noble von Finckenstein was the world and all that it contained. All the experience and the hope and the endless pleasures. He was the promised paradise, holding the key in his hands, and together, they were striding toward that Eden. In a moment, he would reach out and open what had been locked to her for her entire life. With him, she was special and had a future that would obliterate her past. And what more did she need beyond what he had already given? His love for her contained everything she needed. Perhaps that was why she did not ask and investigate and pry.

After what she had heard from von Brinckmann, she felt she would have to talk to von Finckenstein about his family. She would have to find out whether that was indeed how things were for him as well, whether he identified with what she had heard, whether he, too, lived that way. He would have to tell her what his stance was and what his family's stance was on this matter. She still wanted him and knew he loved her, and for her, this was the heart of the matter. She would never settle for less.

***

For several months now, von Finckenstein had been in Medlitz. He was staying at his estate with his sisters and mothers. She had only received a handful of letters from him, which were sparse and unsatisfying. Memories of their last evening together surfaced in Rahel every night when she ended her day and was about to bring it to a close.

On the evening before he left for Medlitz, he had cried. She had demanded that he take a stand and pressured and pressured him until he finally broke down. She wanted him to act like a man, like a person of authority, asking him to exercise that authority on her. But the more she asked, the further he retreated into himself until, for a single moment, she thought he was about to dissipate into the air and disappear.

"Don't you know what you are to me?" she accused him. "You are the entire world to me and even more. I've placed my life and my whole being in your hands. There is not a single thing that I did not open up to you."

"You fell in love with a count and now I am nothing," he said with pain. "I sit here among all your intellectual friends and force myself to be one of them. For you! All for you! And you, you do not appreciate my efforts and constantly push me more and more as if I am a beast of burden whose final destiny lies at the edge of a mountain."

Rahel was shocked by the image he had come up with. By his ingratitude toward all her efforts. "Look how much progress you've made from the day we met. Look how many things you've learned. You yourself told me that, with your own lips. Are your lips and your heart not equal?"

"Do you think I don't know or hear the things your friends say about me? I hear them very well and I know you hear them too."

"Those things do not affect me. They mean nothing to me. I value one thing only and that is my love for you and your love for me. All the rest is folly. No more and no less."

He was not certain.

He was not certain of himself, of his love, or of hers.

"Just tell me that you love me like always and everything will be whole. Set a date and we will complete our covenant, which we forged with this ring." This was her request when she realized how things might unfold, as she waved her hand, emphasizing the diamond on her finger. "Tell me that you love me." She was nearly begging. But her count looked at her with hollow eyes, as if asking her to toss him out of her home and end things between them. To do the work for him. As usual.

Rahel pulled him to her as her tears were about to erupt. He wanted to object but as always acquiesced to her and clung to her body. He wiped the tears from her eyes and kissed them one by one, feeling the saltiness in his mouth. And Rahel, overcome by her emotions, pulled his clothes off and, whispering in his ear, instructed him to do the same. And whispered to him where to lead her and whispered where to touch her and exactly when. And whispered that she loved him even if he no longer loved her.

And he remained silent.

All of Rahel's words slid off him. He only wished to close his eyes and wake up in his own home, in his comfortable estate, beside his sisters, who admired him, and beside his mother, who treated him as if he were still a small, spoiled boy. Where he did not have to justify himself or be someone he was not.

And after all, what did Rahel ask for on that night when her body was clinging to his own, like during their first night? She wanted to make up and to love. She outlined their future for him and told him about a calm, pleasant life. She envisioned them touring the world together and undergoing experiences together and even dared to mention children.

Karl von Finckenstein did not respond and when he thought she was already asleep, allowed himself to discharge his tension and to cry again.

In the morning, he rose before she awakened, put on his clothes and left the house. For one moment, he remained standing outside, watching as one who knew something in his heart, and then he walked off.

25 | 1800

"*An evil demon is disrupting our lives,*" Dorothea wrote to Rahel. She and Schlegel had been living in Jena for several months, in the home of his brother August and his wife Caroline. During this period, Dorothea herself began to write; she was sharply self-critical, sometimes to a paralyzing degree, but despite it all, she wrote faithfully and with great joy.

"*This predicament prevents every good thing, even my work, as I must spend plenty of time in Caroline's company, and therefore cannot give my room its proper due. I am sure you will understand how much this fact appalls me; my entire existence depends upon it. If I cannot work, I do not want to live.*"

For six weeks now, Caroline had been ill. The doctor called it "a disease of the nerves" and Dorothea tried to ease her suffering, tend to her and be of use in the household that provided her with food and shelter. Several days after they arrived, organized their possessions and found their place there, Dorothea embarked on the work of writing. She wrote articles and criticisms and even translated several texts, and received payment for all of these, which, even if it was not particularly generous, helped with their dire financial situation. Every penny that came into their pockets helped. Now she had to cease writing and devote herself to her position as a nurse, escorting, encouraging and serving, fluffing pillows, reading stories and ensuring the house was quiet and harmonious.

"*I have no interest in the acclaim of the writer. I write for money first and foremost. I want to be able to earn money by writing, so that Friedrich will no longer have to write for a living. What I do resides within those borders: creating quietly and earning my keep as an artist, even humbly, until he can."*

Despite all that she said and wrote, which, of course, had some truth to it, Dorothea's writing was characterized by joy, creativity and pleasure. And when Caroline began to recover, Dorothea attacked the task at full speed. This was not letter writing, which, after all, she had done when she was married to Simon Veit. This was a different sort of writing, of criticism and opinion pieces. It was respectable and Schlegel appreciated and admired this writing of hers. But it might have been precisely her impressive capabilities and the fact that she managed to sell her articles that made him slow down, take a rest, not rushing into publication and relying on the money she made and on the meager monthly income allotted to her from Simon Veit based on the interest on her property.

Dorothea loved Schlegel with all her heart, but this trait she discerned in him now, of slowing down and perhaps laziness, evoked her fury.

"After all, you can compose something from the immense repertoire of materials at your disposal. What is the purpose of the stacks of paper you're accumulating?"

Their first serious fight since they became a couple started out as a regular conversation and very quickly devolved into loud, discordant tones and great anger on both sides. Even her embarrassing divorce and the harsh criticism leveled against *Lucinda*, which everyone suspected of being autobiographical, causing them to flee Berlin, had not resulted in such disputes and problems in communication between the two of them as did the fact of Schlegel's laziness, revealed to Dorothea from the moment they first shared accommodations. Dorothea admired his whole being and his talent and expected him to sear the world with his words of wisdom, his poems and the essays he wrote. However, for several months now, he had not produced anything to send out into the world and she was consumed with disappointment. If he had suffered from some form of writer's block, she would understand, but that was not the problem.

The more her frustration grew, the greater was her desire to write more and more, as if she wished to escape from one reality to another. Pages full of her round, cramped handwriting stacked up on her desk, coalescing into *Florentine*, a new novel that seemed to be writing itself. On the blank page, she could create and destroy worlds, change reality and alter the ways of the world. And in the new world coming together under her hands, there were two female rulers who were in utter contrast to the rulers she knew, the exact opposite of the Prince of Rheinsberg, who had left a fiercely negative impression on her during her last visit there. Back then, other than a letter to Rahel describing all she saw, she could not change a thing. But now, in her new world, she changed things around and created women rulers concerned about the welfare of their subjects, who opened up their courtyards and turned them into a public space, women rulers whom the public did not fear, but rather admired and respected. The hero she created escaped from the treacherous maws of Catholicism, with its selfish representatives and obedient acolytes. She put all her emotions, wishes and dreams into this world.

As the days went by, she found herself increasingly satisfied, and soon, the task of writing would come to an end, and her satisfaction turned into fear.

***

Schlegel was an avid supporter of her writing and tried to bring about the publication of the novel.

He wrote to Schleiermacher, telling him about the offers they had received: "*Unger offered royalties of two Louis D'or*[25] *for* Florentine. *The first volume will be ready soon and we have a spark of hope in the financial realm as well.*"

Friederike Unger was a savvy woman who owned a publishing house. Schlegel and Dorothea knew that Friederike loathed Dorothea, and

---

25 Louis D'Or gold coins were French currency in circulation before the Revolution.

therefore concealed the fact that Dorothea had written *Florentine*. They even handed over the manuscript to be copied so that Unger would be unable to recognize Dorothea's handwriting. But despite all this, the transaction did not go through. Unger evaded them using various excuses, piled up obstacles in their path and reneged on her promises.

"Unger the Cat smelled where the novel came from and was despicable enough to allow herself this pathetic revenge," Dorothea wrote to Henriette, who replied, "*Unger's disdain is not reserved only for you, dear Dorothea, but extends to all Jewish women who dare to climb up the social ladder. We are guilty of lack of taste, mediocrity and faulty education, or so she says. She does not even dare publicize this opinion of hers under her own signature. She is low enough to publish her opinions anonymously and considers us all to be idiots.*"

Dorothea had been familiar with the printing industry and the world of publishing for many years now, starting with the years she was a girl living in the house of her father, Moses Mendelssohn. She knew prominent men who had come to her father's home in order to publish his writing, as well as the procedures involved in this task. She was familiar with the legal aspects and matters of copyright and also knew the cunning of those financiers by whom the writer was held captive, like a hostage. Therefore, she did not give up on her attempts at achieving publication until, at last, a decent publisher who was willing to publish her *Florentine* was found.

"*Bohan willingly offered to give me 200 Reichsthaler*[26] *immediately in September, and in addition, also provided us with the most accommodating terms regarding the design and print,*" she wrote to Henriette, each word emanating joy and happiness. Her bliss was twofold, both because a novel she had written was being published and because she would be fairly compensated for it. She wrote an introduction of sorts at the beginning of the novel:

"*I happily recall that joyful, felicitous morning when I first remembered the little stories in this book. They had lain dormant in my soul like violets*

---

26   German currency.

during the winter. A new spring and the return of the sun awakened them all. With cheerful, enthused eagerness, I wrote down the first pages and placed them on my desk with such bliss and innocence, as if I had completed the entire composition."

Her excitement was not tempered in the slightest by the fact that her name would not appear on the novel; rather, Frederick Schlegel would be credited as its editor. Neither was her happiness diminished when the sensitive, moving introduction she had written was omitted from the first edition, due to considerations that were unknown to her. However, from the moment the book emerged into the world, many emotions began to flood her, until she began to fear she might come down with the very same illness that had afflicted Caroline just a short time ago. At first, she felt maternal about her creation, comparing the manifestation of the hero of *Florentine* to the actual act of giving birth she had experienced in the past. It was such an emotional and intimate experience to her that she referred to her protagonist as "my good Florentine," and "my stepson Florentine."

However, from the moment the books emerged from the printing press onto shelves and libraries, she was afflicted with anxiety, and the tension filling her transformed the expressions of love into explicit disdain. Instantly, the book she had brought forth turned into a "stray weed," a "wild growth."

"*I had a proper laugh when I saw the silly book on parchment,*" she wrote to her brother-in-law August.

She sent two copies to Schleiermacher and to Henriette, including an identical dedication to both of them:

"*With beating heart and blushing face—from me to you.*"

There was no originality to this statement, which was commonly used and clichéd as a frequent expression of publication anxiety. The talented Dorothea used it as if she were any unexceptional writer, as if she had no imagination or skill, as if she had not just completed a utopian, groundbreaking novel about an ideal society.

26 | 1801

Count von Finckenstein had been staying for some time at his family estate alongside his mother and sisters. He thought that once he returned home and was far from Rahel, he would manage to organize his thoughts and impose order upon the emotions that left him distraught. One moment, he wanted to sever all ties with the woman who had pressured him to shed his skin and change for her, and the next, he thought he would never find anyone like her. She was good to him and, after all, what was she asking of him? To open his mind somewhat to other ideas? To read a bit more and try to understand? To take an active part in her and her friends' cultural world? Why couldn't he be like his noble peers who had managed to make such a change? What was wrong with him? He did not share his deliberations and questions with his sisters or his mother, keeping them to himself. They could not understand what he was going through, as they were still held captive by their opinions on class and religion and other things that did not trouble him at all. And in any case, what did they have to do with what took place in the literary salons of Rahel and others like her? They excelled at criticizing anything that was foreign to and different from them and gossiping about it, and now they were doubling their efforts. They were constantly trying to convince him to leave Rahel, until he could no longer bear it and tried to avoid contact with them entirely. He wanted to distance himself from Rahel's pressure and instead, received ample portions of pressure from them instead.

As the days went by, he found himself missing Rahel more and more. His distance from her and his sisters' harsh statements about her blurred the difficult feelings that rose within him every time he disappointed her, while emphasizing other things—the intimacy between them, her wit, her desire to utterly dedicate herself to him when they were together. There was something about their relationship that he had not known until that moment. Rahel was flesh and blood, not part of the scenery in which he lived, including the trivial love affairs he had had until he met her. Now, from a distance, he realized it was a significant relationship. He had grown used to Rahel fighting for him and fighting on his behalf and was accustomed to her never giving up, and therefore this time, as well, he asked her to decide for him in the letter he sent her. He added that he was willing to give all of it up for her, if she only asked.

"*You must decide on your own*," she wrote back, sending the letter to his home in Teplitz. "*I will do nothing more.*"

With every word she wrote down, she felt herself shattering again and again into tiny fragments that she knew could not be put together again. And this shattering brought heartache with it, which then evoked great anger. And when she sat down to write what she wrote, the writing implement in her fingers seemed to take over her thoughts, taking on autonomy, and already, words she might regret later but were unable to stop were being written on the page:

"*Be something and I will acknowledge you. After all, you cannot find any pleasure in me. I have terrorized you, and therefore I find no pleasure in you, either.*" She knew in her heart that for some time now, things between them had been signed and sealed and currently they were only experiencing the final throes of dying.

He had not expected her to write anything like what she had, and read the words again and again. He had not believed that Rahel, who had clung to him and fought for him and was willing to shed her skin for their relationship, would give in. And not only did she give in, but gave up. Every word she wrote expressed her insult. Insult over who he was, insult over her surrender. Finally, he understood that like Rahel, he, too, had given up.

She insisted that he be the one to decide, as this was the only way he could express his true love for her, and he could not do so, perhaps in order to shirk responsibility for his own emotions.

"You never truly loved me," he replied. "It was all a game, all intended to teach me, to educate me, to make me worthy of you." Even in his response, he refused to take responsibility for his part in their rift.

The contents of his letter made it clear to Rahel that he did not have the strength to face the challenges stemming from their relationship on his own. She realized that not only had she lost him, but had lost an entire world, as well. A world that had explicitly rejected her and had now done so in full view of everyone.

***

"What I did not receive I can forget. But I cannot forget what happened to me. My God protects the others from realizing it. It is all over. Only life, idiotic and insensitive, goes on. You do not die of grief or misery. Day after day, you wake up, behave as people around you behave and then go to bed. In the ridiculous day-to-day, greater trouble dissipates into nothing."

At first, she tried not to feel, walking around as if nothing had happened. As if it was nothing. She sealed up her heart and did not think, keeping herself busy with trivial, unimportant occupations. She met people, went to the theater, and for a moment, imagined things were still as they were and that nothing had happened. But as the days went by, shame climbed inside her, wrapping itself around her and tightening and refusing to relinquish its hold. Shame and misery and shock. Her heart had been trampled along with its desires and she could not believe that such a blow had indeed arrived and struck her down. Her, of all people. Now it was the reality of her life and a done deal. And, as proof, misery, sorrow, loss and grief came and settled within her, all leading to illness. Many weeks had gone by since it was all over and done with and luckily for her, sickness came and took her inside her home, far from the eyes of her friends, far from society, in which she suddenly felt ashamed. All her confidence, all her indifference to gossip, to what was said or thought about her, all disappeared as if it had never existed.

She could blame no one but herself. She had let herself down, not only because of the happiness that had been taken from her, but because she had not truly managed to understand the essence of her beloved. And how could she blame him? After all, he was acting according to that same essence, that same innate nature. She should have known what that nature was, recognized the character that precluded their covenant from materializing. She had been blind and stubborn and that was her fault. But what solace was there in that fault? Guilt and shame consumed her and exhausted her health. And now, here came the incessant cough and the high fever that brought visions with it and words said in retrospect and self-recrimination and blazing hatred for herself and for her accursed origin—the reason for all this grief she had known since the day she was born.

This shame that burned every part of her body was familiar to her. It was the same shame Rahel knew from the past, from the birthday celebration she had organized for herself after claiming her independence. She experienced the same sensation of public humiliation now as well, and all she wanted was to disappear. To thrust herself into one of those furnaces that melted the bones of the Christian dead, or to die slowly in her bed, embraced by illness, until she disappeared from the world, and all her troubles along with her.

***

One morning, she heard a knock on the door, one that started within a dream and did not cease even when Rahel opened her eyes and woke up. After much knocking, when she realized there was no one home to open the door, she roused herself from the bed, put on the dressing gown that had lain unused for many days on her chair and slowly walked down the stairs, exhausted and weak, holding on to the banister so as not to fall.

At the entrance to the house, elegant and dressed to the nines, stood Countess Caroline von Schlabrendorf. She occasionally visited Rahel's drawing room in the attic and was the kind of woman who utterly disdained anyone's opinion. When she felt like traveling on her own, she did not wait to find a chaperone but rather put on male attire and embarked on her journey. "I put on men's clothing when I do not wish to be reminded at every single moment that I am a woman," she once vocally declared.

"Look at yourself," she scolded Rahel. "One might think you were the only one in the entire world whose heart has been broken."

Rahel stood before her in all her wretchedness and Caroline, who was known for her stubborn, argumentative nature, continued to berate her. Once she was done, she ordered her to bathe and get dressed and promptly informed her that she was taking her with her to Paris.

Despite Rahel's great respect for the countess, and although what she said was the absolute truth, she was ill. She explained to the countess why she could not travel, but the countess interrupted her, whispering in her ear, "You must come with me, you must." She was nearly begging, and also sounded somewhat frightened. "The matter cannot be delayed even one more day." When she phrased it in that manner, her friend's bleak situation gradually became clearer. She was not concerned about Rahel's heartache, but about the thing that was even now growing inside her and would soon be impossible to get rid of.

The affairs that Caroline conducted were not discreet; she went out to cavort with her lovers while her husband passed his time among King Frederick William the Second's entourage of mystics. She tended to her business while he tended to his. But even with such an arrangement, there were rules that could not be broken, and now she tottered upon a thin line and might cross it at any minute.

Rahel was wise enough to understand that the trip to Paris was indeed meant to expel something from Carloline's body but was also an excellent opportunity for her, too, to rid herself of that which so oppressed her and drained her of her strength.

***

"What I want now, the thing I yearn for, is to no longer be troubled by myself, to no longer monitor my own happiness or unhappiness, but to be something that is unquestionable. Just like planet Earth—something whose reality testifies that everyone walks upon it."

Rahel wrote these words on the day her feet first stepped upon the sidewalks of gay Paris, and she meant every one of them. Paris. She had heard of it, read about it, seen it in paintings, but had never thought it to be so different from her Berlin. The Berlin that had turned its back upon her.

After a while, she wrote to Henriette, to whom she had not had time to bid farewell:

"When you are not in your country, meaning when you are outside your homeland, loving life is easy. There, no one knows you. Your life is entirely in your own hands and you are the master, or perhaps I should say mistress, of your own affairs. You have left the basic knowledge that you are unhappy somewhere behind you and now, when that knowledge is not in evidence, the matter is dimmer, distant, and new possibilities are opening up. It is easy to forget yourself when that notorious birth of yours is unfamiliar, is of no consequence and no one recognizes it. A foreign land is a good thing and it is good to be a foreigner there, to be no one, with no name, with no pedigree, with nothing serving as a reminder of who you are."

Rahel decided to forget herself through the beautiful things Paris had to offer: the walks through well-tended gardens, attending the ostentatiously designed theater, the coffeehouses that were bustling at all hours of the day and night and the French salons that bored her, but where she found pleasure nevertheless.

"No happiness can be derived from people," she told Caroline one evening as they were sitting on the hotel balcony. "Pleasant waters and a pleasant climate, those are the most beautiful things in the world. They are what is truly good."

Pleasant waters and a pleasant climate were the last things that interested Caroline, who felt very bad after the procedure she had undergone. But for Rahel, matters were about to change.

27 | 1801

In the transcript he presented at Rabbinical Court during the divorce proceedings, under the item specifying the reason, Simon Veit wrote, *"My wife, Brendel, wishes to divorce me."* There was nothing in this laconic sentence that could hint at his emotions. His heart was broken and a sense of failure had taken over him, and yet he did not seek to disown her completely in order to get back at her, but neither was he particularly generous when it came to property. Dorothea had relinquished nearly everything relating to her previous life with him, and was also willing to give up the little she had left. However, Simon Veit allowed her to take several items from the house, and Dorothea chose to take the piano and the handsome desk she had received as a gift from her friend von Brinckmann. In addition, Veit promised her she would receive a certain monthly income. "All your property will be deposited and you will only receive the interest from it," he said, and she, who only wished to depart for her new life with her beloved Schlegel, accepted it.

Now she needed to take on the burden of their livelihood, and it was clear to her that it was actually Schlegel's laziness, which so annoyed her and resulted in financial distress for both of them, that had awakened an immense force coming from within her, motivating her to produce a lot of worthy writing.

She wrote novels, essays and translations, adding on critiques as well. Her fingers were full of letters and words and paragraphs, ideas in German and French rushed through her mind, and there was even more that she did not have time to do. And yet in a letter she sent to von Brinckmann, she wrote that she needed additional translation work, asking him—out of the pride she still retained—to keep her need for wages a secret. She asked him not to publicize their financial distress as she had had enough of gossip, of people gloating at their expense and wishing to condemn them. She wanted to keep her affairs strictly to herself.

And although she published her work under Schlegel's name, willingly obliterating herself for him, many knew her literary work, which garnered her much praise.

Writer and poet Clemens Brentano asked her to grant her opinion regarding his manuscripts. Critic and translator Ludwig Tieck, later recognized as the forefather of German Romanticism, wrote to her about literature, and other friends promised they would find writing work for her. And the work did come. Sometimes Dorothea found herself battling the clock, whose hands abused her; she also had to tend to her young son, whom she raised and nurtured, not to mention the house, which she always took care to keep tidy and clean and ready at every moment for Schlegel, since she did not know exactly when he would return from his journeys. And occasionally, she had to rest from all this, lay her head on the pillow, and put up her feet and pick up a good book and delve into it.

Sometimes, she remembered her days with Veit, when all she had to do was nurture her children. She did not withhold even an iota of attention from them and invested greatly in their upbringing, learning and education. At such moments, when she recalled the comfort that had once been and had since evaporated, she would also experience a sense of frustration, loneliness and sterility of the heart as a reminder. She had risked it all when she left him and if she had to do it again, she would, repeating it endlessly.

***

Life in Paris was good to Rahel. Her heartache gradually diminished and was replaced by something new, arousing and thrilling—a young man who was different than anything she knew. Someone who swept her along in his wake. She, who was not pretty in the slightest. She, who was older than him by eight years. She, whose heart was already wounded and steeped with disappointment.

"He is a twenty-two-year-old Roman. He has the head of a robber and bruises on his neck and legs. He is as beautiful as a god and belongs to the divine breed," Rahel wrote of him to von Brinckmann. *"Love without pretensions."* She also convinced herself that this time would be different, although from an objective perspective, it seemed like a nearly exact replication of her previous experience with love.

"The loveliest quarry of my life," she defined him to Caroline, who was neck-deep in her own misfortune.

The "god" she had just encountered was named Wilhelm Bockelmann. She met him through her friend David Veit. David had heard that his pal Bockelmann was planning to come to Paris on a business trip and insisted that he visit his oldest friend, Rahel Levin, who was also staying there at the time.

There was no spiritual quality to him. Nor did he possess exceptional logic, or an aspiration to be someone he was not. Furthermore, he did not know her past but only who she was now, in Paris. He was young and vibrant and vital and exceptionally handsome and she was open to a new adventure.

It was true that Bockelmann was not particularly complex, but he did have a sense for reading the person across from him. "You have an unusual ability to change and the capacity to learn and a desire to encounter a new world and take it inside you," he told her decisively. Compared to her, he was worldly, and she felt ready to learn the ways of the world from him, as if she were newly hatched. In Berlin, any desire to change her ran straight into a locked door and unequivocal resistance. But now, in Paris, after committing to availing herself to all the good things the city had to offer, she embraced everything he said and took it to heart.

The first thing Bockelmann told her was about Veit's conversion to Christianity. Rahel had learned of it from Veit's latest letter, but she enjoyed hearing Bockelmann's report, which, unlike others, conveyed no judgment or condemnation. In fact, he expressed no opinion on the matter at all, as if it were a simple surgical procedure like having a mole removed. Rahel, who had had enough of Berlin's hypocrisy and the gossip that had lately been her fare, appreciated this approach.

They strolled along together for days at a time without opening a book or a newspaper, them and the city and its natural surroundings and the people they did not know and did not wish to know. Bockelmann taught Rahel simple things, such as spending hours and hours watching a flock of ducks floating back and forth on the greenish river, or enjoying the good rays of the sun during the exact hours when they were not too hot but still caressed the bare skin. He taught her to lean back and allow things to reach her on their own.

"It's possible to attain things from the world even if you are entirely passive," he told her early on, after they had spent only a few days together. His sharp instincts instantly recognized her desire to propel herself forward, her impatience, the tenseness that kept her from pleasure, inflicting her with a rigidity that took over her body and her spirit.

"If you're not moving forward, you disappear. It's like death. Even worse," she replied.

"I'll help you find the part inside you that always makes you collide with yourself," he assured her, and although outwardly, she agreed, secretly, she laughed at his innocence. *When you're young, you think you can bend the world to your will,* she thought to herself.

"When you're still, the existence of things remains tangible, and those things will come and touch you and embrace you," he promised her. She, in turn, promised herself to surrender, to give herself over to him completely. It was not because she possessed the innocence of one who was blinded by love, but precisely out of the certainty that she would not allow herself to fall again. She had always been a disciplined student, and remained one now as well; she memorized all that he taught her and took it in. She succumbed to her new love, which was good and thrilling, but also had an expiration date that was known in advance.

She surrendered to young Bockelmann and to the pleasant passivity and to the sunny days and to the water and to the starlight and found that her heart was lighter, as were her body and spirit.

She loved him during their walks through Paris's romantic streets, loved him when they sat still across from each other, loved him during the lunches set out on checkered blankets that were laid out on the ground during their picnics and the late dinners in Parisian cafés. She loved him when they returned from the opera or from the concert or from the nocturnal stroll through the illuminated streets. And she loved him especially between the sheets and the covers and the lacy linens. Even when he slept like a god and she was left awake to watch him expel his coarse, graceful breaths, she loved him.

With her Roman god, she became young and carefree and almost managed to erase from her memory Berlin's gray days, her illnesses, the tongues wagging in condemnation and all that had been. In a letter to Henriette, she wrote, *"Up to now, I have loved people through my strength, but I love him through his strength."*

After two months, she set him free to continue on his path. "I demand nothing from you and demand nothing from myself as well, not even loving you, no loyalty, nothing. You will take the world inside you without me and I will do the same without you."

Perhaps this time, too, she had followed the body and passion, but she had walked in consciously, and while she gave herself over completely, she also knew how to let go and how to free herself when the time was right.

Once again, she was left alone, she and her churning interiority.

"Death and silence and evil and fear are the entire world. The entire sunlit world," she wrote in her notebook after they parted ways.

28 | 1802

It had been twelve years since Markus Levin's death and just like her friend David Veit and other Jews throughout Germany, Ludwig, Rahel's younger brother, decided to convert from Judaism to Christianity. He did so after years of debates and deliberations regarding the idea, until, at last, he gathered the courage.

When Ludwig told her about his intention, he said, "It isn't fair to place a heavy burden such as Judaism on your children. It would be better if I could give up this hypocrisy, but if a person has additional aspirations in this life, he has no other choice."

She did not need to be persuaded.

The first step was changing the family name of Levin to Robert. He could not be a Christian with such a Jewish name, and therefore chose to shed that name, which had been a part of many generations and had now been cut off. The second step was accepting Christianity in a special ceremony in a church.

***

Three years after her father's death, Rahel had already taken her first steps in rebelling against religion, and wrote about it to David Veit.

"*Yesterday, during the Sabbath, in full daylight, I took a regal carriage to rehearsals at the opera, at two-thirty in the afternoon. No one saw me.*

I would deny it and will deny it to anyone, even the person who helped me disembark from the carriage! I believe one can act so, that one must act so, in my situation."

And David Veit wrote back, *"If you are traveling on the Sabbath, you must not deny it. Otherwise, I will conclude that you do not wish to contribute a thing to the reformation of the Jews."*

And indeed, just as he had written, Rahel did not see her action as a social or political statement. She was focused on herself and all she cared about was concealing her Judaism, a Judaism of laws and prayers and limitations and 'thou shall,' but mostly 'thou shalt not.' Because, despite all the prohibitions that this God's believers had taken on, He abused them, sentencing His followers to life in the margins, a life of constant persecution and humiliation. This was the life from which she wanted to forge an escape, just as her younger brother Ludwig was now doing.

She knew that even if the Jews adopted the customs of their Christian Berliner friends, they would still remain "the sons of Moses." The Jews did all they could to assimilate. They sometimes attended church and commemorated Christmas with decorated fir trees and gifts, with moving liturgical music in the background. But Rahel knew that despite all this, they could not be rid of the mark imprinted upon them and the biases against them. They would never be able to live in a world where opportunities were open to them.

***

Lately, different voices were being heard, as if the autumn wind now blowing had dispersed them throughout Berlin. If in the past the voices had claimed that Jews would be accepted by society if they assimilated, now, things had changed. The voices were speaking differently. Now they said that if Jews stopped believing and behaving in the Jewish way, if they ceased their strange actions and their divisive attire, then they could become full-fledged Germans.

Years earlier, along with the Humboldt brothers, Caroline von Dacheröden, Deborah Veit and many others, Henriette had founded the Virtue Society. Rahel, too, joined them.

The society strived for one sentimental goal—honest correspondence, an exchange of secrets and a desire to achieve moral perfection. Unlike various other societies and groups in Berlin, in this society, everything was free and uninhibited. When they met or parted, they sealed it with a kiss or two on the cheek, and members addressed each other in a friendly manner, without the rigid, notorious German formalities. In their society, all secrets were laid out in letters, with no screening, no shame, no judgment and no religious biases.

"On paper, we bare our soul. Each of us bares his or her own soul. If you are seeking practicalities, you should know there is no practicality to these letters, other than one thing. Happiness. Happiness that brings love. There are no secrets. It does not matter if you are a member of the Mosaic religion or not. There are no limitations. Everything is on the page," Henriette explained to her, and for a while, the group members were her closest friends.

Now, Rahel understood how naïve that had been. In retrospect, the Virtue Society seemed to belong to a different world, to a life that held promise.

The letters she had exchanged with her friends were piled in a bundled stack in one of the corners of her room. It had been many years since she undid that bundle, which seemed to have become one of the items of furniture in the room. The society had been abandoned, its members growing older and their opinions changing. Shortly after she returned from Paris, in a fit of nostalgia, she had, some time ago, retrieved an old letter sent to her by Wilhelm von Humboldt, who had been one of her fellow society members and a close friend.

Dear Rahel,

You Jewish women, you possess so much charm and curiosity and great beauty, and you know all this, and express it with no shame or modesty. My heart grows bitter, my days are bleak and my desire for my unattainable one is insatiable. At night I lie with my eyes open and fantasize. Fantasies that the page would not bear and even if it would, I would not dare to put them in writing for modesty's sake. You Jewish women. And especially the one who reciprocates and does not reciprocate, filling my house with letters brimming with sweet words, letters written in the Hebrew alphabet—words of love. For the sake of secrecy, I do my best to reply to her in that same holy language, which ensures discretion, but for what purpose? Letters upon letters, words upon words burn my bleeding heart.

Logic cannot conceive of it. After all, she was the one who complained that her marriage lacks inner harmony, claiming that it was a happy relationship but not a happy marriage. She was the one who cried tears when she revealed that each time she expressed love for her husband, he dismisses it as a childish action. Why, then, does she spurn me and what should I do? I am afraid, Rahel, afraid that my love will undermine my reason, that my love will cause me to act as Werther did.

Rahel did not remember how she had replied to him or what she had advised him to do, and in any case, it no longer mattered now that William von Humboldt, he who had revealed the secrets of his heart and his tortuous love for Henriette to her, had some time ago married Caroline, and both of them, who had seemed sympathetic to Jews, actually preferred the newly prevailing views, and these views were not at all sympathetic to Jews.

Caroline accused Jewish women, salon women, of intellectual ambition, which she viewed as a desire to accrue cultural and political power. And while Caroline made her declarations inside her own home, her husband Wilhelm found masculine ears and newspapers in which to express such sentiments. He had changed his tune and publicly voiced his criticism to anyone who was willing to listen.

"There comes a time when a person needs to relinquish intellect," von Humboldt said to his friend Friedrich von Gentz, while the latter was, in fact, praising Rahel, calling her "the most intellectual woman on earth." Von Humboldt viewed her somewhat differently, choosing to call her "a monster" as she represented all that was wrong about a woman. Such statements were not an exception or unusual. Apparently, more and more people, some of them regular salon visitors, had been swept up in criticizing Rahel's conduct and that of her friends, like a wave that had risen and proved unstoppable.

Heinrich von Kleist, a prominent Romantic writer and playwright who was already gaining esteem, was also a regular patron of the salons each time he visited Berlin. He often described the pleasure he found there, now writing to his sister Ulrich, *"It is only rarely that I go out in society. Jewish society might have been my favorite if the Jews were not presumptuous in their attitude toward their culture."*

Jewish friends could be helpful in various ways, but friendship with them could definitely not be based on the virtues of their character. This was what Rahel had been trying to escape from her entire life, and yet it was what haunted her once more. She thought that when she found respected friends among the ranks of high society, she would feel differently, that this thing with which she had been born would diminish. "When there are good times, it does not matter if you are Jewish or beautiful." she once told Dorothea. But now the good times were gradually fading away and her Judaism was haunting her once more.

Apparently, being rejected by the count—who, unlike his friends, did not say a word against her or against her Judaism—was only the opening shot for further rejections by aristocrats who had no compunctions about showing up in her attic, kissing her hand and listening to what she had to say, and later criticizing her behind her back, as if she were a common Jewish woman like all the other Jewish women in that crammed district.

If she had not known how many years her brother Ludwig had been concerned with the question of religious conversion, she would have thought that the recent ill winds had caused him to take action, that the anti-Jewish sentiments had been the final factor that swayed him. But she knew that Ludwig's conversion to Christianity was the culmination of a very long mental process. And she herself, despite her contempt for her Judaism, still did not dare to take this step.

***

Dorothea and Schlegel lived together in Berlin, then in Jena, and had now arrived in Paris. She followed him wherever he wished to go, her essence blending into his. Once an independent, autonomous woman, free-thinking and possessing a boundless creativity, she had subjugated herself before one whose genius was now expressed only sporadically, his talent flickering in and out of existence. She had willingly filled all her horizons with him alone.

In Paris, her worldview changed somewhat. The licentiousness she encountered, the freedom of people with no boundaries, stunned and repulsed her. Dorothea was no prude. After all, she herself was nurtured by lust, which had motivated her to abandon the setting in which she should have resided for the rest of her days. But a process of returning to religion began to ripen within her. Her family had ostracized her, her young son lived with her and Schlegel, who was not her husband, and now Paris seemed to dwarf her own sins, while also emphasizing a lack of human inhibition that repelled her. She had matured and now suddenly saw all this as immoral, distasteful. Paris was loose, free of any inhibitions. In its streets and alleyways, sex was commodified openly and shamelessly. It was a city whose nightly effervescence devolved into senselessness, whose excretions filled the streets. Paris, in which drinking, smoking, dancing and playing cards were the essence of life, in which day turned into night and night turned into day. Paris, in which fashion was always changing and shop windows were windows into the lustful souls of its residents. This Paris began to spark new thoughts within Dorothea regarding her actions and their consequences. For the first time, feelings of guilt arose and grew within her with regard to Veit, whom, during the years they spent together, she had learned to despise as if he were the root of all evil.

"*Freedom? No more than debauchery,*" she wrote to Rahel after Rahel wrote to her about wondrous Paris, with which she had fallen in love. And now she herself was living in debauchery, with a man to whom she was not married, for which she despised herself. He wanted to marry her, even back in those initial days in Berlin, although he stated in advance that he did not know whether he could be faithful to her. He wanted to marry her and she could not, because of the condition Veit had stipulated. She was not permitted to marry Schlegel because he was not Jewish. Now, in view of the Parisian debauchery assaulting her from every corner and from every alleyway, an intense need to be respectable rose within her. At least within her home. As if she were asking some higher authority to confirm the relationship in which she was living.

Even back in her days in Jena, it had occurred to her to convert. She found that the beautiful Christian paintings lifted her spirits and that the heavenly music in church imbued her with calm. But all of these were passing fancies, disappearing as quickly as they had appeared. "Christianity is a passing fad in the Romantic worldview," she told Schlegel. "It rose to prominence and quickly faded away again."

Now, in Paris, these same thoughts returned to her once more. Thoughts born out of a desire to address the compunctions gnawing at her. And out of the condemnation of her family, which withheld financial prosperity due to a relationship they frowned upon. And out of the French debauchery around her, she sought a response and appeared to have found it in the scripture in Luther's translation.

"*I have been diligently reading the Old and New Testament and find that, in my view, Protestant Christianity is indeed purer and preferable to Catholicism. To me, the latter is too similar to the old Judaism, which I despise. Protestantism seems to me like the religion of Christ and the religion of culture. If I can make a determination based on scripture, then in my heart, I am utterly Protestant,"* Dorothea wrote to her old friend, Pastor Schleiermacher, and the more she read and delved into these texts, the more she began to vocally condemn the French society in which she was living, which she called "debauched." She also condemned her family members, whom she described as "narrow-minded Jews" as they refused to acknowledge her relationship with Schlegel. She reserved special condemnation for her brother Abraham, whom she called "an emotionless barbarian." Her other comments concerning him made her sound as if she were one of the voices swept in by the spirit of the times. "He is no better in any way than any Berlin Jew, other than having finer undergarments and a coarser impudence."

29 | 1803

Henriette was sitting in the armchair in the living room with her good friend Friedrich Schleiermacher by her side. He was holding her hand and not letting go, as if doing so would cause his friend to be sucked into some dark place from which she would be unable to return. A pastor was the last thing needed here, and some of the bearded Jewish dignitaries filling the house had already begun to whisper behind his back and express their dissatisfaction, but due to the circumstances, they did no more than quietly mumble prayers. Henriette was immersed in the large armchair reserved for her husband alone. She had never sat in it—not when he was at work, not when he traveled for meetings outside of Berlin and not when the drawing room, where he saw his guests, was overflowing with people. Even then, the armchair was reserved for him alone. Now she sat in it, small and shriveled, her body appearing to shrink from one moment to the next.

It had started out as another ordinary morning. Henriette awoke alongside her husband and when she saw that he was asleep, she rose quietly and thought she would let him sleep on for a while longer as the evening before, he had complained that he was not feeling well. Such complaints had become a matter of routine since his illness had descended upon them. Once, he would never complain about anything, but since becoming ill, he had turned into a different person. He complained in the evenings when he went to bed and in the mornings when he woke up and also in the afternoons between five o'clock tea and early dinner, which he had barely touched lately. His complaints were not explicit, but rather consisted of hollow looks he hoped to conceal from her and moans that would involuntarily escape him. These concerned her most of all. At dinner, they had talked about traveling to the hot springs, which would do him good. Although both of them knew there would no longer be any improvement. But there was something hopeful about this daily conversation that allowed them both to keep going, thanks to the plans they were making. Such plans reinvigorated her, filling her with renewed joy and providing an opportunity to order an additional dress from the seamstress and purchase another pair of shoes and, mostly, to deny the circumstances in which she found herself.

It all began with a bothersome cough that started out small and gradually developed into something more intense. Henriette asked Markus to go see his doctor as the coughing was lasting too long, but he, as one who had been working as a physician his entire life, believed he was immune to the strange illnesses to which his patients were subject, or perhaps he knew. Henriette did not back down and nagged as she always did when she wanted something, but Markus was recalcitrant on this matter, and every day, came up with another excuse for failing to do as she asked.

Several months went by, and it was only when he began to feel actual pain in his body that he went in for an examination. When he returned home that day, he looked different. An old man. Henriette understood immediately, but Markus dismissed her with a vague explanation about a temporary matter and asked to go rest.

When he met his doctor again, she asked to come along and he no longer had the strength to resist her. When they returned, she immediately departed for Rahel's home in order to ease her burden and find solace.

"When the doctor said that he was dying, I also wanted to die. After we returned home, I hurried off to the drawing room and started to walk around in circles. Do you know what I was mumbling to myself the whole time? *You're still so young. What will you do?* And then I wished that someone would arrive and hand me some implement so that I could kill myself."

Rahel gazed at Henriette. It was so like her to think about herself even in such difficult moments. Her husband was dying from a terrible disease, and she, instead of thinking about his agony, about the pain he was feeling and the sense of missing out that he was certainly experiencing due to the knowledge he would soon be gone from this world, was only thinking about one thing—about Henriette.

"Right now, you have to focus on your dying husband, who will certainly need all the support he can get," she told her, and Henriette wiped away her tears and agreed, as if she had suddenly realized how selfish she was being and how little time they had.

Yet it was hard to judge Henriette. For twenty-four years, she had been living with Markus Herz and knew no life without him. She had transitioned from her father's custody to Markus's. The thought that suddenly, there would be no one to care for her was terrifying. Friedrich, sitting next to her, promised her that he would care for her. Rahel and Dorothea, who had happened to come by the evening before to tend to some matter in Berlin, sat by her side and tried to console her. But these attempts only vexed her. How could they know what she was feeling in her heart? After all, Rahel had never shared her life with a husband and Dorothea was living her life happily with her Schlegel. Were their words hollow? Henriette's pain turned into great anger. Not just at her friends, but at everyone, and this anger gradually took hold of her. She knew that very soon, after his death, they would all return to their homes and to their own affairs and she would be left alone, just as her mother and Fromet, Dorothea's mother, had been. If she had children to support or who could support her, her suffering would certainly be eased. She knew her suffering had only begun.

She wanted them all to go away and leave her with the dead Markus, who was laid out in their bed, waiting to be taken away to his eternal resting place. She wanted them to go away, but knew that at this stage, she had to share her parting from him with many Berliners. Her husband was greatly respected both by his patients and by the students who attended his lectures. Even her friends liked him. Everyone appreciated him and admired him, even if they did not always agree with his opinions, which were too rational and old-fashioned for them. And who was she to keep them from saying goodbye to him?

In the late afternoon hours, Markus was taken to his eternal rest. Henriette stood at some distance from the forming pit. She could not come any closer. The gravesite was reserved exclusively for men until the pit was dug, and the prayers required upon the occasion were recited. If Markus, her doctor, were here now, he would give her some sedative, an inhalant or a numbing injection to dull the tempest intensifying inside her the closer they came to the moment when he would be buried in the pit. But Markus was not there. Without him, there was no one to sweeten the bitterness that had taken hold of her throat, the pain that pinched her innards. Her aching head and her broken heart wanted to leap into the pit so that her exhausted body could rest alongside her husband, and together they would sleep forever. That way, she would not have to feel a thing, would not have to think or worry. Hands closed around her shoulders, pulling her back. Someone held her and stopped her from following through with her plan; she did not even know who it was. She heard wails of heartbreaking sobbing and it took her time to realize the sounds were coming from inside her. From the heart of a helpless girl.

***

"Feign thyself to be a mourner, and put on now mourning apparel, and anoint not thyself with oil, but be as a woman that had a long time mourned for the dead."[27]

During the days of the *shiva*, she did not change her clothes and did not bathe in water and did not brush her hair and did not powder her face, in accordance with Jewish custom. For her, this was a kind of death in itself, but she carried it out as if she had always been a devout, observant daughter of Israel.

During the seven days of mourning, Henriette found the strength within

---

27 2 Samuel 14:2

herself to play host to the visitors arriving to console her, to accept their consolations and hear stories about Markus, stories from patients he had cured and from friends to whom he had been a good listener, and from those whom he had helped to find a specialist or a place to seek some sort of help, and other, similar tales. This was what Dr. Herz had been like in life, and this was what he was like in death.

Throughout these days, Dorothea took care to come and be with her. No one knew about Markus shunning her. Since that day when Markus had asked Henriette to shun Dorothea, something had broken between them. Things were no longer the way they had been. Henriette resented Markus—although she did not say a thing—and felt some emotion toward him shuttering within her heart. To her, he was no longer the man she had married and with whom she had lived all these years. All the good things he had done for her over the years were dwarfed by this single action. In one moment, after instructing her to erase a friendship of years, he had become a different man, a man she did not know. He went on as usual, as if nothing had happened, as if the instruction he gave her was a simple, everyday request, like his occasional requests to buy or order something. He went on as usual and she, too, went on as usual, seemingly, and did not dare talk to him about it again. She continued her correspondence with Dorothea without his knowledge, asking Dorothea to address the letters to Rahel's house. But with every letter that arrived, anger accrued within her regarding his imperious manner, and just as she decided to confront him about it and be insistent, he grew ill. If he had known that Dorothea would take care of Henriette during the days of the *shiva*, helping her deal with all the visitors, he would surely have lost his mind. But he was dead and she was the one making the rules now.

✳✳✳

While Henriette's life as a married woman came to an end, something new began for Rahel.

She was invited to a ball held in one of Berlin's respected houses. She did not know the homeowners, but with balls of this kind, such an acquaintance was not required. She debated whether to go to the ball.

Since returning from Paris, a few months before Markus Herz's death, she had found Berlin boring and its people appeared cold to her. She did not remember Berlin that way. Everyone was still where she had left them a year ago—the same conversations, the same gossip and the same arrogance characterizing people who considered themselves to be at the very heart of culture. Rahel no longer saw the point of her frequent outings and social engagements, and thought that this ball, too, would probably resemble all the previous balls and the ones yet to come, full of pompous, self-important Berliners. And yet she made herself go. The thought of being at home on her own while all her friends were out and about was too much for her.

When she entered the large, elegant house with von Brinckmann, he introduced her to its owner—one of the most important government ministers in Berlin, and the minister insisted that they stand beside him and receive the guests. Rahel knew some of them and was introduced to others by the minister, who seemed pleased with the occasion. Whereas she knew nothing about him, he had actually heard of her and realized she was special. She stood beside him for quite a while until her feet started to ache and she began to drift off to seek somewhere to sit down. At that exact moment, the minister raised his voice as if he were a herald and ceremoniously introduced the next guest, "Don Raphael d'Urquijo, the Spanish attaché in Berlin."

Rahel turned around and all she could see was a pair of black eyes gazing at her. Eyes that were drawn as if in a painting by Velázquez. One moment they were burning and the next they were shining with a glow; one moment they were deep, full of meaning, and the next they were like a dark, bottomless well. The Spaniard, Don Raphael d'Urquijo, had dark skin and coal-black hair just like hers, his entire essence blazing with the mysterious quality of one who was born in a different country and whose speech rolled upon his tongue with a sound that pleased the listener, or at least pleased her.

Don Raphael held her hand, kissing it lightly, and immediately, as was the custom among the French, brought his face to hers and planted three kisses upon her cheeks, as if they were old friends. The scent of masculine perfume wafted to her nose, accompanied by the smell of sweetish, intoxicating sweat and some spice whose source she could not assess. Throughout this time, the Spaniard stared at her with his black eyes and she returned his stare with her own black eyes. He did not speak German and she did not speak Spanish, and so on that evening, broken, halting French was their only common language and would have to suffice.

That night, after the ball ended and Rahel returned home, she sat down immediately to write to Dorothea.

"His rare beauty, the noble charm of his origin, and in addition, the directness and animalistic quality of a child of nature. I must confess, all these affect my soul, which yearns for love every single time. His entire external essence screams 'Basque,' gentility and nobility and a power it is evident he must rein in. And the words, even the most simple of words, contain an affection I cannot resist—although I do not understand a thing in this language." She would have been happy to share all this with Henriette as well, but it seemed inappropriate.

Don Raphael d'Urquijo entered her life like a tempest. "A gift from heaven," she referred to her new affair when describing it to her friends.

She told Dorothea, "God had provided my soul with what nature and circumstances have withheld from me. I knew it, but up to now, I did not know that God has granted me inexpressible happiness, the immense, perfect happiness of revealing this soul."

If she could rid herself of her rigid upbringing, of the strict German manners, of the need to be in full control at every moment of her life, she would wish to be like him. To take off her clothes without order and without one additional thought, to lie down to sleep without thinking of tomorrow's tasks, without planning, without setting the number of pages to be written or the number of pages to be read. She would wish to wake up slowly and linger for a few more moments in bed, to eat her breakfast and her lunch there with her hair undone and her nightgown rumpled. She would wish to make love like he did, forcefully, gently and forcefully, again and again until the bookshelves trembled. She would wish to be a girl dependent upon her beloved, penniless, lacking in knowledge, lacking in personality, to raise her eyes and say amen. She would wish to have him all to herself, to have him inspire jealousy within her, to secure him under lock and key like a prisoner, so that he did not look at anyone else and would not see a thing, so that he would have nothing in his life other than her.

That was what she would wish.

And her Spaniard? From the beginning, he was tortured. His conscience tormented him because of a beloved he had left behind in Spain and he tormented himself because he had betrayed her with his new beloved—Rahel Levin. The more his conscience tortured him, the more he found in Rahel a source of solace and embraces, while also increasingly blaming her. He would curl up inside her like a helpless child, cursing himself for his betrayal and blaming her for it as well. He blamed her for his inability to resist temptation. Blamed her for the fact that since the first moment, he had drowned in her eyes. Blamed her for bewitching him, until now he was helpless in her clutches, like a vessel, like an object. Because of her, he was trapped, he claimed, and despite his love for her, he found ways to taunt her. He repeated these taunts in Spanish, in that rapid, rolling intonation, again and again. Then he would say the same things again in French, more slowly. And Rahel, her heart overflowed; as far as she was concerned these utterances were not taunts but words of love, and she would never ask anything else of this world that gave and took and gave again.

She had received this gift when she thought she would never love again. That was what she felt and believed whole-heartedly. No one would take him from her, not that wretched beloved in Spain and not any higher power, whatever it might be.

30 | 1804

Henriette prepared to return to her usual routine. She knew it would take some time before she could have visitors over and thought that for Markus's sake, she should resume doing so as soon as possible. The literary salon was their shared venture, something they had started together and that had been held in their home for a long time. She had to exhibit strength, which meant carrying on. She also knew that deep inside, she needed her salon like oxygen. She needed her friends' admiration, admiration she attained by playing the host in the living room of her home as if it were a stage. She needed that attention in order to keep going, in order to feel loved, in order to live.

For twenty-four years, Henriette and Markus had lived together and throughout that time, he took care of her as if she were still the girl he first met at his friend and teacher Dr. de Lemos's home. He took care of her as if he were her father, provided her every need and fulfilled her every whim. And as for her, all she had to do was admire his character, as she had done since their wedding day. She had thought the only pain she would know since the day he departed would be the pain of missing him, and thought that pain would certainly be joined by the pain of loneliness, as she had been left on her own. Therefore, she carefully prepared for that loneliness. She read books and journals and articles and visited her close friends and also invited them for afternoon tea. She wrote letters and replied to the letters she got and continued to dedicate significant time to nurturing her appearance, to the lace dresses and to visiting her friend the barber, and to tending to her nails and to visiting her usual seamstress to view the latest fabrics and ribbons that had arrived. For a handful of moments, these things did indeed fill her time and thoughts, but she never imagined there would be another, unbearable pain with which she would have to cope.

Now she sat with Simon Veit, and their conversation left her stunned and helpless. She had invited him over in order to consult with him about the next stage of her new life, as she had understood that now there would be no one to do things for her and realized she had to grow up and pick up the reins herself. She opened her and Markus's accounting books to him, meticulously written in round, clear handwriting that matched her husband's exacting nature, and asked him to take a look at what she did not understand at all. Simon Veit immersed himself in the pages, conducting calculations, and throughout this time, Henriette sat in her new dress across from him and still had no idea.

"There is no money."

Simon did not know how to reveal to her what he had found in the books, but decided to say it in the only way she could understand: directly. These words were enough to cause her world, which was already shaky, to collapse.

There had been nothing she asked of her husband that she did not receive. Not a single fruit had been missing from their table, there had not been a single sweet or other food item they had had to do without. There was not a play they had not seen or an opera they had missed and there was not a single dress she wanted that had not been sewn for her or a single jewel that caught her eye that she did not receive. These now rested in an elegant box on her night table, testifying to all that had been lost.

"Everything that came in, went out."

There was no need for further explanations. Henriette felt as if Markus had died a second time. Once again, the heaviness she had known from the day of the funeral settled within her belly, joined by a sensation as if something was wrapping itself around her neck, like a vice clamping down on her and, in a moment, she would be unable to breathe. It was unadulterated fear.

She was no longer anyone's girl. She did not belong to her father, who had turned to ashes and dust a long time ago, or to a husband whose remains were surely being consumed by worms. She was a woman who was no longer young, and in the absence of a man to support her, she had to support herself, as well as her widowed mother, who had been living in her home even when Markus was still alive, and her sister, for whom a match had yet to be found. And this entire burden was weighing down on her slender shoulders.

Schleiermacher suggested that she accept a government position. He was willing to use his connections to ensure it would happen. But both of them knew that for such a position, which might indeed provide Henriette with financial stability, she would have to change her name and convert to Christianity. Jews were not allowed to hold government positions and this edict could not be bypassed.

"This might be an opportunity for you." Schleiermacher was trying to convince her to convert. This was not the first time, although since Markus had passed away, he had let the matter go to some extent as he did not want to add any more pressure to what she was already experiencing after being widowed. But now he found the chance to resume his attempts, and she, too, had much to gain from proceeding. Henriette refused. Even if she tried to think about it logically or to imagine herself taking that step, her mother's image rose before her eyes. She knew her mother would be unable to bear it if she converted and Henriette, in turn, did not wish to cause her further sorrow. After all, their urn of sorrow was already full, even overflowing.

***

Dorothea, in contrast, was already on the other side. She no longer had to debate, having already taken action. On April 6 of the previous year, she had been baptized. This allowed her to marry, on the very same day, the man within whose soul her own soul had become entwined, in seams that could not be undone, despite her family's objections.

Some time after her baptism, Dorothea wrote in her diary, *"The moment I took on the holy baptism, my father's image was revealed to me."* However, even her father could no longer stop her.

It did not take long before the Protestant religion into which she was baptized lost the calm, peaceful effect it had had on her for a while, and the Romantic group to which she and Schlegel belonged was progressing consistently in the direction of Catholicism, as did Schlegel's worldview. Nearly all their friends were already Catholic, particularly the ones to whom they were close, such as the brothers Sulpiz and Melchior Boiserée, natives of Cologne, who stayed in their home and left a great impression on both of them. Dorothea did keep up her friendship with Rahel and Henriette, but her life was in Paris, and the distance from Berlin was immense, and not just because of the many kilometers. Her life was here, alongside Schlegel and their new friends, who constantly discussed the connection between the Middle Ages and Catholicism. It was the old religion, the "true" one, all ceremony and grandeur, with a classicism that corresponded well with the arts. They viewed Protestantism as the root of all evil in the world, a flattening of ancient, medieval Christianity, where literature, art, architecture and music all began to develop.

The connection to this deep primal quality affected her. It was true that she was now a married, respectable Protestant, as she had strived to be, and yet she and her husband still felt that something was missing in their lives. The Catholicism that Dorothea had once condemned, the Catholicism resembling the Judaism she so despised, now no longer seemed as despicable to them as it once had. Perhaps this was what they had been missing.

Sulpiz and Melchior urged them to come live beside them in Cologne and the two of them packed up their possessions and returned to their homeland along with Dorothea's young son. They were now a couple, a family living a decent Christian life in Germany.

***

The nineteenth century did not begin well for Jews. Wilhelm Grattenauer, a German lawyer, published a treatise that became so popular that it was printed again and again, in which he warned against the Jewish threat in Germany.

"The nature and essence of Judaism do not benefit the state's goals and the wellbeing of its residents; they are very dangerous."

He accused wealthy Jews of carelessly spending their fortune on frivolous pleasures instead of helping their Jewish brothers and sisters whose circumstances were more lowly. And although he condemned them for this fact, he hoped that such reckless spending would cause them to lose their fortune and their social status. With regard to women such as Rahel, he stated, *"Not only have their attempts to improve themselves failed to cohere into a genteel style, but their attitude toward culture is opportunistic. They wish to control high culture, with one goal only—to boast to men of this fact… Whether in Paris or in Berlin or in Vienna, Jewish women could not learn what proper manners are even if they keep company with princesses and counts and as many gentlemen as they wish. Wealth, culture, influential friends—none of these can erase the stench of Judaism."*

Rahel had heard plenty of racist, misanthropic denigrations in her life, but this sort of folly was something new. Although she tried to distance herself from her Judaism, to oppose it and to turn her back upon it, these statements still affected her.

The words actually hurt her. She was used to the old variety of anti-Semitism, and now the hatred was gradually transforming.

And despite all this, her attic was full of guests who came and went and enjoyed her company and she went out and spent time with her friends and wrote them letters and received letters in return and the life she loved went on, despite her Judaism.

If she had known that von Brinckmann, her closest friend, had publicly quoted Grattenauer, her heart would have broken within her. He knew how important he was to her; after all, she had once told him, "If I lost you, I would lose a significant part of myself, as you know a side of me that no one else knows and that side must be acknowledged. Otherwise, it is dead." But she did not know he was voicing such opinions and in any case, she was now focused on her Spanish affair and all the rest, important though it might be, was relegated to the background.

31 | 1804

"Does one who trusts love consider it to be life?"

— Goethe

Rahel wanted to love d'Urquijo the way he loved her: loudly. She had never experienced such an emotional tempest. No one had ever claimed her with wild passion like he did. And he had only one request in return for his love—to have her all to himself.

The liaison with Rahel, which began as a betrayal of his Spanish beloved, now became a consummate affair. His beloved parted from him easily. Now, without the compunctions he had initially experienced, their relationship seemed perfect to Rahel.

Since that fatal encounter in the minister's house, his body still thrilled her just as much as it had during their first night, as did the sound of his language and his blazing, fiery eyes. Every part of him thrilled her, from his toes to the crown of his head. And the moment his foot stepped upon her threshold, she forgot herself. She allowed herself to dwell amidst his ardent kisses and his darting tongue, amidst his yelling and complaints, allowing him to mold her for himself. Anything he asked, anything he said, she did. As if she was living for his love. Something changed within her. She was no longer the Rahel of self-improvement and study, not that knowledgeable, witty being, one whose mind was full of Kant and Lessing and Goethe and Fichte. Now she was d'Urquijo's Rahel.

When he arrived, the world swayed, as if a storm had come to the doorway with him, beginning to swirl the air, threatening to pick up everything in the room along with it on a ferocious spiral. He paced back and forth, waving his hands and speaking in a high voice, telling her about an argument he had, or a fight, or about someone who had angered him, and his mouth would contract, as did his forehead, two creases appearing upon it. All Rahel wanted at the moment was to touch them; perhaps that way, she could silence the snarling beast within him, a beast she loved. But he persisted and his stories repeated themselves again and again. She already knew it did not matter what she said; he would not listen anyway. She already realized he did not possess that capability and forgave him for it, as in her eyes, he was like someone who could not be tamed.

In moments of harmony, a peace descended upon them, almost like religious sanctity. Then she wished to live that way forever, bidding farewell to her world and to any other world that was external to them. Then the storm within him would ease somewhat as well. He laid his head in her lap, the way he did during their first days as a couple, and Rahel would stroke his black, tangled hair gently and softly. If she asked to read him something, he refused, and if she wanted to tell him about something that had taken place between her friends, he covered his ears, and when she wanted to express her opinion about something he said, he refused to hear it. He wanted her solely for himself, to have her stroke and pamper and dedicate all her time to him. To be present for him. Her entire being for him.

***

D'Urquijo's fits of jealousy were already a routine matter. He accused her of conducting relationships behind his back and of preferring her many friends to him. He accused her of spending her time reading and writing instead of dedicating her full attention to the man she claimed to love so much. She tried to convince him that this was not true, but all her attempts at persuasion merely fueled his rage and increased his anger and shouting.

"It's the Spanish way of loving," he claimed to her when she tried to explain to him that there were other paths in love. But he only added that her way was "chilly." Her honeyed letters and her words of love were not enough for him. He needed to feel her at every single moment. "When you're with me, I need to receive your full attention and if I don't, I cannot love you."

"I wish I was like one of the Spanish girls, wild and full of passion. The kind who yells and kicks and curses. Then I would fulfill all his expectations," she wrote to David Veit, and he replied gently and with no reproach, unlike his usual custom.

"You are who you are and as I understand, he is insane and jealous by nature. This jealousy will lead you into the darkness, and you would be better off ridding yourself of it and of him as soon as possible."

"Loyalty is an issue, of course; it is a state of love. Without a spirit of trust, one cannot love at all—cannot live, I might say."

And although she understood what David Veit was telling her, she was not ready. She still saw in her beloved all that had been in him on that day when his black eyes enflamed her heart. Her love for him had not diminished since that day, and might even have increased. When he passed the threshold of her home and came inside, her heart skipped a beat and her body tensed. She sought the touch of his hand and his caresses and wild kisses, her body against her own and his breaths, which smelled of tobacco as well as an exotic spice she could not name.

Friedrich von Gentz, who, for a short period had been more than a friend, also told her honestly, after meeting the lover whose traits she had praised and extoled as sublime, "Your love, I thought it was charming, magical, divine. But between the love and the object at which it is directed exists, to my taste, a boundless chasm. I constantly judged him kindly and with goodwill, but I believe there is no particular depth to his character. He always slides complacently down to the mundane, regular course of life, and based on what I saw, there is no singular point in him that allows me to guess that he is capable of enflaming your passion. D'Urquijo seems to me like a very ordinary man."

Rahel responded to this assessment with great anger, accusing him of being motivated purely by jealousy.

The next morning, she packed her things and moved to the countryside, far from her many friends, far from the theater and the opera and the cafés, far from the attic at 54 Jägerstrasse, to a place where she could exist solely for his sake. Although her friends were important and precious to her, D'Urquijo surpassed them all. She was willing to suffer the loneliness that had once so scared her and give up the major achievement of her life—the salon—in order to win his love. Now she took advantage of the great amount of time at her disposal to read and write letters, and in between, she endlessly missed her beloved, whose comings and goings she could never anticipate.

Rahel was not the type of person to give up. She had been a fighter ever since the day she was placed in a wooden box and expected to relinquish her soul to the Creator. She had not done so and refused to do so now as well, and all that she asked of her Spanish beloved was to love her in his own way and allow her to love him in her own way.

"I was made to love you and that's all. The miracle I seek is that you love me! Yes, I believe in it but this is not a lot. Do not separate intelligence from emotion," she begged him. "I am simple to the point of stupidity, while you attribute me with behaviors with which I have nothing to do. And what control do I have over someone wishing to hold my hand?"

Her friends called him "the second Finckenstein." However, other than the love the two men withheld from her, there was no connection whatsoever between him and Finckenstein. "Innocent as an ax that chops off the heads of wonderful men was the Spaniard, and there was not an iota of decency or education in him of the type possessed by the count," they said. There were also whispers exchanged behind her back about his Spanish beloved having gotten rid of him easily, as if he were an old garment, about him being generally despised and even keeping a simple girl in one of the alleyways of Berlin. These whispers did not reach Rahel's ears; she was detached and isolated and tried not to have many guests over. One of the many virtues of her life in the country was the fact that gossip did not reach her. That buzz from the cultured Berliners, who, even more than they liked to discuss a new poem or a groundbreaking play or an opera they had watched, liked to talk about their friends, serving up these friends and their lives and ripping them to shreds with revolting sanctimony. Instead of the venom spread by those who considered themselves her friends, and who had until recently inhabited her drawing room, she had flowers and birds. Fruit trees and the scent of the grass trampled under her feet as she paced in the yard of her house, back and forth, back and forth.

***

The little money Henriette had left was gradually dissipating like her doctor. The life she had lived thus far contained nothing that could have prepared her for what was coming. Yet, despite it all, she wished to retain control of her life, bracing herself and deciding to take her fate into her own hands, although she had still not managed to get anything from the Berlin Widows' Fund.

In the meantime, the rumors spread everywhere, and now there was something new to gossip about. Her friend Ludwig Börne sent her an urgent letter when he was staying in Halle in order to complete his studies:

"*Recently, Mrs. Reille told me that you were the subject of talk at a social gathering and were said to be living in a palace in Berlin, with a princess, a duchess or even a queen.*"

"*I know most of the ordinary people would be very pleased if I, unhappy with the forced austerity in my life, would become dependent upon them,*" Henriette replied.

If she had an unruly temperament, she would have burst out in vocal laughter and would not have stopped until tears burst from her eyes. But, as that was not her nature, she merely smiled and briefly contemplated the fact that her life, of which nothing was left, still inspired so much interest, and outside of Berlin, no less.

"I do not live in a palace, dear Ludwig, but in a small house, and I have no special connections with any princess, beyond the fact that I teach English to the young princess of Courland in return for financial remuneration."

She nearly signed the letter, but after thinking about it some more, she decided to add some praise for her employers. *"The duchess herself, as well as the princes and princesses who are a part of her household and family, treat me with great respect, and even deign to sit and eat at one table with a bourgeois woman—a Jewish woman."*

After all, he would surely go and disclose the contents of the letter at one of those social gatherings, and if he did, it would be better if they all knew she was respected and that her employers were respected as well. Perhaps this would contribute, directly or indirectly, to her livelihood, although she did not really believe it.

Several days later, she received a visit from an old friend, Count Alexander von Dohna. They had known each other back in the days when they were both members of their closed secret society—the Virtue Society, where they exchanged letters suffused with secrets, opinions and emotions. Since the society had fallen apart, Henriette had watched von Dohna climb the professional and social ladder until he became one of the most prominent people in Berlin, and for this, she was proud of him. She was also proud of herself for the fact that they remained good friends. For some time now, he had been Prussia's minister of the interior, and now he stood in her drawing room, tall, broad shouldered and meticulously dressed. He had sent her a brief letter that morning.

"I will arrive between six and seven. No need for any special preparations."

Von Dohna had not visited her since Markus's funeral, and she had no complaints about this as she knew he was busy and concerned with the matter of Prussia, which was gradually changing. He entered carrying a basket full of all manners of bounty, which both embarrassed and pleased her. Although she had not discussed her private affairs with anyone other than Schleiermacher, who had become her confidante, the rumors of her financial situation had spread, making their way to Count von Dohna as well.

They sat in the yard, illuminated by twilight. Henriette wore a pale yellow dress with an embroidered hem, her coal-black hair tied back with lace ribbons in the same hue. Von Dohna was clad in his elegant suit, its buttons shining, his white shirt gleaming and prominent under his opulent velvet jacket.

Alexander opened his mouth and before he could say a word, cleared his throat as a light flush covered his face.

"I know it has not been long since you were widowed and that sorrow still dwells in your home." Henriette nodded in agreement, as if confirming his statement, and von Dohna continued. "You are a handsome, vibrant woman and should live pleasantly and fearlessly. I am a wealthy man, as you know, and can provide you with all the convenience you will need."

Now Henriette already realized where things were heading and although she felt a certain excitement, she kept silent, waiting for him to conclude his speech while continuously holding a handkerchief and worrying at its edges.

"What I want, Henriette. What I desire. What I am trying to say is…" He could not utter the words. Across from her sat a man who had roamed the world, met high-ranking, important people, a man respected and esteemed by all, and here he was, trying to say something simple, and unable to dislodge the words from his mouth.

Henriette remembered her marriage to Markus. Things had been done so differently then. Everything had been agreed upon in advance and had come to her as a done deal. And despite this, she had found pleasure in her life with him, and he had made all her wishes come true. Her friend von Dohna, whom she admired, would also surely be able to make her wishes come true, and her life could return to being easy and comfortable as it had been thus far. He was a respected citizen of Berlin. He was very handsome and younger than her. If she married him, she would be guaranteed a rich, adventurous social life.

However, despite intensely missing Markus and the life she once had, there was something liberating about freedom, about the independence enforced upon her, about the opportunity to decide for herself. She could still taste the bitter flavor of Markus's instruction to relinquish her good friend, and it served as a warning sign of what marriage might bring about for her, no matter how good it was. She was certain that if Markus were still alive, they would certainly go through many more clashes for that reason. It was true that her financial situation left much to be desired, but she considered Dorothea, whose standard of living had declined and yet who had gained so much. Primarily, she had gained herself, but had also won the passionate love she always believed she deserved. Perhaps such a love was also waiting for her down the road, and although that was not her main focus, she wanted to leave the door open.

Now, despite the proposal that had surprised her and somewhat unsettled her equanimity, she managed to come to her senses and realized that money, convenience and a respectable status were all things she had already possessed, but independence and passionate love were not. As much as she appreciated von Dohna, she had never thought of him as someone with whom she could tumble into bed, someone who would see her nude or touch her. They had been friends for so many years that she could not imagine a different sort of relationship between them. And yet despite all the reasons she gave herself for refusing his proposal, the last thing she wanted was to quarrel with a powerful man like him. She knew that in the future, she would certainly need him to use his connections on her behalf and that it was important to ensure he stayed on her side. Furthermore, she knew how a man who was hurt tended to respond. After all, she had often had to reject besotted suitors and had frequently been subject to the harshest insults precisely from those who claimed to love her. The line between love and hate was very thin, and she had to be very careful in what she said to a friend who had her best interest at heart and had surely planned his proposal for so long that his excitement was preventing him from uttering it.

"I appreciate you greatly, my dear friend," she told von Dohna. "There are not many whom I esteem. You are one of the only ones and I'm sure you know it, and nevertheless, I am forced to decline your very flattering proposal."

He did not kneel, in accordance with the custom that was becoming prevalent among the young people within Berlin's high society, and therefore, was spared the indignity. He simply sat in the armchair across from her and listened.

"You know that in order to marry you, I would first have to be baptized, and that I cannot do."

Von Dohna could not oppose such a claim and neither could he be angry at her. She had been born to the religion of Moses while he had been born to that of Christ, and these days, in Berlin, mixed marriages were strictly prohibited. And despite all his privileges as a member of the ruling class, even he could not violate that law.

Henriette had indeed flirted with the idea of converting, but had gone no further, and also knew she could not do so to her mother. Furthermore, she knew it was the only way not to evoke his animosity. Who could tell—she might have need of his connections in the future.

32 | 1804

"From the bottom of my heart, I despise this Enlightenment of our age. Nothing good, nothing good has yet to emerge from it. I prefer Catholicism simply because it is so ancient. Anything new is worthless."

So wrote Dorothea in her diary a short time after the couple returned to Germany. They now lived in the city of Cologne, in the shadow of its fabulous cathedral, the immense edifice whose construction began in 1248 and continued for over five-hundred years. Now, following the revival of Romantic nostalgia, there was talk of the work being completed soon, and Dorothea, who had fallen in love with the cathedral, found herself highly curious about the next stages of its construction.

She liked life in Cologne. She had many friends there who welcomed her and considered her a boon companion, and she valued them greatly, as she found herself alone on many days while Schlegel rambled about, busy with his own affairs. For some time now, she had noticed that although she still loved him and sought his company, something in their relationship had changed. And when she delved deeper into herself again and again in order to figure it out, she realized he was no longer her idol, and in a single moment, it seemed as if a new hollow gaped within her.

Up to that point, she had invested her entire being in him, even enmeshing herself with him. But now, confronted with this realization, she sought new meaning and justification for her life. She feared a return to those days in her life with Veit that were full of nothing and nullity, and the more she looked for direction, the more she found herself attracted to the cathedral in whose shadow she dwelled constantly. It contained an entire world that had left its marks and imprinted its impressions upon it. The art adorning the site allowed visitors to see the stories of creation with their own eyes. The cathedral projected the gravity of one to which generations upon generations had come and gone. The eternal quality of one who had watched wars break out and cease and remained standing, stable and proud, with its sharpened turrets soaring into the sky, with its arcing facades and its spires, majesty and grandeur comprised entirely of aesthetic worship. Primarily, she was won over by the sensation that came upon her as she faced the ancient Gothic architecture. She, Dorothea, so puny and unimportant, and the large, elegant cathedral. Her own insignificance called out to her from every corner and from that insignificance, she gradually and utterly gave herself over to religion and to the Christian faith. All that she deemed bourgeois, frivolous, Jewish, she now disdained. Her essence became an utter contrast to the Age of Enlightenment, with its presumptuous reliance on reason, and as she was seeking justification for her life, she sought an authority that would show her the way, that would disperse the despair of loneliness that threatened her and frightened her so much.

Before too long, Dorothea began to attend every Sunday mass. Excited and dressed up, she left for her cathedral, eager to hear the pastor's sermon. Mass, she had learned, was one of the sacraments of the Catholic Church, and as she sat there on the wooden pew, she could feel the invisible grace touch her, settling into her body each time anew. And every Sunday, after concluding his sermon, the pastor raised the sacramental bread and the goblet of wine in front of his parishioners, and these became the body and blood of Christ. When the pastor sipped a bit, the parishioners knew it was a sign to line up quietly and wait, one by one, to receive the wafer—the host. Dorothea, who took care to arrive at the cathedral a bit early every time in order to secure a seat close by, also stood in line, waiting and knowing she was among the first to receive grace. She could have sworn that the moment the wafer touched her tongue, something took place in her body and a sacred peace filled her.

"Take, eat; this is my body... Drink ye all of it; For this is my blood of the new testament, which is shed for many for the remission of sins,"[28] the priest said, and all her sins were forgiven and disappeared and peace descended upon her. She knew that if this peace left her, she would return to the cathedral on the coming Sunday, and that peace would return to her once more.

Her life was taking place according to a predetermined design. She was now sure of it. The rift with Veit and her illegal love for Schlegel were what had led her into the fold of the Church. And as for mass, it had settled into the hollow that had gaped inside her and had now taken the place of the genius of her beloved Friedrich Schlegel. Dorothea had invested her all in Schlegel. She had alienated herself from her family and from her friends. She had gained an entire world that had filled her for a while, a world in which there was room for her to develop and reach achievements she had never thought she would reach, a world in which she loved intensely and was equally loved, and all the intensity she had felt in previous years had weakened and become routine, mundane, something to which she had gotten used and which no longer thrilled her as it once did. Her writing had become work she had to do, which did not always align with what she wanted. And as for Schlegel, although she still considered him to be talented, once she got to know him in depth, including his laziness and fears and small infidelities and his restlessness, he no longer seemed like a genius to her. Perhaps acknowledging that life was mostly gray, despite all the sparks, was what had caused a chasm of meaninglessness to gape open inside her. Dorothea realized she could not live her life that way, and what she found in the cathedral filled her more than she could have hoped. She now dedicated her entire being to mass, and in her diary, she wrote:

"Do I have faith within me? I do not dare assert that yet, but I know I do have honest faith in faith." She realized that without faith, the world to her was a wasteland and no more.

***

---

28 Matthew 26: 26-28

Weeks passed from the time Rahel left Berlin until she visited the city once more. On a pleasant, spring-like evening, when the air outside was exactly warm enough, she strolled hand-in-hand with her Spanish lover in the Tiergarten, after they had set a time to meet following more than two weeks in which they had not seen each other. Two weeks that seemed like an eternity to her.

Her spirits were high and his mood seemed elevated as well, because of something he did not tell her. He wanted her to coerce him and entreat him again and again until he had no choice. Perhaps if she did, he would tell her about the sweaty nights of love with his new beloved, who greeted him with laughter each time he came to see her, effaced herself for his sake and was entirely his the whole time they were together. He would tell her that everything he had not found in her, he found in this simple woman who had no expectations from life other than the anticipation that he come to her and tell her his interesting stories and shake up her world. He would tell Rahel that this uneducated woman did not try to change him and reproach him or tell him how he should love her and how he should behave with her. He would say that with her, he could yell and curse and she did not hold all that against him. It had been some time since he last saw Rahel, and time was not in her favor regarding the gauge of D'Urquijo's love; he sought thrills and storms, and despite all that, he was still unwilling to give her up.

They walked hand-in-hand like a pair of lovers. An elderly couple and their young grandson, holding a toy in his hand, passed by them. And now came a noisy group of boys and a large family that reminded her of the Mendelssohns of her childhood. Rahel pleasurably took in the sights and sounds. They reminded her why she loved Berlin so much. Now a young damsel passed by across from them, her beauty unusually pleasing.

"Look, so much beauty," Rahel said, wishing to direct her beloved's attention. "I have to meet this young woman and know who she is."

"And what about the one by your side?" D'Urquijo suddenly raised his voice senselessly. "If you found the will to invest the same energy in the one by your side, things would look different."

Rahel tried to shush him with smiles and by pointing out that they were in the middle of the park, but this seemed only to further inflame his already turbulent spirit.

"Who is this stranger to you? And why do you need to know more people? Am I not enough for you? You constantly seek to know more and more people, to consort with your friends again and again when I am here, with you."

Rahel sighed and said nothing. She knew that ultimately, the rage would subside, as in all his other outbursts, and knew that, as always, she would manage to appease him somehow. But now, with the crowd around them, looks were directed at them and words were whispered among the spectators, and she even saw an impolite finger pointed at them. And the sense of insult was already climbing up, up from her stomach and soon she would be unable to control it. A sharp pain pierced her throat and something prickly settled there, searing and burning and bitter.

All she could do at that moment was take in air. And so, slowly, she filled her lungs in an attempt to clear her mind of some discordant voice that was digging in, trying to hush it. And now she felt the tears, threatening to erupt at any moment, and she did her best to hold them back as well, since what else did she have left? This, and nothing else. But she could not silence the sighs rising from her, and these served as fuel for D'Urquijo, feeding the thing that was perpetually burning within him.

If there was one thing he hated about her, it was her Germanic restraint, and he knew she could not uproot it even if she tried as hard as she could. If only she would yell or erupt at him or even hit him, here, in front of everyone. Then he would know that she had passion and turbulence in her, however hidden they might be. But the more he abused her, the more she shrunk back, the more quiet she was, the more she surrendered. All of this was the exact opposite of why he had fallen in love with her in the first place. He saw her as a rebellious woman, a breaker of boundaries, brave, but when faced with him, her strength betrayed her. Or so he felt. She evoked in him only an increasing desire to hurt her.

"Von Finckenstein treated you badly, too. You should be used to it by now." He took advantage of her open heart and the fact that, right from the start, she had revealed all her secrets to him, in order to now use them against her, like a thief. For several moments, all the voices within her grew silent and the stabbing disappeared, and it seemed as if it were only the two of them in the world, and a peace of sorts engulfed her, a peace whose origin she did not know.

"If those words were said on a stage, the audience would be appalled and burst into tears," she said with detachment.

"That's true." He grew silent for several moments, then added, "But this should free you and show you we cannot be together."

Many times, he had told her he loved her but did not respect her, and she did not listen. He accused her again and again of being unfaithful to him and she wanted to prove that he was wrong. But only now, when the two of them stood among people's gazes, did she understand that he did not love her. Only now could she release her grip on him.

She was brave. Braver than others. They were afraid to be happy. Afraid to follow their happiness all the way while she, when staying was called for, she stayed, held on, fought. She gave herself over to love completely, as she gave herself over to everything in her life, as she gave herself over to books, as she gave herself over to her friends. But when it was time to go, she went. And Rahel knew the time had come. She had to go. She would now give herself over to the grief inherent in this parting of ways and would not look back.

PART THREE

"Upon life's labyrinthine path once more
Is heard the sigh, and grief revives anew;
The friends are told, who, in their hour of pride,
Deceived by fortune, vanished from my side."

— Goethe[29]

---

29 From "Dedication," in *The Poems of Goethe*, translated by Edgar Alfred Bowring. https://www.gutenberg.org/cache/epub/1287/pg1287.html

33 | 1806

On October 24, Rahel made an appointment to meet the seamstress at her home, at the intersection of Friedrichstrasse and Krausenstrasse. They had set the meeting for eleven a.m. and precisely on time, she knocked on Rahel's door. A moment after the door closed behind her, George, the seamstress's nine-year-old son, entered the house, highly animated, and pointed outside.

Rahel and his mother hurried to the doorway and witnessed a scene that seemed to have been taken straight from the theater stage. About fifty meters away, a French soldier was mounted on his horse. His face was tan, he was wearing a sable coat, and a pipe was thrust in his mouth. Rahel, who had already visited France several times, was accustomed to the sight of French soldiers, but her friend the seamstress and her young son, who had apparently never left Berlin, were thrilled by the sight and even more thrilled by the fact that the soldier's face bore a friendly smile and his lips were uttering a greeting. The three of them thus lingered on the street, which was gradually filling with neighbors and passersby, all of them waiting to see what the French conqueror, who seemed to have arrived all alone on his horse, had to say.

Before too long, sounds of loud trumpets echoed down the street. Young George covered his ears with his hands in order to shield himself from the volume of the sound produced by the trumpets, which was still increasing. Suddenly, the soldier turned and disappeared. It was obvious that something was about to take place, but this caused no concern. The French smile of the soldier, who did not look threatening, made it clear to the citizens standing around on the streets that Napoleon's soldiers were not about to slaughter them. Nevertheless, a chill ran down Rahel's spine. Gradually, more and more soldiers appeared, a whole battalion wearing royal red passing by them and striding with pride after the trumpeters, who were riding horses. All of them wore shiny clothes and sported French haircuts that were very different from those of the Prussian soldiers. They marched with their head held high, fading away at the end of Leipziger Strasse.

The next day, Rahel stayed home. She heard that throngs of Berliners were flooding Halle Bridge in order to watch the French Army officially enter Berlin. She, who had never liked such mass gatherings, preferred to stay home. She did not want to be a part of the crowded Berliner horde, even if it was a historical day and even if she herself secretly welcomed the newcomers and was excited by the bounty brought along by a nation she had always liked. She wished that the revolution taking place in France would affect Germany as well, that the old order would collapse, to be replaced by a new order under which she would have the same rights as her Christian friends in the bourgeoisie, the aristocracy, the upper class, and in general. However, despite her excitement, she preferred to be on her own now, relying on her brother Ludwig, who had chosen to spend that day with the masses on the bridge, to tell her in detail about all that would take place.

The French soldiers were not wearing the braided powdered wigs that the Prussian soldiers wore on their heads. Someone in the crowd on the bridge joked that it was probably those clumsy wigs that had brought about the Prussians' defeat. This witticism did not land well and one of the spectators in the crowd began to beat the jokester, soon joined by several others. But the greatest surprise was undoubtedly the uniform, which stood in stark contrast to the elegant blue of the Prussian fighters.

"Napoleon's men sported dirty uniforms and torn linen trousers," Ludwig told Rahel, who, a day earlier, had seen orderly, well-dressed soldiers. She could not envision the image he was describing.

"This is one of the oddest days I've ever experienced," Ludwig added, "and not just because of the filthy uniforms, but because of all their unbearable behavior. As if they had no discipline."

Rahel smiled. She knew the French and they were an utter contrast to the Germans living beside her. Yet Ludwig, too, had been to Paris, and therefore she marveled at his great surprise.

"One of the soldiers fed a filthy dog with a piece of bread impaled on the end of his bayonet, and a metal spoon dangled from a string tied to his red hat."

"Savages." Rahel laughed, but Ludwig did not find it funny in the slightest.

"It seems impossible that these scrawny men defeated our proud warriors," he said. "And judging by the crowd on the bridge, the first day of this humiliating occupation was full of enthusiasm."

Rahel still could not see things the way he did. To her, there was nothing humiliating about the French occupation.

***

When rumors of Napoleon approaching Berlin first began to spread, Rahel noticed that every evening, someone was missing from her attic salon. Her friends disappeared without a letter or an explanation regarding the reason for their absence, and they did not return the next evening, either. Gradually, the gatherings in her home emptied out until they became sparse, reminding her of her earliest days. However, at that time, she had been imbued with hope, while now she felt that it was the end of an era. After October 27, precisely the day on which Napoleon entered the city on his horse through the Brandenburg Gate, Rahel sent letters to all her friends informing them that she would no longer host gatherings in her home. She did not say a thing that was not already obvious to everyone, merely preempting the inevitable, thus holding on to the bit of self-respect she still retained.

Everything grew silent. The salon was still. No one came or went, as if it had all been forgotten, as if it had never happened. As if it was all a pleasant dream to be recalled fondly until it dispersed and disappeared. No more high-spirited gatherings, no more attending plays or concerts together, no more groups united around Romanticism. Now there were other matters, such as, for example, The German-Christian Club. Rahel was convinced that its rules had been created specifically in order to exclude her, her friends and other Jewish women from the gatherings, so that they would not take part in the new intellectual discourse, so that they would not sully the holy-of-holies of the reviving German nation. She heard that Friedrich von Gentz and Fichte, whom she so admired, as well as many others, frequently attended the club, which met at a tavern, pampering their stomachs with fine Berlin beer. No more simple tea in an attic. The old days were no more.

The German-Christian Club was not the only place she was not invited. Her many friends distanced themselves from her. The fact that she was just as much of a patriot as they were did her no good, and the fact that she loathed her Judaism almost as much as they did was no help either, not to mention the fact that her intellectual knowledge was much broader than most of theirs. The very fact that she was a woman, and Jewish as well, was enough for them. Even if they had allowed her to take part in those gatherings, what good would it have done? She would have been forced to hear about the moral corruption of the Jews, about their bodily odors, about their hereditary diseases and their ignorance. She would have been forced to join a chorus of German folk songs and witness all their smugness and self-satisfaction, as well as their hatred and malice toward all that was not purely German.

Later, she would write in her diary, *"Our ship went down in the year 1806. The same ship that contained the finest pleasures, the best things in life."*

***

From the day that French soldier entered Berlin on his horse, an idea had sprouted within Rahel—that this might be the beginning of a Europe that would be united and whole for everyone. Napoleon, who brought the message of freedom, effortlessly conquered more and more countries, and soon he would establish one big, united Europe, with equal rights for every citizen, male and female. She had never dedicated much time to politics. But now, for the first time in her life, politics imbued her with the hope that Europe would embrace her as an equal and would be for her what Prussia had never been—a homeland, a place where her ancient origins were of interest to no one.

She began to study French with the help of her new friend, Henri Campan, a clerk in the occupying French force, who did not dwell at all on the question of her origin. She had some familiarity with the language, could read and write a little, speak a little, and yet she wanted to know more. Campan taught her the language that represented Europeanism to her, and in return, she introduced him to the work of Schelgel, Goethe, and other German poets and writers.

"Napoleon has won and I have joined the victor," she said. She was swept up in the hope for complete equality, for the possibility of social reform that would save her from the inferiority of her origin. In her mind, she envisioned a Germany that would be as free of class as France and its liberated citizens.

When her brother Markus heard what she had said, he mocked her. "For quite a while, you lived under the patronage of one great personage and now you are moving on to the next one." He meant to call out her naïveté, to show her that she tended to fill up with false hopes inspired by leaders who never benefited her. Frederick the Great, the leader of Prussia, had not granted the Jews any rights, but she had never spoken against him. She had always thought the fault lay with the Jews themselves, due to the way they separated themselves from the German people, as well as additional reasons that were a part of their nature. Now she saw Napoleon as a great savior. This new loyalty struck Markus as premature, not to mention excessive.

Ludwig, too, sat her down for a conversation one evening. "Wake up," he said to her. He was not angry, but rather concerned. He wanted her to see reality as it actually was, before it was too late. Unlike her, he was realistic in his view of German resistance to the occupation and the hope for change that would beget a gradually strengthening nationalism.

"The days when you could say all that is in your heart are gone. Look around you. Where have all your friends gone? The aristocrats, the poets, the writers? All the ones who are not Jewish? Where has von Gentz, who worshipped the ground you walked on, disappeared to?"

Rahel knew they were right, but she was so busy with the loneliness enforced upon her, with her self-pity, so busy hating the history she came from and admiring the new conqueror, that she imagined all his subjects as equal, and did not see things as they really were.

Friedrich von Gentz, who had been a part of her life, who admired her mind, her spirit, all of her, he who had spent time at her gatherings and later in her bed as well, was now a regular visitor of the Supper Club, founded by von Arnim, von Kleist, Brentano and Muller, whom she had also hosted in her home in the past. She had also served them tea and cookies and shared with them her love for Goethe and for Romanticism, which they had in common. And not only had he joined them, but he also contributed to their cause and helped them choose the forty-six Berliners (half of them aristocrats) for the new emerging club, where membership was restricted.

"*No entry to Jews, ignoramuses or Frenchmen,*" the ground rules stated. And in tiny letters, added on at the bottom of the placard, the matter of Jews was meticulously clarified. "*No entry to converted Jews, up to three generations back.*"

All these clubs, popping up in every corner of fiery, inflamed Berlin, spread poison whose toxicity could already be felt, and yet, despite all this, Rahel did not give up on Germany and dreamt of a change that was still to come.

As far as she was concerned, the change had to arrive. After all, it was inconceivable that she had come so far only to return to her point of origin.

She felt as if she had been given a gift, but only for a limited time, only in order to provide her with a glimpse into a world that could have been her world, a taste of something she could no longer reconstruct. Perhaps everything repeated itself after all. Her status had returned to nothing, her friends had dispersed and spurned her and she was left on her own. For whole days at a time, she sat and silently bemoaned her situation; outwardly, she projected strength, while internally, she was gradually fading away.

34 | 1808

"Your primary duty, Germans, is to cast out anything that originates from outside the country, be it ideas, fashion or culture. You will thus continue to fulfill your mission, the nation's mission, with which it was tasked, to unite Old Europe's social regime with the true religion and thus ring in a new era in history, an era that is utterly different from the ancient era that has perished."

— Johann Gottlieb Fichte, *Addresses to the German Nation*

It had been two years since Napoleon conquered Germany and the winds of change had become a reality. A thousand years of history in which nothing had changed instantly became something new. "The Holy Roman Empire of the German Nation"[30] had died off, to be replaced by "The German Confederacy," in which the countries of Central Europe were united in an attempt to create a single national entity. This attempt created two extremes, each tugging in a different direction. The conservatives, including the military aristocracy and the landowners, strived to preserve the old order, while the liberal nationalists—the bourgeoisie—sought to establish

---

30 The Holy Roman Empire was a national entity. Unlike France or England, it did not develop into a centralized nation-state, but remained a super-entity comprising autonomous territories, ruled by princes, ruled by clerics, under the direct rule of the Kaiser, some of which existed as republics. All this persisted until Napoleon's occupation, when the change began.

reforms and changes that would benefit general welfare and strived for a common German identity.

Rahel was well familiar with Johann Gottlieb Fichte. She had first met him in Jena in 1794 and after a single lecture, in which he had brought up the idea of the "absolute I," she knew these things had been inside her all along and found their way out through this man, who spoke before his large audience with great fervor.

"It is easier to bring most people to see themselves as a chunk of lava on the moon than to think of themselves as an 'I.' Therefore, they did not understand Kant and did not perceive his spirit."

These were the opening words of his lecture in Jena that day and she had not forgotten them. Rahel remembered the sensation that had taken hold of her, the excitement of something familiar, lost and then found after a long period of searching. She remained in her seat after the lecture ended, waiting for the audience to disperse, and throughout that time, other statements from the lecture echoed in her ears, and one sentence in particular felt as if it had been carved from the depths of her soul and replicated: "The 'I' is not a part of the world, but rather exists beyond the world as a power in its own right." This was precisely the "I" into which she dug and delved and burrowed endlessly, asking questions and raising doubts and examining and often berating. From it came pleasure and anguish and loneliness and frustration at high intensities that were autonomous of anything else.

Later, just as Fichte—who was older than her by only nine years—was on his way out, she approached him and introduced herself. She complimented him on the depth of his lecture, on the innovative quality of his thoughts and the courage to share them with others, and finally invited him to visit her in Berlin and meet her friends. He was polite and listened to what she had to say attentively, despite the late hour. And although this forced him to huddle with many members of his audience, all men, finally, he even offered to escort her out. At the time, she did not think he would actually come to visit her attic; she hoped he would, but certainly did not expect it. But his promise to do so was enough, although she thought he would certainly soon forget it.

She did not know if he remembered that promise he had made but in 1799, some time after she returned from Teplitz, Fichte came to one of the Tuesday gatherings in the attic and continued attending occasionally. At the time, Rahel had already read almost all of his publications and was tracking the development of his ideas. She was an avid fan and now, following the acute patriotism that he had contracted, she remembered that on one of the shelves in her home was a little booklet he had written containing words of enthusiastic praise by one who had felt the need to passionately defend the French Revolution.

Rahel had put an end to her salon gatherings and Fichte had left for Königsberg. And after the conquering French soldiers took off for Spain and the peace treaty was signed, he returned to Berlin brandishing *Addresses to the German Nation*. At that point in time, after the "pivot" she had made, as her brother claimed, she wished to hear him speak, to go back in time somewhat and imagine that all was as it had once been. She wished to benefit from his wisdom, even if it seemed he had now abandoned the "I" in favor of the "We." In the lectures she attended, he spoke about society, portraying it as "the necessary condition for the development of the individual!" And he stated that the means for advancing society was intelligent national education. "The greatest danger threatening a nation," he said, "is getting caught up in the spirit of enslavement, when the individual forgets what the nation means to him and does not feel that the nation is the basis for the entire essence and meaning of his life. The meaning of life cannot be that we eat and sleep and work and have children whose fate will once again be identical to ours; our destiny is to be part of a great collective—surpassing the individual."

Rahel wanted to be a part of that nation, to belong. No more loneliness, enforced or voluntary, but rather part of a whole. She had been born and raised here, and especially loved the spirit of the people to whom she so longed to belong once more. Some time ago, she had read something written by author Jean Paul Richter: *"The English rule the seas, the French rule the land, but the kingdom of the spirit is ruled by the Germans."* And the same spirit she revered in her attic for so many years, that same spirit was what made her a German like all other Germans whose very marrow now burned with nationalism, spreading like a fire that soon would not be contained. She wanted to return her many friends to her and to go back to the happy days she once knew.

"*Hurrah, hurrah for Fichte! With teary eyes, I read in your letter that, in Paris, you are reading our esteemed teacher, that perfect man! He drew out and produced from me the best of me, pollinated it and claimed it as a deposit. He called to me, 'You are not alone,'*" she wrote to her brother Ludwig when he was in Paris, before he started attending the lectures with her. Even if she was left alone in the world, even if she was cast off and rejected, she would still have her inner world, that world imbued with spirit that no one could harm.

Ludwig, in turn, replied with a furious letter.

"*It has not been long since you expressed your support for Napoleon and already you have pivoted back and you approve of Fichte's whims. What about those declarations that loving one's country was not enough? What about your declarations that your past should be identical to that of the country?*"

"*This is not poison, but rather patriotism, and what sort of harm might grow from a nation that seeks unity, independence and a new path for itself?*" Rahel wrote to Ludwig, who had been staying in Paris after she rediscovered Germany, a discovery that instilled within her a new spirit and enthusiasm to which she held fast.

35 | 1808

Dorothea was utterly immersed in her religion. For her, there was no "my country" or "your country." The Napoleonic Wars took place around her, and the German people stood tall and discovered nationalistic feelings within themselves that they had never felt before. But in Dorothea's reality, none of that happened. She created a world of her own for herself and in it, she saw her life only as present and past, with no future. For her, there was only the divine providence of God and His emissary and His worldwide church.

Now, she also condemned her close friends, in addition to her family. Of Schleiermacher, who, following the occupation, had turned into a zealous patriot, she wrote, *"I never truly trusted that Calvinist."* And of Goethe, whom she admired and who had been an inspiration and a role model to her, she wrote, *"He is a pagan, and the man must be dismissed."* She had renounced her family when she abandoned her husband and child, renounced them when she converted to Protestantism, and now she was also renouncing her good friends, the ones who had stood by her when everyone condemned her due to her choices and those of her beloved. And she was whole-hearted with not a speck of regret in her.

During the last two years, Dorothea had lived in the shadow of the cathedral as a Protestant, and now she began to urge Schlegel to seek refuge in the bosom of Catholicism along with her. She felt like a Catholic in every sense of the word. All that was left was the baptism ceremony, which would put an end to her previous life and open up a world of atonement and redemption to her.

Schlegel did not require much persuasion. On the intended day, they entered the church, accompanied by their friends the Boiserée brothers, all of them smartly dressed. Dorothea held Schlegel's hand, his face now reminding her of the young man she had first met, the same one she fell in love with, and her heart skipped a beat. She was meeting the priest at noon, and as the time approached, she no longer had the patience to be leisurely, and therefore hastened her steps, pulling Schlegel along with her until he, too, felt the same urgency.

Despite the cathedral's immense size, Dorothea navigated its inner passages effortlessly. She knew every door, every nook and cranny, every turn, and was already leading the group in her clattering high heels to the baptistery, where the baptism ceremony would take place.

There, in that sprawling hall designed in the shape of a cross, the priest was waiting, dressed in his robe, cinctured with a tasseled belt. He smiled, asked how they were doing, shook their hands pleasantly and invited them to the baptismal font. Dorothea felt nearly breathless, her heart pounding with the excitement of one who was about to assume membership in an ancient order.

"Go ye therefore, and teach all nations, baptizing them in the name of the Father, and of the Son, and of the Holy Ghost,"[31] she recited the verses from Matthew, adding a quote from Luke, "I indeed baptize you with water... He shall baptize you with the Holy Ghost."[32] And already, holy water was being drizzled on her forehead, sanctified by the priest.

"In the name of the Father, the Son and the Holy Ghost," the priest said in ringing Latin, crossed himself and drizzled the holy water on Schlegel's forehead as well, three times.

Now only one ceremony remained—the confirmation ceremony, in which they would add a saint's name to their own names in order to protect them.

---

31 Matthew 28:19

32 Luke 3:16

***

The preparations for the festival of Christ were at their peak, and it appeared as if Germany, undergoing a wave of nationalism, was particularly festive. Houses were decorated with Germanic symbols and folk songs rang from every corner. Notice boards displayed manifestos calling for patriotism. And on this holiday, as the chasm between Jews and Germans gradually widened, the desire to convert surged within Henriette once more.

Schleiermacher had never applied pressure on her on the topic of religion, although they had conducted many conversations on the matter, and although she agreed with his claims in support of Christianity. But despite all these conversations, which always ended with mutual agreement that Schleiermacher's Christianity was indeed superior, this year as well, Henriette took no significant steps in the matter, temporizing in adopting his religion as her own.

In the past, she had condemned her Jewish brethren who freed themselves from the yoke of Judaism but did not declare that they denounced its God. Back then, when she was younger, she criticized the arrogance of those *Neuisraeliten*, New Israelites, a reference to those who had abandoned religious observance but not their identity as Jews, clinging to it although it was hollow for them. She did not understand why they insisted on clinging to Judaism while not carrying out any of its religious edicts, when they were faced with a wonderful alternative in the form of Christianity. Now she realized they did so out of respect for their father and mother, a reluctance to betray their family and friends, and a fear that they would be condemned as possessing dubious morality.

She was following their lead precisely. After all, secretly, Christ had been dwelling within her for quite a while now, and this "religion of the heart" provided her with support and succor, filling her entire being. And what was left for her in this life? What real solace could she seek other than that emotion, that sensation, that orientation of the soul surrendering to the self, to the infinite?

Schleiermacher himself said repeatedly that the true nature of religion was the individual's awareness of the divinity within himself. And who, if not her, acutely felt that divinity standing by her side? Was that not enough? Did she need religion's outer trappings? After all, inside her, there was no place at all, however narrow and confined and concealed, left for her Judaism. And still, she procrastinated.

The last few years had not made things easier for her. Since she was widowed and after being forced to reject her friend Count von Dohna's generous proposal, she had no choice but to continue making do on her own. The grandeur of her luxurious home had wilted long ago. It was no longer well-maintained as it had once been, and housemaids and domestic servants no longer scurried around there. Lately, she had felt that Berlin no longer afforded her the ability to express her talents and make a living off them.

Despite the time that had passed since her husband's death, the upheavals she had undergone and the compromises she had been forced to make in her life, there was one thing on which she was unwilling to compromise: her attire and hairdo, and her shoes and jewelry. From her perspective, the shoe should match the overcoat, and the ribbons adorning her coal-black hair should match the hem of her dress, and the hues of the fur overcoat should match the necklaces around her neck and the bracelets on her wrists, and every color and shade should be complemented to create full harmony. The same applied to her scarf and the kerchief on her head and her embroidered handkerchiefs and any visible apparel, as well as the concealed items.

Her style and beauty retained their youthful quality, and she refused to change them. Unlike women who got married and adopted a more mature style appropriate to their new status, Henriette had no interest in that. She did not surrender to passing time, wishing to stay young.

The Angel of Death had come for her husband only five years ago, when it was still early for him to depart from her. He had taken then and persisted constantly in taking. Taking from the young and the old and from infants and those who had yet to emerge into the world. First, he took their beauty, and then their health, and finally, he took their soul and did not cease. He did not distinguish between the good and those who spread evil, between those who contributed added value to the world and those whom no one was willing to defend.

She wished to somewhat delay passing time's gnawing at her flesh, and therefore cast off anything that might hasten the ensuing damages, and in her social encounters as well, preferred the company of the young. And the young men, they sought her proximity due to her beauty and wisdom and extensive knowledge of foreign languages, poetry and literature. But more than all that, there was actually a different thing they wanted. Did she not see it? Did her heart not stir within her as well? Did she not yearn to live as part of a couple once more, or at least enjoy the pleasures of the body?

The men, they approached and she sent them away until she once more became the topic of conversation and rumors and talk, of Henriette, whose beauty could be enjoyed as if through a display window, as if she were a china doll. Some time ago, a poem had been published by Ludwig, Rahel's younger brother, called "Court Advisor Yette Herz."

"Like the goddess Juno she is immense / Egyptian Marchioness / with many virtues blessed / loyal more than loving / forcefully charming / a hundredfold more heartless / noble and painless / robust and cold / too young for one so old."

She took it upon herself to serve as a mother, sister and confidante to those young men, and like any task she took upon herself, she dedicated her full intention and attention to this one as well. However, she was so focused on her desire to give of herself, to guide and instruct, that she failed to notice what was going on around her.

Rahel heard the gossip concerning Henriette, the insults flung at her and the accusations raised against her, and wrote her a letter intended to support her, but which could also have been interpreted as a defense of what she had heard, which only enhanced Henriette's sense of insult. *"You must acknowledge your good qualities and your flaws. If you acknowledge your flaws, nothing can get to you. Take your relationship with von Humboldt, for* example. You exchanged letters upon letters many years ago, your words of love written in the holy language. He even learned the complicated Hebrew alphabet for you, and was willing to do more. Meanwhile, you exhibited emotions toward him, but they were not authentic. Look inside yourself and tell me whether or not this is true."

Rahel did not want to add to Henriette's sorrow, and therefore did not mention the words published anonymously more than a decade ago. Then as now, they were intended to taunt Henriette for being unavailable, for holding herself back solely for her own designs and for possessing purely selfish needs, such as studying languages and nourishing her intellect and mostly cultivating her appearance.

"This Madam Moses is Jewish, and when it comes to her, you have probably noticed that she had acquired, with great effort, so much grace that she evokes unusual resentment for this reason. In this society, she is the true beautiful spirit. Ever since the days of her youth, she has frequently consorted with brilliant minds that have left her with a decent amount of general, vigorous aesthetic ideas, which she now conveys, penny by penny, to any new acquaintance. She always appears masquerading as some character from Goethe, and is particularly fond of taking on the form of the princess from 'Torquato Tasso.' Therefore, she is also studying Latin now. If Goethe did not fit the character to the measurements of her body, she cuts it to size herself in accordance with the latest fashion. However, her favored lovers claim that when she is alone with them, she is, indeed, Madam Moses."

'Moses' was a distinctly Jewish name; it was not, it was true, Henriette's name, but everyone knew she was the subject of the piece. Then, there had been someone to defend her—her father and husband—but now she had been left on her own. Now it was easier for everyone to gossip about her and tell stories that did not contain a shred of truth, and German nationalism, which had raised its head, further encouraged it.

And yet there was still a bit of merit to the accusations. Henriette always escaped to books and words and self-care and surrounded herself with friends and acquaintances, and all those who worshipped her for her beauty and intelligence and wit covered up the truth hiding inside her, a seed implanted deep inside her, comprised entirely of the need to be acknowledged, to be seen. After all, she was not fertile like Dorothea or strong like Rahel, who sucked life inside her at full force. All she had was her beauty, which would soon disappear as well.

"My unjustified notoriety as a sophisticated woman of the world, as if lovers fall at my feet, as if I have plenty of money, in addition to my Judaism, all these obstruct me in Germany. Therefore, I have no choice but to travel abroad," she told Rahel one evening when the two of them were sitting on their own in Henriette's drawing room, which was dimly lit.

"I'm sure it's all in your head and that soon you will find a good household where you can convey your great knowledge to tots in fancy dress," Rahel replied, although she was far from certain about this, but did not want to further sadden her friend.

"Mrs. Charlotte von Katten was seeking a governess for her children and asked me to look for one," Henriette said. "I wanted to suggest myself, but suddenly it occurred to me that my Judaism might not suit old Mrs. Christina Theodora Katten, and that Mrs. Charlotte might find it odd, and so I did not dare."

Some time later, Henriette sent a letter to Rahel in which she told her she had indeed been appointed to the position there, and Rahel was happy for her. But only a short time later, Rahel heard that Henriette had left her position and Berlin and moved to the island of Rügen without telling anyone.

Henriette left for Rügen following a letter from Schleiermacher, in which he urged her to come work as a governess for his brother's children. "*My sister-in-law is a convivial, pleasant woman. You will find much depth in your conversations with her.*" He went on to praise the Baltic sea air, describing the limestone from which the entire island was made and the summers in which all the residents of the island came down to the beach. "*And although the water is cold, the sun caresses the body and its rays are beneficial to it. And so you can forget your troubles somewhat and give yourself over to the pleasure of study and the excitement of a new life,*" he promised her.

Before packing her possessions and departing, she lingered to sit down and think, after which she put her thoughts into words and sent them to Schleiermacher.

"I think I will be brave enough to easily overcome parting from my relatives and peacefully leave behind the four walls in which I was mistress. But I am afraid that when the moment comes, I will need all my strength to continue standing tall. With a certain measure of sacrifice, I have maintained my liberty thus far; it will not be easy to give it up. My friends are bemoaning my desire to leave Berlin, but I shall do what I believe I have to do."

36 | 1808

"Yet, I should be like some old violin / That broken once, and mended, sings again / With softer tone, but with a greater sound."

— Frederik Paludan-Müller[33]

For several weeks now, Rahel had been packing all her possessions. She folded dresses into one suitcase and slips into another and shoes and bedspreads and curtains whose hems showed tiny holes. She folded and packed and closed and, on every suitcase and trunk, noted the items included within.

Her mother had not been living with her for several months now, since a major fight broke out between them. They had always fought over anything and everything. However, lately, the fighting had grown more intense. Rahel felt that her mother was interfering in every little thing, criticized everything and, from day to day, became more and more dissatisfied. Her mother, in turn, constantly claimed that Rahel ignored her, that she was dismissive of her and that she was not being treated as she deserved. Perhaps

---

33 From "Two Sonnets" in *A Book of Danish Verse: Translated in the Original Meters*, translated by S. Foster Damon and Robert Silliman Hillyer: https://www.google.com/books/edition/A_Book_of_Danish_Verse/G3hMAAAAMAAJ?hl=en&gbpv=1

for this reason, she was also seeking attention in another way, as if she were gradually becoming a little girl. Perhaps it was tension related to the changes unfolding in Germany, perhaps it was Rahel's loneliness, or perhaps it was the financial pressure that pushed both of them into impatience. The first to leave was her mother, who moved into Markus's house. However, after a few months, Rahel found out that she was unable to maintain the upkeep of the large house, once full of people and family members, now standing empty and neglected. Her brother Markus's failing business was now an open secret, and the house on Jägerstrasse was put up for sale.

From now on, 22 Charlottenstrasse would be her new home. It was not as large but not as shabby, and with unfamiliar neighbors.

"I am sitting at the tea table in my home, with only my dictionaries. I do not serve tea often. This is the extent to which everything has changed! I have never been more alone than I am now. To an absolute degree. I have never been so bored."

She wondered to whom she should address these lines. To those who no longer came, did not write and did not answer her letters? Some of them were busy with Prussian folk songs and with turning their backs upon the days of the past, while others have been in exile in Königsberg along with the administration's clerks for the past two years. After her good friends Friedrich von Gentz and Wilhelm and Caroline von Humboldt had publicly abandoned her, setting an example for many others, she was left alone. And to whom would she address those bitter lines? To Henriette, who was fighting to make a living? To Philippine, whose husband had fled after a bankruptcy, leaving her penniless? Or perhaps to Dorothea, who for some time now had been living her life in a world full of saints?

During her first night in her new room, she had a dream in which she was dead. In the dream, she was with her two friends Bettina von Arnim and Caroline von Humboldt and all of them ascended to heaven together. And as she did in life, in death, too, she wished to investigate and ask them about the essence of their lives. "Did you experience unrequited love?" The two of them nodded and burst out in tears, their hearts now unburdened. "Did you experience betrayal? Illness? Fear? Worry?" she continued, and each time, the two women replied, "Yes." Finally, one question remained unasked: "Did you experience disgrace?" Immediately when she asked, the space turned silent and the two of them looked at her in a way she could not initially interpret. Slowly, the two women began to drift away from her until she was left on her own. Now she knew. Her Judaism was a burden she would always carry alone and that would remain imprinted solely upon her own heart.

At that moment, Rahel woke from her sleep and realized that the words she had written could never be sent. Until that moment, she had thought she could address them to her friend David Veit, but it had been a long time since she had written to him and he had written to her, and in general, since he converted, his life had improved, while she remained at the same point where her life had started. She now remembered that in one of his letters to her, he had teased her by saying she could get along well without her friends, that, after all, they were just different versions of herself. He always claimed she sought friends who resembled her.

***

Several months passed and Rahel adjusted to her new residence. Now it was a pleasant routine to which she no longer objected and might even have welcomed. Every day during the afternoon, Karl August Varnhagen von Ense arrived at her home on Charlottenstrasse, and the two of them sat together, sipped tea and exchanged opinions. Sometimes he brought some fruit or a pastry he had purchased on the way, sometimes a bottle of cheap wine, and sometimes he brought a new book or some controversial article.

Spring had now arrived, the days grew long, and they could go out and stroll the streets, take in the fresh air and see how Berlin had reawakened. As if it had fallen into a deep sleep since Napoleon entered the Brandenburg Gate, and now that his soldiers had departed once and for all and the French occupation had come to an end, it seemed as if the arriving spring was the first one.

The two of them crossed the park, still engulfed with coolness, with the scent of flowers frolicking in the air, peeking and disappearing. They walked along the boulevard, where new stores were born from day to day, their windows a breathtaking show. Sometimes they would venture further, all the way to the row of alehouses from which the voices of men and the notes of a piano were emanating. Throughout their walk, the conversation flowed and curved, turning here and there, one topic pursuing another, and only the scenery changed, day turning into twilight then dark, and already they were on their way back, having a hard time understanding how the time had gone by so quickly.

There was nothing distinct about von Ense's appearance. He was tall and awkward, his fair hair wavy and thick and his broad forehead hinting at the fact that his intelligence level exceeded that of his peers. He was only twenty-seven and his knowledge surprised her, although she noticed his opinions were flexible and he greatly relied on the opinions of others. However, she dismissed all this, even after he showed her the bad poems he had written and the novels that had not ripened into pieces that met reasonable literary standards, which were pointless and shallow. What won him quite a few points with her was his love for her literary idol Goethe, as well as a simple, painful fact—her loneliness. She was so lonely that she agreed to accept von Ense's company despite these flaws. But there was something about the way he listened to her, the way he remembered whatever she told him in the most minute details, the gentle way he treated her and the fact that he put her needs before his own; all these made her keep him by her side.

She did not know it, but he had needed three random meetings with her before he dared approach her and introduce himself to her. The first time, he was nineteen years old, working as a tutor, while she was conducting her tempestuous relationship with d'Urquijo. The second time he met her, he was secretly engaged to the widow Fanny Herz. Even then, Rahel had left an intense impression on him, which was further enhanced when he discovered that his admired teacher Schleiermacher, no less, was an avid fan of hers. After he happened to encounter her in one of Fichte's lectures, he decided he had to meet her in person and lurked in wait for her during one of her strolls through the city, having thought in advance of what he would say to her.

Rahel thought their relationship would consist of him making her time more pleasant with conversation and an exchange of opinions, while she could help a young soul like him to weather the upheavals of life and its battles; as she soon found out, for him, such upheavals were quite common.

Being around him reminded her of her adventure in Paris with Wilhelm Bockelmann, which freed her from the deep grief she had been experiencing in those days, and was good and pleasant. She clearly remembered that the love Bockelmann had declared at the time had been the infatuation and erotic enthusiasm of a young man, and perhaps that was the case now as well. And how would she know? After losing herself within her life with d'Urquijo, she no longer trusted herself. She had to be careful with her heart, which was already broken and glued together and reconstructed again and again and if it shattered once more, it might no longer be able to heal.

Von Ense knew he did not have the knowledge she possessed, the insights, the analytic ability, the wit, the kindness, the passion that burned within her; all of these were not a part of his life, of his essence.

"My soul came into the world in extreme poverty, whereas others in this earthly society have been given stake to start with, or at any rate can be given it at any time, I have had to draw timidly back from the game. All is emptiness in me, real emptiness most of the time. I can neither represent relationships as a system nor endow the element with individual life in the form of wit. No springs bubble forth in me.... but in this total vacuity I am always open. A ray of sunlight, a movement, an aspect of beauty or even only of strength, will not escape me, I only wait for something to happen. I am the beggar by the wayside." he told her.

Rahel, who had been preoccupied with introspection, examination and questions her entire life, who had always worshipped the "I" and sustained an entire world within herself, listened, and her heart went out to the young man standing across from her and declaring to her that he was empty and hollow. It was obvious that he, too, examined and interrogated himself and was resigned to what was within him, and furthermore, to what was not within him. He was willing to accept from the world what the world was willing to give. And the world had given her to him so that he could live through her eyes.

37 | 1808

It had been only several months since the water was drizzled onto the foreheads of Dorothea and Schlegel, and a new life had opened before her. It was obvious that Catholicism enchanted Dorothea.

"How can I describe to you the unbelievable wealth that has been revealed to me in the treasures of the Catholic faith," she wrote to Schlegel, who was on the road, leaving her behind in Cologne. Her life had now been entrusted to the saints and she was less troubled by her husband's absence, as she was entirely immersed in her new religion.

In the corner of a well-lit room in their home stood the shrine she had constructed—a small, intimate prayer booth where rosaries, pictures of the saints, candles, and mementos purchased at various churches were all proudly displayed. Every day, she ascended to the shrine and said her prayers; every day, she became as one with the saints and a feeling of calm and security engulfed her.

Now that she had a new life, she took on an important task: to bring those she held dear closer to the true faith.

First and foremost, she wanted to secure redemption for her sons, Jonah, the eldest, and Philipp, the youngest. In order to achieve this, she had to bring them closer to the church. She knew that on this matter, Simon Veit would not give in without a battle, and therefore, she would have to be creative in shifting the balance in favor of the Catholic Church.

With Philipp, she was not required to make much of an effort. He was close to her and had been living with her since she closed the house door behind her years ago. Her world was his world. With Jonah, it was more complicated. He had stayed with his father after the divorce. She did not see him much as he lived a two days' drive away from her and for some time now, had been busy studying business with Abraham Mendelssohn, her younger brother. If she was only forced to deal with the physical distance, she could have overcome it easily, but the mental distance was an obstacle as well. Her brother Abraham was a consummate rationalist, and the entire manner in which he did business was based on common sense. It seemed as if the more Dorothea connected to her heart and delved into her internal essence, the more Abraham distanced himself from his own heart and relied upon his mind, and Jonah was influenced by this.

"A person is better off using his brain. It is the strongest tool with which nature provided him," he told her, and it was clear to her that this sentiment originated with Abraham.

Therefore, Dorothea sent an urgent letter to kind, accommodating Veit and asked him to allow Jonah to spend time with her and with his younger brother Philipp. She also asked him to allow the boys to make their way toward salvation, the same salvation she had found for herself.

"Quite a while has passed and you have found a place in your heart to hold back regarding my behavior. Your heart is a kind one and there are not many like it, and therefore I ask that you allow the boys to be saved. I beg you to allow them to accept the religion of Christ."

She sent off the letter and wanted to believe that like every other time, this time, too, he would find it in his heart to honor her wishes, that he would understand what she was saying, and once he saw her happiness, would also believe that this was indeed the way.

The kind, even-tempered Simon Veit, whose will collapsed again and again when confronted with Dorothea's wishes, went against his nature this time and found within himself new power to resist, now turning its full force against her and against the idea of renouncing the Jewish religion.

When he read her request, he found himself missing the small study group of which he had been a part for some time before Moses Mendelssohn passed away. Participants in those meetings had included Dorothea's younger brother Joseph, as well as Bernard Wiesel, a family friend, and of course, Moses Mendelssohn, his beloved father-in-law. The pleasant memory alone was now enough to fill him with the same excitement he had felt back then, when he woke up early in the morning, as violet rays were still illuminating the sky, and stillness still cradled the streets. He remembered how, during those hours, the four of them were eagerly anticipating the study session, especially Moses Mendelssohn, whose illness, which had already left its mark upon him, was still dormant at that hour, allowing his thoughts to emerge from the fog it created. They conversed and discussed a chosen topic, or listened to a lecture from Moses Mendelssohn. Veit now recalled one of those many conversations, in which Mendelssohn had discussed one of the greatest dangers—that of losing faith in God.

He did not propound upon the edicts of Judaism or analyze the contents of the Torah or lecture on divine revelation. He merely presented them with a series of rational proofs, seasoning them with the basics of philosophy and mostly expounding on his unique worldview, which posited that the existence of God was a supreme eternal truth, as anyone could attain understanding with the force of reason, and therefore rationality and wisdom were not reserved exclusively for the members of the Mosaic religion.

Now that he thought about what Mendelssohn had said and about his extreme openness, he understood where Dorothea's freedom of thought had originated and where it had come from—a freedom he himself did not possess. It was a whole world that was closed to him, like many other worlds that were indecipherable to one who had been raised to obey and appease and carry out the edicts of an ancient god. And despite all this, he was a Jew, as his parents and grandparents and great-grandparents had been, and his children would be Jews as well; rationalists or Romantics, they might pick this or that school of thought, but their Judaism was an element he would not allow to be abandoned in favor of Christianity, which he considered pagan.

"They were born Jewish, to the religion of Moses and Israel, and will die that way as well," he promised her in a particularly harsh letter, perhaps the only such letter he had ever sent her.

* * *

Henriette took only two items with her wherever she went. Two portraits. One was the painting by Anna Therbusch and the other was a neoclassic bust of her sculpted by Johann Gottfried Schadow. She received such enthusiastic praise for these pieces. "Juno the Goddess," she was called, as well as "the classic girl goddess." She had been so proud when her father told her that the bust sculpted in her image was the first modeled on a Jewish woman. She had been so proud, and this pride begat the idea within her that her future would not be like that of all Jews, that she was meant for greater things. She was certain of it.

She knew there was no point in clinging to the past; it was dead and gone, remaining only as a story written many years ago. A story that was still on the page and could be delved into, allowing one to forget the here and now for a while. Therefore, she thought, wherever she went, these pieces would remain by her side at all times, as something pleasant—no more than that.

She continued to live in the present and tried to make the best of it using her skills and the connections of her friends.

Some time ago, Schleiermacher had helped her by introducing her to one of the biggest publishers in Berlin. She had translated a few pieces from German to English, which were now languishing uselessly in her writing desk. Schleiermacher needed to use his powers of persuasion as she was uncertain regarding their quality; however, after she acquiesced and sent the manuscripts to the publisher, he agreed to publish them and even paid a fair price for them. If her name had appeared on the translations, which she had toiled over attentively and meticulously, she could have been more satisfied. But she knew that even if she asked, it would not happen. Few men, like Schleiermacher, encouraged women to study and write and publish.

Most, of them, as she already knew—after hosting quite a few of them in her home—even if they wished to appear liberal and open to change, became closed-minded when faced with a woman, especially if she was well-educated and a talented writer. However, she did not complain; after all, she had received money that she needed in return for her work, and now, as Schleiermacher was preparing to marry Henriette von Willich, she could sew herself a new dress and purchase a pair of shoes. Perhaps the money would suffice to allow her to add a wedding present for the couple.

Henriette had already traversed a great distance from her previous life, but occasionally, when she contemplated it, she remembered the fierce triad of friendship she had shared with Rahel and Dorothea, and thought about the fact that although she and Dorothea had never been similar in any way, as time went by, she had found that they had some things in common. Both of them wrote for a living and both of them had already taken steps toward Christianity. However, unlike Dorothea, Henriette had yet to be baptized and did not know if she would do so anytime soon, or at all. Yet this did not matter to her in the slightest as, inside, she was full and brimming with the Christian philosophy.

Christianity endowed her with love, a focus on interpersonal relationships, doing good. She was already living by all these principles and had now begun to study scripture as well, which allowed her to resign herself to her fate and find happiness in what the world sent her way. Scripture imbued her life with peace and taught her to be grateful for what she had.

She was grateful to the past for a life full of beauty, and grateful to her friend Schleiermacher for standing by her constantly, and grateful to the publisher who accepted her work and even paid her for it, and grateful to God, who was by her side, even though she had still not done what was required of her by taking steps in His direction.

***

Finally, Simon Veit gave in. Forced to choose between relinquishing his two children, who were his whole world, and accepting them as they elected to live, he made the choice that accorded with his character.

"Let us lower the curtain on what happened between us and relegate it to the past. I will not stop loving both of you and doing all I can for you, even if we do not agree with regard to religion. My dear son, as long as it is merely religion that separates us yet we stand united in our moral principles, there will never be any barrier between us. Now, after you have converted to a different religion, do not think that those millions of people who follow other religious principles are poor sinners whom God despises and that they have no part in eternal salvation. Such a thought has often separated friend from friend, a father from his son, a happy husband from his beloved wife, and has only caused damage."

Simon Veit had always believed in the path of compromise, other than the spirit of resistance that had inhabited him for a short while, and this time, too, he conceded for the sake of his family. Using her intelligence and her powers of persuasion, Dorothea finally managed to position both her children by her side. With Philipp, this was quick and easy. He admired his mother and wished to be like her. With Jonah, things proved more difficult and required persuasion, which took longer. But at last this task, too, was completed, and both boys converted to Christianity. When it happened, Simon Veit threw his hands in the air and surrendered, even reneging on his threat of withdrawing his financial support from his children. He went even further by deciding to draw closer to their world.

He would never convert; he was a Jew and would remain that way until his last day on this earth. However, when it came to his sons' cultural world, he sought to learn and understand what he could not back in the days when they were children, as he was young and caught up in other matters that claimed his time. Now, he traveled to them and kept company with them and dedicated the time to getting to know them. He watched and saw how they occupied themselves with the craft of painting, and the closer he grew to them, the more he could feel the inspiration that engulfed them as they sat across from the taut canvas.

Jonah held the brush in his left hand, his strokes gentle and confident. His left hand had always been his dominant one, and Veit and Dorothea had always received plenty of advice from those around them regarding their son's "handicap." When he was five years old, a distant relative suggested tying Jonah's left hand behind his back, thus forcing him to use his right hand and strengthen it. Naturally, this piece of advice was promptly relegated to oblivion, along with the relative who had dared suggest it. When he reached the age of thirteen and was bound by the requirements of the Jewish religion, a query was sent to the rabbi in order to find out on which arm he should lay the *tefillin*. As there were so many opinions and answers, the question ignited widespread controversy in the synagogue. *Chazal*[34] claimed that a man must lay the *tefillin* upon his weak arm, and therefore Jonah must lay it on his right, while most laid it on their left. The Kabbalah's[35] interpretation claimed that one should not divert from the custom practiced by most people, and therefore Jonah should lay the *tefillin* on his right arm. Another rabbi claimed that a man who was left-handed should lay two sets of *tefillin*—one on his right arm, so as to fulfill the edict of the law verbatim, and once it was removed, lay it on his left arm one more time without saying the blessing, in order to carry out the edict according to the *Halakha*.[36] Finally, the rabbi decreed that he must lay it upon his weak hand, meaning the one that was not used for writing, in accordance with *Chazal's* suggestion.

---

34 Chazal is an acronym from Hebrew meaning "Our sages, may their memory be blessed." It refers to all Jewish sages of the Mishna, Tosefta and Talmud eras, spanning from the times of the final 300 years of the Second Temple of Jerusalem until the seventh century CE, or c. 250 BCE – c. 625 CE.

35 Kabbalah, literally meaning "reception, tradition or correspondence," is an esoteric school of thought within Jewish mysticism.

36 The *Halakah* is the collective body of Jewish religious laws, which is derived from the written and oral Torah. *Halakha* is based on biblical commandments (*mitzvot*), subsequent Talmudic and rabbinic laws, and the customs and traditions which were compiled in many Jewish texts.

Simon Veit watched how Jonah held his brush in his left hand and focused upon his art, painting and illustrating and shifting it here and there, sometimes in broad strokes and sometimes with great precision, holding his breath so that his hand would not shake while he was trying to draw an ultra-thin line or a dot. And throughout the time when he was painting, a sacred peace descended upon his face, of a kind his father had never seen on him before. It was obvious that the act of painting emerged from his heart, and therefore Veit wished to do something for his own sake. The time had come, he thought, for him to address his cultural defects and grow better at a world with which he had had no contact until now. And from the moment he reached a decision, something opened within him. He learned to develop an appreciation for art in himself, diligently reading poetry and literature with the help of a tutor, who praised him for his rigor and his rapid progress. Who would have believed that the same Veit, "pleasant but uninspired," as Dorothea often described him to her friends, now exhibited interest in the very things that had interested her in the past? Who would have believed that calculated, stodgy Veit, who saw everything in terms of profit and loss, would become a man of intellectual depth and true understanding?

And as time went by, as he stood across from one of his younger son Philipp's paintings, he could now analyze the color palette and the composition and appreciate and know that his son's paintings were unusual and were not painted according to the conventions of the Vienna Academy of Fine Arts, where Jonah had been studying for some time now.

Jonah and Philipp, who had lived in Rome for a while and then in Vienna for a while, studying the intricacies of painting there, wrote of their father in their letters to Dorothea with love and warmth, and with a sense of respect and appreciation. They reported that from day to day, he grew more fluent in art, literature and poetry. Dorothea's Christian essence flinched back when she read all that they wrote and the way in which they wrote it. If he had been coarse and stingy, if he had been cruel and evil, then she could have justified all that she had done to him, justified drifting away from him and steering her children away from his sphere of influence. But now, how could she explain it to herself? And as much as she thought about it and about Simon Veit and about the way he had treated her every day of their lives, about his exemplary fatherhood, she still could not explain to herself how Veit had conducted himself like an absolute Christian while insisting on staying Jewish. Gradually, she realized that she had no choice but to ask him to forgive her, even if it entailed humiliation for her.

38 | 1809

"The beggar." This was Rahel's nickname for her new friend Karl August Varnhagen von Ense, whom she viewed as a stranger standing and watching the world from the side of the road, nameless, faceless, devoid of history.

She regaled him with the entire story of her life, with no fear of exposing herself, of baring herself, as he had no title and no status and no work and belonged to no milieu; he had no identity or name and could not threaten her existence in any way. He listened and expressed interest and gradually found himself immersed in her tale, in the twists and turns of her life, in the ups and especially the downs, which, time after time, threatened to shatter her but never succeeded. The more he got to know her, the further he made his way into the crevices of her life, the more he abandoned his status as an external observer. He was now facing a whole life, full and complex, which she had placed in his hands, a life that, much as he tried, he never could have imagined on his own.

Rahel's life had always been an open book; she had never concealed a thing and did not fear criticism, judgement or gossip. Not back in the days when she traveled by carriage on the Sabbath in plain sight, not when she had been abandoned by her first fiancé and not when she had been betrayed by her second fiancé. Something about his alien quality and the way he was willing to open himself up to her stories, something about his innocence and the elemental nature of one who had nothing, something about the fact that he was interested in her, made her share her history with him and want to stay by his side. He was her only friend during the time when her world was transforming.

"If I could live by your side," he told her one evening when they were strolling down the boulevard, engulfed by a pleasant stillness, "if you would allow me to see what you see and listen to what you have to say, life would seem as if it has inclined toward me with good intention. Life itself will seem sufficient to me."

There was no pretense to him. Not when he revealed his emptiness to her, not when he told her he "lacked the capacity for great passion," and not when he confessed that he admired the passion in her, her wit, her ability to love and her dedication to misery. He further admitted that as he had not been blessed with many skills and had not had many experiences in his life, he filled up on others' lives, and now that he had found a full, whole life to cling to, he was satisfied. Rahel agreed and presented him with three thousand letters. These letters laid out her life in black ink. He read them again and again and was fulfilled. He felt the complexities of life through her words, the joys and the knowledge and the anguish and the heartache. He read the wit with which Rahel analyzed works of art, adding her own comments and expressing her disappointment with the ones that did not meet what she saw as proper standards. He read how she consoled her friends, both male and female, sometimes even reprimanding them and putting one of them in his or her place. And he read the reactions of her friends, who replied with letters full of interest and pleasure.

He then told everyone about her letters with much pride, talking about her with open admiration that caused his friends to mock him. "The prophet of a woman," they called him, comparing him to a priest charmed by his disciples. However, he did not care, since now he was no longer "the beggar" to Rahel, but rather a person in his own right.

"I want to be your emissary," he told her one evening. She found this both flattering and embarrassing simultaneously.

"This is the role in which I feel best. I feel it would be fulfilling my destiny in many ways! I spoke about you at Stefan's house, as the third glory of the Jewish nation, the first and second chronologically being Christ and Spinoza, but you the first as far as content goes. They accused me of idolatry, but Stefan was nevertheless delighted with my fervor.

"Please take care," she said with utter seriousness, "take care not to make a fool of yourself." She was familiar with the hypocrisy of society and was certain that his friend Stefan, or anyone else listening to his enthusiasm, was not at all pleased with his words of praise for a Jewish woman. Especially these days, when her status was not what it had once been and when women throughout the reforming Germany had retreated back to their ancient role. Therefore, she warned him and begged him to cool his fervor, at least externally.

"He has none of the natives' sense of honor," she told her brother Ludwig. She was referring to the accursed Spanish concept of honor that had notched her heart and left it with scars that would remain there until the day she died. Von Ense was no longer a stranger to her. His devotion and dedication to her eased her loneliness. Although initially she had not been attracted to him and had thought there was nothing to him, now she felt close to him. She wrote to Henriette, *"My wounded, raging heart does not have the strength to love alone. I have had two previous loves; in one I was loved and not understood, and in the other I was understood but not loved, and in both, I was endlessly lonely."*

Distant Henriette warned, *"He might be exploiting you. Perhaps he is displaying you, as in a store window; he wishes to be well-known and famous by exposing your life to whoever is interested. Will your heart withstand being shattered again? Can you contain the disappointment yet again? In this case, the signs are obvious rather than being gradually revealed until your heart is already attached to him. You can still disengage, return to the beginning without being harmed."*

"Of course he is exploiting me," Rahel replied, "just as I am exploiting him. Is there a relationship that is not based on exploitation? And what is the alternative, waiting between my four walls until the current climate changes?"

***

Less than a year had passed since Rahel's mother left the house they shared and moved in with Markus. He had encouraged her to leave the big house in which she lived with Rahel and move to his residence. This provided him with a small victory of sorts over his big sister, who always bested him. The move happened following a major fight he had with Rahel. He reduced the monthly allowance he gave her, which evoked her fury. She blamed him for their financial situation and for failing to manage the business he had taken upon himself to run after their father passed away. While he, who had been carrying the entire family on his back since their father's death, battling the constantly changing zeitgeist and their dwindling fortune, was thoroughly offended.

"What do you understand about business management?" he accused her.

"I understand stinginess, and although I don't have a lot of good things to say about our father, I can say he was anything but stingy." Rahel knew this was not accurate and that their father had been quite a miser within his home. But from the midst of her feelings of helplessness, she only wanted to lash out at Markus.

"The fact that I take care of the money and don't scatter it around as you might want me to do does not indicate stinginess but rather frugality."

"They are one and the same." Rahel laughed mockingly.

That fight had only a single result—a major falling out between the siblings. And several months later, when their mother continued to update him on her various financial disagreements with Rahel, he urged her to relocate to his home. It was a convenient arrangement for Markus as, beyond his victory over his sister, it also allowed him to significantly decrease his financial support for his mother.

Markus thought that was the end of the matter and never imagined that his troubles were only beginning. First, there was his mother's irritability, a kind of constant dissatisfaction with everything. If he served her hot tea, she claimed it was too hot, and if chicken was served for dinner, she complained there was no beef. When he sat beside her and talked to her, she complained he was interrupting her reading and when she was sitting alone on the drawing room sofa, she was hurt if no one came over to ask how she was. Then she began coughing frequently, disrupting the sleep of Markus and the members of his household, and a doctor was periodically summoned to examine her. All the expenses he had saved when he had brought her over to stay with him were now being spent on the doctor's visits and the expensive medications he prescribed, which piled up on the chest of drawers next to her bed, unused.

One morning, he confessed to his wife. "Now I understand what Rahel was going through and appreciate her more than I ever did before, despite my anger at her. For years, she lived with Mother and I never heard a single complaint from her. It's true, she often said she wasn't easy, but she didn't elaborate and I didn't ask. Why did I have to intervene in their relationship when I have quite enough on my plate?"

After the acute cough, her appetite began to disappear. She no longer complained about the chicken and the temperature of the soup, or a lack of salt, or the peas that were served day after day. She tasted a bit and left the rest uneaten. After a while, her words grew confused. She forgot what she had said just a moment ago. Finally, she stopped recognizing the members of the household. Rahel was the only one she remembered, frequently asking about her.

The guilt for failing to update Rahel on their mother's condition would stay with him forever. Had he not seen how she grew worse from day to day? Had he denied what was happening or was he simply busy dealing daily with his diminishing business? Was he so immersed in his anger that he denied his older sister her last days with her mother? He could not answer all these questions, and even if he wanted to, he was now busy with preparations for the funeral.

When Rahel heard the news, she recalled how she had walked back home from her father's funeral and, even during that walk, ideas regarding the rest of her life were already sprouting within her, as if something had opened up and a world full of possibility was laid out at her feet. Now, she did not feel any relief but rather a sense of oppression over her mother's disappearance from her life in a single day. One moment her mother had been full of life, ready for battle and for endless confrontations with her, her mind clear and her words sharp, and the next she was being wrapped up in a shroud, lying among clods of dirt, and soon industrious worms would show up to nibble at her body. If Rahel had known this would happen, perhaps she would have tried to reconcile with her, or at the very least would have shown up to say goodbye. But the previous year had passed swiftly and the fact that her mother was living with Markus, to whom she had not spoken since their big fight, distanced her even more.

The entreaties of Ludwig and her sister Rose, who had arrived from Amsterdam at the last moment and had managed to spend some time with their mother before she passed away, fell upon deaf ears. They begged Rahel to stay and spend the days of the *shiva* with them, knowing that if she returned to her home on Charlottenstrasse, she would be alone with her thoughts there, which might submerge her into a state of depression. However, all Rahel wanted was to distance herself from the Jewish mourning rite of rending garments and from the bearded officials who would soon arrive, filling the drawing room with the murmur of prayers. She wanted to distance herself from know-it-alls who wanted to impose their mourning customs on others, and to avoid hearing arguments about the way the bereaved should express grief and what should and should not be done. She felt that she could not cope with the visitors' pity and their hypocrisy and their desire to depart as soon as possible after fulfilling the religious obligation of consoling the grieving family. All she wanted was to climb into her bed and curl up there and glide into a sleep that would carry her to any place that was not Markus's house.

Their mother's death did not manage to heal the rift that had formed between Markus and Rahel but only made it worse. The fact that he had concealed her illness now only further inflamed Rahel's existing anger at him, causing that slim chance of reconciliation to disappear as well. Rahel thought to herself that she would never manage to forgive him.

They did not exchange a word with each other during the funeral or after it and once their mother was buried, and Rahel hurried off to her home with no intention of coming back. And so it came to be that during all the days of the *shiva*, she ensconced herself in her house, not going anywhere, and no one came to see her, and in fact, without meaning to do so, these days of confinement came to serve as her private *shiva*.

***

Karl August Varnhagen von Ense's entire being was wrapped up in Rahel's letters and he felt that he needed them like a strong drink. However, the more he read her letters, the more unworthy of her he felt—unworthy of being by her side. He was not sufficiently educated; after all, he had abandoned his studies rather than completing them. He did blame this on the war that had broken out, causing the lecturers and the students to be banished from Halle, and yet, even if the circumstances were to blame—and in his heart of hearts he knew they were not solely to blame—the fact remained that he had been left without a formal education, and while he could have been a doctor, he was nothing. How would he be worthy of spending time with her without a certificate of graduation from a university? With no profession, without the ability to make an honorable living, without being someone who was as worthy as she was? Despite his deliberations, he continued to read, avidly drinking down her words. Only the letters between her and d'Urquijo remained locked to him.

Now, after a period in which her life had been laid out before him like a tablecloth covering a table seating many diners, Rahel felt that she could share them with him.

They had already grown closer and after her mother's death, she felt that she was alone in the world. Now, she had no father and no mother and had renounced her roots and although she had her siblings, she was not speaking to Markus, Rose had returned to Amsterdam, and Ludwig was roaming the world. Each of them was living their life, busy with their own affairs. The only one by her side was "the beggar" who admired her and her life, and she had grown used to his presence. He did not hide a thing from her either, and she encouraged it. Her life was exposed to him and therefore it was appropriate for his life to be exposed to her as well. Therefore, he occasionally told her about Fanny Herz, the fiancée he had left behind in Hamburg.

Finally, she presented him with her most private letters. "No one, past or future, can arouse the passion in me that I felt with d'Urquijo," she confessed shamelessly, and earnestly asked, "Let's not let our relationship spoil due to such attempts that are destined to fail."

She entrusted him with the letters of the Spaniard who had done whatever he wished with her heart, while privately knowing that these letters might ultimately come between them. And yet, as if toying with her fate rather than surrendering to it, she added one more comment, a warning, as if foreseeing the future.

"Don't be too willing to let me go."

And as she had feared, the letters she had handed over had an effect upon him, setting him off, and as he read them again and again, something seemed to ignite in him, and he began to speak more about his fiancée Fanny, about their intimate letters and the sadness her suffering caused him, and as a result, Rahel gradually came to a decision. She would not allow his fiancée to steal him from her. She would fight with all her might. And, after all, she did know how to fight.

She wanted to believe that he truly was a modern man, the kind of person who had contributed to the disintegration of ailing Europe, like the ones who could love two women and be dedicated to them as if they were one, as if it were natural. Such thoughts flooded her as she tried to look into herself and decide how to proceed. Her heart had already begun to grow attached to him, bringing about the sort of heartache that accompanied such relationships. After days of deliberation, she realized she could not hold on to him when he wanted to go.

"You must see her, this woman. Every night I become stronger, more lucid, firmer, delving deeper into myself. I cannot stand weakness, vulnerability, ambivalence, illness or self-pity in my soul. You must live with her. If wounds ensue, they must wholly heal, whether through a happy life together or through a parting of ways. If you love me, it will all turn out well. I can no longer fight for anyone and conquering happiness always disgusted me."

Von Ense, who had still not managed to sort through his own thoughts and the whirlwind of emotions that had shaken him up from the day he read her and d'Urquijo's letters, could not decide where he should be. Should he stay with Rahel or return to his fiancée Fanny as Rahel was urging him to do? He only felt that he was being backed into a corner, and this feeling wreaked havoc upon him.

"You are hard," he dared to tell her one evening when she once again suggested that he leave. Although he was already familiar with her honesty, his insecurity made him feel as if she wished to get rid of him.

"You think I'm hard? But I am a miserable woman! Always against myself! I don't want to present you with two suffering women, and so one of them is as tough as iron. Even now when you must leave me, I will not complain. If you come, I'll be happy and you know I do not like hesitancy. It's the limitation of my nature."

Finally, he left. He left her alone in Berlin, with the possibility that she would lose him forever hovering over her head.

39 | 1811

"You must enjoy love and the happiness it brings. This is not an exaggeration or sentimentality or self-sacrifice on my part, and I do not possess the values of dedication and sacrifice. However, if you truly did love, I will help crown you! I will return your love with great affection, as you have often seen. I can spend my life with you—this is how serious and enthused I am, and this is now my only passion. I will dedicate it to you with pleasure and immense satisfaction. I will acknowledge your entire value. I am faithful to you out of inclination, out of love, out of the choice considered to be the best one. I have no claim on you. I am your friend, as male friends might be. With all due respect to you, you have no obligation to me at all."

August read the letter again and again, and meanwhile, his fiancée Fanny rocked in the rocking chair in her yard. For some time now, he had been with her in Hamburg. He had left Rahel and all her letters behind and returned to his fiancée, who had been patiently waiting for him. They had already strolled on the bank of the Elbe River, crossed countless bridges during their walks and visited St. Nicholas Church, whose turrets were visible from afar. Every Sunday, they sat in a café and chatted, sometimes on their own and recently joined by friends as well. He enjoyed her company but could not keep from comparing the two women he loved. He compared the way each of them talked and their topics of conversation, compared the way each of them treated him, how each embraced and kissed him and even compared the way they made love to him.

He expected that from day to day, he would love Fanny more and told himself he had to get used to her again after being away from her for so long, knowing he had to give it time, and yet at every step and at any moment during the day, he could not help but compare the two. Sometimes he felt he was nearly losing his mind, but ordered himself to be patient.

And so the days went by. The enthusiasm of his return began to dissolve. This process was exacerbated by Rahel's letters, which troubled his peace of mind. He read them again and again and felt flattered and confused and still, he remained determined to continue living with his beloved, if only things would work out for them.

However, during the last few weeks, their relationship had deteriorated. He avoided spending time with her under the premise of various excuses, and she taunted him and insulted him and then turned ingratiating, trying to make up, while he could no longer stand her games and tricks and stopped himself again and again from leaving her.

But one evening, while Fanny was swaying in her rocking chair in the yard of the house, August stood up, and something within him stopped him from going out to her and sitting by her side, as she expected him to do every evening. At that moment he realized that even if Rahel were not waiting for him in Berlin, his marriage to Fanny was doomed to failure.

He decided to end his relationship with her and annul their engagement. After he did so, one thing loosened its grip on him, but something else settled upon his heart, just as he had decided that he must return to Berlin, to Rahel who was waiting for him: how could he share his life with Rahel when he was still a student, one who had not even completed his studies? He had no money, position or status. Fanny had no financial constraints, while he knew he would have to provide for Rahel.

***

Despite it all, he returned to Berlin.

For a short time, he was with Rahel, and her days filled with meaning and pleasure once more. But all that soon ended, and now she was lonely again. He traveled to Tübingen to complete the medical training he had begun. He owed it to himself if he wanted to achieve something in life, if he wanted to live by her side. Rahel encouraged him to do it, to develop and learn and grow. These were things she valued greatly. But although she supported and encouraged him, other thoughts nestled in her heart. Could he be someone in his own right? And if he completed his studies, how would it serve her? And what would happen with all that he knew about her from the letters she had shown him? And if he became "someone," would he include her in his plans? She sighed. Suddenly, it occurred to her that she had brought about his desertion. When he first met her, he was convinced he was beyond head-over-heels in love with her, and she, in her stupidity, had extinguished his love with statements and declarations like "she could never love again after d'Urquijo" or that "love was no longer of use" to her. Now he was far from her, and she hoped that it was actually through love and pining and craving and yearning that she could return him to her.

As he had promised, he wrote her many letters, but they were full of empty words and phrases, and none of them managed to convey what he truly wanted to tell her. Before every letter he wrote, he envisioned her letters, written tastefully and with elevated language, full of sensitivity and wisdom and humor. All her letters reflected more interesting friends and a vibrant, exciting social life. While he could find no way to be original. His letters were a replication and an echo of what she wrote to him. In his last letters, he referred to the uncertainty in his life, planting discreet hints about freedom. After all, it was Rahel herself who talked incessantly about this freedom. In the aftermath of her relationship with d'Urquijo, she was zealous about her freedom and expected to receive it from whoever was by her side. Therefore, he began to demand the same exact freedom, and she was willing to grant it in return. But why did he need that freedom, she wondered. After all, he was now alone in Tübingen, with no company or love interest. But this changed and one day she received a letter in which he wrote that he had met a young woman in Hamburg and felt a commitment to her.

August was not the type to be able to live alone, on his own. He found nothing inside himself and was forced to seek it externally. The emptiness that threatened to take over him frightened him more than anything else, and he had yet to find something to fill that space that not his correspondence with Rahel, nor his studies could. And out of the fear of being left alone and the distance, which also had an effect upon him, he had found someone to occupy him.

Rahel refused to believe what she was reading. She tried to understand why he had written what he did; was it the truth, or was he merely seeking her attention? But nothing she told herself managed to soothe her. Since the arrival of the letter, a gray cloud had settled over her head, and she felt that their relationship was about to turn into another wretched love affair. Therefore, she immediately sent out a letter in which she asked to gain a better understanding of what was going on.

"I demand that you tell me what you are planning to do about this."

However, August evaded her questions and continued to send her letters that said nothing and further intensified her uncertainty.

Did she love him, or perhaps her love was equivalent to his evasions? Perhaps she merely needed him just as he needed her? Perhaps she was holding on to nothing? Did she wish to maintain a hold on her past through him? After all, she herself escaped him at night into dreams, places whose secrets were reserved for her alone. Dreams in which August had no part. Ones that were not documented in any letter and never would be.

The more she thought about it, the more she realized that the fact that he had never let her down, unlike other men she had been with, was to his credit, and she appreciated him for it, and therefore did not wish to impose an ultimatum upon him. But lack of clarity was something that had always shaken her up and she could not resign herself to it. As it did every time, her inner integrity was the deciding factor, along with her attraction to absolute truth.

"I declare you free! However, pausing in the midst of actualization means not finishing it, which has nothing to do with being free or not being free.

Anyone who wishes to dance the fandango[37] and stops in mid-dance because he finds it strange or because he does not have the courage to go on does not derive an act of freedom from it. And for a moment, I thought I was not alone! I am again, in some sense!"

After writing to him, she had no doubt that the words of reprimand she had included would be the closing note of their relationship. And although she was very sorry for it, she felt a certain relief as well.

"Nothing in your words insults me," he wrote back. "*I look upon them bravely although I feel myself shriveling, becoming smaller and smaller under their gaze. But your truth is not a terrible thing to me as it is in harmony with the truth in me.*"

Rahel had not expected him to write what he did. She was used to the fragile masculine logic, which was not equipped to withstand criticism and needed to justify itself at any cost. She now realized that the fact that he agreed with her and accepted her comments actually testified that he possessed a healthy logic, to which he listened, and, in addition, he had also adopted a rational line of thought. There were no personal or emotional whims in his heart and although she had known this previously, she had now received further confirmation of that fact.

After all of her previous relationships with men, this was the first time in her life that her partner's otherness did not constitute doom for her. This otherness was what saved their relationship. She realized that she had found the thing that made up for the hollowness within him, for that emptiness of which he boasted, and this allowed Rahel to receive what she had fervently yearned for.

"*Dear August, (I am complimenting you now!) since no one I know on this earth has more accurate powers of judgment, such perfect perception regarding the nature and the scope of my entire being than you. Yes, you are also the most cultured person.*"

On that distant day when he stopped her during her stroll after meticulously planning his approach, she had never imagined that it would be him,

---

37   The fandango is an uninhibited Spanish dance.

of all people, who would be her best friend until the day she died. He, who was no one special, who was the utter antithesis to everything she believed a person should possess, had been gifted with the ability to understand her better than any lover she had ever had.

***

Henriette was holding *The Sorrows of Young Werther*. Ever since she married Markus, the book had been pushed aside, displaced by the books that Markus recommended. Now she opened it at random and the words that had been seared into her mind years ago sprung up across from her, igniting a yearning for the past.

"I am ready to confess that I prize [dancing] above all other amusements. If anything disturbs me, I go to the piano, play an air to which I have danced, and all goes right again directly."[38]

When she heard what had happened, she was immediately drawn to the trunk under her bed and took out the book she was holding now, the one that had accompanied her throughout the years of her youth. Heinrich von Kleist, whom she had known from the salon gatherings, had been found shot on the bank of the river alongside his good friend Henriette Vogel. The thought of the two of them lying lifelessly beside the river shook her up and would not let go. Was she turning to Werther to seek answers for what Kleist had done, or was she perhaps only seeking to escape back to the days when she could dream and imagine and think it would all come true in the future, and all the worries could fade away with dancing and frolicking?

Von Kleist, who had killed his friend Henriette Vogel and then committed suicide, left a fierce impression on her. Rumors claimed that his friend Henriette was very ill and had asked him to take her life and put her out of her misery, and von Kleist, who was close to her and sensitive to her suffering, consented to do so for her.

---

38 Goethe, *The Sorrows of Young Werther*. Translated by R.D. Boylan. https://www.gutenberg.org/files/2527/2527-h/2527-h.htm

Naturally, and without meaning to do so, Henriette thought about Markus and about his illness. Was it the same disease from which Henriette Vogel had suffered? Was it truly incurable?

What would have happened to her if Markus had asked her to do the same thing for him? Would she do it? Yet Markus had been Jewish and although he had not been deeply observant like her father, he would never have asked her to violate the most severe prohibition of the Jewish religion, *"And surely your blood of your lives will I require."*[39] Christianity, to which she had grown much closer, also prohibited the taking of life, and therefore she could find no loophole or logic regarding the action that unsettled her peace of mind and shook her up in a way she could not understand.

Rahel, who had known von Kleist and was his friend, wrote to Henriette some time later that she understood what he had done, adding that she supported him. She supported murder that eased torment and the taking of a life in this manner. She was the only person who supported this idea while the deed was condemned by all.

As time went by, rumors concerning the murder-suicide swelled further, refusing to die off. Some said it happened following the threat of closing faced by the newspaper *Berliner Abendblätter*, which von Kleist edited and through which had managed to evoke fierce patriotic sentiments within the nation. Others claimed it resulted from the rejection of his plays by Berlin's official theater, and although they were produced in the private theater of Prince Antoni Radziwill and his wife Louise, this did not satisfy him. Was he motivated by failure? Was it depression? Did he not find gratification in the "Supper Club" he established with four of his friends, which met with great success in awakening Berlin? Or perhaps it was only self-sacrifice for one who could no longer be saved?

He was a successful man, at least from Henriette's perspective, with countless options open to him; he could do as he wished. And yet, apparently he did not sufficiently appreciate his life and did not grant himself the opportunity to enjoy it.

---

39 Genesis 9:5

"If only I were offered the same possibilities," Henriette wrote Rahel, adding what had already been said and was well-known and unchangeable—if she were a successful man like von Kleist, a reputable author and playwright, the whole world would be open to her. She would not give it all up by taking her life. She would nurture the possibility of developing, of succeeding, of making decent wages and doing anything she wished.

Rahel replied with a quote from Epicurus: *"Death is nothing to us, since, when we exist, death is not present to us; and when death is present, then we have no existence. It is no concern, then, either of the living or of the dead, since to the one it has no existence, and the other class has no existence itself."*[40]

Rahel's opinion was that when everything ended, pain ended as well. She added that every person was entitled to put an end to his pain—be it a pain of the body or a pain of the heart.

Henriette continued to seek answers in *Werther*, as if it were the bible of suicides. Therefore, she turned to his last words, written before the fatal shot that put an end to his life.

"All is silent around me, and my soul is calm. I thank thee, O God, that thou bestowest strength and courage upon me in these last moments!"[41]

Suddenly, she did not understand how, back then, she had admired the deed that seemed daring to them, one that swept along many in its wake and was considered an act of bravery.

Some time later, she wrote to Rahel, *"True courage is to stay and brave it all and embrace the pains of the heart and the pains of the body and overcome them all or not. That, to me, is courage."*

---

[40] From Diogenes Laertius, *The Lives and Opinions of Eminent Philosophers*. Translated by C.D. Yonge. https://www.gutenberg.org/files/57342/57342-h/57342-h.htm

[41] Goethe, *The Sorrows of Young Werther*. Translated by R.D. Boylan. https://www.gutenberg.org/files/2527/2527-h/2527-h.htm

40 | 1812

It had been some time since Rahel and August had last seen each other. They thought they might be able to meet mid-way for a few days, perhaps in Frankfurt or in Leipzig in October, but this did not come to pass. They then resolved to meet at the end of January, but Rahel grew ill and it took her a while to recuperate. August actually wanted to come and nurse her back to health, but she firmly implored him not to come. She would recover soon, she told him, and the moment she felt strong enough, she would come to Tübingen. Such a journey was not cheap and although she did not have much money, August had even less. She wanted to make the effort for him, even if it meant she would have to live frugally for many weeks.

The month of February arrived, followed by March, and now April was nearly here, and they had still not managed to set up the meeting they sought. A few days together, that was all they wanted, and the great difficulty in executing such a thing threatened to cause them to quarrel. If they were incapable of this, what would happen later on?

One morning, when the summer sun was abusing Rahel, who was sitting in her garden, a carriage stopped in front of her house. There was not much traffic in the area and the sound of hooves clattering against the ground and whinnying horses told her that something was going on. Rahel marked the page in the book she was reading with a bookmark, its top embroidered with her initials, rose and strode to the gate to take a look.

August was at the gate. He had had enough of talking and attempts to set up a meeting, and once he heard that two of his fellow students had been urgently summoned back to Berlin due to a death in the family, he joined them and had not had time to send a letter announcing his arrival. Surprised and moved, she extended both arms to him, ready to embrace him. When she gazed at him, after a long time in which she had not seen him, she sensed that something in him had changed. The knowledge sprouted inside her that in a few years, when he returned from Tübingen after completing his studies, he would be the man who could take care of her. As much as she had grown used to taking care of herself, something in this knowledge made his sudden arrival complete.

In the many letters they exchanged after weathering the crisis in their relationship, August asked her to be his fiancée. She agreed, but although they considered themselves engaged and committed to one another until the day they could marry, despite it all, August wished to hold an engagement ceremony.

The ceremony they held was symbolic, taking place with only the two of them on that same evening. He sought out her left hand, held on to her ring finger and placed a slim gold ring upon it. He then stroked the finger, wanting to tell her that it was the origin of the *vena amoris*, the vein of love that led to the heart. But as he was certain that she already knew the story, he kept his silence, also not wanting to make the ceremony too sentimental, a trait he avoided assiduously. And Rahel, deeply thrilled by the gesture and the surprise of his arrival, was now surprised by the delicate ring he had purchased with money that she did not know how he had obtained. And after they went to bed, and after she began to hear August's weary breaths—as the day had doubtlessly been full of excitement for him, as well—she could not help but compare it to her engagement to von Finckenstein and to the diamond ring he had purchased for her, and to her engagement to d'Urquijo, sealed between starched sheets, with no ring, but with great passion and turbulent emotions.

***

The news of her mother's death reached Dorothea a short time after she returned home from the Sunday sacrament, when she was still dwelling in sanctity.

Her mother had been left alone in the house in which her father died. She was found lifeless, her body as cold as ice, sitting on the same sofa on which her husband had also taken his last breaths. Every evening, she sat on that sofa and read the Book of Psalms, as if she wanted to stay close to her husband, and this had been the case on her last evening as well. She had never forgiven Dorothea and did not want to hear any explanation from a heretic daughter who had shamed her family again and again, but had never stopped loving her in her heart and worrying about her conflicted soul.

As the years went by, Dorothea became more conciliatory. She took care to stay in closer touch with all her family members and tried to avoid discussing matters of religion with them. Privately, she worried about their wellbeing and welfare and happiness, both in this world and in the one to come. The same Romantic who wished to reject and remove any shackle forced upon her independent spirit by Jewish law and rationalism now urged and encouraged and recommended praying at regular intervals. She aimed to subjugate the soul to the higher will of someone other than herself and took it upon herself to find salvation for those who had yet to find it. In recent years, she had particularly worried about her mother, left alone in her home.

She resigned herself to her mother's reprimands, which were present in every letter she received from her, and ultimately understood where such admonishments were coming from. After all, she was a mother and had used every possible tactic and method she saw fit so that her sons would shed the Mosaic religion and be baptized into divine grace. She knew the heartache of a wrong choice; after all, she had felt that pain every day on behalf of her brother Joseph and her sister Recha and her friends, who had yet to become the sons of the Holy Church.

Now Dorothea was left alone in the world, with no one to berate her with reprimands, no one to express wordless disappointment, no one to love her unconditionally like her mother loved her. Her sorrow over the death of her mother was diffused into greater sorrow for the fact that she had not attained the yearned-for salvation.

"Pray for your grandmother, Johannes," Dorothea commander her oldest son. "Pray for the ascension of her soul, with pure intent."

Although she wanted to attend the funeral, she did not have time, and thus was spared the sight of her mother's body being lowered into the pit as if she were an object that must be disposed of. She was spared the *shiva*, the rending of garments, the avoidance of bathing the body and spending time among all the bearded officials. She tried to bring about the ascension of her mother's soul through her prayers and those of her son Jonah, and what was in her heart would stay there, between her and Christ; He was the only one to whom she was accountable.

Her mother's death shook her up and accelerated her desire to forgive. She was taking in the fact that her day, too, would come, and she could not know when and how it would arrive, and felt she must make haste. Some time later, she wrote to Simon Veit, *"You are guilty of nothing."* She thus absolved him of any blame, taking upon herself the sin she had committed many years ago.

41 | 1813

An eternity seemed to have elapsed since the day Napoleon entered Germany. He was now confronting the sixth anti-French coalition, uniting many countries, including the Austrian Empire, Sweden, Britain, Prussia, the Russian Empire, Spain and Portugal, all sharing one goal—to defeat Bonaparte, who seemed invincible.

August, who had completed his studies, became a captain in the Imperial Russian Army, and no one could condemn him for his lack of loyalty to the German nation, as before taking on the role, he had first made certain that there was complete cooperation between Germany and Russia. His military service evoked patriotic sentiments within him that Rahel could not find within herself. She was a stranger within this nation, within this place. Even the decree issued about a year ago, declaring a law that granted rights to Jews, did not fill her with hope. She did not take part in the great joy that followed the easing of restrictions and the bestowal of citizenship upon the Jews of Germany. After all, the Prussian nation still had a hard time accepting them. Not every decree was enforced and not every promise was fulfilled. And when it came to broken promises, she already had plenty of experience.

Therefore, she wrote to August, *"Do not forget that after this period, a different one will come for those left alive and everything will return to the old, rotting order, and the masters of the land will laugh at all the rest."*

She implored him and requested that every promise he had received or would receive, as well as any achievement he attained from this war, would immediately be officially legalized and approved and documented in the records, as, after all, *"people are mortal, especially in wartime."* August claimed she was a pessimist, asking her to look at things in a positive light, but she maintained her stance of viewing everything on a proper scale. She found the decree idiotic and mocked the Jews' choice to cling to these rights and look away from what they were not given: "The fact that we are called Germans and that we are Germans now is all a matter of luck, and blowing it all out of proportion will result in all this folly exploding."

This was what she thought and believed and she did not hide it. She said so to August before he departed for Hamburg, where he was stationed, and made sure to repeat it to her family, now her only company, as they had been back in the days of her childhood. She did love them and had made her peace with Markus as well, but their company was not enough for her, and she waited for the first opportunity to make her escape.

***

Despite the difficulty and horrors it entailed, the war created opportunities as well. Like August, she, too, wished to believe it. In the meantime, the sounds of war were approaching Berlin and soon its effects, too, would be visible and certainly discernable everywhere. Markus suggested she join him and his family on their way to Wroclaw, where things were still quiet, and August implored her to travel and continue on to Prague. There, he promised, he would provide her with a room to lodge in and an allowance. After she consented to his request, he even sent her money for the journey. She had believed in him and now he was honoring the debt, which moved her greatly. She was not used to people, much less her romantic partners, keeping their promises. She was indeed wary of leaving, but did so, as he had asked her to do. She escaped Berlin, and her dispiriting existence there, with Markus and his family, straight into the arms of August, who took care of her. He had made a promise and kept it and therefore, her love for him continued to grow.

***

She was a foreigner in Prague as well. However, there, her foreignness did not attract attention. The city was full of soldiers, men and throngs who had escaped the wasting clutches of the war, just as she had. She had been naïve when she thought the war would stop far from her, when in fact, it persisted and progressed and had sent thousands of its wounded as a vanguard. The days were filled with activity. She volunteered to treat the wounded and helped gather funds and possessions to aid those who were left destitute and helpless. Here, at last, she had an advantage, as she was accustomed to enforced exile, to the foreignness into which she had been born in her home in Germany. While others found it difficult, she herself barely felt that alienation. Here, they were all foreigners, all passersby; they were like her and she was like them.

"*In this foreign place, I cannot invite people to my home, I cannot communicate, but at least I have the title and status of a foreigner, and naturally, the consequence of this is that I am accepted. Any disruption, any pain of regret for the past, has faded away,*" she wrote to August, and he was pleased with his choice to bring her to Prague and even more pleased when he managed to discern some change between the lines, to pick up on a dash of her wit as well as some cheer.

"I believe this is how it is with my mood. It is constantly there, only it is suppressed," she responded to his optimistic sentiments. "*The sum total of the old experiences moves rapidly out of the depths inside me; I feel the rapid motion acutely, as if there was a gushing inside me. I was depressed for too long; I have always said so. Now, as I have not died and my essence has not been killed within me, it lives on like someone saved from being buried alive. Life is something stubborn and beautiful, you know.*"

In Prague, she began to tend to the wounded who were part of the coalition with Germany. She was the only one in her family who volunteered to join the war effort. Germany had never rewarded any of them and they were not certain it ever would, and therefore they found no desire within themselves to help. And yet there were plenty of volunteers. Thousands of Jewish men flocked to the war, doing their best to prove that they were equal to their German brethren. They accepted the rights, but furthermore, also took on the duties and wished to publicize this fact, to show everyone that they were doing their part in contributing to the national effort, as if they had forgotten that debts to Germany had always been paid in money and in property and with the body. This was the case for both the men and for the women, who toiled constantly to provide their services for anything that was needed.

"If the Christians only gave as generously as the Jews do, there would finally be no more distress here," she wrote in her diary.

***

After spending some time outside of Germany, she began to identify with the sentiments that had surfaced in August with regard to their home country. When she lived in Germany, she could not see it. Now, after attaining some distance from her past and all that the country symbolized for her, something else began to dawn within her. Perhaps it was homesickness, perhaps it was the wounded to whom she tended, or perhaps the fact that they were all united against a common enemy.

She began to feel a sympathy of sorts, but only for those who spoke about the war with respect for the enemy, for those who equipped themselves with the understanding that this enemy, too, was human. Yes, this was the main thing for her. It was proper for the virtues to be retained even when the battle was bloody, for morality and fairness to be applied even toward those who rose to kill you. With those who spoke in this manner, she found the ability within herself to support them. This was how she viewed humanity, gradually giving rise to the same sentiment within her that August had experienced long before her, aimed at the German nation. And Rahel began to open up to the idea of the opportunity that August had recognized in the war. The impact of the years he had spent at the university was evident in everything he said or wrote to her.

"Nobility, titles, being born to a certain status, are no longer brought up anywhere, but academic studies or a real position are highly esteemed and immediately recognized. With all due respect, this war offers us the greatest hope, and the mental climate that will ensue from all this will certainly be more important than all the changes to the borders."

This opportunity appeared out of the rank that August had managed to fit into after great effort, the bourgeoisie, which had begun to assert itself. And with this self-assertion Rahel, too, could identify.

42 | 1815

"There's Goethe!" Rahel was as excited as a child. She stood in the middle of a bustling street, an uncontrollable cry escaping her lips. Her face grew flushed as a result of the embarrassment she had brought upon herself, although he had not heard. Even some time after he had disappeared down the alley, her legs were still shaking, an inexplicable heaviness spread through her arms and her back was covered with a cold sweat. After the heat in her face subsided, her complexion assumed an even paler hue than it had before she saw him, and now she looked like a walking corpse.

He had not seen her, but she did not experience a sense of missing out due to this fact. She did not require a conversation with him, as he flowed within her blood; his thoughts were her own, and that was enough for her. Her admiration was not dependent upon an encounter with him.

Perhaps it was for the best that he had not heard, for if he had noticed her, the awkwardness would have forced him to pause from his own occupations, politely approach her and dedicate some of his precious time to her, and who was she to cause him to delay his essential business?

"I have received endlessly from him, while he has received nothing from me," she wrote to August after returning to the house where she was staying in Frankfurt.

***

Three days went by and the impression of the meeting remained imprinted upon her. She had made a date to go to the theater with several friends later and had just woken up from a light afternoon nap. As she was about to put on her dress, she heard a knock at the door.

She was not expecting anyone at that hour and assumed the visitor was seeking someone else, and therefore did not pay much attention to the knock. However, immediately afterward, she heard another knock on the door to her room. She opened the door slightly, and two words were whispered to her, and in a single moment, her knees grew weak once more. *Calm down!* she commanded herself, thinking that if she were to start getting dressed now, it would take quite a while. She had to put on her slip and then the dress and lace it up and button it. Under all that, there was also the matter of her stockings and putting on her shoes. She would have to brush her hair, disheveled from sleep. It was not proper to leave him waiting for her. Therefore, she pulled her dressing gown down from the hook and put it on over her nightgown. She quickly plaited her hair into a long braid and hurried down the stairs.

Despite the many words within her, there was not a single word to describe the moment in which she appeared in her hosts' drawing room clad in her dressing gown. Goethe was standing there, apologizing for showing up without notice. He was apologizing to her! "I heard that you were in Frankfurt, and it was important to me to make time to spend in your company."

In her company!

And so the two of them sat, he dressed in his best finery, and that bright aura she had drawn around his name her whole life hovered right there over his head, illuminating him as if he were one of the saints. While she, little Mrs. Levin, whose hands he had kissed just a moment ago, sat there in her dressing gown.

"*I sacrificed myself so as not to leave him waiting even for a moment,*" she would later note in her letter to August.

And at night, when she lay in her bed, her eyes closed, she thought that

Goethe's very presence had bestowed her with a noble title that no god from Mount Olympus could have granted her. She was proud of this visit, proud with every fiber of her being.

"Goethe saw me!"

43 | 1816

Over the years, after each of them retreated into her own life, the only thing that could bring Rahel, Henriette and Dorothea together was the death of someone close. But this time, none of their relatives had passed away, and yet they still met. As if a guiding hand wished to unite them, they met spontaneously in Berlin.

They were no longer the girls they once were, no longer tending toward uncontrollable laughter and mischievous wildness, and yet they joked and rejoiced and reminisced about days gone by, days that evoked mixed emotions within them. They alternated between then and now, filling in the gaps and adding what they had not had time to cover in their letters.

The first thing they talked about was precisely the thing from which they had wished to distance themselves for most of their lives—the Jews and their situation. The three of them were already rooted in the Christian world, but still had unbreakable ties to people within the Jewish community. Henriette, who had already distanced herself from Judaism, but had yet to be baptized, as her mother was still alive, mentioned her friend Karl Ludwig Börne, whom they knew as Judah Leib. He had been a frequent guest in the home she shared with the late Markus, who had taken him under his wing. Börne deliberated on the question of conversion, wishing to find greater worldly success. About two years ago, when they had discussed the matter, Henriette had thought that after the decrees of emancipation were issued, baptism might no longer be required. She knew his wish to convert was motivated solely by practical considerations, and now, if the Jews were granted rights, perhaps it might prove unnecessary. However, then, the whole matter of emancipation began to fade away, and the dispensations and rights granted to Jews began to disappear completely. After a while, her friend's rights were revoked as well; everything that had been working in his favor gradually dissipated and he was left devoid of rights and of employment, and it was clear to Henriette that there would be no choice but to proceed with the religious conversion.

What Rahel and Henriette remembered about Leib was actually his intense infatuation with Henriette and his pathetic attempt to commit suicide after her husband's death, when he thought she would reciprocate his affections and was rejected. She did not accept his advances, as had been her custom with all her suitors since being widowed.

"Even today," she told them, "I have quite a few suitors, and all of them wish to rescue me from a life of poverty."

Rahel did not understand why she insisted on remaining a widow. "After all, you've always been conservative on this topic. You were happy to be married and faithfully filled the role of wife. You referred to it as 'a calling' and were even sorry for your sister who did not fulfill this 'calling' for herself."

Dorothea agreed with Rahel, but also vividly remembered the intense pressure Henriette had put upon her to leave her wretched marriage, quite a while before Schlegel came along.

"Marriage must be based on true appreciation. The husband must know how to appreciate his wife's mind. If it is characterized by friendship and bonds of affection—if it possesses all that—then I am an avid supporter. However, we are well aware that very few men treat their wives that way and that the wives are willing to serve as an ornament and a mere source of pleasure to their husbands, so long as they maintain the status quo and do not rock the boat."

Dorothea and Rahel agreed with her, but mostly marveled at the change that had occurred in her. However, to Henriette, this seemed natural.

Immediately after she was widowed, the desire to take charge of her fate and manage her own affairs as she saw fit had surfaced within her. She did not know the source of this desire, but from the moment it arrived, she did not want to relinquish it.

"Fortune or misfortune has situated us alone, without a supportive environment. We do not feel stable ground under our feet and therefore we sway. While seeking support, we often believe we have indeed found it and then we rely upon it and sink down."

She had always known that her marriage involved luck. Although it had not been perfect, it had provided her with all that she could ask for, and once it was over, she decided she would only rely on herself.

"Time has changed us," Dorothea said, placing her hand on Rahel's shoulder. "See, you, too, thought that you would not get married, and ultimately you did."

Rahel nodded. She had written to them of her decision to marry August two years ago and both of them wished her happiness and luck. But now, as they sat together by the warming fireplace, she could tell them in detail how it had happened and what had motivated her to marry precisely the man who seemed farthest from her.

Alexander von Maravic, the man who inserted himself between her and August and inspired much jealousy in him, the man who had almost come between them, was actually the one who had ultimately made her come to her senses and realize that August was the man with whom she wanted to share her life.

It was actually August who had introduced her to Alexander von Maravic. He was a young, handsome nobleman, although his soul was conflicted and fiery. He voluntarily enlisted in the Prussian Army fighting against Napoleon, but did not do so out of patriotism or identification with his homeland, but rather out of a death wish and pure hatred for the world. Even during their first meeting, Maravic was direct and wore no masks, thus winning Rahel's heart: "I live badly. I'm too isolated, too mechanical. No relationships, no hope, and my inner strength nearly collapses when faced with colorless death, which closes in on me from all directions."

Rahel, for whom morbidity was a middle name, felt that she had encountered a person who experienced the world just as she did. It seemed as if his existence in the world was also an accident of sorts. Just like her, he had been born to a tradition he could not escape, and was just as trapped as she was in a world that evoked disgust and repulsion in him. As the two of them grew closer, her relationship with August began to dissipate, and Rahel felt that she had found her soulmate. Thanks to him, she learned how to take a step back and view the world from an independent perspective. Thanks to him, she could emerge from herself, from her inner burrowing, and look at things from above, with no emotional involvement. He taught her to feel the contempt he felt for the class to which he belonged, the class she had always aspired to join. He taught her to understand it was all worthless, speaking again and again of the degeneration of the world and of the "detachment and emptiness" of the present. And as she was so focused on his life, his actions, his thoughts, his intentions and his entire being, all of her introspection and obsessive preoccupation with her feelings came to a stop at the time, as if she no longer needed them.

The rift between them formed when he began to declare that enlightenment had doomed the world to disaster. While she, her entire existence depended upon enlightenment. It was the only thing that allowed her a full life, that promoted her status and allowed her to get to know other classes, that connected her to all her acquaintances and friends and lovers. And now he had also turned his back on the world she came from and to which she belonged. And if that was not enough, he had also begun to malign August, whom he knew from back in their days at the university.

"He claimed he was vulgar, petty in his opinions and meager in the energy of his willpower. He said his vulgarity was repulsive and embarrassing. And he also said there was no true greatness to him." She had never revealed all this, not to Dorothea or to Henriette. Perhaps she was ashamed of allowing a man whose entire essence was comprised of contempt for the world to infiltrate her heart, or of actually loving him despite all of that.

But it was actually Maravic's claims that caused her to understand several things about August. "It's true that he was not a nobleman, but he was a liberal and an intellectual, a member of the middle class of enlightenment, who believed fiercely in the rights of the lower classes. He himself was opposed to the nobility as a class and to rising through the ranks based on birthright. It was only through August that I realized that the nobility, in which I have always so strongly believed and to which I was so attracted, would not serve my interests, and could not promote me and deliver me to the better world I have always sought for myself."

Dorothea did not have much to share beyond what she had already written to them in her letters. Her life was conducted within a pattern she had set for herself. Schlegel traveled frequently. Her children lived their lives elsewhere, and she filled her days with writing and prayer. The storms had subsided, making room for a stillness she had never known before. Even if she were to be left alone, she said, she would be satisfied with her life.

Ultimately, they relied only on themselves, as well as relying on their new god, who took on a different form for each of them. Henriette consoled herself with the concept of a higher authority, and did not trouble her mind with attempts to find a rational explanation for the world in which she lived. She had accepted Christianity, and although she had not yet been baptized, she knew it was only a matter of time and that she would ultimately do so. Dorothea devoted her days as a Catholic to fortifying her faith, wishing to attain eternal life and the promise of heaven. While Rahel, certain as she might be in her new religion, was in no hurry to entrust her entire being to it. On the day she married August, she was baptized into the Christian faith. Ludwig, her younger brother to whom she was close, was the only one she invited to stand by her side and give her away to her future husband. She did not sleep all night; something was fluttering within her and despite her ability to dig deep and examine her own mind, she could not manage to understand whether these were flutters of resistance or excitement. She had long despised the Jewish religion and was utterly certain of August, and yet these flutters deprived her of sleep, and in the morning, she woke bleary-eyed. All she wanted was to get it all over with and be done with it, as if it were a surgical medical procedure, such as having a mole removed. From the moment the baptism ceremony came to an end, followed by the wedding ceremony, she felt relief.

Just as she had not given herself over to Judaism, so, too, did she not hurry to give herself over to Christianity. She asked questions and investigated, and did not malign human intelligence, as her two friends did, although this was the Church's decree. This intelligence belonged solely to human beings, and they were the only ones empowered to make use of it, Rahel believed. But all this did not contradict her affinity for prayer. On the contrary, she appreciated it and avidly believed it was prayer that brought the soul directly to God, who was revealed to each and every person in the process.

And today, as had been the case in the past as well, similarity was not what brought them closer to each other, and difference was not what tore them apart. They were as close as if they had never parted.

44 | 1819

Several months after the moving reunion in Berlin, Henriette's mother passed away, and nothing more remained for her there. No parents or siblings or friends. Therefore, she decided to accept the position she had been offered and traveled to Rome. But first, she did what she had been waiting to do for some time—the baptism ceremony.

The ceremony was held privately for her, with only Schleiermacher present. She wished to be baptized privately not because she was ambivalent about her decision, but because she saw no need to flaunt her choice to those who considered her a member of the community—her Jewish friends. Therefore, she left the neighborhood where she was living and scheduled the event at a location far from the eyes of her acquaintances, in the outskirts of Berlin. The ceremony was held early in the morning, while the chill of the night still lingered in the air and few people were out and about on the streets. Schleiermacher arrived to pick her up in a carriage he had paid for in advance, and she waited on the threshold of her home in a festive outfit.

She had not slept a wink all night. Would she feel a change after the baptism? Would she be more religious? More devout? After all, her faith had been full and complete for a long time now, and the ritual was a mere formality. And yet she was gripped by excitement that reminded her of the day before her wedding. Then, she was unsure what lay before her and what awaited her in life after committing to a man she did not know. But now, she knew this God as well as the religion He had produced, and she knew His messenger, Christ, she knew His scripture and the tenets of His faith. She had renounced her Judaism some time ago and had no desire to stay within its bounds. And yet the occasion unsettled her, and she wished to be done with it as soon as possible and move on with her life.

After the ceremony, she began her life as a Protestant, in Rome, to which she ventured following an offer of employment. Dorothea, too, was living in Rome and insisted on sharing her home with Henriette. The house was not large but it had enough rooms for her and Schlegel, who came and went, and for her children, who were adults with lives of their own, and now for Henriette, who had always stood by her as well. Life in Rome provided them with interesting encounters and quite a few acquaintances from Old Berlin.

One evening, Dorothea invited some friends over. Schlegel was on one of his journeys; she was not certain if he was in Berlin or in Jena or in Helle or elsewhere. For some time now, she had had a hard time tracking his wanderings and chose to focus utterly on writing, reading and translating, and on her life as a Catholic. But that day, the air was pleasant and the chill had been replaced by a breeze bearing the scent of fresh flowers, and all this created an awakening of sorts within her. Perhaps it was related to the imminent spring, perhaps to the presence of her good friend, or perhaps she wished to somewhat recreate those days in Berlin.

That evening, Barthold Georg Niebuhr, a historian serving as an ambassador to the Pope's court, showed up in the company of a handsome young man. Niebuhr introduced him, praising him effusively. "Immanuel Bekker. He was carrying out a uniquely important task until a short while ago. I would not be overstating the case if I said that the spiritual future of Germany as a whole hung in the balance, and he handled the matter in the best possible way, saving our rich culture."

Meanwhile, Immanuel Bekker stood there as if rooted to the wooden floor of the tiny drawing room, as if he were not there. He did not make a sound, or even flash a small, polite smile. The praise heaped upon him by the man who had opened his home to him and accommodated him under his roof seemed to mean nothing to him. He was the son of a metalsmith from Berlin, and his entire life was now dedicated to seeking out and copying manuscripts looted by the conquering French. Once this task came to an end, and he managed to return many manuscripts to libraries and archives, the Berlin Academy of Arts gave him a new assignment, and for him it was a job like any other.

"A major, annotated edition of the writings of Aristotle is forthcoming soon, and who is better for the task than Immanuel Bekker, an expert at searching archives and digging around in libraries?" Niebuhr asked. He did not truly expect an answer, exuberantly adding, "For three years, he stayed in Paris and did not see daylight. For twelve hours a day, he would sit and copy the manuscripts impudently seized by the conquerors. And after three years, he looked as if he had been living in underground burrows, and was instructed, upon doctor's orders, to spend as much time in the sunlight as possible."

Henriette had heard of Immanuel Bekker from her good friend Schleiermacher, who had taken him under his wing, but she had yet to meet him. She liked him immediately, and soon found out that the feeling was mutual.

"'What is a friend? A single soul dwelling in two bodies,'" he quoted Aristotle to her and Henriette felt ready to become one single, whole soul with him. He was pleasant and did not speak much. When she mentioned it to Schleiermacher, he jokingly replied, "He can be silent in seven languages." And indeed, he was usually silent, but not constantly silent. And when he was not, he spoke wisely and filled her heart with curiosity, whispering words of love, complimenting her appearance and making her feel younger. Things went easily with him and he sometimes reminded her of her late husband. They did not resemble each other physically or in their areas of interest. She was older than him by twenty-one years, and yet something in him felt familiar and safe to her. Some time after they met, she opened her heart to him, but one fear snuck in—she was afraid of the moment when she would have to take off her clothes in his presence, when she was no longer as young as she once was, her skin no longer taut like it once was, and the same was true of her belly. Beyond that, intimate relations were not something she relished, then or now.

And yet, he was young and virile and sought her opinion and her knowledge, but also her proximity and her body. He did so considerately and gently, but also out of the lust of the young, of those who were motivated by hunger. And she thought of Rahel, of the love affairs that had raised her to heights that few had experienced, but had also propelled her into the depths of hell.

She recalled that Rahel had once maligned her to Dorothea: "Madam Herz spends her life dressed to the nines and does not know that undressing is also an option, and what one feels while doing so." At the time, when Dorothea had told her about it, she reacted with disinterest, as if it did not affect her, but now she thought that Rahel was right. If she wanted to allow her relationship with Immanuel Bekker to develop, she would have to undress and feel and experience and give of herself and accept the passion in which he desired to sweep her up. And the more she thought about it, the more she found that it was very difficult for her to do so.

***

Quite a while had passed since Dorothea's first days in Berlin with her husband Simon and now, from amidst her life in Rome, she sometimes felt as if it was just a story in one of her books. At certain moments, she actually felt penitent and remorseful, hoping for forgiveness.

Dorothea had given Veit two good, talented sons and he could honestly say their mother had endowed them with a spirit of imagination and creativity and the fearlessness of one who did not follow the beaten path.

He funded Philipp's studies at the Dresden Academy and, with his money, also allowed him to learn the fundamentals of painting from Caspar David Friedrich, one of the best German Romantic painters of the era. When Philipp exhausted his studies there, he uprooted to Vienna and Veit paid for his studies there as well. However, he did not find his place at the Vienna Academy of Fine Arts either and dropped out along with a group of friends from the Romantic school, all of whom moved to Rome in order to live in the abandoned Sant'Isidoro monastery.

"Dear Father," Philipp wrote. *"All our activity is done in opposition, mostly to Neoclassicism, as well as to the mundane manner of teaching at the Academy. Free thought is not accepted here and there is no focus on developing the creative spirit. And what do we seek? To return to that golden era of values that are dominated by the spirit; no more shallow virtuosity, no more of the same old thing. We seek to paint from a decent point of view."*

Veit admired their courage in going against the current; it was the courage of the young. He thought of himself and of the time when he was their age and did not find even a pinch of that courage in himself. Their group now resided in the monastery, its members living an ascetic life, all their days dedicated to opposing the mainstream, a course of action that was not benefiting them at the moment, its future consequences still unclear. But Veit did not see fit to object in any way. He knew that, like their mother, they would follow their truth all the way.

His Jonah—now named Johannes—had also joined a group that had adopted the derogatory nickname used against it. They were called "the Nazarenes" and had turned this term of mockery into their trademark.

"We are mocked for our antiquated style, for the painted figures wearing biblical, pre-Renaissance garb. We are mocked for our way of life and for turning our back on academia. For us, there is one truth that incorporates values, the spirit of religion and its innocence. Values that once existed and were lost, and now we wish to revive them with our art. If they mock us—very well then, let them mock us. 'Whosoever shall smite thee on thy right cheek, turn to him the other also.'"[42]

Perhaps something of their father's nature had clung to them as well, and they had adopted his mild, easy temperament, in addition to the daring they got from their mother, causing them to turn away from turbulence.

---

42 Matthew 5:39

But now, he could admit to Dorothea that not only had he forgiven her, but he was also proud of the education she had given them, which he never could have done.

"I forgive and have forgiven long ago. After all, from the first moment you were introduced to me, your soul seemed conflicted and roiling to me, your mind and heart battling each other."

This was his nature, it was more convenient and pleasant for him that way, and the body was loose, with no tension there. This was his nature both in the past and perpetually. And in this spirit, he could take in good, positive things and always be pleased with his lot and with all that his God—the God of Moses—had provided him.

***

"Hierosolyma est perdita."[43]

It had only been a short time since Rahel left Karlsruhe with August, and although she had been very sorry when he was called to leave his position and return to Berlin, she was now glad that they had left in time and had not been forced to witness evil raging in the streets with their own eyes.

Her brother Ludwig reported to her from Karlsruhe, where his fiancée Friederike lived. During those days, they sat at home with the windows shuttered and did not venture outside, fearing they would be harmed. And although several months had gone by since Ludwig had converted, and he was now utterly a Christian, he still knew that his Jewish appearance might betray him, and also knew that no one would take the time to inquire what his religion was and when he had been baptized.

The Jews of Karlsruhe had been the first to feel the wrath of their neighbors, who vented their rage at them mercilessly. They burst out into the streets in a preplanned or spontaneous manner, full of hatred and bitterness, equipped with a sense of superiority. Among them were students

---

43 Latin: "Jerusalem is lost."

and professors and business owners and commoners—and all of them were armed with the same purpose, as well as with various implements of destruction. They marauded against the Jews and their property in any way they saw fit, with no one to stop them.

"*Hep! Hep! Jude verreck!*"[44] they called out loudly and rhythmically, and their voices did not weaken even when they invested more energy and power in the task of whipping.

"*This is amazing. How did the commoners come upon that expression, 'hep hep'?*[45] *They cannot possibly know its source. No doubt, this riot was incited by an educated mob.*"

The riots then spread. Swiftly and systematically, the plague of hatred also reached central and southern Germany. In Franconia, Jews were exiled from their homes, and in Frankfurt, many escaped to the border with Denmark. Throughout this time, the German people maintained their silence and the Jews did as well. They resigned themselves to their fate silently.

Hep! Hep! Destruction and death for every Jew!
If you don't flee, your end is near!

For two days, Ludwig and his fiancée heard the calls rising from the street, calls that the police did not manage or did not want to quell. Stunned, he forcefully stopped himself from venturing out and violently assaulting the passersby who strolled down the street, indifferent, while Jews were beaten in front of their eyes. It was quite enough that they walked by and read the banners pasted to the walls on the streets, calling for a massacre of the Jews. Read them and nodded in agreement or in silent agreement, none of them stopping to tear off the banners and put an end to the wild, uninhibited riot.

"The true extent of people's corruption and their limited sense of law

---

44 German: "Death to all Jews."

45 An acronym of the Latin phrase *Hierosolyma est perdita*, attributed to Roman soldiers during the siege upon Jerusalem in 70 AD, or to marauders in the Rhineland during the crusades. The use of Latin is considered to be confined to the educated.

and justice—not to mention love for their fellow man—is indicated by the fact that no outrage was expressed regarding these incidents, not even in the official press… I've heard that the residents of the city raged at Brünker for promptly closing the beer halls. They threatened to topple him off his horse."

After the riots subsided somewhat, Ludwig went out to see what had happened with his own eyes, writing to Rahel, who was in Berlin: "*I did not want to stay in one place for fear that I would be arrested, and therefore walked all the way to Walhorngasse. There I spotted the city commander, General Brünker, riding his horse, and as shouting was still ringing out occasionally, he instructed his unit, 'Let the bastards shout if they insist on it, but the moment they do anything foolish, strike at them!' All the residents of the city stood at their open windows and I slowly approached the houses so I could hear what they were saying and get a sense of their frame of mind.*

"*Inside the doorways, children were playing, gleeful and giggling. They surveyed the events of the day with childish interest. But none of the men or the women scolded them or even conducted a serious conversation with them. The chance of encountering a priest was even lower, although I believe there should have been pastors there, expounding on the value of love.*"

Rahel's written response took longer than usual to arrive, due to the riots.

"*I feel infinite sadness on behalf of the Jews. This is something I have never experienced before. What are masses of people banished from their homes to do? Are they trying to detain them only to continue humiliating and torturing them? It seems as if the Germans desperately need the Jews as scapegoats that are convenient to hate. I know the nature of my country. Sadly, for three years now, I have been saying that the Jews will be attacked; I have witnesses. Supposedly, the Germans are deeply offended, and why? Because the most cultured, peace-loving and disciplined nation, with their hypocritical love for Christianity (and may the Lord forgive me for my sins) and for medieval times due to their poetry, art and atrocities, has been inciting people to carry out the only atrocity to which they can still be incited: to strike at the Jews! All the newspapers have been hinting at it for years—professors Paris, Reise, whatever their names are… The source of their hatred is not religious fervor. How can they hate other faiths when they do not even like their own?"*

She also added, on quite a different note, that she and August had decided to re-establish the gatherings in the living room of her home. No more meetings in a shabby attic, but rather a respectable lodging on Französische Strasse. And although at the moment her husband did not have any official position due to his opinions, which were too subversive for the administration, they were making do and subsisting at a reasonable standard of living.

She concluded with an anecdote about her good friend Henriette Herz. "*A while ago, Immanuel Bekker proposed to her. He is younger than her by twenty-one years, and nevertheless, she is seriously considering accepting. I wish her all the best and much happiness.*"

45 | 1823

"Henriette visited me this morning," von Humboldt told his wife as they sat down for lunch. "The comet has turned bright for her and if it persists, some of her wrinkles will disappear along with it. She was a lot more beautiful than usual. Immanuel Bekker has now proposed to her, and I tried to dissuade her from marrying him. If it wasn't for the matter of the age difference, she would do it, believe me. She admitted that she enjoys leaving that sort of impression even now, and I find it quite natural. I myself would enjoy it if people still found me attractive at my age."

***

Henriette declined Immanuel Bekker's proposal. No one knew whether she had been convinced by von Humboldt's appeal or whether she had made up her mind on her own. She now lived alone in Berlin, in a small apartment according to her financial means, its rooms dim and narrow, and it seemed as if her only difficulty was with the betrayal of the body.

She felt pain from the passing of time, from aging and wear. For her, the most meaningful conversion in her life was not the religious one but rather the conversion she herself had undergone—from child to youth, to adult and to the old woman she now was. It seemed as if the more she fought off time, the more it abused her. In this, it joined the people around her and their comments about the way she dressed, which they believed did not match her age at all. And all this was said behind her back.

But there were other voices as well, at least from her friends.

"People make fun of dear old lady Herz. There is something odd about that woman; she does not wish to grow old and does not do so. She does not want to look old, and no one treats her that way, either," her long-time friend Ludwig Börne wrote to one of his friends. However, even if she had read these words, she would still have remained convinced of one thing: for her, it was all over.

It was Schleiermacher who came up with the idea that she document her life on paper, an idea she initially opposed. But after rethinking it and listening to his logical considerations, she was won over.

"The bright, black eyes turned lighter and dim. The shiny black hair turned white. The white pearly teeth turned black and flawed, and the full oval face turned lean and long." These were the opening words to the story of her life.

After writing down what oppressed her, the way she saw herself, she seemed recharged and returned to the beginning. Writing brought her back to her happy days as a cheerful, carefree girl, and mostly back to her father.

"My father was a Portuguese Jew. His own father fled Portugal with many of his religious friends so as not to be persecuted by the Inquisition."

It was important to her to tell the tale of the man who had brought her into the world, who had loved her so and showered her with warmth and love, who had taught her everything she knew until the day he gave her away in marriage, who had taught her about investing in her appearance and about refinement.

"As per the fashion of the time, his attire was elegant, sewn of fine fabric, his clothes made of silk, velvet and similar materials. The best linen, a wig with its hair pulled back and a good tricorne hat. Although this outfit had begun to seem old-fashioned, even back then, he was very handsome in this garb, to such an extent that the older physicians began to indulge themselves with such suits as well."

And her mother? What would she say about her sickly mother, with the red eyes that not even her husband the doctor could cure? Her father had explained to her that this reddishness was caused by the problem of the ingrown lashes, which injured the eye, but she had once heard that it was a result of long hours of crying after the premature death of her firstborn son. Either way, it did not soften her heart and she had no compassion for her.

"*My mother was said to be very beautiful, although, I must confess, I did not discern any remains of her beauty, ever again.*"

Perhaps it was a result of the lack of understanding between the two, perhaps due to many years of having no common ground and no shortage of conflict. Perhaps it was due to her mother's appearance, which was simple and unappealing, entirely and constantly severe. She always wished her father had a wife like the women who rode around in carriages, with elegant hats, the kind who caused all heads to turn. She thought her father's elegance demanded a beauty to stand by his side, and in her childhood, did not understand how he resigned himself to the woman who served as his wife but did not hold a candle to him.

She then also wrote about her husband, Dr. Markus Herz, whose inner qualities overshadowed his homely appearance.

***

Since Rahel and August had returned to Berlin from Karlsruhe, August had been unable to procure a government position. At first, he persisted in trying, but wherever he went, he was rejected with typical Berlin politeness. "On reserve" was the term for his professional status, and he was promised that when a position befitting of his skills opened up, he would be summoned to staff it.

From the first moment, Rahel told him that he would have to get used to the situation, which would not change anytime soon. After all, he had never concealed his liberal views, and since the riots, people who held such opinions were unwanted in the corridors of power. While less focused on political aspirations, he wished to resume his status as a respected member of society, to belong once more. He did not want to impact history but merely to take part in it again, and yet the world seemed to mock the both of them. The very liberalism that had been the first trait that Rahel so appreciated in her husband now caused them to be rejected once more. After many failed attempts and the realization that no position would be found for him in these times, he resigned himself to the situation and hoped that things would return to their previous state as soon as possible. He consoled himself with the knowledge that they were still entitled to his state pension from Prussia and did not have to worry about their livelihood.

Now both of them were settled in Berlin, busy writing and hosting guests in their home. In the previous year, they had already published a manuscript comprised of selected quotes by Angelus Silesius, a Baroque sixteenth-century mystic. Rahel had always found him enchanting and swept August along in the idea of compiling his sayings in a manuscript to which they would add their own interpretations and comments.

"The moment man thinks about it, he immediately finds the true god within him, in himself. In the same way that he did not make himself, the creative imagination, the great splendor, the eternal wonder," Rahel wrote in a comment on one of his poems. Like Angelus, she, too, believed that God was in the soul itself, which is where she sensed him in full force.

Another thinker she was never willing to relinquish was Goethe. His writing now served as a focus for the social gatherings they hosted in their home. Only last week, she had found herself fervently defending his work against the new-old attitude currently spreading, in which he was once again facing the same accusations of betraying his homeland. "Old Goethe," the angry youths called him. "He is conservative and opposes the revolution. He did not take part in the war against Napoleon the Conqueror back in the day, not as a poet and certainly not as a fighter, and the same is true today as well." This was the sentiment conveyed, one way or another, and his patriotism came to be questioned. He, who wrote poems and plays and essays and stories for his homeland, was now referred to as "an Olympic personality," one who floats about in elevated spheres, ignoring the burning necessities of life. And all the things said about him reached

Rahel's drawing room only so that she could reject them and offer her own interpretations of the claims raised against him.

"He cannot be a supporter of the French Revolution, as its horrors brought him great misery. He himself wrote about it. It is also well known that as a poet, he is opposed to all political poetry. He views it as limiting one's horizons, dependency upon political parties and narrow-mindedness." When she spoke of Goethe, of his poems, his writing and his essence, explaining and interpreting him and living through his eyes, there was nothing around her other than herself and him.

***

After three years, perhaps the most wonderful she had ever known in her life, the same old tune began to play inside her, bringing restlessness in its wake, and her dissatisfaction threatened to seize control of her once more.

"I do not like anything here, nothing here grants me pleasure," she said again and again. "No one should return to his country of origin after being far from it for a long while."

August was pleased with his lot and sought no more than what he had. It was true that he would have been happier if he could find another position, but although he held no official position, he and Rahel lived as a part of society and were appreciated and sought out by others. All this, along with their shared task of writing, was enough for him.

However, Rahel continued to complain. "All these are ghosts," she told him accusingly when her frustration grew. He did not understand its cause and she did not further reveal her heart, a topic she could only write about to her good friends.

"My life is reserved and boring! I am bored to tears."

She had expected that once she shed her Judaism, she could live like the rest of the Berliners, thought that if he agreed to the condition she posed to him before they married, that he would not impose even a single limitation upon her as his wife (a condition that he fulfilled, of course), her marriage would be perfect. However, gradually, she was overcome by the creeping realization that she had shed much more than she meant to and now all that was left of her was a role played by someone else, who was not her. Did Rahel miss all the turbulence and the emotional upheaval? All the little scandals she had piled upon herself? In certain moments, she thought her marriage had exerted a price that was too steep.

46 | 1825

August had planned the meeting and Rahel knew she could not avoid it. Although he was aware of her reservations, this time he chose to ignore them. Just as he had outdone himself when he planned the trip to Weimar, leaving Rahel thrilled, he did the same by setting up and organizing the meeting with the idol whom they worshipped together. Although he did not know Goethe personally and had never met him, he knew which connections to make use of in order to set the plan in motion, and also knew that the moment Goethe heard it was Rahel, he would not refuse.

"If you want to, come, and if you're not interested in coming along, I will understand and travel on my own," he told her, even though he did not mean what he said. He knew very well that without Rahel, the meeting would be pointless.

And so it came to be that precisely ten years after that wretched meeting, when Rahel had been clad in a robe, she met Goethe again, this time in his drawing room, now wearing a dress sewn for her well in advance, her hair elegantly done, a pair of pearl earrings adorning her earlobes and light lace gloves covering her small hands.

"Little Levi," Goethe called out when the two of them entered his home, adding with a wink, "I debated whether to greet the two of you in a dressing gown or to bother to get dressed." They laughed. Once again, Rahel's face was covered with the same flush that had flooded her when she stood on the sidewalk and called out to him; however, this time it was unaccompanied by a weakness in the knees and a cold sweat. She was not stricken by shock; she was utterly ready to speak. She had thought in advance of what she would say, what they would talk about and how the conversation would develop. She had determined which topics she should express her opinion on, and which ones she should not comment upon. For whole days before the meeting, she imagined his home, the way he would host them, the refreshments he would serve on the drawing room table. However, fertile as her imagination might be, it did not approach reality in any way.

When the carriage stopped across from his house, they had to climb four steps. The house was located on Frauenplan Street and built in a Baroque style. The front door was visible from the street and nothing about it indicated what was to be found inside.

They climbed the stairs and after knocking on the heavy door, whose color matched the first-story windows, it was opened. A woman dressed in a maid's uniform greeted the Varnhagens. She wore a small apron pinned to her gray dress, and a hat with jagged ends was perched upon her head. With a measured, polite smile, the woman invited the couple into a foyer of sorts, wordlessly instructing them to turn right. Upstairs, at the top of a staircase, their esteemed host, Johann Wolfgang Goethe, awaited them, and with no preliminary pleasantries, he began to tell them the history of the staircase on which he was standing, which they would soon find themselves climbing as well.

"It was the first thing I did when I received the house from Emperor Karl August—one of the fundamental changes I wished to make, all under the influence of Ancient Greece, the Romans and, of course, the Renaissance, which was absorbed into my blood after a two-year stay in Italy. It was a dream come true—born of a desire that anyone who went up and down these stairs would never grow tired of them."

The house resembled a gallery of works of art. Across from the staircase, recessed into the wall, were two identically sized indentations containing classical black statues depicting the human form, replicas of the Apollo Belvedere. After climbing the staircase, a ceiling mural in breathtaking hues was revealed to them. "It was painted by Johann Heinrich Meyer, my advisor in matters of art and the person in charge of the renovation of the house," Goethe told them. Apparently, he was accustomed to serving as a guide for those touring his home. The mural depicted Iris, the winged messenger of the gods, descending to the earth upon the rainbow and honoring the era with a hundred symbols of peace. "Oh, how I wanted peace to arrive in those terrible times. How happy I was to return to my home after it was all over and discover Iris on the ceiling of my house. Wholeness, harmony and humanity are, as you know, the values at the core of the classical conception of art that I developed here in Weimar after my trip to Italy."

Rahel had never imagined that during the first hour of their visit, before they would even be offered a drink, the meeting would focus upon art rather than writing. The finest artists, both famous and less famous, served as a daily accompaniment to their friend's life within his home. *When you live in the shadow of such works of art, it is no wonder that you are full and rich,* Rahel thought to herself. The tour imbued her with a miraculous feeling.

At the center of the yellow room they reached at the end of the tour, stood a large dining table bearing a pitcher containing a steaming beverage and matching china cups, some cookies and a large platter of fruit. The room could obviously host a large number of visitors, but currently, only the three of them were there, surrounded by simple carvings in blue and yellow frames, which told the story of Cupid and Psyche.

Rahel did not require an explanation regarding the meaning of the yellow color of the walls. After all, it was all written down and explained in *Theory of Colors*, which he had published in 1810. Goethe, too, did not tend toward explanations; he was convinced that they had indeed read his *Theory*, and knew that it described that shade of yellow as "cheerful, vibrant and somewhat stimulating."

The back garden was the most surprising element of the entire visit. It consisted of five areas, each of which was bordered by flower beds and a box of hedges. Something different grew in each area: potatoes, cauliflower, even asparagus and artichokes. Cherry and peach trees, with grapes growing upon lattices affixed to the house's southern wall. The highlight of it all was Goethe's botanical experiments.

A transparent bed served as his observation post, from which he could track the development of the families of wild plants that he cultivated and expand his understanding of their botanical classification.

> *Wonderment fresh dost thou feel, as soon as the stem rears the flower*
> *Over the scaffolding frail of the alternating leaves.*
> *But this glory is only the new creation's foreteller,*
> *Yes, the leaf with its hues feeleth the hand all divine,*
> *And on a sudden contracteth itself.*[46]

Just as they were about to bid farewell to their wonderful host, Rahel brought up an impudent request, "To peek at your study, Goethe."

August wanted to bury himself at that moment, but Rahel's passion led her quite frequently in her life, and did so this time as well. "Your work is what gave me justification for the tribulations of life, for the values I believe in, which others might call delusional visions. I must, this one time, see where those works were created."

If Goethe was already tired, he did not show it, merely directing them with a smile toward his study.

"To be surrounded by a room full of comfortable, tasteful furniture is a condition that prevents me from thinking and causes me to be in a passive state," he said as they entered his study. And indeed, the gulf between the ascetic study that had produced masterpieces from him and the other parts of the house was immense. The furniture was simple and served the exact function for which the carpenter had created it. Nothing hung on the walls

---

46 From "The Metamorphosis of Plants," in *The Poems of Goethe*, translated by Edgar Alfred Bowring. https://www.gutenberg.org/cache/epub/1287/pg1287.html

other than essential items such as the list for the gardener, which swayed in the wind on the left transom of the window. On the table, which was particularly long, were scattered, in a supremely orderly manner, various items that probably served Goethe's scientific inquiries. There was also a small pillow lying on the table. "To place my hand there when I read for a long time," he explained without being asked.

The study walls were painted green. Rahel smiled, interpreting what her eyes were seeing. "Green brings true satisfaction."

Goethe smiled, and August did not say a word.

***

"Everything was said and done. He really is flowing in my blood!" Rahel said after they parted from their host and were waiting for the carriage to come and collect them. August wrapped his hand around hers and neither of them knew this would be the last time they would meet him.

Later that evening, as they sat to sip their last cup of tea, Rahel said, "What won my heart most of all was that miraculous, heartbreaking garden, especially when you are aware of the fact that the person in charge of the vegetable garden and the fruit trees was Christiane, his late wife."

47 | 1829

Dorothea was busy from morning to night, surrounded by pages, letters, lists, all of which she thoroughly sorted through. When she sat down to eat or drink something or to rest from the intensive work, she thought that death was inconsiderate. It emerged from some corner and took control with no preparation. If her Schlegel had been ill, then she could have prepared for the worst; she would have nursed him and taken care of him and would have had the time to bid him farewell. Perhaps she would have told him all that she had not had the time to say, or perhaps she would only have sat with him in silence, after everything had already been said. But death came swiftly and snatched her beloved. He was so young, with so many things still inside him to bestow upon the world, but now this possibility had been permanently sealed off.

His body had already disappeared from the house. He had been buried and his clothes distributed to whoever wanted them. Many tears had been shed and had already dried, with only a few left behind to emerge occasionally, surprisingly, just like accursed death.

Her mother, Fromet, snuck into her thoughts, along with the inevitable comparison between the two of them. Fromet's husband had also departed swiftly, and a loneliness that filled her days had been imposed upon her as well. Like her, Fromet, too, had to deal with piles upon piles of notes left behind by her husband, Moses Mendelssohn. Dorothea remembered how Fromet had tried to impose order upon them, but the deeper she dug in, the more she felt as if she was being swallowed up and had been unable to take control of it all. How was she supposed to know what to do with everything after having served tea and cookies all her days, catering to the palate of their guests? How was she supposed to know if she only lingered beside things, rather than venturing inside them? And how was she supposed to negotiate and converse with the publishers? What should she ask for, how much, from whom? After all, the publishers, both back then and today, only wished to double and triple their profits, and she, the great Mendelssohn's little wife, had no experience with all that. If it wasn't for David Friedlander, who helped a little, and other good people, nothing would have happened at all.

Dorothea meticulously sorted through sentences, words, letters, envisioning Schlegel sitting and writing, here in Rome, in Halle, in Jena, in Paris and in other locations, remembering how she had packed his suitcases for him, mended the clothes than needed mending, sewn new shirts for him and occasionally ordered a coat or new shoes. She recalled preparing fare for the road for him, putting the good paper she had purchased for him in his document case along with quality writing implements, making sure he would lack nothing.

And yet, she was not Fromet. She was, without a doubt, equipped with the required skills. After all, she was responsible for many publications and works that had appeared under Schlegel's name and also knew how to bargain and knew what an acceptable offer was and what the appropriate wage was. She was also fluent in the art of editing and soon could start working on his book *The Philosophy of Language* and publish it. She had indeed set an immense task for herself.

It was true that his body was dead, and this could not be altered, but his soul continued to pulse within her, as did his spirit. The more she published of his works and his wisdom, the more eternal he would become for her, continuing to live many years after she, too, returned her soul to her maker. Death had indeed taken him just as it had taken her father; however, the two of them lived on within the leather covers, amidst the letters and words and between the pages that emitted the scent of ink.

***

For some time now, Henriette had dwelled in the bosom of Christianity, which had been good to her. However, there was one matter to which she had a hard time resigning herself within her faith. For her, there was one God; she had granted Him access into her heart and He was enough for her. His son Jesus was secondary to her. She did not understand how Jesus had been accorded such a central position in the Christian world while all the good was carried out by God anyway. It was to Him that she spoke and from Him that she drew strength and encouragement. He was the one who performed miracles and listened to her prayers and sustained her soul, and most of all, it was He who dwelled in her heart and in her entire body.

If she were to speak of it openly, she would set the entire Christian world against her. Therefore, she allowed herself to question Christ's position only with her close friend Schleiermacher. She knew he would not condemn her for her opinions and would continue to love her despite it all.

"They position the one who called himself human above the one who sent him to us as a savior—they pray almost exclusively to him. He no longer stands there as a mediator but as a god."

After writing her words, she read them again and felt some regret over them. She regretted writing her criticism precisely to the person who had brought her closer to the religion that granted her solace each and every day, and most of all, to one who had been educated in the institutions of the same church. Was she being ungrateful?

Therefore, she did not send the letter. But the sentiment burned inside her and when she met Schleiermacher some time later, she sat down with him to discuss the matter.

"They address their prayers to the Son instead of to God himself and forget that Christ is only His emissary."

Schleiermacher was not angry. He was also not angry when she used the word "cult." He explained to her that Christ "was sent with a mission from that same God—to provide salvation for humanity as a whole. And therefore, he was given the tools and entrusted with the authority as well as the ability to work miracles, and even beyond."

Henriette was not easily convinced, and it was important to her to express her opinion, while simultaneously making an effort to study the Christian religion. She had begun doing so back when she was Jewish and continued even now when she was utterly a Christian, in her body, in her thoughts and in the way she conducted herself in the world.

She wished to understand the essence, as the deeper she delved into carrying out the religious edicts, the stronger and more entrenched she became in Christianity, the greater her salvation would be once death came to claim her. Henriette wanted to get into heaven. She imagined paradise as aesthetical and pleasing to the eye, the way she liked to see herself, and yearned to be accepted there for her eternal rest.

48 | March 7, 1833

Hushed on the hill
Is the breeze;
Scarce by the zephyr
The trees
Softly are pressed;
The woodbird's asleep on the bough.
Wait, then, and thou
Soon wilt find rest.

— Goethe[47]

Dorothea and Henriette stood beside Rahel's bed. Her body was gaunt and her black hair had gone white some time ago. Only her eyes were full of vitality, as if refusing to say goodbye. Henriette and Dorothea knew that this time, the only prayers for her would be hymns that would send her soul off to eternal life after she bid farewell to her body.

A long time had passed since Rahel arrived in the world; shortly after she had emerged from her mother's belly, was already wreaking havoc, coming and yet not coming, deciding and yet not deciding, and everyone had to

---

47 From "The Same," in *The Poems of Goethe*, translated by Edgar Alfred Bowring. https://www.gutenberg.org/cache/epub/1287/pg1287.html

wait, standing around her and expecting the worst. Now, neither Henriette's father nor Moses Mendelssohn was with them to grant them support and explain what was not always explainable. Also absent were their mothers and brothers and sisters and the bearded officials. Dorothea and Henriette stood on their own. They had been with her when she came into the world and they were with her now, when she was about to depart from it.

Dorothea extended her hand to Rahel, as if wishing to recreate that touch, the embrace of the tiny fingers of the infant who had been suspended between heaven and earth back then. She could almost feel the thrill she had felt back then when Rahel's tiny finger wrapped around her hand.

Dorothea had been like a little mother to her in her earliest days and remained there for her now even when she had nothing left to give. And the thrill of recalling that primal experience was replaced by the sensation of something that was about to vanish from her forever, a great sense of oppression settling within her body. It was not right for mothers to bury their daughters. But she knew that soon, the "commending ceremony" would arrive and Rahel would be commended to God, and the pastor would say "ashes to ashes, dust to dust," on her behalf, and everyone would say Amen.

"My dear August," Rahel whispered, her voice nearly inaudible. "I thought about Christ and cried for his agony. I felt it, for the first time, I felt it, that He was my brother. And Mary, her suffering was so great! She saw her beloved son suffering but did not give in; she stood by the cross! I could not have done that! I could not have been so strong and held on to my Judaism as Christ held on to Christianity. I admit how weak I am."

Her Jewish roots and that two-thousand-year-old pain rose to face her, wishing to appease her, and she cursed them and fled from them and denied them and even converted them, but they did not abandon her. And in her last breaths, they wished to show her what she had refused to see during her entire life. In one moment, it all became clear.

"Such history…" she whispered in a voice that was gradually fading away, a smile of resignation dawning upon her face. "A refugee from Egypt and from the Land of Israel."

August listened. With one hand, he grasped her own hand, as if wishing to keep her with him for a bit longer, while his other hand held a pen. He knew these were her last words and wrote them down despite his emotional turmoil, despite the tears blurring his vision, although he wanted to toss it all away and be collected, along with her, into the place where she was going. For years now, he had taken care to document every word and sentence, every saying and anecdote she uttered. He had committed to doing so for her. It was the mission of his life. Therefore, he did so now, as well, torn between the emotions that flooded him and cold logic.

Dorothea gazed at them. It had only been four years since her Schlegel died abruptly on one of his journeys, and she had not been there to say goodbye to him, to speak last words to him or even just to caress his hand, just as August was now doing for Rahel. And although the taste of missing out was already starting to gnaw at her, she was thankful for the fact that she was granted these moments with Rahel.

Henriette listened to Rahel and her thoughts wandered to her own death, which had been preoccupying her for some time, and whose timing she could not foresee. Rahel's comments about Jesus and Mary and the cross awoke something within her, which she had to write down in the little notebook that was always in her reticule, in order to include it in her autobiography. She borrowed a writing implement from Rahel's desk.

"*This person—myself—is happy and endowed with rights. A person who has experienced the beauty in the light of faith and whose essence has at last ascended, and is thus not forced to die unfulfilled by sublime, delightful faith. I thank the mercy of God that allowed me to experience this happiness as well.*" She returned the pen to Rahel's desk and looked at her. Now, she thought, the Creator could claim her as well.

Rahel was gaunt and thin, her skin nearly transparent. It appeared as if, since last March, her condition had been gradually deteriorating. As if she had not resigned herself to Goethe's death. He had passed away exactly a year earlier, when spring was near, and darkness had descended upon her world. It did not matter to her that he had been eighty-three years old, in his golden years, and that he had created an entire, complete world for her and for humanity as a whole. The news had hit her hard and from that day on, she retreated into herself and began to wither away. "If only he had lived to enjoy publishing the second part of *Faust*. He worked for it all his life and did not enjoy the fruits of his labor."

Her hand was still in August's hand, her breathing heavy. Dorothea and Henriette approached her bed, coming as close as they could. They knew she would not depart without saying one last thing and wished to capture her words, just as August did.

And Rahel retained the same quality in death that had characterized her in life—she stared the truth in the face, fearlessly and shamelessly, and said:

"What was, for such a long time in my life, my greatest shame, my bitterest misery and misfortune—the fact that I was born Jewish—I would now not give up for any price."

End

Bibliography

Arendt, Hannah. *Rahel Varnhagen: The Life of a Jewess*. Johns Hopkins University Press, 1997

Arendt, Hannah. *Reflections on Literature and Culture*. Stanford University Press, 2007.

Elon, Amos. *The Pity of It All: A Portrait of Jews in Germany, 1743–1933*. Metropolitan Books, 2002.

Finer, Shmuel. *Moses Mendelssohn: Sage of Modernity*. Yale University Press, 2010.

Goethe, Johann Wolfgang. *Conversations of Goethe with Johann Peter Eckermann*, De Capo Press, 1998

Finer, Shmuel. *The Origins of Jewish Secularization in Eighteenth-Century Europe*. University of Pennsylvania Press, 2010

Goethe, Johann Wolfgang. *Erotic Poems*. Oxford University Press, 1999.

Goethe, Johann Wolfgang. *From My Life: Poetry and Truth*. Princeton University Press, 1994.

Goethe, Johann Wolfgang. *The Poems of Goethe*, translated by Edgar Alfred Bowring. https://www.gutenberg.org/cache/epub/1287/pg1287.html

Goethe, Johann Wolfgang. *The Sorrows of Young Werther.* Translated by R.D. Boylan. https://www.gutenberg.org/files/2527/2527-h/2527-h.htm

Hertz, Deborah. *Jewish High Society in Old Regime Berlin.* Yale University Press, 1988.

Key, Ellen Karolina Sofia. *Rahel Varnhagen: A Portrait.* Palala Press, 2016.

Laertius, Diogenes. *The Lives and Opinions of Eminent Philosophers.* Translated by C.D. Yonge. https://www.gutenberg.org/files/57342/57342-h/57342-h.htm

Lowenstein, Steven M. *The Berlin Jewish Community: Enlightenment, Family and Crisis 1770–1830.* Oxford University Press, 1994.

Naimark-Goldberg, Natalie. *Jewish Women in Enlightenment Berlin.* The Littman Library of Jewish Civilization in association with Liverpool University Press, 2016.

Schlegel, Friedrich. *Philosophical Fragments.* University of Minnesota Press, 1991.

Weissberg, Liliane. *Life As A Goddess: Henriette Herz Writes Her Autobiography.* Bar-Ilan University, 2001.

In Hebrew:

Bergman, Samuel Hugo. *The Annals of New Philosophy: From the Enlightenment Era to Immanuel Kant.* Bialik Institute, 1973.

Bergman, Samuel Hugo. *The Annals of New Philosophy: Jacobi, Fichte, Schilling.* Bialik Institute, 1977.

Kaplan, Marion (ed.), *Existence in an Era of Change: The Everyday Life of Jews in Germany 1618–1945.* Zalman Shazar Center, 2008.

Luker, Malka. *The Face of Romance: Germany, France, England.* Bialik Institute, 1962.

Meir, Michael. *The Emergence of the Modern Jew: Jewish Identity and European Culture in Germany, 1749–1824*. Carmel Publishing, 1990.

Neiger, Shmuel. *Criticism and Its Problems: Between Author, Critic and Reader*. Bialik Institute, 1957.

Rubin, Noga. *The Conqueror of Hearts*. HaKibbutz HaMeuchad, 2013.

Wassermann, Henry. *But Germany, Where Is It?* Open University of Israel, 2001.

Made in the USA
Monee, IL
05 March 2023

29200095R00204